I0661486

JULES VERNE

AROUND THE WORLD IN EIGHTY DAYS

THE FULL ACCOUNT

THE OTHER LOG OF PHILEAS FOGG

PHILIP JOSÉ FARMER

JULES VERNE

AROUND THE WORLD
IN EIGHTY DAYS

THE FULL ACCOUNT

THE OTHER LOG OF
PHILEAS FOGG

PHILIP JOSÉ
FARMER

Meteor House

The Full Account

copyright © 2023 by Meteor House. All Rights Reseved.

"Jules Verne's Extraordinary Voyages Around the World"
copyright © 2023 by Henry G. Franke III. All Rights Reseved.

Foreword copyright © 1973, 2023 by the PJ Farmer Family Trust.
All Rights Reseved.

Introduction copyright © 1973, 2023 by the PJ Farmer Family Trust.
All Rights Reseved.

The Other Log of Phileas Fogg copyright © 1973, 2023 by the
PJ Farmer Family Trust. All Rights Reseved.

"Only a Coincidence: Phileas Fogg, Philip José Farmer, and the Wold Newton
Family" copyright © 2012, 2023 by Win Scott Eckert. All Rights Reseved.

"A Chronology of Major Events Pertinent to *The Other Log of Phileas Fogg*"
copyright © 2012, 2023 by Win Scott Eckert. All Rights Reseved.

"Being an Account of the Delay at Green River, Wyoming of Phileas Fogg,
World Traveler" © 2016, 2023 by Win Scott Eckert. All Rights Reseved.

"Passing through the Hands of Steel" © 2012, 2023 by Dennis E. Power

The article "A Submersible Subterfuge or Proof Impositive" by H. W. Starr
appeared in *Leaves from the Copper Beeches*, published for The Sons of the
Copper Beaches Scion Society of the Baker Street Irregulars by Livingston
Publishing Co., Narberth, Pa., 1959. All Rights Reseved.

Cover design and signature page copyright ©2023 by M. S. Corley.
All Rights Reseved.

Interior illustrations (pages 129, 145, 169, 290, 339, 432, and back cover)
copyright ©1982, 2023 by Rick J. Bryant. All Rights Reseved.

Interior illustrations (pages 8, 24, 28, 296, and 392) copyright ©1973, 2023
by Jack Gaughan. Every effort has been made to trace the copyright holders
and obtain permission to reproduce this material.

Meteor House

ISBN 978-1-945427-29-9
First Trade Paperback Edition

This is for the late Professor H. W. Starr, a brilliant Sherlogician who made *Voyages Extraordinaires* of the mind. It is also dedicated to the members of the Sherlock Holmes scion society of Peoria, The Hansoms of John Clayton.

Acknowledgments

I thank Bill Starr for his permission to use some of the elements of his article, "A Submersible Subterfuge," in this narrative-behind-the-narrative. I am also grateful to him and to the following for the permission to reprint the article as an addendum: Julian Wolff, M.D., commissionaire and editor of *The Baker Street Journal*, and Edgar P. Smith, president of The Baker Street Irregulars, Inc. I thank Jack Tracy, a regular Irregular, for his permission to use his discovery of the identity of "a very tall dark man, with a heavy stoop" in his article, "Some Thoughts on the Suicide Club," *The Baker Street Journal*, vol. 22 (New Series).

A Note from the Publisher on
Publication of The Full Account

Welcome to this, a special, one-of-a-kind edition that stitches together the classic novel *Around the World in Eighty Days* with its companion novel *The Other Log of Phileas Fogg*.

For the first time, you can read the original exploits, as described by Verne, interleaved with Farmer's explosive exposé of what actually initiated the adventure, and which in the process, describes some of the more audacious (but omitted by Verne) escapades that Fogg and his travelling companions were party to.

It's probably no surprise that producing a single narrative out of two separate publications, written some one hundred years apart, has given rise to some challenges. We, at Meteor House, felt using complete texts honored the source material but this does mean there are times when the independent texts repeat each other—sometimes in very close proximity. Rather than edit these down we have chosen to leave both texts intact, giving the reader the choice to read each account of the wonderful adventure separately from each other, or, to experience them as one full narrative. On occasion, Farmer, who probably never envisaged a volume such as this, recaps Verne's side of the adventure so as to aid the reader. Although we could have edited these short passages out we decided to leave them intact. The two texts are slightly, but noticeably, differently formatted to aid the reader. However, it is only by comparing the events in the respective books in "real time" that the full wonder of the story truly stands out.

We feel it will add to the experience of the reader if a few further notes are recorded here that explain some of the decisions made concerning elements of the text.

Firstly, Verne's account is presented in British English to reflect the translation used. On the other hand, *The Other Log* is presented in American English, as published. Also, we've adopted the more common title of *Around the World in Eighty Days*. (Originally, the translated title was rendered as *Round the World in Eighty Days*.)

While we have used complete texts of both novels, we have corrected any objective errors. We have done this after extensive research and with confidence that we are doing the right thing by the authors. An example is the spelling of Savile Row. Verne, and many of his subsequent translators, spelled it as "Saville"—we have corrected this.

One thing you will immediately notice as you read this account is the archaic language of the Verne translation. We took expert advice on the best translation to use (knowing how poorly Verne was treated by some early English language translators) and although this is an old translation, it does add an element of depth to the historical setting of the novel. Of course, Farmer, when writing up *The Other Log* had to consider the audience of the 1970s. In the Verne version, we see words like "bed-room" and "look-out" hyphenated; the [Stock] Exchange abbreviated to 'Change; idiosyncratic speech introducers; a lowercase letter following an exclamatory interjection; archaic place name and religious spellings. Language evolves, and spellings, names, and syntax change over time. Although we are not using the words as Verne wrote them but rather relying on a translation, albeit contemporaneous, it still felt important to maintain much of the words and format that define that era.

We should remember that Verne was primarily a novelist and he sometimes changed or omitted small details to make the story more exciting. Verne's tale was initially published serially, and the author had an eager reading public to entice, tease, and satisfy. Farmer notes this in his own telling of the story and, of course, Farmer had access to the hidden account and thereby access to information about which Verne, or any biographer or translator of Verne, never knew. As Farmer says in his narrative, ". . . this is not a novel but a reconstruction of a true story . . ." (p. 75) and "Verne knew nothing of what was taking place behind the scenes." (p. 38)

THE FULL ACCOUNT

You will note that, occasionally, Farmer uses a dollar amount, rather than a sterling figure in the Verne translation. We are sure Farmer did this deliberately to help us understand the exchange rate at that time, which was approximately five dollars to the pound sterling. It is probably also worth noting that the £50,000 stolen from The Bank of England in 1872 would, today, equate to over £4,000,000.

At the end of Farmer's telling of this story, he asks the reader to consider the coincidence of his initials to those of Mr. Fogg. Anyone who is in possession of the 1982 Tor edition cannot help but marvel at the resemblance of the illustrations of Fogg to that of Farmer himself. Of course, we may ask, is there an atavistic likeness between Farmer and Fogg? Perhaps they are directly related as proposed by Win Scott Eckert in his "Only a Coincidence: Phileas Fogg, Philip José Farmer, and the Wold Newton Family" article, included in this volume. Or may they even be the same person?—see "The Time Distorter" by Paul Spiteri (*Farmerphile: The Magazine of Philip José Farmer* no. 15, January 2009). And if either of these are true, does that mean Farmer was an Eridanean? Anyone reading *Other Log* and who is familiar with Verne's account (or has the benefit of reading this edition) cannot help but wonder at some of the discrepancies between the two accounts. Some can easily be explained as being two different interpretations of the one true adventure, but some are more than differing viewpoints. Take, for example, Farmer indicating that Inspector Fix did not have a warrant when arresting Mr. Fogg. This so blatantly contradicts Verne's telling that we can only conclude this was a deliberate act by Farmer. That it was a coded message, deliberately inserted by Farmer into his text, to pass on an instruction, or some information, to the diaspora of Eridaneans. For what better way to communicate to unknown, hidden, secretive members of that Race than by a book easily procured at any bookshop? And who can tell what other messages Farmer included in this, and others of his books? As publishers of Farmer, and custodians of some of his private files, we occasionally have access to information we cannot readily share. But we can hint, and you can extrapolate.

Anyone wanting to delve further into the overall timeline will find "A Chronology of Major Events Pertinent to *The Other Log of Phileas Fogg"* by Win Scott Eckert an invaluable resource. This detailed timeline not only summarises some of the key events in Fogg's famous journey but positions that trek around the world against other events in the Eridanean/Capellean war, as well as major events in the Wold Newton Family.

Finally, Meteor House would like to record our appreciation to Kim Turk, Jason Scott Aiken, and Sean Lee Levin, for their input into how best Meteor House should present *The Full Account.*

Of course, any errors or omissions in the final text are the sole responsibility of Meteor House.

TABLE OF CONTENTS

JULES VERNE'S EXTRAORDINARY
VOYAGES AROUND THE WORLD
HENRY G. FRANKE III

Over the years, the French novelist and playwright Jules Verne has gained the unwarranted reputation as an author of unsophisticated adventure stories best left to children. This view has been particularly enduring in the United States, in large part due to poor English translations and, occasionally, outright censorship, leaving many of his stories uneven and gutted as published in the U.S. However, Jules Verne was both a multifaceted writer and a complicated man, arguably having more in common with Philip José Farmer than a cursory review might suggest.

Jules Verne is credited with establishing the geographic and scientific adventure novel, but he also routinely added his personal social, political, and ethical perspectives to these stories. Verne was a lover of wordplay and cryptograms, adept at humor and irony—sophisticated elements of storytelling that, unfortunately, rarely survived translation from the French. The author, born in February 1828, lived through the French Revolutions of 1830 and 1848 and emerged as a republican rather than a monarchist. France's defeat in the Franco-Prussian War in early 1871, which led to the short-lived revolutionary Paris Commune government and its violent suppression, added to the traumatic events that reshaped the nation. The author continued to decry European imperialism and colonialism, even as he praised the ingenuity, initiative, and strong work ethic of Americans.

15

These political beliefs appeared in his fiction, prompting many a British translation to modify or remove Verne's more democratic and anti-imperial references. The author's views on the likelihood of the beneficial applications of science and technology transitioned from optimistic to pessimistic about halfway through his writing career, which also impacted the enthusiasm for his later stories. British publishers, finding views expressed in his books late in life of greater concern, simply decided to forego publishing them rather than taking the time to censor them. American editions often relied on British translations, even if incompetent or marked by heavy-handed editing. Even when American translations were undertaken, there was still a reasonable chance that they suffered from the same shortfalls. The issue of problematic English translations for many of Verne's novels was finally highlighted in analyses of the author's work starting in the 1970s. Eminent Verne scholar Walter James Miller wrote in his foreword to the 1976 Cromwell annotated edition of *Twenty Thousand Leagues under the Sea*, "The English-speaking world has never had a chance to know the real Jules Verne."

The rehabilitation of Jules Verne's reputation in the U.S., along with the publication of improved English translations of his stories, has progressed since Miller's admonition first appeared. But at the time Philip José Farmer's *The Other Log of Phileas Fogg* was published in 1973, the "original log"—*Around the World in Eighty Days*, one of Verne's most popular novels—was still appearing in editions of varying quality in the U.S.

Farmer scholar Michael Croteau reports, "To my knowledge, Farmer does not mention which edition of [*Around the World*] he read. He first read it in 1929, so that would have been in English since he was eleven. He said he reread it four or five times by 1938, then reread it around 1971, but he didn't mention reading it in French." It happens that there were reasonably good English translations available in 1929. Arthur B. Evans, editor of *Science Fiction Studies* and a Verne scholar, noted that the "best public domain translation was published by Hutchinson, which came out in the 1870s but whose translator is not known." (This translation appears in the book you are now holding.)

Jules Verne's circuitous path to becoming a world-famous novelist started when he was quite young. He penned poetry, songs, short stories, and plays, a fair amount appearing in *Musée des Familles* ("Museum of Families"), a magazine published in Paris. Even at an early age, his desire was to be a playwright, but his father, a lawyer, wanted his son to follow in his footsteps. Verne moved to Paris in 1847 to study law, earning his degree in 1849. However, the theater remained his passion for years to come. He stayed on in Paris so that he could work in theater and be close to major literary and theater personalities, such as Alexander Dumas and his son. But 1862 would prove to be the pivotal year to his literary future, when, at age thirty-four, he completed the novel *Five Weeks in a Balloon*. As Verne sought out a number of editors in Paris, the very influential editor and publisher Pierre-Jules Hetzel reviewed the manuscript and recommended changes that would garner his acceptance. The story was published in January 1863, beginning a lifelong association with Hetzel (and then his son, after Hetzel died in 1886).

Hetzel would be a de facto collaborator on Verne's novels. He was the first to see the author's manuscripts, directing revisions to meet his editorial standards. During the first couple of years of his relationship with Hetzel, Verne still pursued a wider range of literary interests. In 1863 the author offered Hetzel the story *Paris in the Twentieth Century*, which presented a dystopian vision of the far future. Hetzel rejected the story as too negative and farfetched for his audience, concerned that releasing the tale would damage the emerging novelist's standing. Hetzel's desire was for contemporary stories applying grounded science, not fanciful predictions, and so Verne dropped a promising genre. (*Paris in the Twentieth Century* was finally published in France in 1994.)

A devotee of American writer Edgar Allan Poe, Verne published "Edgar Poe and His Works," an extensive essay appearing in four installments in the magazine *Musée des Familles* in 1864 (interestingly, Verne could only read the American's stories as translated into French). Poe's influence on Verne was long-lasting, prompting him to write *The Sphinx of the Ice* (1897), a sequel to Poe's *Narrative of Arthur Gordon Pym of Nantucket* (1838). Some critics believe that, long before this, Poe's short story, "Three Sundays in a Week" (1841), helped to inspire *Around the World in Eighty Days* (1873). Poe's use of cryptograms in his tales prompted Verne to make these secret messages a key element in such novels as *Journey to the Center of the Earth* (1864) and *The Jangada* (1881). Poe's "The Gold Bug" (1843) might have played a role in Verne writing *The Children of Captain Grant* (1867).

But Hetzel kept Verne focused on the type of fiction he wanted from the author. Verne's output in the first dozen years also included what would become his most famous stories (all dates shown are for hardcover publication): *Five Weeks in a Balloon* (1863), *Journey to the Center of the Earth* (1864), *From the Earth to the Moon* (1865), *The Voyages and Adventures of Captain Hatteras* (1866), *The Children of Captain Grant* (1867), *Twenty Thousand Leagues under the Sea* (1870), *Around the Moon* (1870), *A Floating City* (1871), *The Adventures of Three Russians and Three Englishmen in Southern Africa* (1872), *The Fur Country* (1873), *Around the World in Eighty Days* (1873), the short story collection *Doctor Ox* (1874), and *The Mysterious Island* (1875).

With the publication of Verne's fourth novel for Hetzel, *The Voyages and Adventures of Captain Hatteras*, the editor decided to formally name the series of stories *Voyages Extraordinaires* (the "Extraordinary Voyages") telling his readers that the goal of these tales was "to outline all the geographical, geological, physical, historical, and astronomical knowledge amassed by modern science and to recount, in an entertaining and picturesque format that is his own, the history of the universe" (as translated by Arthur Evans in his 1988 study, *Jules Verne Rediscovered*). The targeted audience was the educated French family (that is, families whose members could read and write). Thus Hetzel expected Verne's stories to foster good family values. The editor/publisher quickly installed a new, long-term contract with the author, requiring 200,000 words a year—basically two novels a year. Yet Verne, despite his growing popularity, was not well-paid. In all, fifty-four books in the series were published between 1863 and the author's death in 1905, along with a short-story collection and seven individual short stories included separately with different novels. An additional eight novels were published posthumously under his name between 1905 and 1919, although his son Michel Verne (generally with his father's prior approval) had extensively revised them and, in one case, had written a story in its entirety. A posthumous short-story collection was made up of pieces completed or revised by Michel.

Hetzel followed a standard publishing schedule for nearly all of Verne's stories. They were first serialized in a magazine, usually Hetzel's biweekly *Magasin d'Éducation et de récréation* ("Magazine of Education and Recreation," renamed in 1864 from his *Bibliothèque illustrée des Familles*, or "The Family Illustrated Library"). Verne's tales were profusely illustrated by such talented staff artists as Édouard Riou, Léon Benett, and George Roux. Once serialization was completed, stories quickly moved to book publication, first in lower-priced editions and then on to quality hardcovers with scores of illustrations. Many of these novels soon appeared in England and the United States by various publishers in any number of translations, often without consideration of copyrights or proper reimbursement to Hetzel.

Even though he is often called the "Father of Science Fiction," Verne himself did not consider the stories in the Extraordinary Voyages series to be speculative or even profoundly predictive of the future, but instead tales grounded in scientific facts and trends evident to any capable observer. Just as Philip José Farmer was a polyglot, Verne was also interested in a wide range of topics. He studied newspapers and journals daily, recording whatever he read that might be used in future stories. He also traveled extensively throughout Europe, including on his own yacht.

The author certainly resented the heavy editorial hand Hetzel applied to his stories and the limits placed on him as to what he could write. Reviews of Verne's papers and the correspondence between author and editor confirm that Hetzel personally reworked manuscripts, sometimes through multiple drafts. Verne regained some independence when he again turned to scripting plays. This time, the popularity of these new works not only added to his fame, but made him a wealthy man.

Writing in collaboration with French playwright and showman d'Ennery (a pseudonym of Adolphe Philippe), Verne first adapted *Around the World in Eighty Days* in 1874. With d'Ennery's flair for staging, the play was produced as a *pièce de grand spectacle*, an extravaganza complete with scores of cast members, live elephants, sumptuous costumes, and more. The original production in Paris ran for 415 performances from November 7, 1874, to December 20, 1875. Verne and d'Ennery then adapted two more of Verne's novels, *The Children of Captain Grant* in 1878 and *Michel Strogoff* in 1880. Both were also great successes. All three plays were staged around the world, including in the U.S.

In *The Other Log of Phileas Fogg*, Farmer added to Verne's original plot in *Around the World in Eighty Days* by bringing over characters and situations from other Verne novels (most notably Captain Nemo). This provided greater depth to Farmer's plotline involving an extended extraterrestrial presence on Earth, with two factions in a life-and-death struggle for dominance. Farmer had a major affinity and talent for interweaving together characters, plots, and chronologies taken from multiple stories. *The Other Log* provided him another opportunity for this, this time collaborating in absentia with one of his favorite authors. Farmer likely appreciated that Verne himself had carried storylines and personalities from novel to novel, notably with his trilogy linked to Captain Nemo and his trilogy featuring the Baltimore Gun Club, along with Verne's sequel to Poe's only novel.

Farmer would have been disconcerted by the discrepancies between the timelines and date references in the first trilogy, comprising *The Children of Captain Grant*, *Twenty Thousand Leagues under the Sea*, and *The Mysterious Island*. These inconsistencies were not an accident; Verne and Hetzel were aware of them, and footnotes in the latter novel actually pointed them out. Apparently, Hetzel's plot guidelines for the second two novels led to these issues after the release of the first story.

Most readers are unaware that Verne had plans to write stories that would involve more of his characters from previous novels. In early 1875, Jules Verne considered bringing together many individuals from across his Extraordinary Voyages for a new narrative. This story would have included Phileas Fogg from *Around the World in Eighty Days*, Samuel Fergusson from *Five Weeks in a Balloon*, Pierre Aronnax from *Twenty Thousand Leagues under the Sea*, Dr. Clawbonny from *The Voyages and Adventures of Captain Hatteras*, and others. This group would have traveled around the world in a heavier-than-air flying machine. However, later that year Alphonse Brown's first novel *La Conquête de l'air* ("The Conquest of the Air") was published, employing a similar plot idea. With this, Verne stopped work on his own novel.

Verne revisited the idea of a crossover of his characters in early 1880, but this time in a play with a new and different plot. He approached d'Ennery with this proposal in February 1880. They worked together on this play at the same time they were scripting the adaptation of Verne's novel *Michel Strogoff.* The play with the original storyline, titled *Journey Though the Impossible*, premiered in Paris on November 25, 1882, with a successful run of ninety-seven performances ending in 1883. D'Ennery staged it as another extravaganza, complete with music and songs, ballets, opulent costumes, and lavish sets.

Hetzel, however, thought that the story was foolish. While he published all three of the Verne/d'Ennery stage adaptations of Extraordinary Voyages novels together in *The Journeys on Stage* in 1881, Hetzel had no interest in *Journey Through the Impossible.* The complete play finally appeared in print for the first time in 2003, and in an English translation rather than in French. In his introduction to this publication, Verne scholar Jean-Michel Margot highlighted the uniqueness of the play: "[I]n no other work by Verne are science fiction and fantasy so present." Each act of the three-act play was set in a fantastic location, first "The Center of the Earth," then "The Bottom of the Sea," including Atlantis, and finally "The Planet Altor," which is then destroyed. Margot noted that this play was written during the years of Verne's transition from a champion of the benefits of new technologies to a cynic concerned that advances in science would be misused.

The basic plot involves a contest between good and evil for possession of George Hatteras, the son of Captain Hatteras, the discoverer of the North Pole in Verne's *The Voyages and Adventures of Captain Hatteras* (and who subsequently went mad). George is accompanied by his fiancée Eva. Evil is personified by Doctor Ox, from the short story "Doctor Ox," and who is also a rival for Eva's affection. Good is embodied by Volsius. Over the course of the story, Volsius works through avatars of Otto Lidenbrock (*Journey to the Center of the Earth*), then Captain Nemo (*Twenty Thousand Leagues under the Sea* and *The Mysterious Island*), and finally Michael Arden (*From the Earth to the Moon* and *Around the Moon*). Impey Barbicane and J. T. Maston of the Baltimore Gun Club help them reach the planet Altor. Comic relief is supplied by Tartelet (based on a character in *The School of Robinsons*). These characters were already familiar to the public thanks to their appearance in Verne's books, increasing interest in attending a performance of the show.

Philip José Farmer would certainly have been fascinated by *Journey Through the Impossible*, perhaps the most Farmer-like of Jules Verne's tales, with its allegorical premise, crossover characters and settings, and science fiction elements. Similarly, *The Other Log of Phileas Fogg* might not have been all that startling to Verne.

Postscript: The North American Jules Verne Society (NAJVS), founded in 1993, is a non-profit corporation dedicated to promoting interest in Jules Verne and his writings. NAJVS had led the publication of Journey Through the Impossible, *and since then has published the first English translations of several of Verne's works. For more information about the Society, go to http://www.najvs.org.*

FOREWORD

I first read Verne's *Around the World in Eighty Days* in 1929. Between then and 1938 I reread it perhaps four or five times. I saw Todd's movie version and enjoyed it immensely, but about thirty-three years passed before I read the book again. I found it to be even more charming than I'd remembered and was amazed at how well it stood up. It's a true classic—of its own genre—though not in a class with *The Brothers Karamazov* or *Moby Dick*, of course. But I saw certain elements in it that had escaped me in my youthful reading days.

After pondering on these elements for several months, I concluded that *Around the World in Eighty Days* had two stories. One was the exterior, the easily observable, reported by Verne as an interesting but unsinister adventure tale. The other was esoteric, behind-the-scenes, and full of dangerous implications for humanity. There was a science fiction story in *Days* which Verne, the father of science fiction, had not told. He had not done so because, one, he did not know of it, or, two, he dared not reveal it, or, three, he suspected something was amiss but could only hint at it.

Why were Fogg's origins so shrouded in mystery? Why was his life conducted as if he were a wound-up robot? Did he have clairvoyance or a brain which could compute the degrees of probability of future events and so act accordingly? Why did all the clocks of London strike at ten minutes to nine when Fogg got off the train at the end of his trip?

Philip José Farmer

P. Fogg

INTRODUCTION

How much did Jules Verne know of the real story behind *Around the World in Eighty Days*?

He could not have had all the facts. If he had, he would have been afraid to write the story in any form. Yet, he drops so many hints and ambiguities about Phileas Fogg that he must have suspected something. No other account of the famous global dash, and there were many of these, contain any such allusions or obliquities.

Did Verne get a glimpse into Fogg's secret notebook, the other log of his eighty-day voyage? It doesn't seem likely. He may have heard of it somehow and gotten from someone a few passages from it. But if he had, he would have been no more informed, though much more puzzled, than before. The secret log was written in the syllabary symbols of Eridanean A. Only one of the ancient blood, or an enemy Capellean, or a human foster-child, could read this. None of these would have imparted to a mere human the information in the strange writing.

There are always traitors, of course. Sentiency implies both loyalty and treachery.

Consider a few of Verne's hints about Phileas Fogg. He might live a thousand years without growing old. His admission to the exclusive Reform Club was mysterious. The bankers Baring had recommended him, but why did they do so? No one knew where Fogg or his money came from. Yet the reluctance of the upper-class mid-Victorian Englishman to accept anyone without a "good" family background or money is well known. He seemed to be a creature of absolutely undeviating habits. Not only could the neighbors set their clocks by his routine, they must have wondered if he were truly human and not a clockwork robot. Certainly, he seemed either inhuman or unhuman.

Yet he had a heart. He himself admitted that he had one, when he could afford it. He could sit unmoving for hour after hour as if he were a big frog watching unblinkingly for the juicy flies of time.

And had he traveled, this man who confined his activities to a very small area of the world? He seems to have known most of the world, even the far-off places.

"The unforeseen does not exist," he was heard to say more than once. Does this mean he had clairvoyance? Or does it indicate something more credible but far more sinister? Why did this Englishman, fixed on a track like a locomotive of the Great Western, suddenly jump the track and take off across the horizon?

Why? There are many whys which Verne does not answer.

The existence of Mr. Fogg's other log was not known until 1947 when the house at No. 7, Savile Row, Burlington Gardens, London, was undergoing some repairs. This house, as everybody knows, was once occupied by the famous and witty but penniless playwright and Member of Parliament, Richard Brinsley Sheridan. He died in distressing circumstances in 1816, not in 1814, as Verne says. During the tearing down of a wardrobe wall, a small diary was found in a hollow space between two walls. This seems to have been in good condition until a hole in the roof permitted water to flow over it. Some of the pages were entirely ruined and parts of others were illegible. Enough of the unknown writing was left to become a *cause célébre* among cryptographers and linguists the world over.

In 1962, the writing was recognized as neither a code or cipher but a hitherto unknown language. This would still be untranslatable if it had not been for the discovery of some notebooks in a house in rural Derbyshire. This was in the manor once owned by a Sir Heraclitus Fogg, baronet. These consisted of notes written to help an English-speaking child learn the language. With these referents, a noted linguist of the University of Oxford, Sir Beowulf William Clayton, fourth baronet, tackled the material found in No. 7, Savile Row. He managed to translate at least a third of what was left.

THE FULL ACCOUNT

I was the first to hear about the translation because it was my researches[1] into the life of General Sir William Clayton, first baronet, father of Phileas Fogg, which enabled Fogg's childhood home to be located and, hence, the illuminating notebooks.

The long-abandoned Fogg Hall was searched by my English colleague, the aforementioned linguist, a great-grandson of Sir William Clayton by his tenth wife, Margaret Shaw. Sir Beowulf's investigation resulted in the finding of the child's parallel texts and the consequent partial translations. From the notes furnished me by Sir Beowulf I have reconstructed the story behind Verne's story: *The Other Log of Phileas Fogg*.

---

[1] *Tarzan Alive, A Definitive Biography of Lord Greystoke*, Doubleday Books, 1972

J. Passepartout

CHAPTER I

IN WHICH PHILEAS FOGG AND PASSEPARTOUT COME
TOGETHER, THE ONE AS MASTER, THE OTHER AS SERVANT

In the year 1872, No. 7 in Savile Row, Burlington Gardens, the house in which Sheridan died in 1814, was inhabited by Phileas Fogg, Esq., one of the most eccentric and noticeable members of the Reform Club, although he seemed to be especially careful to do nothing which could attract any one's attention. Yet Phileas Fogg, an enigmatical personage, of whom nothing was known, except that he was very well bred and moved in very good society, was destined to rival in notoriety one of the greatest orators who have honoured this country; he was said to be like Byron in the face, for his feet were faultless, but a Byron with moustache and whiskers, a Byron without emotions, who might have lived for a thousand years without growing old. Certainly an Englishman, perhaps Phileas Fogg was no Londoner; no one had ever seen him on 'Change or at the Bank, or in any city office; none of the docks near London had ever opened their gates to any vessel freighted or chartered by Phileas Fogg; his name was not to be found on the direction of any company, nor had it ever been heard at any of the Inns of Court, neither at the Temple, nor at Lincoln's Inn, nor Gray's Inn; he had never pleaded in the Court of Chancery, nor the Queen's Bench, nor the Exchequer, nor in any Ecclesiastical Court. He was neither a manufacturer nor a broker, neither merchant nor agriculturist; he was not a Fellow of the Royal Society, nor of any other society enjoying the direct patronage of Her Gracious Majesty, nor did he belong to any of the societies which swarm in London, from the Harmonic to the Entomologist, which latter was founded chiefly with the object of destroying noxious insects. Phileas Fogg was a member of the Reform Club, that was all. Should any one express astonishment that such a mysterious gentleman should belong to a club so exclusive, the reply is that he was proposed by one of the Messrs. Baring with whom he banked.

Was Phileas Fogg a rich man? Without doubt. But how he became so the best informed were unable to say, and Mr. Fogg himself was the last person likely to afford any information on the subject. He was neither extravagant nor stingy, for whenever a subscription was needed for any noble, useful or benevolent object, he gave it without observation and sometimes anonymously. On the whole no one could be less communicative than he—he spoke as seldom as possible, and his silence made him appear more mysterious still—his every-day life was open to every one's observation, but what he did was so mathematically regular, that imagination was fairly at a loss. Had he ever travelled? Very probably, for no one was better acquainted with the world; there was no spot on the globe, however distant, with which he did not seem to be specially acquainted. Sometimes, but in a few well-chosen words, he would correct many conjectures circulating in the club respecting lost or missing travellers; he would point out what probabilities there were of their re-appearance, and his words seemed inspired by second sight, so often did the event justify his prediction. He was a man who must have been everywhere, at least in the spirit.

There was one thing certain, and that was, for many years Phileas Fogg had not left London; those who knew him best bore witness that—if it was the most direct way which he took every day to or from his own house to the club—no one could report he had ever seen him, anywhere else. His sole occupation was to read the daily papers and play his rubber. He often played at this silent game, which suited his disposition so well he often won, but his winnings were always devoted to charitable purposes. Besides, it must be observed, Mr. Fogg ardently played for the sake of the game and not to win money, which was in his eyes a struggle, a fight against obstacles, but a struggle involving neither exercise nor fatigue, and that coincided with his disposition.

The world attributed neither wife nor children to Phileas Fogg—which may be the case with very respectable people—nor relations nor friends, which is much more unusual. Phileas Fogg lived alone in his house in Savile Row, and no one ever visited him. Of his domestic life nothing whatever was known. One single servant attended to his wants. Breakfast and dinner he took at his club, at hours to which he was punctual as a chronometer, in the same room, at the same table, never inviting another member or a stranger to dine with him; he used to go home exactly at twelve o'clock to bed, without ever making use of one of those comfortable bed-rooms which the Reform Club offers its members. He passed ten out of the twenty-four hours at home, either in sleeping or in dressing himself. If he ever walked about it was up and down the entrance hall with its inlaid floor, or in the round gallery, above which rose the dome with blue glass windows, supported by twenty columns of red porphyry. When he dined all the culinary resources of the club were taxed to supply his table; the most solemn-looking servants, in noiseless shoes, correctly dressed in black, waited upon him; his dinner was served up in china made especially for the club; the table linen was of the finest Saxon damask; the wines he drank were in the most elaborately-designed decanters, and kept at the proper temperature in ice imported from America at a great expense. If living thus constituted eccentricity, it must be confessed there is some good in it.

The house in Savile Row, without being sumptuous, was extremely comfortable, and its occupant's regular habits rendered his servant's duty very easy. Nevertheless, Phileas Fogg expected rigorous punctuality from his only domestic. That very day, the 2nd of October, Phileas Fogg had discharged James Foster, for he had been guilty of bringing in his shaving water at eighty-four degrees of Fahrenheit instead of eighty-six, and he was then expecting his successor, who was to make his appearance between eleven and half-past.

Phileas Fogg was sitting firmly in his armchair, his feet close together like a soldier on parade, his hands resting on his knees, as he watched the hands of the clock—a very complicated affair which showed the hours, minutes, seconds, days of the week, the months, and the years. As the clock struck half past eleven, Mr. Fogg would, according to his daily practice, leave his house for the Reform Club.

At that moment there was a knock at the door of the room where Phileas Fogg was sitting.

The discharged valet, James Foster, showed himself.

"The new servant, sir," said he.

A young fellow about thirty walked in and made his bow.

"You are a Frenchman, and your name is John?" asked Fogg.

"Jean, if you please, sir," replied the new comer; "Jean Passepartout, a surname which has stuck to me on account of my ability for getting out of troubles. I consider myself a respectable man, sir, but to tell you the truth my occupations have been various. I have been a strolling singer, circus rider, rope dancer, like Leotard and Blondin, and to turn my talents to better account—I was lately serjeant in the Paris fire brigade. It is now five years since I left France, and, having a taste for family life, became a valet in England. Now, finding myself out of place, and having heard that Mr. Fogg was the most regular and quiet gentleman in the United Kingdom, I have come to offer my services to you, sir, in the hope of living in peace, and of forgetting the very name of Passepartout."

"Passepartout suits me," replied the gentleman. "You have been well recommended to me—you are aware of my terms?"

"Yes, sir."

"Very well; what time is it by your watch?"

"Five and twenty minutes past eleven," replied Passepartout, dragging an enormous silver watch from his fob.

"You are slow," said Mr. Fogg.

"I beg your pardon, sir, the thing is impossible."

"You are four minutes slow. Never mind, it is sufficient to know that it is so. Now then, from this moment, twenty-nine minutes past eleven in the morning of Wednesday, the 2nd of October, you are in my service."

Having said so much, Phileas Fogg rose, took his hat in his left hand, placed it on his head like an automaton, and disappeared without saying another word. Passepartout heard the street door shut once, it was his master leaving the house; then a second time, it was his predecessor, James Foster, who also left in his turn. Passepartout remained alone in the house in Savile Row.

THE OTHER LOG OF PHILEAS FOGG

Phileas Fogg was said by Verne to be a bearded Byron, one who was so tranquil that he might live a thousand years without getting old. Was this statement about his possible longevity just a coincidence, a flying thought which chance happened to fit with the wings of truth?

A millennium of life was exactly what Fogg had been promised. In 1872 he was said to be about forty years of age, and so he was. But the Eridanean elixir does not effect its work until the body is about forty years old, and then it rapidly takes hold. Today, Fogg would look as if he had aged perhaps a year or two, if he is still alive. The chances are that he is alive and well somewhere in England. Can anyone point to a gravestone on which is carved his name, the date of his birth, 1832, followed by the date of his death? They cannot.

Mr. Fogg was tall and well shaped and had a handsome face,

which is to be expected from one who so closely resembles Byron. His hair and whiskers were light, which may mean in Vernese that he was blond or had light brown hair. The color of his eyes is not mentioned by Verne. A Scotland Yard report, however, still available to the researcher who is diligent enough to dig for it, gives them as dark gray. This is to be expected in a member of a family noted for its gray eyes.

His face was pale, a natural consequence of exposure to the sun for only once a day during the time it takes to step off one-thousand-and-one-hundred-and-fifty-one consecutive paces. His teeth, unlike the typical Englishman's of that day, were magnificent. He had lost none to the dental decay which afflicted the people of Albion in the mid-nineteenth century. This quality, like the gray eyes, seems to have been a genetic factor. On the other hand, since he was given a number of elixirs during his childhood, the dental health may have resulted from a drug which originated light-years and millennia away.

At the time this story opens, Wednesday, 2 October, 1872, Mr. Fogg seemed to have no relatives. He lived at No. 7, Savile Row, where the only other occupant was his valet. He had acquaintances but no close friends. His sole recreations were the walk from his house to the Reform Club, reading the newspapers, and playing whist. According to Verne, he had been living like a pendulum on a clock for many years. Actually, the "many years" were only four, from 1868 to 1872. But his presence was so full of "thereness" that people thought of him as an old fixture, like the milk wagon or even a house.

Fogg demanded that his shaving water be exactly at 86° Fahrenheit. On this morning, his man, James Forster, appeared at the right time with the water, at thirty-seven minutes past nine. He set the bowl down by the basin, and Mr. Fogg removed the thermometer from its water. It registered 84° F. There was no excuse for this deficiency. Few though his duties were, they must be performed precisely at the precise time. He was to awake his master exactly at eight in the morning. Twenty-three minutes later, he was to appear with a tray on which were tea and toast. Verne does not say that these had to be at a certain temperature, but we may assume that they had to be. Ten minutes later, Forster would remove these. There remained for him only the shaving water at 9:37 A.M. and the dressing of his master at twenty minutes to nine.

At 11:30 A.M., no few seconds given or taken, Mr. Fogg would go out the front door, and he would come back through it as the clocks of London struck midnight. Between his departure and arrival, his servant had little to do. He did have to clean up a little, arrange for a cleaning woman to come in once a week, ensure that his master's clothes were cleaned and pressed, the beds made, pay a few bills, and so on. Except for the unhuman requirements of the schedule, James Forster was his own master.

Or was he?

Why, for instance, did Forster deliver the shaving water at two degrees less than that required? All he had to do was to check the thermometer. Why didn't he, when he knew it was so important?

The answer is that he *did* check it. Mr. Forster had waited until the temperature of the water had dropped to 86° before carrying it out of the kitchen. He knew very well that by the time he reached the bathroom on the third floor, the water would be below the desired temperature. Nor did he look perturbed when informed by Fogg that he was dismissed.

Fogg should have looked upset, since the metronome of his life had been checked. All was out of order, and while it is true that not many people would be disturbed by a mere two degree difference in their shaving water, Mr. Fogg regarded such as serious. But his serene expression changed only slightly. His eyebrows raised as if they were a pair of wings reluctantly flapped by a bird accustomed to gliding all its life. Then the eyebrows came down, and Fogg said, in a voice which was cold but not outraged, "You will leave as soon as I have acquired a new valet. You will inquire at some suitable agency for your successor, and I will interview the applicants. I will be here for that purpose until eleven-twenty-five."

Forster said, "Yes, sir. Very good, sir. And may I ask about my recommendation?"

"You have been satisfactory up to this moment," Mr. Fogg said. "I will state that in unmistakable terms for any would-be employers. But I must also state exactly why I was forced to dismiss you."

Mr. Forster did not reply, but he surely must have been thinking that very few employers would regard two degrees of Fahrenheit as anything serious or even worth commenting on.

Neither man smiled at the end of this conversation, though it's difficult to understand how they could refrain. Though there were no witnesses and no one could possibly have seen or overheard them, neither let down his guard. If there had been a hidden camera or electronic ears, nothing untoward would have been recorded. Of course, in 1872, neither of these devices existed.

Or did they?

What about the very slight whirring that could be heard in this house when neither man was speaking? To what could that be attributed? And what about the large mirror in Mr. Fogg's bedroom? Could this possibly be a one-way piece of glass, and could there be equipment behind it, equipment which even 1972 A.D. might find very advanced indeed?

Whether or not the house was bugged, it was certain that Fogg and Forster never said a word or made a gesture which was not expected from people of their class and in this situation. There was nothing to indicate that 2°F. could be a signal for the dismissal of one servant and the hiring of another. Or that the famous bet made in the Reform Club was also the result of this signal.

This may be an excellent reason for Mr. Fogg's eccentricity of undeviatingness. To fire a man because he offers water two degrees off the standard is to be eccentric. Such behavior in a "normal" man would at once attract attention. But such behavior was to be expected from Mr. Fogg. Indeed, if he had not reacted as he did, he would have been regarded suspiciously by any hypothetical hidden observer.

At twenty minutes before ten, Forster assisted Fogg to dress. Fifteen minutes later, Forster left the house and took a cab to the employment agency specializing in valets, footmen, maids, and cooks for the well-to-do.

Phileas Fogg sat down in his armchair and assumed his habitual posture. His spine was straight; his shoulder blades were firmly pressed against the back of the chair. His feet were close together. His hands were placed palm down on his knees. His eyes were fixed upon a large clock across the room. This instrument indicated not only the customary seconds, minutes, and hours, but the day, month, and year. He did not move except for the rise and fall of chest associated with every living mammal, even Mr. Fogg, when he is breathing normally, and for the blinking of the eyelids. Despite what is said about the unblinking gaze of villains in the penny dreadfuls of 1872 or 1972, no one with eyesight can do without blinking. The results are too painful. And so Mr. Fogg blinked, as he would have voluntarily done even if he had not been naturally required to do so.

He doubted that there were any concealed spies, human or mechanical, in the house, but it was possible. He lived as if he were an automaton—almost like Mr. Poe's mechanical chess player—for two reasons. One, he had been taught to do so by his foster-father. Two, though he lived quietly, he did so conspicuously. There were few aware of his existence, but these few were very aware. His very standingoutness, however, was the quality to allay the suspicions of the enemy. They would believe that their enemies would be doing all they could to appear normal, to merge into the human herd. Therefore, Mr. Fogg, by his behavior, would convince them that he could not possibly be hiding from them.

Despite this theory, there was some evidence that Fogg was under surveillance. And so Fogg, whether in company or alone, always acted as Fogg should. He had done so for such a long time that he would have found it unnatural to do otherwise.

The image was he, and he was the image.

But this was to change very soon. It may be that the premonition of this, indeed, the certainty, made his heart beat faster.

Perhaps.

But was it not this man who said, "The unforeseen does not exist"? Was he, as he sat unmoving in the chair, using his brain as a computer to extrapolate the most likely of the futures? Did his unusual training as a child enable him to switch certain neural circuits and stimulate certain patterns in his brain into computing unconsciously and with all the speed of modern electronic brains? Could he visualize the statistical chances of an occurrence *in potentia*? Fogg never says so in his log, but there are some statements that sound as if he were referring indirectly to such a talent. If he could do this, then he must have known that he could not be sure that such and such a thing would be inevitable. And so, though in a sense the future contains no unforeseens, it holds no inevitabilities. If it did, and these could be anticipated, one side or the other in this secret war would long ago have acknowledged defeat. In fact, the war might have been over before it began, since computation would show both sides who would eventually win.

There was a rap on the door—foreseen? James Forster opened the door and said, "The new servant."

Why did Forster thus announce the applicant? The new man had not yet been interviewed, let alone hired. Why would Forster speak as if the matter were settled? Was it a slip on his part, and the matter had indeed been predetermined?

If so, Fogg's expression did not change, and Verne says nothing of Forster's. Why should he? Verne knew nothing of what was taking place behind the scenes.

A man entered and bowed. He was short and stockily built; had a pleasant face with red cheeks and bright blue eyes; his hair was brown and always looked windblown.

Mr. Fogg said, "You are a Frenchman, I believe, and your name is John?"

"Jean, if monsieur pleases. Jean Passepartout . . ."

Fogg had given the first code of inquiry when he had asked him if his name were John. And the Parisian had replied with the password when he said his name was Passepartout. Just as the name of Fogg indicated a certain role in the organization, by a happy coincidence, so Passepartout indicated his role. But the Frenchman's name was not the one with which he had been born. He had been dubbed Passepartout—"Passes everywhere"—for a good reason. It indicated more than the Frenchman's wanderlust and instability.

Passepartout, at Fogg's request, gave his background. He had been a wandering minstrel, though not necessarily of rags and tatters. He had also ridden horses in circuses, and he had danced on the high wire, like the famous Blondin. If Passepartout could emulate the feats of this fellow Gaul, as he hinted he could, then he should have stuck to the tightrope. It was Blondin who first crossed above Niagara Falls on a wire 160 feet above the water and 1,100 feet long. This he did many times, blindfolded, on stilts, carrying a man on his back, sitting down on a chair and eating a meal, and so on. Only eleven years ago he had appeared at the Crystal Palace in London and there, wearing stilts, had somersaulted on a rope 170 feet above the ground.

It was not to be supposed that Passepartout was the equal of Blondin, but he may not have been far behind in skill. In any event, he had quit the high wire to teach gymnastics for a while. Then he became a fireman in Paris, but he had quit that five years before to take up valeting in England.

Surely this was a strange switch of professions, but he explained that he was tired of the dangerous and the unsettling. He desired the quiet life. He was now out of a position, but, hearing of Mr. Fogg, than whom no one led a more strictly scheduled and peaceful life, he had presented himself as a desirable valet. He did not even want to use the name of Passepartout anymore.

Mr. Fogg said, "Passepartout suits me. You are well recommended to me. I hear a good report of you."

This was strange, because from whom and when would Mr. Fogg have heard about Passepartout? Until a few hours ago, he had not even thought about getting a new servant. Since he had fired Forster and sent him out to get another servant, he had communicated with no one. He had neither inserted an ad in the papers, written a letter and received a reply, nor used the telephone. The latter he did not have, since Mr. Alexander Graham Bell was only twenty-six years old and a little less than four years from filing his patent on the electric speaking telephone.

Mr. Fogg could have sent Forster out to the nearest telegraph office, but Verne says nothing of this. No, just as Forster's introduction of Passepartout was a slip on his part, so Fogg's comment on the recommendation was his slip. The question is, were these slips intentionally made to affect the hypothetical hidden observer in a certain fashion? If the unforeseen truly did not exist for Fogg, would he have slipped? And if Fogg made a mistake on purpose, then it's safe to presume that Forster did so, too. This means that all three, Fogg, Passepartout, and Forster, were cognizant of a certain plan.

"You know my conditions?" Fogg said.

The Frenchman's answer indicated that Forster had filled him in on the way from the agency.

Fogg then asked Passepartout what time it was. The Frenchman drew an enormous silver watch from his vest pocket, looked at it, and said, "Twenty-five minutes after eleven."

"You are too slow," Mr. Fogg said.

Passepartout replied that that was impossible.

Fogg said, coldly, "You are four minutes too slow. No matter. It's enough to mention this error. Now from this moment, twenty-nine minutes after eleven o'clock, this Wednesday, the second of October, you are in my service."

Phileas Fogg rose, took his hat in his left hand, put it on his head, and walked out.

Mr. Fogg was thoroughly satisfied that Passepartout was the man sent to help him in his new venture, whatever that was to be. Forster had checked him with certain passphrases at the agency. The bit about Passepartout's watch being slow had been another method of identification. In addition, the Frenchman's name had indicated his function, and the "enormous" watch was so large because it contained more than a timepiece. Mr. Fogg's taking his hat with his left hand had been the final signal, since he was right-handed. If he were left-handed, he would have used the right. Passepartout had observed his last confirmation and so was also pleased.

After Fogg left the room, he stood listening for a moment. The door to the street shut. That would be his ally and master leaving at exactly 11:30 A.M. A few seconds later, the door closed again. That would be James Forster going to wherever the plan dictated. There Forster would make another move in the secret and martial chess game that had been going on for two hundred years between the Eridaneans and the Capelleans.

CHAPTER II

IN WHICH PASSEPARTOUT ARRIVES AT THE CONCLUSION
THAT HE HAS AT LAST FOUND HIS IDEA OF A MASTER

Assuredly," said Passepartout to himself, though rather startled at first, "I have seen people at Madame Tussaud's quite as lively as my new master." During the few minutes' interview which he had with Phileas Fogg, Passepartout had rapidly but carefully observed his future master. He might have been forty: he was handsome, tall, rather inclined to be stout, with light hair and whiskers, an unwrinkled brow, rather pale, with very fine teeth. He possessed in a high degree what physiognomists call "repose in action," a faculty common to all who are more disposed to work than to talk. Calm, phlegmatic, and clear-eyed, he was the type of the Englishman so well portrayed by Angelica Kauffman. Judged from the actions of his every-day life, he seemed as well regulated a being as one of Earnshaw's or Leroy's chronometers. In fact, Phileas Fogg was the personification of punctuality, which was perceptible even in "the expression of his hands and feet," for in men as in animals the members are expressive organs of passion.

Phileas Fogg was one of those mathematically precise people who, never in a hurry and yet always ready, are economical in their movements. He never made a stride too long, and always took the shortest road; he never stared about him; he used no superfluous gestures; he had never been seen either excited or at a loss; he was the most leisurely man in the world, and yet always punctual. At the same time it must be understood that he lived alone, and apart from all social ties; he knew that in life one must have one's share of rubs, and as they must more or less retard one, he encountered as few as he could.

As to Jean, called Passepartout, a genuine Parisian from Paris, during the five years he had passed in England, and acted as a London valet, he had been on the vain look-out for a master to whom he could attach himself.

Passepartout was not one of those Trontias or Mascarillos who, with their noses in the air and impudence on their faces, are only insolent rascals. No, Passepartout was a good fellow, with a pleasant face, rather projecting lips, good-natured, obliging, with one of those round heads which we like to see on a friend's shoulders; his eyes were blue, his complexion fresh, chest open, strongly built and of great strength, which had been greatly developed by his early career. His brown hair was rather rough; if the sculptors of antiquity had eighteen different modes of arranging Minerva's locks, Passepartout had but one for his own — three applications of a coarse comb sufficed.

The smallest amount of prudence would not allow me to say that the expansive disposition of this man would harmonize with that of Phileas Fogg. Was Passepartout likely to be the thoroughly exact servant his master required? That would only be seen on trial. After a youth spent in wandering about the world he was in want of a quiet life. Having heard Englishmen's preciseness and proverbial coolness highly spoken of, he came to England to seek his fortune. But till then he had not prospered. He had been in ten different employments, but all his masters had been either capricious or irregular, running after adventures, or rushing about from place to place which did not suit Passepartout at all. His last master, young Lord Longferry, member of Parliament, after passing his nights in the Haymarket oyster-shop, was often brought back to his rooms on a policeman's shoulders. Now Passepartout, who was sincerely desirous of respecting his master, risked a few respectful observations, which were taken ill, and he left. About that time he heard that Mr. Fogg was in want of a servant, so he made some inquiries about that gentleman. A person whose life was so regular, who never slept out, never travelled, was never one day away from home, must suit him. He offered his services, which were accepted as we have seen. Passepartout, at half-past eleven, found himself alone in the house in Savile Row; he therefore inspected it from garret to cellar. The house was clean, well arranged for its size, modestly furnished, and pleased him. It was like a snail's shell lighted and heated by gas which was sufficient for both purposes. He had no difficulty in discovering his own room on the second floor—it suited him exactly; electric bells and speaking tubes put him in communication with the other rooms in the house; and on a chimney-piece an electric clock agreed to a second with a similar one in his master's bedroom.

"That is just the thing for me," thought Passepartout.

He also observed a notice above the clock, detailing his daily duties from eight in the morning until twelve at night, at which hour his methodical master retired to bed; everything was set down, anticipated, and regulated. Passepartout found amusement in studying this programme and learning its different articles by heart.

His master's wardrobe was equally well arranged. All his clothes were numbered, and a list kept of them, and the date when, according to the season, they were to be worn. The same regulations applied to his boots and shoes.

On the whole there was in this house in Savile Row—which must have been a temple dedicated to disorder while the illustrious but dissipated Sheridan lived in it—a degree of comfort and luxury which announced an easy fortune. There were neither books nor book-cases, for these would have been useless to Mr. Fogg, as the Reform Club possessed two libraries, one for lighter reading, the other devoted to legal and political works. In his bedroom stood an iron safe, both burglar and fire-proof—there were neither fire-arms nor fishing-rods, nor sporting implements of any description, nor warlike weapons—everything bore the signs of most peaceful habits.

After having examined all these details, Passepartout rubbed his hands, a smile of satisfaction stole over his face, and he exclaimed aloud—

"This is just what I wanted! Mr. Fogg and I will get on perfectly well together. A regular machine! Well, I don't mind attending to a machine!"

CHAPTER III

A CONVERSATION WHICH MAY COST PHILEAS FOGG DEAR

Phileas Fogg had left his house in Savile Row at half-past eleven, and having set his right foot five hundred and seventy-five times before his left, and his left five hundred and seventy-six times before his right, he reached the Reform Club, a grand structure in Pall Mall which cannot have cost less than one hundred and twenty thousand pounds in building.

Phileas Fogg immediately betook himself to the coffee-room, the nine windows of which overlooked a garden in which the trees already bore the tints of autumn. There he seated himself in his accustomed place, and there his breakfast awaited him.

At forty-seven minutes past twelve this gentleman rose, and directed his steps towards the drawing-room, a sumptuous apartment, ornamented with richly-framed pictures. There a servant brought him an uncut copy of the *Times*, which Fogg unfolded so dexterously as to betray great acquaintance with that difficult operation. Reading this paper occupied Phileas Fogg until a quarter to four, and then the *Standard*, which he read next, took up his time until dinner, of which he partook in the same manner as his breakfast.

At twenty minutes to six he reappeared in the drawing-room, and was soon absorbed in the perusal of the *Morning Post*. Half an hour afterwards several members came in and stood by the fire. They were Phileas Fogg's habitual partners, and, like him, great whist players. Andrew Stuart, the engineer, John Sullivan and Samuel Fallentin, bankers, Thomas Flanagan, the brewer, and Gauthier Ralph, one of the directors of the Bank of England, all persons of wealth and consideration, even in a club which comprises among its members men most eminent in manufactures or finance.

"Well, Ralph," asked Thomas Flanagan, "how about this robbery?"

"Why," observed Stuart, "the bank will lose its money."

"I hope not," said Gauthier Ralph; "I trust we shall catch the thief—most expert detectives have been sent to America and all over Europe, and to every principal port, and the gentleman will find it hard work to escape them."

"But have you any description of the thief?" asked Stuart.

"In the first place he is no thief," replied Ralph, very seriously.

"What, no thief! an individual who walks off with fifty-five thousand pounds in bank notes?"

"No," said Gauthier Ralph.

"I suppose you would call him a speculator," said John Sullivan.

"The *Morning Post* declares he is some gentleman."

The person who made this observation was none other than Phileas Fogg, from behind the sheet of paper which he was reading. He rose at the same time and saluted his friends, who bowed in return.

The circumstance above mentioned, which had been discussed in the daily papers, had occurred on the 29th of September, three days previously—a bundle of bank notes, amounting to fifty-five thousand pounds, had been stolen from the counter of the chief cashier of the Bank of England.

By way of answer to those who expressed astonishment that such a robbery should have been committed with such ease, the deputy-governor, Gauthier Ralph, merely said that at that moment the cashier was busy entering the receipt of a sum of three-and-sixpence, and could not have his eyes everywhere at once.

Here we may be allowed to make an observation which makes the fact more easy of explanation, viz., that wonderful institution, the Bank of England, seems to rely very much on public honesty—no guards, no sentries, no iron bars—gold, silver, and notes are freely exposed to view, and are, we may say, at the mercy of the first comer. It would not be proper to distrust the respectability of those passing through the office. One of the shrewdest observers of English customs tells the following story:—In one of the rooms in the bank, where he happened to find himself one day, he had the curiosity to take a closer view of an ingot of gold, weighing from seven to eight pounds, which was lying on the cashier's table; he took it up, examined it, and passed it on to his neighbour, and he to another, till at last the ingot was passed from hand to hand along a dark passage, and only found its way back to the table after an absence of half an hour, without the cashier having once looked round.

But on the 29th of September things happened very differently, the roll of notes did not find its way back, and when the great clock in the drawing office struck five, announcing the hour of closing, the Bank of England had nothing for it but to pay the fifty-five thousand pounds to the account of profit and loss.

As soon as the theft was discovered the most experienced detectives were sent to the principal ports, to Liverpool, Glasgow, Le Havre, Suez, Brindisi, New York, &c., with a promise, if successful, of a reward of two thousand pounds and five percent on the amount recovered. While a preliminary investigation was pending these detectives were directed to keep a look-out on all travellers either coming or going.

Now, according to the *Morning Post*, there was reason to believe the author of the robbery was not connected with any ordinary band of thieves. The day of the robbery a gentlemanlike, well-dressed man had been noticed moving about in the drawing office, where the theft had been committed. The inquiry had elicited a tolerably correct description of this gentleman, which had been immediately despatched to all the detectives employed at home and abroad. Some of the most sanguine, and Gauthier Ralph was one, thought themselves justified in hoping the robber would not escape. As may be supposed, this was for the moment the topic of conversation all over England. The chances of catching the thief were discussed everywhere; nor was it surprising to hear of it in the Reform Club, the more so that one of the deputy governors of the bank was there himself. Mr. Gauthier Ralph would not believe there could be any doubt of the result, stimulated as were the agents' zeal and intelligence by the amount of the reward offered. But his partner, Andrew Stuart, was far from feeling the same confidence, so the conversation was continued between these gentlemen at the whist table, Stuart opposite Flanagan, Fallentin opposite Phileas Fogg. During the game there was nothing said, but between the rubbers the conversation was more animated than ever.

"I maintain," said Stuart, "that the chances are in the thief's favour, who must be a clever fellow."

"Nonsense," said Ralph, "there is not a single country where he can hide himself."

"Indeed!"

"Where can he go?"

"I can't say," replied Stuart, "but the world is wide enough."

"It was so once," said Phileas, in a low tone. Then, as he passed the cards over to Flanagan, he added, "It is your turn to cut."

The discussion ceased while the cards were played. Andrew Stuart soon began again.

"How once? has the earth grown smaller by chance?"

"Certainly it has," replied Gauthier Ralph, "I am of the same opinion as Mr. Fogg. The earth has grown smaller, since one can travel over it in a tenth of the time it required to do so a century ago; and this it is which in our case will greatly facilitate our search."

"But it will also contribute to the escape for the thief."

"It is your turn to play, Mr. Stuart," said Fogg.

But Stuart was incredulous, and as soon as the game was over—

"I must confess, Mr. Ralph," he began, "it is very amusing to hear you say the earth is become smaller. So, because you can now travel round it in three months—"

"In eighty days and no more," said Phileas Fogg.

"Yes, gentlemen," added John Sullivan, "in eighty days, since the line has been opened between Rothal and Alahabad on the great India Peninsula railway; and this is how the *Morning Post* makes the calculation:

From London to Suez by Mont Cenis and Brindisi, railway and steamboats	7 days
Suez to Bombay, steamer	13 "
Bombay to Calcutta, railway	3 "
Calcutta to Hong-kong, steamer	13 "
Hong-kong to Yokohama, steamer	6 "
Yokohama to San Francisco, steamer	22 "
San Francisco to New York, railway	7 "
New York to London, steamer and railway	9 "
Total	80 days."

"Yes, eighty days," cried Andrew Stuart, who in his excitement trumped his partner's best card; "but that does not take into the calculation bad weather, contrary winds, shipwrecks, railway accidents, and the like."

"It includes everything," said Phileas, playing a card as he spoke, for by this time the discussion had ceased to respect the game.

"Even if the Hindus and the Indians were to pull up the rails?" cried Andrew Stuart; "if they were to stop the trains, plunder the baggage cars, and scalp the passengers?"

"Everything included," replied Phileas Fogg, throwing down his cards, adding, "The two best trumps."

Andrew Stuart, whose turn it was to shuffle the cards, said, as he picked them up—

"Theoretically, Mr. Fogg, you are right, but practically—"

"Practically, too, Mr. Stuart."

"I should like to see you do it."

"That depends upon yourself. Let us go together."

"God forbid!" cried Stuart; "but I would not mind betting four thousand pounds that such a journey, to be carried out as above, would be impossible."

"On the contrary, quite possible," replied Mr. Fogg.

"Well then, do it."

"Round the world in eighty days?"

"Yes."

"I will."

"When?"

"Now; only I warn you I shall do it at your expense."

"You are mad!" cried Andrew Stuart, who began to be vexed at his partner's obstinacy; "go on playing."

"Deal again, then," said Fogg, "there is a misdeal."

Stuart took up the cards with a feverish hand; then, suddenly laying them down on the table—

"Yes, Mr. Fogg, I will lay you four thousand pounds!"

"My dear Stuart," said Fallentin, "be quiet; it is only a joke!"

"When I offer to bet, I mean it," said Stuart, very seriously.

"I take it," replied Fogg; then, turning to the others, "I have twenty thousand pounds lying at Baring's; I will risk them with pleasure."

"Twenty thousand pounds!" cried John Sullivan, "which the least unforeseen accident may cause you to lose!"

"There is no such thing as 'the unforeseen,'" quietly answered Fogg.

"But this period of eighty days is calculated as the minimum space of time."

"A well-employed minimum, which will be amply sufficient."

"But that you may not exceed it, you will have to jump with the accuracy of a time-piece from railway to steamer and from steamers into railway carriages."

"I shall be as punctual as a time-piece."

"It can only be a joke on your part."

"A true Englishman never jokes about anything so serious as a bet," replied Phileas Fogg. "I will bet any one that likes twenty thousand pounds that I make the round of the world in eighty days or less, say nineteen hundred and twenty hours, or one hundred and fifteen thousand two hundred minutes. Will you take it?"

"We take it," replied Stuart, Fallentin, Sullivan, Flanagan, and Ralph, after some consultation.

"Good," said Fogg. "The train for Dover starts at a quarter to nine; I shall go by it this very evening," replied Phileas Fogg. "Now," said he, looking at a pocket almanack, "this is Wednesday, the 2nd of October, I must be back here in this drawing-room of the Reform Club on Saturday, the 21st of December, at a quarter to nine in the evening, failing which the twenty thousand, now lying in my name at Baring Brothers, will become yours by right, gentlemen. Here is a cheque for that amount."

A memorandum of the bet was drawn up and signed on the spot by the six parties. Phileas Fogg was perfectly cool. He certainly had not made the bet for the sake of winning the money, and had only risked these twenty thousand pounds, half his fortune, because he foresaw he would have to spend the other half in carrying out this difficult, if not impossible, project successfully. As for his adversaries, they seemed excited, not so much on account of the value of the stakes, as because they felt a scruple in betting against their friend under conditions which seemed so unfavourable to him.

It was striking seven. They proposed to Mr. Fogg to leave off playing to give him time to make his preparations for leaving London.

"I am always prepared," calmly replied that gentleman, as he dealt. "Diamonds are trumps," said he. "It is your lead, Stuart."

THE OTHER LOG OF PHILEAS FOGG

The Reform Club toward which Mr. Fogg proceeded at an exact velocity was only one-thousand-and-one-hundred-and-fifty-one paces from Mr. Fogg's house on Savile Row. Verne does not say what transpired during Fogg's walk. For him, the ordinary would not have been worth describing, and the extraordinary was not reported to him. However, the ordinary of our day and Fogg's may be contrasted for the benefit of the reader. The Londoner of 1872 had his own brand of smog. Indeed, the word, formed from smoke and fog, is of London origin. The smoke of hundreds of thousands of industrial and domestic furnaces and stoves burning soft coal often darkened the skies and laid a sooty film over everything. It also gave the London air a rather acrid odor and doubtless contributed to the generation of tuberculosis and other diseases of the lung.

Another odor, not unpleasant under certain conditions and when in not too great quantities, emanated from the horse droppings. These littered the streets from West End to East End. During the dry periods, clouds of manure rose to mingle with coal dust and dirt dust as the wheels of carriages struck the piles. Mingled with these were the huge and pestiferous horseflies that were once a familiar and seemingly permanent part of the civilized world. This, however, was October, and the chilly nights of the past few weeks had considerably discouraged the activities of these insects.

Mr. Fogg walked on the sidewalk from No. 7, Savile Row, turned left onto Vigo Street, after a few paces crossed Vigo to Sackville Street, and proceeded along it until he came to Piccadilly. Having traversed this with no apparent attention to the hansoms and vans which filled this main thoroughfare (London traffic was a nuisance and a danger a century ago), he walked eastward until he reached the narrow Church Street. Here he turned right and, coming to Jermyn Street, turned right again, walked a few paces, and then went across Jermyn to enter the Duke of York's. This led him to St. James Square. Having passed along this, he crossed Pall Mall to the Reform Club. This imposing and famed edifice is neighbor to the Traveler's Club, which admits no one as a member who has not journeyed at least five-hundred miles in a straight line from London. Although Mr.

Fogg could easily have joined this club both before and after his dash around the globe, he was never a member.

Across Pall Mall at an angle was the Athenaeum Club, devoted to bringing together the practitioners of the fine arts and sciences and their eminent patrons. This is the institution called the Diogenes Club in the Sherlock Holmes stories. However, at this time, Mycroft Holmes, its future member, was only twenty-six years old and his brother Sherlock was a mere eighteen. Yet, the paths of the younger Holmes and of one of the many pedestrians on Pall Mall that day were to cross many years later.

Although Fogg seemed to look neither to left nor to right, as if he were riding a rail and did not have to steer himself, he was missing little. Thus, he saw a tall, broadshouldered gentleman of about forty years of age standing in a doorway and lighting up a cheroot. Only the keenest of observers could have noted that Fogg's stride checked ever so slightly. And only a nearby and very perceptive person would have detected a minute paling of Mr. Fogg's skin.

His lips opened a tiny bit, and a name breathed out.

He did not otherwise betray himself. He walked on steadily as if he were a planet in its orbit and could be perturbed by nothing less than the sun going nova.

But behind that serene face millions of microscopic novas were exploding as neuron after neuron and neural circuit after circuit lit up. Could it indeed be *he*? Or had he been mistaken? After all, the man had been across the street and in the shadow of a deep doorway. The features had been indistinguishable. The physique certainly resembled the man whose name Fogg had exhaled. The safety match with which he lit his cigar could have illuminated his features in the shadow of the doorway, but the hand which held it shielded them. Nor could Fogg determine if the fellow had an unusual distance between his eyes.

Moreover, Fogg's glance had been too brief to allow him any rechecking of his first impression. And, the further he got from the man, the less he thought that it could be he. Why would he stand where he might be seen? What purpose could he have in letting Fogg know that he was alive and shadowing him? Was it bravado? Or was he trying to stampede the unstampedable?

And how could he be alive? How had he escaped? As far as Fogg knew, he and three others were the only survivors. Still, at one time he had thought he was the only one not drowned, but he had found out later that others had had good fortune, too. The other survivors were French and Canadian and there was not much chance that they would ever see him again. To make sure that they did not recognize him if they did encounter him, he had grown his beard.

Despite an intensive investigation, no evidence had been found that anybody else had gotten away alive from the maelstrom. However, that could mean that the Capelleans had kept their secret a secret. They were very good at that.

Perhaps, Fogg thought, this was why everything was so suddenly upset, Forster ordered to an unknown destination, and Passepartout appearing with his distorter, the only one in the possession of the Eridaneans.

He walked on up the steps of the Reform Club. It was true that he had foreseen this possibility of other survivors, but he had calculated that the odds against this were so high as to make the event extremely unlikely.

But if anyone could survive, that fellow would be the one. He, Fogg, might have allowed his wishes to interfere with his mathematics.

The Reform Club was political in origin, being founded by the Liberals of both houses of Parliament to help push through the Reform Bill, 1830–32. This was not what we of today would regard as a democratic measure. It redistributed the seats in Parliament, giving the new middle classes of the industrial cities the representation they had lacked, and getting rid of the "rotten boroughs." It failed to satisfy the radicals (whom we should regard as very conservative indeed by modern standards), but it was a step closer to true representative government. Why Fogg chose this club rather than another is not known. He seemed to have no interest at all in politics. At least, Verne records no opinions of his, and a diligent search has failed to find his name on any registry of voters.

The club itself was housed in a magnificent structure, the architectural style of which was pure Italian, supposedly based on the famous Farnese Palace at Rome, designed by Michelangelo. It contained six floors and one-hundred-and-thirty-four apartments.

In the center was a great hall fifty-six feet by fifty feet, as high as the building itself. Adjoining the drawing room are a library and a cardroom. It was the latter that Fogg intended as his final destination.

In the meantime, he made a scheduled stop at the dining room, the nine windows of which opened onto a garden. He sat at the table which had been laid out for him, and he ate his breakfast, for which he had to give no order since it never varied.

At thirteen minutes to one, he rose and walked to the large hall. He sat down there and a servant handed him the *Times*. Fogg read the paper until fifteen minutes to four o'clock. Without Fogg's requesting it, he was handed the *Standard*. He then ate a dinner the menu for which deviated no more than that of his breakfast. Mr. Fogg then repaired to the washroom, an event which Verne discreetly omits to mention. Since his internal actions were as well governed as his outer, Mr. Fogg reappeared in the reading room at the scheduled time: twenty minutes before six. He sat down to read the *Morning Post*, and continued to do so until half an hour had passed. An acute observer, however, would have noticed that he raised his eyes from the paper more times than usual, and he might have deduced that Mr. Fogg was looking for someone. This someone, if he appeared, caused no visible reaction in Mr. Fogg.

Apparently, whatever the signal of the 2°F. meant, events were proceeding slowly. If there was frenzy or desperation behind the plan, it was not obvious. Mr. Fogg read every word of the three publications with a remarkable swiftness. This was even more remarkable considering the lack of practice at other kinds of literature. Nobody at the club had ever seen Fogg read anything but the journals, and he certainly did not read at home since No. 7, Savile Row lacked books of any kind. And yet, he seemed to have been everywhere and to know everything about the most remote of places. From where had he gotten his knowledge?

He did not seem to be looking for anything in particular in his perusal of the papers. Yet his eyes did slow down sometimes and retrack. The delays were caused by certain items, accounts of strange happenings in every niche of the globe. They were the sort of thing put in to fill space, though certainly calculated to interest most human beings. Fogg was putting them together with other accounts in today's papers and also with those he had read in the past. He was trying to construct a coherent picture from them. He was especially interested in the stories of weird or unusual marine phenomena. Stories about sea serpents or missing or overdue ships caught his attention. Nor did he neglect the terrestrial, especially unmotivated murders or disappearances.

At ten minutes after six, five members stopped to talk before the fireplace and rid themselves of the chilliness of the autumn evening. These were Andrew Stuart, an engineer; two bankers, Sullivan and Fallentin; a brewer, Flanagan; and a director of the Bank of England, Gauthier Ralph. Mr. Fogg was aware of their presence, but, since he was not finished reading, he did not address them.

Mr. Flanagan asked Mr. Ralph what he thought about the robbery.

Stuart answered for Ralph, stating that the Bank of England would lose its money.

Ralph replied that the bank expected to get the robber. The best of detectives had been sent to all the large ports of America and Europe, and the robber would have to be very slippery indeed to elude the hawks of the law.

Stuart said, "But do you have a description?"

Ralph said, "In the first place, he is no robber."

Stuart was astounded. "What! A chap who makes off with fifty-five thousand pounds is no robber?"

"No."

"Perhaps, then, he is a manufacturer?"

"The *Morning Post* reports that he is a gentleman."

No one smiled at this last remark, which was made by Phileas Fogg. He rose, bowed to his whist partners, and indulged in a conversation about the robbery. Three days before, a package of bank notes had been picked up by a gentleman from the principal cashier's table. It was not the gentleman's, but he did not return it. So, in a sense, it was his. At least, it would be until he was caught.

As Verne observes, "The Bank of England has a touching confidence in the honesty of the public." No one even knew that the fifty-five thousand pounds were missing until the bank was closed and the books were balanced. No guards stood by, ready to defend the institution from illegal activities. The cashier had noticed the

THE FULL ACCOUNT

man taking the money but had thought nothing of it until the loss was discovered.

However, the Bank of England quickly took action when it found its confidence, not to mention the money, misplaced. Detectives were hurried off to Liverpool, Glasgow, Le Havre, Suez, Brindisi, New York, and other parts. The natural zeal of the manhunters was sharpened by a reward of two thousand pounds plus five percent on the recovered sum. They were not proceeding blindly, since they had been provided with an excellent description of the gentleman who had taken the money.

Ralph, as a bank official, thought it unthinkable that the man would not soon be caught. Stuart, the engineer, disputed his conclusion, even after the whist game had started. He had for partner Mr. Flanagan, while Fogg's was Fallentin. Of course, they did not converse until after the first rubber was over. Stuart then said, "I maintain that chance favors the thief, who has to be a shrewd chap."

Ralph said, "But where can he fly to? No country is safe for him." Stuart exclaimed with disbelief.

"Where would he go?" Ralph said.

Stuart snorted and said, "I don't know. The world is big enough."

And having provided an opening for Fogg, he waited.

Stuart is derived from "steward," one who manages. And Stuart was an engineer in both a public and a private sense. He was, in fact, Fogg's superior, for all Fogg knew, the head of the entire Eridanean Race. He was the steward, and he was chief engineer of the Race, natal and adopted.

"The world is big enough," Stuart repeated.

Fogg said in a low voice, "It once was."

He handed the reshuffled cards to Flanagan.

"Cut, sir."

After the rubber, Stuart said, "What does your 'once' mean? Has the world grown smaller?"

Ralph said, "Indeed, I agree with Mr. Fogg. The world has grown somewhat smaller. A man can now go around it ten times more quickly than he could a hundred years ago. That is why the search for the thief is more likely to succeed."

Stuart said, "But that is also why it is easier for the thief to get away."

"Be so good as to play, Mr. Stuart," Fogg said.

No one except Stuart was aware of the double meaning in this request.

Stuart was, it must be confessed, as keen a cardsharper as could be found. Even if he had had no native talent, he would have had to be dull indeed not to have profited by one hundred and fifty years of practice. Despite his ability to crook the cards, he was always honest. That is, he was unless the occasion required otherwise. In this case, the occasion required. And so Stuart laid down as his first card that which he had selected, the jack of diamonds. To all except Stuart and Fogg, it meant that diamonds would be trumps. To Fogg it was an order to bet, to take a dare, though not with the cards. What bet, what dare? That depended on Stuart's conversation and Fogg's ability to interpret.

When this rubber was over, Stuart said, "You have a strange way, Ralph, of proving that the world has gotten smaller. Thus, because you can go around it in three months . . ."

"Eighty days," Fogg said.

Sullivan interrupted with a long explanation of why it would only take eighty days. The Great Indian Peninsula Railway had just opened a new section between Rothal and Allahabad, and this would reduce the traveling time enough to make it possible. The *Morning Post* itself had made out a schedule whereby an intrepid, and lucky, traveler might proceed from London and circle the globe with enough speed to be back in London in eleven weeks and three days.

Stuart became so excited at this that he made a false deal. At least, he seemed to be excited. Fogg knew that the trey of diamonds meant: *On the track. Go ahead.*

Stuart then said that the schedule did not take into account bad weather, contrary winds, shipwrecks, railroad accidents, and other likely events.

"All included," Fogg said. He had kept on playing even though the others had stopped.

Stuart was insistent. "Suppose the Hindus or American Indians pull up the rails? Suppose they stop the trains, clean out the baggage cars, scalp the passengers?"

"All included," Fogg replied calmly. He threw down his cards. "Two trumps."

The others looked surprised, not at his cards but at his talkativeness. And they found his attitude irritating. The mirror-smooth calmness and assumption of authority had been noticed by them before, but in general he was a decent chap. His peccadilloes were minor and forgivable because he was an eccentric. Englishmen then loved eccentrics, or at least respected them. But the world was much bigger then and there was room for the unconventionals.

It was Stuart's turn to deal. While shuffling, he said, "Theoretically, you're right, Mr. Fogg. But practically . . ."

"Practically also, Mr. Stuart."

Mr. Stuart had hoped that someone besides himself would initiate the bet. Since this did not now seem likely, he would have to do it. He hoped that the inevitable Capellean—who was he? The servant nearby? Fallentin? Flanagan? Perhaps, perish the thought, Fogg himself?—would think that the bet had arisen naturally. Of course, they were on to Fogg now or at least suspected him. But he did not want them to suspect Stuart. Or, at least, to suspect no more than they did Fallentin, Flanagan, or Ralph.

In a somewhat indignant manner, he said, "I'd like to see you do it within eighty days.

"That," Fogg said, "depends on you. Shall we go?"

Stuart replied that he would bet four thousand pounds that it could not be done.

Fogg calmly insisted that it was quite possible. One thing led to another, and so the famous wager was made. Fogg had a deposit of twenty thousand pounds at Baring's. He would risk all of it.

Sullivan cried out, and we may judge the intensity of his passions—real or assumed—by the fact that an English gentleman would raise his voice inside the Reform Club. He cried out that Fogg would lose all by one accidental delay.

Phileas Fogg replied with his curious, and now classical, remark that the unforeseen does not exist.

Stuart may have shot a warning look. Any eavesdropping Capellean would fasten onto this, worry it as if he were a dog and it the bone, and find in the marrow a vast suspicion. He would wonder if some strange hands were being dealt by strange hands at this card table.

Or had Stuart sent the message that Fogg was to talk suspiciously?

The latter seems more likely, since Stuart's plan was to use Fogg as a decoy. The time for laying low was over. Now there was a reason for bringing the enemy out, to mark them, and to put an end to them.

Where Stuart got his idea for exposing Fogg is not known. At least, the other log says nothing about its origin. Probably, Stuart was inspired when he read the model schedule for the eighty-day trip in the *Morning Post*. Fogg would not find out until later why Stuart had decided to launch another campaign.

One of the players protested that eighty days was the least possible time to make the journey.

Mr. Fogg made another classical reply. "A well-used minimum suffices for everything."

Another protest that, if he were to keep within the minimum, he would have to jump mathematically from trains to ships and back again.

Fogg made his third classical reply.

"I will jump—mathematically."

"You are joking."

Fogg's rejoinder was, in effect, that a true Englishman does not joke about such matters.

Convinced by this, the whist players decided to accept the wager.

Mr. Fogg then announced that the train left that evening for Dover at a quarter before nine. He would be on it.

He had not known about the bet until this hour, and he never took the train. How did he know the railway schedules? Had he memorized *Bradshaw's*? In view of his other talents, this seems probable, though he must have done it sometime before 1866, as will be made clear in due course. Thus, he had no way of knowing that trains were still adhering to the schedules of that time. But he would have checked long before boarding, and no doubt he trusted in the resistance against change inherent in the English character.

After consulting his pocket almanac, he said, "Since today is Wednesday, second of October, I shall be due in London, in this very room, on Saturday, the twenty-first of December, at fifteen minutes before nine P.M. Otherwise, the twenty thousand pounds now deposited in my name at Baring's is yours in fact and in right. Here is a check for the amount."

THE FULL ACCOUNT

Mr. Fogg's total fortune was forty thousand pounds, but he foresaw having to spend half of that to win the twenty thousand. And this is so strange that it is surprising that no one has commented on it. Why should an eminently practical man, indeed, a far too practical man, one who conducted his life according to the laws of rational mechanics, make a bet like this? He was a man who had never given way to an impulse. Moreover, even if he won his bet, and this did not seem probable, he would not be a guinea richer than before. And if he lost, he was a pauper.

The only explanation is that he was under orders to make this astonishing and unprecedented move. Even if we did not now have his secret log, we could be certain of that.

As for his forty thousand pounds, the private property of an Eridanean was at the disposal of Stuart when the situation demanded it. Stuart would have sacrificed his own fortune if it were necessary. And so, if Fogg must put his entire wealth in jeopardy, he could assure himself that it was in a good cause.

Far more than money could be lost. He could be killed at any moment. From now on, he would not be an eccentric semi-hermit living obscurely in a tiny area of London. His bet was sure to be publicized quickly. The world would soon be following his journey with hot interest and cool cash.

If Fogg was perturbed by this, he showed not the slightest sign. Of all the party, he was the calmest. The others were quite disturbed. All except Stuart felt that they were taking advantage of their friend with this bet. Stuart's agitation had another cause. He knew what dangers Fogg would be encountering.

Verne says nothing about the whist game from this point on. However, the other log does. Fogg had to let Stuart know that he had seen someone who might or might not be their old enemy. Inasmuch as he was as adept with the cards as Stuart, though he had only thirty-one years of practice, not one hundred and fifty, he had no trouble in dealing out the correct combination. Stuart's eyes widened when he saw his hand, and his lips soundlessly formed the dread name. He looked up at Fogg, who slowly lifted his head and lowered it in affirmation.

When it was Stuart's turn to deal, he gave Fogg cards the order of which said: *Proceed as directed.*

But Fogg knew that Stuart would return to his house as soon as the game was over, and the machinery of investigation would be started.

The game of surprises was not yet over. It may be that Stuart had not planned to impart additional information to Fogg. The less any individual in the Race knew, the less he could tell if he were captured and tortured. Fogg's news may have changed his mind. Fogg needed to be on guard even more than Stuart had suspected. And so, when Stuart dealt again, Fogg read a telegraphic but clear message.

The enemy had found a distorter. In China.

If Fogg were shaken by this, he did not show it, of course, and his log says nothing of his emotional state at this time. But he would have been unhuman if he had not been throbbing with curiosity. Who? How? Was this why he was being ordered to circle the Earth? Was this the reason for the inevitable publicity? Was he the decoy? Or, not actually himself but Passepartout? The enemy was to learn that Passepartout had a distorter, and they would try to get it. One distorter was no good; two were needed for transmission.

Then it occurred to him that the Capelleans did have at least one. Rather, they had had one. But this belonged to the rajah of Bundelcund, who was a traitor. According to Eridanean reports, the rajah had been ordered to give it up for use elsewhere. He had refused and so was marked for death by his former superiors. This did not mean, however, that the rajah had gone over to the Eridaneans. Far from it, as an Eridanean agent had found when he had approached the rajah to enlist him. The agent had died horribly.

No, the rajah was not pro-Eridanean. He was only pro-rajah. Intelligence said that he was mad, that he had intentions of finding another distorter, stealing it, rather, and using both in a revolt against the British. First, he would launch a secret war against the British, using his independent raj as a base of operations. The distorters would transmit thuggees, the worshippers of the goddess of death, Kali, into the fortresses and homes of the British officers. The thuggees would strangle the officers in their beds.

The native grapevine would let all India know that the rajah of

Bundelcund was behind this and that he had a magical means for sending in his assassins and for getting them out. The rajah's magic could not be fought; his stranglers could go everywhere, not only in India but in the world.

Eventually, there would be another great uprising, but this, unlike the Sepoy Revolt which had been suppressed fourteen years ago, would succeed. It would not fail. At least, this is what the rajah would transmit through the grapevine, though he would know that with only two distorters he could conduct only a very limited warfare. Though the initial transmitter could be used anywhere in the world, the receiver had to be planted at the intended destination. If a Britishman were to be assassinated in his bedroom, the receiver had to be put inside the bedroom. This could be done easily enough by the Indian servants, but if the British caught on to the pattern and imposed strict security measures, planting it would become difficult. The rajah knew this and was reported to have told his closest confidant that he would kidnap Queen Victoria herself and use her as a hostage if he had to do so.

This had not only panicked the Eridaneans. The Capelleans were equally affected. The Earthmen must not discover that there existed, and had existed for two hundred years, two groups of nonterrestrial origin among them. The Earthlings would become hysterical; a relentless hunt by all the governments of the globe would be conducted. This, in the opinion of Stuart, and doubtless of the Capellean chief, could have only one end. The extermination of all Eridaneans and Capelleans. Even if a few escaped, they would have to lie low for a long long time, and the recruiting of new members by adoption or education of their own children would be very dangerous.

Stuart, while playing solitaire with Fogg as a kibitzer for a few minutes, had told Fogg this some time ago. He had also predicted that if the two parties had to be quiescent for a long time, the concept of Eridanean and Capellean would just die out. This was especially probable if all those who were non-human were caught and killed. Their human foster-children could not be depended upon to keep alive the idea of the Race and of the ultimate peril.

There were times when Fogg thought that this might be a good idea.

Then he had to upbraid himself. After all, he and the other humans of the Race were doing all this for the good of the peoples of Earth. Though he would be regarded as a traitor by human beings, if they found out about him, he was actually their guardian angel.

Meanwhile, the rajah of Bundelcund threatened the existence of both Eridanean and Capellean. Once he got hold of another distorter, he would start the first phase of his plan to sweep the British out of India. That completed, he would assume the maharajahship of all India. After that, who knew?

Fogg was well aware that his intended route around the world would bring him close to the borders of Bundelcund. Was he supposed to attempt to get the rajah's distorter?

Stuart sent no message about this.

That meant that he had no orders about that particular affair. And if an opportunity arose to get the distorter, he was free to seize it or ignore it. Perhaps Stuart was sending another agent to try for the distorter while the rajah was being distracted by the threat of Fogg. But why would he send Passepartout with Fogg? The Frenchman had the only distorter the Eridaneans possessed. Why put him near the rajah so the rajah could trap him and get his hands on what he needed most?

Of course, Passepartout's device was the one thing which would draw the rajah away from the fortress-palace of the city of Bundelcund. Though he might come out with an army of thuggees, undoubtedly would be accompanied by an army, he would not be in the rear. He would want to make sure that no one else got a chance to get his hands on the distorter. His general, Kanker, knew about the distorters, though apparently he had not been told anything about their origins. Even so, this breach of security had enraged both Capellean and Eridanean. No one, unless he were of the Blood, should have even the slightest hint of the truth. And if Kanker should get greedy and should come into possession of distorters, there was no telling what terrible things would happen.

The rajah was a very wily person, however, and he would make certain precautions to ensure that Kanker would not realize his ambitions, if he should happen to have any.

But accidents happened, and though the rajah might live to be a thousand years old, he was as subject as anyone to a bullet or to disease.

It was quite true, as Verne says, that Passepartout yearned for repose. He had been almost everywhere and done almost everything. Part of this was due to his nature; he was not named Passepartout just because he carried a distorter. Mostly, though, he had gone here and there, performed this and that, at the orders of Stuart. Now, called from his beloved France, he had come to England and taken up a new trade. Ten English houses had seen him as their valet in five years. Verne says he would not take root in any of them. He always found his masters too impulsive and footloose. His latest, young Lord Longferry, had discharged him because he had commented on his lordship's drunkenness. That was true. But Passepartout had deliberately insulted Longferry so that he would be dismissed. His investigations of the young nobleman had turned up nothing suspicious. He seemed to be as innocent of Capelleanism as the previous nine. Passepartout wondered why any of them had been put on Stuart's list, but he did not question Stuart. And when he was commanded to go to Fogg at once and offer his services, he did not ask why.

Not until he had been given a password by Forster at the agency did he suspect that this case was different. On the way in the cab, he was told more but not much. He had no idea that Fogg was going to get an assignment at the Reform Club. Forster could not have told him because Forster did not know this.

This sparseness of information indicates the strictness of the Eridanean security. It also tells of the loneliness that affected most Eridaneans. He or she had few contacts or intimacy with his or her fellows unless a marriage could be arranged or the singularities of a mission permitted such. The true Eridaneans could not even get married with the idea of having children, since the last true Eridanean female had died several decades ago. However, Stuart was zealous in trying to fix situations so that human Eridaneans could become married and so have children. Otherwise, the Race would die out, and the Capelleans would be victor by default. That is, they would have if they had not also had the same problem as their enemies.

Passepartout seldom got his orders by word of mouth. Almost always it was by code transmitted via playing cards. He would be seated in a restaurant catering to people of his class, and a man at a table by his would be playing patience. Passepartout would be observing the cards with the greatest of interest, of course. And so the cards would tell him in telegraphic language what he was to do next. And Passepartout would do it.

He had been in a restaurant in Tours when the cards informed him he was to go to London. While eating oysters in a Cheapside inn, the cards, dealt by a red-faced, fat middle-aged lady, told him to get hired as valet for a Lord Windermere. This was the first of his investigations, all of which had resulted in nothing Capellean. But Passepartout thought that some of the things he had uncovered could be, probably would be, used by the Eridanean chief to the advantage of the Race.

The ninth person he'd worked for had been General Sir William Clayton of Sallust's. Passepartout had not ever actually valeted for the old baronet, since Sir William was absent from the manor of Sallust's House, Oxfordshire. He was away somewhere in southern or south central Africa at this time. Apparently, he was once again looking for the site of the ancient city of Ophir, if Sir William's wife was telling the truth. She was a good-looking woman of thirty-seven years of age, the eleventh wife of the seventy-three-year-old adventurer. Passepartout's predecessor had been fired when he was caught drinking brandy from the master's stock. Lady Martha Clayton had hired the Frenchman to be the baronet's valet when he got back from the Dark Continent. Meanwhile, he was to be both butler and manager of the household, which included a maid, a cook, a gardener, Lady Martha, an infant, William, by Sir William's tenth marriage, and an infant, Martha, by the present wife. Passepartout used "the present" because the baronet's wives did not seem to have much survival value. Except for one who had divorced him, all had died a few years after marrying him. There was no suspicion of foul play in this series of fatalities. The baronet seemed to radiate an aura which attracted beautiful women and then scorched them. Like moths to a light, thought Passepartout.

He did not understand why women kept marrying him, since everybody seemed to know what happened to his wives. But then everybody thinks he or she is special; death isn't going to notice them.

Passepartout was puzzled by his assignment. Sir William's flamboyant lifestyle did not make him a likely candidate for Capelleanship.

Passepartout did not stay long at Sallust's House, however. Apparently, the chief was interested mainly in finding out where Sir William was and how long he would be gone. He had left the country secretly and with no word to his intimates of his destination. But his wife knew, and so Passepartout read, very late at night in the study, a letter she had written but not yet posted to a missionary friend in southeast Africa. She confided to her that Sir William was again on the old quest for Solomon's treasure city. Would her friend report anything she heard about him? Sir William, despite his age, was a remarkably vigorous man, she wrote. (As who should know better than she, who had borne him two children in the past three years, Passepartout thought.) He might be gone a long time. Meantime, their son, Phileas, had died of the colic. But if her friend happened to run into Sir William, she was to say nothing of this. Sir William must not be deterred from his quest.

Passepartout, after five years on the island, was accustomed to the eccentricity of the English. Thus, he was not surprised to find a septuagenarian baronet tramping around in the wilds of Africa after some fabled, doubtless totally nonexistent, city. He was interested when he found out that the dead Phileas was not Sir William's first child of that name. He eavesdropped on Lady Martha's conversations with her crony, the widowed Lady Jane Brandon of nearby Brandon Beeches. And he discovered that Sir William's fourth marriage, in 1832, had resulted in two children, a Phileas and a Roxana. His fourth wife, daughter of an old and noble Devonshire family, had remarried after divorcing Sir William. Lady Martha did not know whom the woman had married, since all her information was based on some scattered remarks by Sir William. She did know that Lady Lorina had hated Sir William so much that she had gotten her new husband to adopt her children. Sir William had not objected to this nor to her wish that he never see her or their children again. This was why, Lady Martha told Lady Jane, Sir William's son by his tenth marriage would inherit the baronetcy. His children by Lady Lorina would inherit nothing. Of course, there had been some legal difficulties, since the title was supposed to go to the eldest surviving son. But that had been taken care of.

Passepartout had thought little of this and some additional information she had let drop. When he had ascertained that Sir William would probably not be back to civilization for a long time, he was removed from the case. After his resignation, he was sent into the service of Lord Longferry, a member of Parliament and a drunk. (In those days, the two were often synonymous.) Passepartout was startled when he found out that Longferry's Christian name was Phileas. Could this be a coincidence? Or was it connected, no doubt in a sinister way, with Sir William and his Phileases?

During his short stay with Longferry, Passepartout managed to spend some time in the reading room of the British Museum. It was necessary to get a recommendation for admittance, but Longferry himself had furnished this. He had laughed when his valet asked him for it, as if a member of the lower classes and a Frenchman at that, could not possibly be interested in intellectual matters. But he had consented to send down a note to the proper authority. Passepartout had then discovered a very definite connection between the Phileases, though its significance had been beyond him at that time. The grandfather of the present Lord Longferry had been a Phileas, the original, in fact. He had been a very close friend of William Clayton in their youth. Both had gone off to fight with Byron and the Greeks in their battle for independence. Captured by the Turks, young Longferry had died of maltreatment (probably of gang rape by the Turks, Passepartout thought) and of a fever. William Clayton had grieved for a long time for his dead friend. He had tried to perpetuate the memory of his friend by naming two sons after him. The first had disappeared, as far as the records went. He looked through the newspapers of 1832 through 1836. He found a notice of Sir William's and Lady Lorina's divorce (which had required an act of Parliament), but he could find nothing about her remarriage.

A record of it had to exist, of course, and Passepartout intended to track it down. But he was ordered, via a game of cards, to quit his present master. He did this by severely reprimanding the noble for having been carried home intoxicated early one morning. Two days later, the cards, dealt out by a beautiful woman of twenty-five, told him to seek immediate employment with a Mr. Phileas Fogg.

Phileas! One more thread, no, cable, rather, in this mysterious network. Passepartout felt frightened. What did all these Phileases mean? Surely an enlightenment would come someday, and what now seemed so complex would turn out to be laughably simple.

When he received his first message, he had assumed that Fogg was another of the long line suspected of being Capellean. But during the trip with Forster to Savile Row, Passepartout knew that he was in a different area of the case. The 2°F. signal told him that both Fogg and Forster were his kind. It only remained to be verified by the code words.

After his new master had left, he inspected the domicile carefully. As the valet, he would have done this anyway, but as an Eridanean he was obligated to, if only for the sake of survival. Verne says that the house seemed to Passepartout like a snail's shell. This is a more appropriate comparison than Verne knew. A snail's shell is not only a comfortable home but a fortress. He scoured No. 7 from cellar to garret to determine more than its layout. He wanted to know how vulnerable it was to attackers and what defenses it contained. Curiously, it was its very accessibility to intruders and its total lack of firearms or weapons of any kind which pleased him. This meant that no attacks were expected, and none were expected because its owner did not dream—apparently—that he had any special need for defense.

"Everything betrayed the most tranquil and peaceable habits," Verne says.

No wonder that Passepartout rubbed his hands and smiled. No wonder that he spoke aloud. "This is exactly what I desired! Oh, we shall get along, Mr. Fogg and I! What a domestic and regular gentleman! A real machine! Well, I don't mind serving a machine!"

He spoke aloud for several reasons. One, he was genuinely pleased. Two, his words were designed to reassure any hidden recorders or observers that he and Fogg were only what they pretended to be. Fogg was a rigidly self-controlled English gentleman, and he was a French itinerant who had finally found a snug and unchanging berth.

Passepartout should have known better. The long string of Phileases should have put him on the alert. But he so needed a rest that he allowed his emotions to overcome his logic.

CHAPTER IV

IN WHICH PHILEAS FOGG ASTOUNDS HIS SERVANT, PASSEPARTOUT

At twenty-five minutes past seven Phileas Fogg, having won about twenty guineas at whist, took leave of his friends, and quitted the Reform Club. In ten minutes he was at home.

Passepartout, who had been carefully getting the programme by heart, was not a little surprised when he saw Mr. Fogg guilty of such a want of punctuality as to appear at such an unusual hour. According to the notice over the clock the tenant of the house in Savile Row could only return home exactly at twelve o'clock.

Phileas Fogg went straight up into his bedroom, then he called Passepartout.

Passepartout made no reply.

"Passepartout!" called out Mr. Fogg, in the same tone.

Passepartout, showed himself this time.

"It is the second time I have had to call you," observed his master.

"It is not twelve yet," said Passepartout, holding out his watch.

"I know it," replied Phileas Fogg, "and I do not blame you. We leave this house for Dover and Calais in ten minutes."

A grimace clouded the Frenchman's round face. It was clear he had not rightly comprehended his master.

"Are you going abroad, sir?" said he.

"Yes," replied Fogg; "we are going round the world."

Passepartout opened his eyes, raised his eyelids and eyebrows, stretched out his arms, while his body seemed to collapse, and showed every symptom of stupefied astonishment.

"Round the world!" he muttered.

"And in eighty days," replied Mr. Fogg; "so you see we have no time to lose."

"The baggage," said Passepartout, unconsciously nodding his head from side to side.

"No baggage at all, only a carpet-bag. Put into it two flannel shirts, three pairs of stockings, the same for yourself; we will buy what we want as we go along. Fetch my mackintosh and travelling rug; take some good shoes, though we shall have little or no walking. Go, and make haste about it."

Passepartout was about to reply, but he could not find words. He left his master's room and went into his own, fell into a chair, and, using an expression which is common enough in his own country, he exclaimed—

"Well, this is rather, rather strong, this is! and I wanted to be quiet at home."

Mechanically he made preparations for starting. Round the world in eighty days! Was his master mad? No. Was it a joke? They were going to Dover, perhaps to Calais; what then? After all it could not be very disagreeable to the good fellow, who, for the last five years, had not set his foot in France. They might, perhaps, go to Paris, and he would be delighted to see the great capital once more. But a gentleman so averse to moving about would surely stop there. Yes, doubtless he would; but it was quite true, nevertheless, he was going somewhere, this very domestic gentleman hitherto.

By eight o'clock Passepartout had got his master's modest travelling equipment ready as well as his own; then, with his spirits still in a perturbed state, he left his room, shut the door carefully, and went down to Mr. Fogg's room.

Mr. Fogg was ready; he carried under his arm his continental *Bradshaw's* guide, which would give him all necessary instructions for his journey. He took the bag from Passepartout and thrust into it a roll of those notes which pass everywhere.

"You have forgotten nothing?"

"Nothing, sir."

"My macintosh and travelling rug?"

"Here, sir."

"All right; take the bag."

Mr. Fogg put the bag into Passepartout's hands.

"And take care of it," he added; "there are twenty thousand pounds in it."

The bag nearly fell out of Passepartout's hands, as if the money had been in gold and very heavy.

Master and servant then went downstairs and left the house, and double-locked the street door.

There is a cab stand at one end of Savile Row. Phileas Fogg and his servant got into a cab, which drove off to Charing Cross Station.

At twenty minutes past eight the cab stopped. Passepartout jumped out, his master followed and paid the cabman. At that moment a poor beggar woman, holding a child by the hand, with her naked feet in the wet, and wearing a tattered bonnet, from which hung a ragged feather, a torn shawl hardly covering her rags, came up to Mr. Fogg and begged.

Mr. Fogg took the twenty guineas he had won at whist out of his pocket and gave them to the beggar woman.

"Here, my good woman," said he, "I am glad to have met you."

Then he went into the station.

Passepartout felt a sensation of moisture about the eyes. His master had advanced a step in his affections. Mr. Fogg then went into the great waiting-room; there Phileas Fogg ordered Passepartout to take two first-class tickets for Paris; then, turning round, he saw his five friends of the Reform Club.

"I am off, gentlemen," said he, "and the various *visas* in my passport will enable you on my return to check off my route."

"Mr. Fogg," replied Gauthier Ralph, very civilly, "that is very unnecessary—we trust entirely to your honour."

"It is better thus," said Mr. Fogg.

"You have not forgotten," said Andrew Stuart, "that you have to be back—"

"In eighty days," replied Mr. Fogg; "on Saturday, the 21st of December, 1872, at a quarter to nine in the evening. Farewell, gentlemen!"

At forty minutes past eight Phileas Fogg and his servant took their seats in the same carriage, five minutes later a shrill whistle was heard, and the train moved out of the station. The night was dark and rainy. Phileas Fogg, ensconced in his corner, did not open his mouth. Passepartout, who was still in a state of bewilderment, mechanically kept a tight hold on the bag containing the bank notes.

But the train had hardly passed Sydenham when Passepartout uttered a cry of despair.

"What's the matter?" asked Mr. Fogg.

"Why, sir, I was in such a hurry I quite forgot—"

"What?"

"To turn off the gas in my room."

"Never mind," coolly replied Mr. Fogg, "I shall stop it out of your wages."

THE OTHER LOG OF PHILEAS FOGG

Imagine his consternation when his master entered the house, not at the prescribed hour of midnight but at ten minutes to eight or somewhere near that. Because of surprise and apprehension, Passepartout said nothing to Mr. Fogg as he went into his bedroom. He had to be called twice before he went into the master's bedroom. Imagine his dismay on hearing that he was to leave with Fogg for Dover and Calais inside the next ten minutes. Picture his near-collapse when he was informed that they were going to journey completely around the Earth in record time. Visualize the lights bursting in his brain and the shivers running through him when he heard that they would be traveling through India. He knew about the rajah of Bundelcund. And they would be taking the distorter so close to him!

At eight o'clock, he was ready. Then he almost collapsed when handed a carpetbag containing the travel expenses. Twenty thousand pounds in bank notes!

So it was true, and here was the result of his investigations into the multi-Phileas! But why had he had to make sure that Sir William Clayton was out of reach of news from the civilized world?

At the end of Savile Row, the two took a cab, which drove rapidly to Charing Cross Station. Presumably, the street at the end of Savile Row was Vigo, since to walk to Conduit would have taken them further away from their destination. The traffic must have been excessively heavy that night, and perhaps an accident delayed them. Verne says that they arrived at the station at twenty minutes after eight. Since the station is less than a mile from Savile Row, the two could have walked there more quickly. Especially since they were not overburdened. Fogg carried *Bradshaw's Continental Railway Steam Transit and General Guide* under one arm, and his valet carried the carpetbag. Though Verne states that Fogg's house contained no books, he must not have counted the *Bradshaw's* as this type of literature. And if Fogg had memorized the *Bradshaw's* for the English railways, he had not done so for the continent. Otherwise, he would not have transported the European guide with him. Or perhaps he had committed this to memory, too, but considered that people would think it strange if he did not use such a reference.

At any rate, we may be sure that Verne was guessing or exaggerating when he said that the cab drove "rapidly" to Charing Cross Station.

However, it could be that Verne's transit time is correct and that something happened on the way which Fogg and his valet would have kept to themselves. Perhaps the Capelleans tried to abduct them. If this were so, then this account is missing an adventure. But Fogg did not record it, and since this is not a novel but a reconstruction of a true story, the gap will regretfully have to be left just that: a gap.

At the entrance to the station, the two were confronted by a wretched beggar woman holding an infant. They were two of the horde that roamed the streets of London. The Western capitals seldom see them now, but then they were an all-too-familiar sight, as common as they are in present-day Bogota, Colombia. The barefooted woman, shivering in the autumnal chill and its fine rain, asked for money.

Mr. Fogg had won twenty guineas at whist, and since he always donated his winnings to charity, and a not inconsiderable sum of his private fortune, he gave her the whole sum.

"Here, my good woman, I'm glad that I met you," he said.

This incident engendered tears in the soft-hearted Passepartout. His master, after all, was human.

Both men, as a matter of fact, being Eridaneans, were much touched by the poverty, disease, and suffering that afflicted the numerous poor of mid-Victorian England. Such a condition would be wiped out once the Eridaneans had set into motion their long-range program. The ideal society toward which they would strive would be modeled on the state which the nonhuman Eridaneans said existed on their home planet. But before that could be brought about, the evil Capelleans must be exterminated.

What Verne does not mention about this incident, but Fogg does, is what the beggar woman exchanged for money. Fogg received a small piece of paper. It was actually a tiny clipping from a newspaper. It was not only meaningless to any Earthling but of no significance to Fogg. It was a few sentences from an article on the bank theft which had been discussed that very evening at the Reform Club.

Fogg pulled out his watch and seemed to be looking at it. In reality, he was absorbing the article, which lay over the front of his watch. His cupped hand prevented anybody but Passepartout from seeing the clipping, and the good Frenchman was looking through tears at the rapidly departing beggar woman and her infant.

The article had been sent by Stuart, of course. But what did it mean? Something to do with him, no doubt, something he would find out in time, though not, he hoped, too late to do him any good.

He snapped the cover of the watch shut, enclosing the folded article in it. Later, he would remove the clipping and swallow it.

THE FULL ACCOUNT

There are times, and this was one, when he wished that communication could be conducted, if not more openly, at least more fully. The short cryptic messages often left him as much in the dark as before, if not more so, and invariably filled him with uneasiness. It was true that he did not have to suffer from anxiety unless he wished to. He could block it off mentally and so retain his inward composure. The price (there is always a price) was that he had to turn the anxiety back on someday. If he didn't, it stayed undiminished in the circuit in which he had placed it. Its current, so to speak, would be added to anxieties previously shuttled in and switched into a sidetrack.

Later anxieties would increase the pressure even more, or, to preserve the analogy, congest the tracks. Sooner or later, and the sooner the better, he had to open the switch and push some of the anxieties out into the main track. If he didn't, he'd suffer derailments, cerebral wrecks. The pain and the brain damage would be terrible. He had been assured of this by that old Eridanean, Sir Heraclitus Fogg, the being who had raised him. Sir Heraclitus knew that would happen from personal experience and from having observed other Eridaneans.

The baronet, long involved in a particularly sticky situation, had blocked off his anxieties and many of his passions. And one day, just after he had killed two Capelleans in the Paris sewers, he had been struck down from within. The pain had lasted for days, and he had been half-blind and paralyzed on his right side for a year. Fortunately, Eridaneans, not humans, had found him. If the latter had come along, and he had been carried off to a hospital and given an examination, he might have been exposed as a nonterrestrial. This had happened a few times before, but the Eridaneans, or the Capelleans, had heard of it and managed to hush it up.

Fogg had been only ten at the time. He still remembered his grief and terror when his foster-father was brought home late at night in a van driven by two Eridaneans. The baronet was the only parent he had, the only one he deeply loved. His mother had died when he was four, slain, according to Sir Heraclitus, by Capelleans. His real father, he knew, had wanted nothing to do with him and so Phileas hated him.

Not long after his mother's death, the baronet had begun to drop hints, to tell little stories of far-off places and distant times. Gradually, Phileas had been shown the truth. And so he had grown up, Earthling by heredity but Eridanean by education, conditioning, and love. He had not known how much by love until his foster-father was brought home from Paris. The thought that he might die or remain paralyzed shocked Phileas. Yet, a few minutes later, he was acting as if nothing ever upset him. He had blocked off the trauma. And he was still paying for it. Sir Heraclitus, when well enough to understand what had happened to his foster-son, had almost had a relapse. Quickly, he described to Phileas the results if he did not start releasing the trauma. It would build up as other anxieties and shocks were added to it. One day, the suppressed hurts would flash forth in a devastating neural current.

What young Phileas had to do was to construct the mental equivalent of a trickle capacitor in his circuits. Thus, he could discharge the load slowly. This would hurt, but it would not be ruinous.

Phileas knew what a capacitor was. He had learned about it in the laboratory in the cellar of the manor. It was far advanced over the Leyden jar or condenser of the time, and he had been sworn to secrecy concerning it.

Phileas did as directed, though not always with one hundred percent control. Unfortunately, he had set up in his neural configurations a regenerative feedback. As fast as he bled off the traumas, these bred new energy. Sir Heraclitus was puzzled by this and finally called in Andrew Stuart. This was when Phileas was twelve, after the blood-sharing ceremony which made him a full-fledged Eridanean. It had also made him a sick one for a while, since the elder Fogg's and Stuart's corpuscles used vanadium, not iron, for oxygen-carriers.

Stuart had said that Phileas' traumas were feeding off early, and as yet unapproachable, traumas. These had been caused by the desertion of his real father and his mother's death. He had blocked these off through natural, though not desirable, means. And a natural block had, in a sense, to be tunneled to.

Meanwhile, Phileas was suffering the daily uneasiness, shocks, and hurts that all flesh, terrestrial or not, was heir to. Storing and discharging these occupied much of his time, and so he had never caught up with the main task. Though he had kept to a strict exterior or physical schedule these last four years, he was far behind on his interior, or psychic, timetable.

From twelve until twenty-one, he had been busy with his education. This was gotten from tutors, both human and conventional, and Eridanean and unconventional. After twenty-one, he was a full-time soldier in the war that had been raging quietly for two centuries.

At thirty-six he had completed a long campaign, though as a spy. He had almost drowned but had been picked up off the coasts of the Lofoten islands by a fisherman. He returned to Fogg Hall to convalesce and await further orders. While there he grew his beard as preparation for his reemergence into the world. His foster-father had become a casualty in the campaign. His bones were on the sea floor, which was just as well if he had to die. Any doctor or anthropologist who got a look at them would be filled with curiosity quenchable only by death.

And his death had been one more great trauma to store and to trickle off later.

Even while Phileas was growing his beard, Stuart was making his long-range plans. This involved Phileas at once, but it also required a schedule which would allow him time for rest and therapy.

Why did Phileas use his own name when he rented out No. 7, Savile Row? No one knows. But in all previous campaigns he had been in disguise and using assumed names. The Capelleans certainly knew nothing of the true nature of Fogg Hall. If they had, they would have raided it. It's probable that Stuart foresaw that, when Fogg made his bet, he would be highly publicized. Fogg would not reveal his background to any inquiring person. But if some zealous reporter or keen detective backtracked, he might find out where he came from. Stuart did not particularly want anyone to uncover Fogg's origins, but he did not care too much if they were. The humans would only find certain facts which would tell them nothing of Fogg's unhuman connections. By the time the Capelleans found out, it would be too late for them.

This was why Passepartout had been sent to determine the

whereabouts of Sir William Clayton. The old baronet was the only one in all the world, outside of a few Eridaneans, who could tell the press where Phileas came from and how he had gotten there. By the time that Sir William returned from Africa and heard the story of the famous dash, the Capelleans would be unable to do anything about it. They would be dead. Or else the Eridaneans would be dead. In either case, it did not matter.

CHAPTER V

IN WHICH A NOVEL DESCRIPTION OF SECURITIES
IS QUOTED ON THE STOCK EXCHANGE

When Phileas Fogg left London he hardly thought what interest his departure would excite. The news of the bet soon became public in the Reform Club, and caused great excitement among the members. From the club it found its way into the daily papers, and from London it soon reached the provincial press. The question of the journey round the world was as much discussed and commented upon as the case of the *Alabama*. Some backed Phileas Fogg, others—and they formed the majority—laid against him. To accomplish the tour of the world, except in theory and on paper, in a maximum of eighty days, with the existing means of communication, was not only impossible, but absurd.

The *Times*, the *Standard*, *Daily News*, *Morning Post*, and twenty other papers declared against Mr. Fogg. The *Morning Post* alone supported him to a certain extent. He was generally looked upon as a maniac; his friends in the club were generally blamed for having accepted a bet which betrayed such a decay of mental powers on the part of the proposer—several passionate but logical articles were written on this question. The interest which any geographical question excites in England is well-known. So there was no want of readers in every class of society for the column devoted to Phileas Fogg in the daily press—at first a few bold spirits—especially the women—took his part, when the *Illustrated London News* published his portrait.

There were some presumptuous enough to declare that stranger things had been seen before now. These were mostly readers of the *Morning Post*. But one could see that paper began to waver. Then a long article appeared on the 7th of October, in the minutes of a sitting of the Royal Geographical Society, clearly proving the folly of the attempt. According to this article everything was against the traveller, obstacles created by men, and arising from natural causes. To insure success there must be a miraculous agreement in the hours of arrivals and departures; an agreement which did not and could not exist. It might be just possible in Europe, where distances are comparatively moderate, to reckon on the arrival of a train at some particular hour; but, when it requires three days to cross the Indian Peninsula, and a week to traverse the United States, how could such a problem, depending on such a train's punctuality, be solved? Then there were accidents to machinery, chances of running off the line, collisions, bad weather, snow, everything against Phileas Fogg. The steamers in winter were at the mercy of storms or fogs. It was not so very seldom that the fastest transatlantic steamers were one or two days behind time. Now, one single cause of delay would be sufficient to break the chain of communication beyond recovery. If he only just missed the steamer by an hour or two he would be obliged to wait for the next one, and in so doing, the success of his undertaking would be seriously compromised.

This article caused a great sensation. It was copied into nearly all the other papers, and the friends of Phileas Fogg were sorely discouraged.

The days immediately following his departure several heavy bets were made on his success or failure. Not only the members of the Reform Club, but the public generally, adopted the course usually followed on such occasions by the English, whose temperament leads them to bet. Phileas Fogg was as much backed as a racehorse, and bonds, bearing his name, were dealt in on the Stock Exchange. Five days after the Geographical Society article appeared, their value diminished; from five premium they now went to twenty, fifty, eighty discount. One supporter, and one only, stood by him. This was the old paralytic Lord Albemarle, who, confined to his armchair, would have given his whole fortune to have been able to accomplish the tour of the world even in ten years' time. He backed Phileas Fogg to the amount of five thousand pounds. When the folly as well as the inutility of the attempt was explained to him, his only reply was—

"If it is to be done, it is as well an Englishman should be the first to do it."

Things were at this pass, Phileas Fogg's patrons were daily decreasing in number, every one, and with reason, was against him, when, a week after his departure, a most unexpected incident drove him completely out of the betting. On that day, at nine in the evening, the Chief Commissioner of Police received the following telegram:

"SUEZ TO LONDON.
"Rowan, Commissioner of Police, Scotland Yard.
"On the track of the bank robber, Phileas Fogg—send warrant to arrest him to Bombay."

The effect of this despatch was that the gentleman disappeared, and his place was occupied by a robber of bank notes; his photograph, which was at the club with those of all the other members, was inspected. Every feature in it resembled the description of the thief. It was observed that Phileas Fogg led a mysterious sort of life—his solitary existence, his sudden departure—and it soon became a self-evident fact that this person, in undertaking to make a tour of the world in eighty days, and in supporting it by a senseless bet, had but one object, which was to throw the police agents off the scent.

Philip José Farmer

The Other Log of Phileas Fogg

As all the world knows, the story of the bet spread from the Reform Club to the newspapers. Except for the *Morning Post*, the English papers declared Fogg's project to be mad. Nevertheless, there were plenty of people who believed in him enough to put their money down on him, and greater faith has no man. The depth of this sincerity may be judged by the fact that "Phileas Fogg bonds" were issued on the Exchange. Verne goes into great detail about how Fogg's stock rose and fell, so there is no need to repeat it here.

However, for those who have forgotten or who may have somehow missed Verne's book, a week after Fogg had left, his stock dropped to zero.

Mr. Rowan, the commissioner of police, Scotland Yard, received a telegram from a Mr. Fix, a detective for the Peninsular and Oriental Company, a shipping and passenger-line.

I'VE FOUND THE BANK ROBBER, PHILEAS FOGG. SEND WITHOUT DELAY WARRANT OF ARREST TO BOMBAY.

The unbelieving commissioner procured a photograph of Fogg from the Reform Club. He compared it with the description of the man who had stolen fifty-five thousand pounds from the Bank of England. The resemblances were too close to be coincidental unless Fogg had a twin. The unknown origin and background of Fogg, his nongregarious lifestyle, and his rocket-like and totally unexpected departure from England reinforced the suspicions of the police. Fogg was the one.

CHAPTER VI

IN WHICH DETECTIVE FIX SHOWS A VERY NATURAL AMOUNT OF IMPATIENCE

This is how the despatch relative to Phileas Fogg had been forwarded.

On Wednesday, October the 9th, the Peninsular and Oriental steamer, *Mongolia*, was expected at Suez at eleven in the morning; the *Mongolia* went regularly from Brindisi through the Suez Canal to Bombay and back. She was a fast vessel, and always made more than the prescribed ten knots an hour.

Two men were waiting on the quay among the crowd of natives and strangers who swarmed in this town, once but a mere hamlet, but which, thanks to M. de Lesseps, may now look forward to a very important future. One of these men was the consular agent of the United Kingdom, established at Suez, who—notwithstanding the unfavourable anticipations of the British Government, and the ominous predictions of Stephenson, the engineer, could now see English vessels pass through the canal every day, and thus shorten by half the old voyage from England to India by the Cape of Good Hope.

The other was a little, thin man, with an intelligent face and a nervous twitching, which continually contracted his eyebrows in a most remarkable manner; he had a quick eye, but he could disguise its expression at will. At this moment he betrayed marks of impatience, as he walked up and down the quay.

This man's name was Fix, and he was one of the detectives who had been sent to different ports after the robbery at the Bank of England. It was the duty of Fix to keep a strict watch over all travellers taking the Suez route, and should any one seem to justify such a proceeding, not to lose sight of him until a warrant for the individual's arrest could reach him.

Exactly two days previously, Fix had received the description of the supposed thief from the head office. It was that of the well-dressed distinguished-looking person who had been seen in the drawing office of the Bank; the detective's zeal was much stimulated by the large reward offered in case of success. He was awaiting the *Mongolia*'s arrival with real impatience.

"Do you say, consul," asked he for the tenth time, "she is sure not to be behind her time?"

"No, Mr. Fix; she was signalled yesterday off Port Said, and the hundred miles of canal are not much for such a fast vessel; the *Mongolia* has always taken the premium of twenty-five pounds given by Government for every twenty-four hours she is in advance of the time contracted for."

"Does she come direct from Brindisi?" asked Fix.

"From Brindisi, where she receives the Indian mails. She left there on Saturday last at five in the evening, so you see she must be here very soon. But I cannot see how you are to recognize your man, if he be on board the *Mongolia*, from the description which has been sent to you."

"Consul," replied Fix, "one can feel the presence of these fellows rather than recognize them. One must have a scent for them which is a compound sense, uniting hearing, seeing and smelling. In the course of my life I have nabbed more than one of these gentlemen, and if the thief is really on board, I can answer for it he will not slip through my fingers."

"I hope not, Mr. Fix, for it is a very considerable robbery."

"A very great robbery," said the detective, enthusiastically—"fifty-five thousand pounds. We do not often get such a chance as this—thieves are degenerating—the breed of Jack Shepherds is nearly lost!"

"Mr. Fix," replied the consul, "you speak so well I wish you success with all my heart; but as I said before, I fear you will find it rather difficult. You know from the description sent you the thief may be very like a respectable man."

"Consul," said the detective, dogmatically, great thieves always look like respectable men. You must see that fellows who look like scoundrels are obliged to be honest or they would be arrested immediately. A good honest face is what we have to unmask, and a difficult job it is, for it is more than a business to do it—it is an art."

From which we see that Fix was not without a certain self-esteem.

By degrees the quay grew more animated. Sailors of various nations, merchants, ship brokers, porters, and fellahs, crowded to meet the steamer which was evidently expected every moment.

The weather was fine but cold, with an easterly wind. A few minarets were visible above the town, in the pale rays of the sun. Northward a long pier ran out for two thousand yards, like an arm into Suez harbour. Several fishing smacks and coasting vessels, some of which still retained the elegant line of the ancient galley, were visible on the Red Sea.

As he wandered up and down among the crowd, Fix could not help casting a professional glance on the passers-by.

It was then about half-past ten.

"This boat is a long time coming," cried he, as he heard the clock at the port strike.

"It cannot be far off," said the consul.

"How long does it stop at Suez?" asked Fix.

"Four hours. Just time to coal. It is thirteen hundred and ten miles from Suez to Aden, at the farther end of the Red Sea, and they must coal here."

"And from Suez does this steamer go to Bombay direct?"

"Direct, without stopping."

"Well," said Fix, "if the thief has taken a passage by this

boat his plan must be to land at Suez, and try to reach the Dutch or French possessions in Asia by some other route. He ought to know he will not be safe in India any more than in England."

"Not unless he is a very clever fellow," replied the consul; "you know a criminal is always safer in London than he would be anywhere else."

Having made this observation, which caused the detective some minutes' reflection, the consul walked off to his office close by. The police agent remained alone, in a state of nervous impatience, aggravated by a presentiment that the thief was on board the *Mongolia*; and, in truth, if the rascal had left England with the intention of gaining the New World, he would have preferred the overland route by India as less likely to be watched than that of the Atlantic.

Fix was not long left to his reflections. A shrill signal whistle announced the steamer's arrival. All the porters and fellahs rushed in a crowd to the edge of the quay in a disorder which augured ill for the members and clothes of the passengers. A dozen boats pushed off to meet the *Mongolia*, whose gigantic hull was soon seen coming down the canal, and it struck eleven just as she took up her moorings in the harbour, and blew off her steam.

There was a large number of passengers; some remained on deck, gazing at the picturesque view of the town; but most of them landed in the boats which had gone alongside the *Mongolia*.

Fix carefully examined all those who came ashore.

At this moment one of the passengers came up to him, after vigorously repulsing the crowd of fellahs, and asked him very civilly to point out the consul's office to him. At the same time the passenger showed him a passport in which he wished to have the English consul's *visa*. Fix instinctively took the passport, and read the description of the holder at a glance.

He could hardly help trembling, for the description was identical with that sent him from Scotland Yard.

"This is not your own passport?" said he, to the man.

"No, it is my master's."

"Where is your master?"

"On board."

"But," observed the detective, "he must take it in person to the consular office to prove his identity."

"Is that absolutely necessary?"

"Indispensable."

"And where is the office?"

"There, at the corner of the square," replied the police agent, pointing to a house about two hundred steps off.

"Then I will go and fetch my master, who won't be best pleased at being disturbed."

Thereupon the passenger made Fix a bow, and returned on board the steamer.

THE OTHER LOG OF PHILEAS FOGG

Fogg's train had taken the two from Charing Cross Station to Dover. On the way, Passepartout suddenly recalled that he had left the gas jet in his room burning. Mr. Fogg coldly replied that it must burn—at Passepartout's expense.

From Dover the two took a boat to Calais, and a train from there through France and Italy. At Brindisi, still on schedule, they boarded the P & O ship, the *Mongolia*. This luxurious liner, fed by coal, driven by steam, docked in Suez, at 11 A.M., Wednesday, the ninth of October, exactly on time. According to Fogg's notebook, the journey thus far had taken 158½ hours or six and a half days. For this period, the other log of Fogg contained only a few phrases, with some enigmatic references.

Stayed in the cabin. P— brought in the meals. Gave P— a description of N—, and P— is looking for him on the ship. Told P— that the color of N—'s eyes may be different. When I served under him, they were black. But they were covered by contact lenses. N— must have an ocular deficiency or he was wearing them to disguise the real color of his eyes. Latter seems improbable. Why would he need a disguise while aboard the N—? But he can't conceal the extraordinarily wide spacing between his eyes unless he pretends to be injured in one eye and wears a bandage. Or, more likely, a large patch over one eye. Told P— to look for these.

Should have killed N— while aboard the N— and taken the consequences. But a thousand years are not easily thrown away. Not conscience but longevity doth make cowards of us all.

At Suez, the man who had sent the telegram to Scotland Yard was waiting on the dock. Mr. Fix was short and thin and had sharp intelligent-looking features, bright foxy eyes, and eyebrows incessantly rising and falling as if subject to shock waves. He was a detective who had been sent to Suez, to apprehend the Bank of England robber if he should be trying to escape via the Eastern route. Mr. Fix had been provided with a good description of the wanted man, but he did not need it. He had known beforehand that the thief and Mr. Fogg looked like twin brothers. He was cursing softly now because his superiors (Capellean, not police) had not permitted him to "find" and arrest Fogg the day after the theft. But no, they wanted to make it appear that Fix had "happened" to come across Fogg during his walk from his house to the Reform.

All must appear natural and unforced. The arrest could take place three or four days after the theft; there was no hurry. First, Mr. Fix must find an excuse for being in Fogg's neighborhood. Then he would "accidentally" see Fogg, note the resemblance to the thief, and take him into custody. There was little chance of keeping him in jail long or of bringing him to trial. This seems to have been overlooked by Verne, though he was only one of many millions who did not consider carefully the weakness of the case against Fogg. Aside from the startling physical similarity of Fogg and the criminal, there were no grounds for charges. Mr. Fogg would have had his valet's testimony that he had been in the house until 11:30 A.M. the morning of the theft. At least two dozen people could testify that he had entered the Reform Club at the regular time and stayed there long after the theft had occurred.

The mystery about the case is why the police or the public paid any attention to Fix's identification of the robber as Fogg. Any policeman on the beat could have established in a short time that Fogg could not possibly have been the culprit. The only explanation for this mistake is that the robbery occurred in the morning and that Forster, the valet, could not be found to testify that his master had indeed been home that morning. Forster must have been sent out of the country on a mission from which Stuart could not recall him even to save Fogg's reputation.

However, why did Fix go to Suez before he knew that Fogg would be leaving England and travelling on the *Mongolia*? The answer is that, though the Capelleans often manipulated people and events, they could not always manage things to suit themselves. Fix, though a Capellean, was also an employee of the police department. When ordered by the police chief to go to Suez, he had to go. He could have played sick and so stayed in the country. But his Capellean superiors must have decided that Fogg might be apprehended by a non-Capellean policeman.

And so Fix took train and steamer to the Red Sea port. Meanwhile, his superiors prepared to tip off the police through an anonymous note. Fogg would be brought in for questioning. If the Capelleans could abduct Forster, Fogg would have no witness to verify that he had been home and not at the Bank of England. As it turned out, the Capelleans had taken too much time to carry out the plot. Forster had disappeared, which was fine for their plans, except that they had hoped to get their hands on him and extract all the information he contained. But Fogg himself had left England.

We may imagine what the Capelleans did, since we are as logical as the Capelleans. This unexpected defeat of their plans might be fortunate. If Fogg were arrested by Fix, Fix would not have to turn him over to the authorities. On the journey back to England, an "escape" by Fogg would be arranged. Fogg would disappear, apparently into hiding. But he would be hidden in some Capellean secret chamber. There the same methods planned for Forster would be applied to Fogg. The original idea had been that Fogg would be held in jail for a day or two before an investigation determined that he must be innocent. But he would be "rescued." He would suppose that those who effected his escape would be Eridaneans. He would discover his error when it was too late for him.

And so Fix received a message that he should intercept Fogg at Suez. Fix was happy about this. He went at once to the British consul and informed him that a passenger who remarkably resembled the thief would soon step off the *Mongolia*. After hurrying back to the dock, he scanned every face of the disembarkers. The man he was looking for did not get off. Fogg, as we know, was discreetly staying in his cabin.

As chance would have it—or was it chance?—a passenger asked him how to get to the consulate. He was a short stocky fellow with thick wild hair, bright blue eyes, and a slight French accent. He showed Fix the passport he was carrying. On reading the description thereon, Fix was startled. It was of the man for whom he was looking. The Frenchman, Passepartout, was taking his master's passport to be stamped by the consul. This was not necessary, since this was British territory. Fogg, however, wished to validate the times and places of his journey so that the bettors of the Reform Club would have no doubt that he was not cheating. This was also unnecessary, since his word was good enough for his friends at the Reform.

He also, we may be sure, wanted the Capelleans to know where he was. Only thus could he make sure that the hunters would not lose his track.

Why, of all the people standing on the wharf, did Passepartout pick Fix to ask the way to the consulate? Was this not more than a coincidence? On the other hand, how would Passepartout have known that Fix was a Capellean? They did not carry placards proclaiming their identity.

Passepartout, however, had had much experience with the police. Just as Fix had bragged to the consul that he could smell a crook, so Passepartout could smell a cop. The Capelleans, like their enemies the Eridaneans, had many of their people in the police departments. They could be very effective there. Being lawmen, they could often act outside the law with impunity if they were discreet. So Passepartout may have calculated that a policeman might also be a Capellean.

It is more likely that Passepartout recognized Fix as a detective and thought that a policeman could give the proper directions. In any event, Fix directed him to the building, which was only two hundred steps away on the corner of the square. Since the British flag would have been flying over it, and there would have been signs indicating its function, it is strange that Passepartout did not see it. So, after all, he may have just been testing out the nervous little Capellean.

Fix informed the valet that, if the passport was to be stamped, its owner must appear in person with it. Passepartout returned to the ship.

CHAPTER VII

WHICH AFFORDS ANOTHER PROOF OF THE USELESSNESS OF PASSPORTS, AS FAR AS THE POLICE ARE CONCERNED

The detective left the quay and hurried to the consul's office, and he was immediately admitted to an interview with that functionary.

"Consul," said he, without further preface, "I have every reason to believe our man has taken a passage on board the *Mongolia*."

And Fix told him what had passed between himself and the servant about the passport.

"Well, Mr. Fix," replied the consul, "I shall not be sorry to see what the rascal is like. But perhaps he may not come to my office at all, if he is what you suppose him to be. No thief would like to leave any traces of his route behind him; and, besides, no passport is requisite for India."

"Consul, if he is as clever as we are led to believe he is, he will come to have his passport *visaed*."

"Yes, the only utility of a passport is to give respectable people trouble, and help rascals to escape."

"I can tell you beforehand his passport will be perfectly regular, but I hope you will refuse to put your stamp on it."

"Why? If it is in order," replied the consul, "I have no right to refuse."

"Nevertheless, I must contrive to keep him here until I can receive a warrant from London for his arrest."

"Well, Mr. Fix, that is your business, but for my part I—"

The consul had no time to say more, a knock at the door was heard, and the clerk ushered in two strangers, one of whom was the servant who had had the conversation with Mr. Fix.

In fact, they were master and servant. The master handed his passport to the consul, and briefly requested him to apply his *visa* to it.

The latter took the passport and read it attentively, while the detective apart watched the stranger anxiously.

When the consul had finished reading the passport—

"Are you Mr. Phileas Fogg?" he asked.

"Yes, sir."

"And this man is your servant?"

"Yes—a Frenchman named Passepartout."

"Do you come straight from London?"

"Yes."

"And you are going?"

"To Bombay."

"Very well. Are you aware that a passport is unnecessary, and this formality quite superfluous?"

"I am quite aware of it," replied Phileas Fogg, "but I wish to prove by your *visa* that I passed through Suez."

"Very well, sir."

And the consul signed and dated the passport, and stamped it officially. Mr. Fogg paid the fee, and after a stiff bow retired, followed by his servant.

"Well?" asked the detective.

"Well," replied the consul, "he seems a very respectable man, as far as I can judge.

"Very possible," replied Fix, "but that is not the question. Don't you think, consul, he is exactly like the party whose description has been forwarded to me?"

"I must say it is; but, as you know, all descriptions—"

"I must know more about him yet," replied Fix, "the servant seems less difficult to decipher than his master. Besides, he is a Frenchman, and he is sure to talk. I shall see you again soon."

So saying, the police agent walked off to try and find Passepartout.

As soon as he left the consul's office Mr. Fogg returned to the quay. There he gave his man several orders, got into a boat, was rowed off to the *Mongolia*, and went to his cabin. Then he took out his note-book, which contained the following dates—

"Left London, Wednesday, October 2nd, at 8.45 P.M.

Arrived in Paris, Thursday, October 3rd, at 7.20 A.M.

Left Paris, Thursday, October 3rd, at 8.40 A.M.

Arrived at Turin by the Mount Cenis Railway, Friday, October 4th, at 6.35 A.M.

Left Turin, Friday, 7.30 A.M.

Arrived at Brindisi, Saturday, October 5th, at 4 P.M.

Embarked on board the *Mongolia*, Saturday, at 5 P.M.

Arrived at Suez, Wednesday, October 9th, at 11 A.M.

Total consumption of hours, 158 1/2, or 6 1/2 days."

Mr. Fogg inscribed these dates in an itinerary arranged in columns, showing from the 2nd of October to the 21st of December, the month, date, day of the arrivals as contracted for at every principal place, such as Paris, Brindisi, Suez, Bombay, Singapore, Hong-kong, Yokohama, San Francisco, New York, Liverpool, and London, which thus allowed him to calculate the time lost or gained at every point of his journey.

In this manner Mr. Fogg always knew exactly how he was situated.

He now put down the date, October 9th, of his arrival at Suez, which, agreeing with the time the vessel was due, showed neither profit nor loss in point of time. Then he breakfasted in his cabin. As to looking at the town, he never thought of it for a moment, being one of that sort of Englishmen who make use of their servants' eyes if they wish to see the countries they pass through.

Philip José Farmer

THE OTHER LOG OF PHILEAS FOGG

Fix at once hastened to the consul. He told him that he believed that the thief was on the *Mongolia*. The consul must detain Fogg when he came to have his passport visaed. Fix needed time to get a warrant for his arrest from London via telegram.

This the consul refused to do. Unless a warrant was on hand, the consul must permit Fogg to go on his way.

The master and servant shortly thereafter appeared, and Fix helplessly observed the stamping of the passport. He decided to follow the two. Fogg had returned to the cabin to eat his breakfast there, but Passepartout was around the wharf.

CHAPTER VIII

IN WHICH PASSEPARTOUT SAYS RATHER MORE THAN WAS ADVISABLE

Fix now fell in with Passepartout, who was strolling about the quay and looking at everything, being allowed the free use of his eyes.

"Well, friend," said Fix, as he came up to him, "is your passport all right?"

"Oh, it is you, is it?" replied the Frenchman; "much obliged, all right."

"Are you seeing what you can of the country?"

"Yes; but we travel so fast that it seems like a dream to me—and here we are at Suez."

"As you say, at Suez."

"In Egypt?"

"Exactly so."

"And in Africa?"

"In Africa."

"In Africa," repeated Passepartout. "I can hardly believe it—only fancy, sir, I thought we were going no farther than Paris, and all I saw of that famous capital was from twenty minutes past seven in the morning to forty minutes past eight, between the stations of the Northern and Lyons railways through the windows of a cab, and during a pouring rain. I am so sorry; I should have liked so much to have seen Pére la Chaise cemetery and the circus in the Champs-Elysées once more."

"You must be in a great hurry," observed the police agent.

"I am not, but my master is. By the by, where can I buy some socks and shirts? We left home without any clothes, with only one carpet bag."

"I will show you where you can find everything you want."

"Thank you, sir," replied Passepartout. "You are really very obliging."

They walked away together. Passepartout continued talking.

"I must be sure not to miss the boat."

"You have plenty of time," said Fix, "it is hardly twelve yet."

Passepartout pulled out his great watch.

"Twelve," said he, "why it is only fifty-two minutes past nine."

"Your watch is slow," said Fix.

"My watch—an heirloom from my great-grandfather!— it does not vary five minutes in twelve months. It is a real chronometer!"

"I see how it is," said Fix. "Yours is London time, which is about two hours behind Suez time. You must take care to set your watch by the hour of noon in each country you come to."

"I alter my watch," cried Passepartout— "not I."

"Well, but it won't agree with the time by the sun if you do not."

"So much the worse for the sun then; he will be wrong, not my watch." So the good fellow thrust his watch into his pocket again.

In a few moments Fix observed—

"You must have left London in a great hurry!"

"I should think we did. Last Wednesday, contrary to his usual habit, Mr. Fogg came home from his club, and three-quarters of an hour after we set off."

"But where is your master going?"

"Straight ahead. He means to go round the world."

"Round the world?" cried Fix.

"Yes, in eighty days. He tells me he has made a bet he can do it, but, between ourselves, I don't believe him; that's all nonsense, there must be some other reason."

"Mr. Fogg must be an eccentric character."

"I think he is."

"Is he not?"

"He must be, he carries a large sum about him in new bank notes, and he does not care what money he spends on the road. For instance, he has promised the *Mongolia*'s chief engineer a handsome sum if we gain some hours on the time we are due at Bombay."

"Have you known him any length of time?"

"I," replied Passepartout—"I only entered his service the day we left."

One can easily conceive the effect of these replies on the overheated imagination of Mr. Fix.

This hurried departure from London, so short a time after the robbery, the large sum in new bank notes he was carrying with him, the hurry he showed to reach distant countries, and the excuse of an improbable bet, all confirmed Fix in his previous ideas, and reasonably so. He continued to question the Frenchman, and soon convinced himself that the man knew nothing whatever about his master, who lived by himself in London, who was said to be rich, though no one knew the sources of his income, that he was a very reserved man, &c., that he became quite certain of one thing, viz., that he, Phileas Fogg, had no intention of going ashore at Suez, and that he really meant to go on to Bombay.

"Is it far to Bombay?" asked Passepartout.

"Some distance," replied the detective, "about ten days' sea voyage."

"Where do you say Bombay is?"

"In India."

"In Asia?"

"Of course."

"The devil it is. I must tell you there is one thing which worries me. My gas burner."

"What gas burner?"

"My burner which I forgot to turn off, and which is now burning at my expense. Now I have made a calculation that it will cost me two shillings every twenty-four hours, exactly sixpence more than my wages come to, and you can understand, if this journey lasts a long time—"

Did Fix understand this tale about the gas? it is not very likely. He paid no further attention to his companion, for he had made up his mind how to act. He left Passepartout making his purchases in the bazaar, recommended him not to miss the *Mongolia*, and hurried back to the consul's office.

"Sir," said he to the consul, "I am no longer in any doubt—I am sure of my man—he passes himself off as an original, and he has undertaken to go round the world in eighty days."

"He is a clever fellow then," said the consul; "so he reckons on returning to London after throwing the police of two continents off the scent."

"We shall see," replied Fix.

"Are you sure that you have made no mistake?" asked the consul again.

"None."

"Then why should this thief have insisted so much on having his passport signed at Suez?"

"Why, that is more than I can tell, consul, but listen to me."

And in a few words he repeated some of the most striking points of his conversation with Passepartout.

"Really," said the consul, "appearances are certainly against this man; how do you propose to act?"

I shall send a telegram to London, desiring them to send me a warrant for this man's arrest direct to Bombay; I shall go on board the *Mongolia*, keep the thief in view to India, and there, being on English ground, I shall very politely tap him on the shoulder and show him my warrant."

Having thus coolly explained his intentions to the consul, the detective took leave of him, and betook himself to the telegraph office; thence he sent the telegram, which we have already seen, to the head-quarters of the police in Scotland Yard.

A quarter of an hour afterwards Fix, with his light travelling bag in his hand, well supplied with money, took a passage on board the *Mongolia*, which was soon steaming at a rapid rate down the Red Sea.

THE OTHER LOG OF PHILEAS FOGG

He readily answered Fix's questions. He told him that since they had left in such a hurry, he must buy some shoes and shirts while in Suez. Fix offered to take him to a shop. Passepartout accepted with thanks. On the way, the Frenchman consulted his watch to make sure he had enough time to shop and then get back to the steamer.

"You have plenty of time," Fix said. "It is only twelve o'clock."

Passepartout was astounded. His watch indicated only eight minutes to ten.

"Your watch is slow," Fix said.

Passepartout exclaimed with disbelief. His watch, he said, did not vary five minutes in a year. It was an heirloom, it had originally belonged to his great-grandfather. And it was true that he was proud of the chronometer as a perfect timepiece. But he also dangled it before Fix to get a reaction which had nothing to do with watches per se. It was necessary to know if the Capellean, if he were one, suspected that a distorter was concealed therein. Fix, however, seemed interested only in Passepartout's lack of knowledge about time zones. He informed him that his watch was still keeping London time. This was two hours behind Suez time. He should regulate his watch at high noon whenever he passed into a different zone.

Passepartout acted as if this suggestion bordered on sacrilege.

"I regulate my watch? Never!"

Fix patiently, if in a nervous manner, said, "Then it won't agree with the sun."

Passepartout's reply was typically Gallic.

"So much the worse for the sun. The sun will be wrong!"

Fix was silenced for a few moments by this vehemence and disregard for natural laws. When he recovered, he said, "You left London suddenly?"

"I believe so! Last Friday at eight o'clock in the evening, Mr.

Fogg came home from his club. Three-quarters of an hour later, we were off!"

"But where is your master going?"

"Always straight ahead. He's going around the world!"

Fix was startled by this. Or, at least, he seemed to be. Perhaps his superiors had not notified him as yet of the wager.

"Around the world?"

Passepartout then told Fix that the trip must take no more than eighty days. As for him, he did not believe the reason given for this unexpected departure from the "snail's shell." There must be another reason for this madness.

This may have convinced Fix that the Frenchman was only an innocent fellow-traveler. If so, he could learn much by being friendly with this fellow.

Whatever Passepartout's role, he was certainly telling the truth about Fogg's intention of going eastward.

"Bombay, is it far from here?" Passepartout said.

"Rather far. It's ten days by sea."

"And in what country is Bombay?"

"India."

"In Asia?"

This ignorance may be excused in a peasant or an illiterate worker in the factory. But would a man whose name means "Goes Everywhere," and who has been everywhere, be so lacking in such elementary geographical knowledge? Hardly. Passepartout was merely continuing to act the role allotted to him. To reinforce this image, he told Fix of the gaslight he had forgotten to turn off. His master was charging him for this, justly, it must be admitted, which meant that he was losing sixpence a day more than he earned.

Fix did not care about the man's troubles. After saying good-bye to the valet, he sent off a telegram for a warrant of arrest. He then packed a small bag and boarded the *Mongolia* a few minutes before it left the dock. He also, we may be sure, sent a coded telegram to his superiors in London. He would receive their reply in the telegraph office in Bombay.

CHAPTER IX

IN WHICH THE RED SEA AND THE INDIAN OCEAN SHOW
THEMSELVES FAVORABLE TO THE CAUSE OF PHILEAS FOGG

The distance between Suez and Aden is exactly thirteen hundred and ten miles, and the company's time tables allow its steamers one hundred and thirty-eight hours to accomplish that distance. The *Mongolia*, with a full head of steam, was going at a rate which promised an arrival before the stipulated time. Most of the passengers who had embarked at Brindisi were bound to India; some were going to Bombay, some to Calcutta *via* Bombay, for since a railway was running across the Indian Peninsula, there was no necessity for going round by Ceylon.

Among the passengers on the *Mongolia* were several civil functionaries and officers of all ranks. Of the latter, some belonged to the British regular army, others were in command of native regiments, all receiving very high pay, even now that the Government had taken the functions of the old East India Company upon itself; sub-lieutenants being paid two hundred and eighty pounds a year, brigadiers two thousand four hundred pounds, and generals four thousand pounds.

They lived very well on board the *Mongolia*, in a society consisting of civil and military authorities and a few young Englishmen, who, with large sums at their disposal, were going out to establish commercial undertakings in foreign lands. The paymaster, the company's confidential agent on board, whose influence was only exceeded by the captain's, kept a sumptuous table. Breakfast, lunch, dinner and supper were equally well served. The lady passengers, and there were a few, changed their dress twice a day; they had music and even dancing when the sea permitted it. But the Red Sea is very changeable and often very rough, as all these long straight gulfs usually are. When the wind came either from the coast of Africa or Asia, the *Mongolia*, a long screw steamer, with the sea on her beam, rolled frightfully. Then the ladies would soon disappear; pianos were silent, no more singing or dancing. All this time, however, in spite of squalls and heavy seas, the steamer made her way through it all to the Straits of Babelmandeb.

What was Phileas Fogg about all this time? One would be justified in supposing that in his anxiety he spent his time in watching the wind as it delayed or favoured the course of the vessel, or speculated on what damage the sea might cause the steamer, oblige him to make for some other port, and so compromise the success of his undertaking.

Not at all, or at least if such a contingency ever occurred to him he showed no trace of it on his face; he always wore the same imperturbable air, which no event, no accident could disturb—he was as guiltless of any emotion as the ship's chronometers; he was seldom seen on deck—he never troubled himself about the Red Sea and its memories of the past, the theatre of the first historical scenes humanity is acquainted with. He never cared for the interesting towns along its shores, whose picturesque outline was to be noticed on the horizon; he never gave a thought to the dangers of that Arabian gulf which the ancient historians, Strabo, Arrian, Arthemidorus, Edrisi, and others, have always mentioned with dread, and which in other days sailors never attempted to navigate without offering propitiatory sacrifices at the outset of their voyage.

What then was this original about during his imprisonment on board the *Mongolia*? In the first place, he took his four meals per diem, allowing neither rolling nor pitching of the vessel to interrupt such a wonderful organization as his. Besides, he played at whist.

Yes! he had fallen in with men as fond of whist as himself; a revenue collector, *en route* to his port at Goa; a clergyman, the Rev. Decimus Smith, returning to Bombay; and a brigadier-general, returning to his command at Benares. These three passengers were as fond of whist as Mr. Fogg, and they used to play for hours, all three as silent as himself. As for Passepartout, sea-sickness was to him unknown; he had a cabin forward, and he fed like a man who did his duty. The truth is, this voyage, and the circumstances attending it, were no longer disagreeable to him; he now rather liked being well fed, well lodged, and visiting foreign parts; besides, he had made up his mind that all this caprice would have an end at Bombay. The day after they left Suez, the 10th of October, he felt quite pleased when he met on deck with the obliging person whose acquaintance he had made when he landed in Egypt.

"If I am not mistaken," said he, addressing him with a smile of welcome, "you are the gentleman who was so kind as to act as my guide at Suez."

"Well," replied the detective, "I thought I knew you again! You are that English original's servant, are you not?"

"Exactly, Mr. —"

"Fix."

"Mr. Fix," continued Passepartout; "delighted to find you on board. And where may you be going?"

"Like you, to Bombay."

"Nothing could be better. Have you ever made this passage before?"

"Several times," replied Fix; "I am an agent of the Peninsular and Oriental Company."

"Then you know India well?"

"Well, I may say I do," replied Fix, who was afraid of committing himself.

"India is a curious place, is it not?"

"Very curious; mosques and minarets, temples and fakirs, pagodas, snakes, tigers, and dancing girls. I hope you will have time to see the country."

"I hope so too, Mr. Fix. You see, a man can hardly be in his right senses to pass his life in jumping from steamer to railway train, and from train again to steamer, on pretence of going round the world in eighty days. No, all these gymnastics will come to an end at Bombay, you may rely on it."

"How is Mr. Fogg?" inquired Fix, in a very natural tone of voice.

"Very well, Mr. Fix, and so am I. I eat like an ogre; it is the sea air."

"And your master? I never see him on deck."

"No, never; he is not at all curious."

"Do you know, Mr. Passepartout, this pretended eighty days' tour may conceal some secret mission, I mean diplomatic, you know."

"Really, Mr. Fix, I must confess I know nothing about it, and, in fact, I would not give half-a-crown to find it out."

Since that meeting Passepartout and Fix often had a conversation together. The police agent was very anxious to be on intimate terms with Mr. Fogg's servant. It might happen to be very useful to him; for that reason he often treated him to a glass of whiskey or bitter beer at the *Mongolia*'s bar, which Passepartout accepted without ceremony, and as often returned, at the same time thinking Fix a very jolly fellow. The steamer, in the meantime, was making a quick passage. On the 13th they sighted Mocha, surrounded by its girdle of ruined walls, above which they could distinguish a few green date-trees. In the distance vast groves of coffee plantations were to be seen. Passepartout was delighted to see this celebrated city; he fancied with its circle of walls and dismantled fortress which looked like the handle, that he could trace in it a resemblance to an enormous coffee cup.

The night following the *Mongolia* passed the Straits of

Babelmandeb, which in Arabic signifies the "Gate of Tears," and the next day, the 14th, it brought up at Steamer Point, at the north-west of Aden harbour, where they had to coal.

It is a very serious matter to supply steamers with coal at such a distance from the mines. The Peninsular and Oriental Company spend eight hundred thousand pounds a year on coal alone. They are obliged to have depots at different ports, and in these distant seas fuel sometimes costs them from three to four pounds a ton.

The *Mongolia* had still a run of sixteen hundred and fifty miles to make before reaching Bombay, and it would take four hours at Steamer Point for her to fill up her coal bunkers.

But this would cause no delay in Phileas Fogg's programme. It had been anticipated. Besides, the *Mongolia* arrived at Aden in the evening of the 14th of October instead of on the morning of the 15th; thus he had a gain of fifteen hours. Mr. Fogg and his servant went ashore; the former wished to have his passport signed and dated. Fix followed him unnoticed. That formality fulfilled, Mr. Fogg returned on board and continued his rubber.

Passepartout, as usual, wandered about among that population of Somanlis, Banyans, Parsees, Jews, Arabs, and Europeans which form the twenty-five thousand inhabitants of Aden. He admired the fortifications which have made this town the Gibraltar of the Indian Ocean, and the magnificent cisterns on which English engineers were still at work, two thousand years after King Solomon's engineers had begun them.

"Curious, very curious," said Passepartout to himself, as he returned on board. "I see the necessity there is to travel if one wishes to see what is new."

At six in the evening the *Mongolia* left Aden harbour, and was soon crossing the Indian Ocean. She had one hundred and sixty-eight hours allowed for the passage from Aden to Bombay. The Indian seas, too, were in her favour. The wind was northeasterly, and her canvas assisted her engines.

Under this pressure of sail the vessel rolled much less. The lady passengers, in fresh toilettes, began to show themselves on deck again. Very soon singing and dancing were once more resumed.

The voyage was thus on the point of coming to a termination most favourably. Passepartout was delighted with the agreeable companion chance had thrown in his way in the person of Mr. Fix.

On Sunday, October the 20th, about twelve, they sighted the coast of India. Two hours afterwards the *Mongolia* was boarded by the pilot. On the horizon a line of hills stood out against the sky; they could now easily distinguish the palm trees which form the background to the town. The steamer entered the harbour formed by the islands of Salcette, Colaba, Elephanta, and Butcher, and at half-past four she came to her moorings alongside the quay at Bombay.

Phileas Fogg was just finishing the thirty-third rubber he had played that day, and he and his partner, having very cleverly made all the thirteen tricks, finished their whist by a Schlem. The *Mongolia* was only due at Bombay on the 22nd of October. Now it was only the 20th when she arrived. Phileas Fogg was thus enabled to set down in his itinerary a gain of two whole days, which he did with the greatest composure.

THE OTHER LOG OF PHILEAS FOGG

The *Mongolia* was scheduled to traverse one thousand three hundred and ten miles in one hundred and thirty-eight hours. Fogg ate his four meals a day, breakfast, lunch, dinner, and supper. During this leg of the trip, he did not stroll on the decks, but he did not entirely confine himself to his cabin. If he had one passion, aside from a desire for regularity, it was for whist. This game, the precursor of bridge, was then the rage of England. He found three equally intense lovers of the cards and spent most of his time with them at the table. These were a tax collector on his way to Goa, a priest, and a brigadier-general in Her Majesty's service at Benares. All were not only excellent players but untalkative, which pleased Fogg. He may have joined them originally to determine if one of them had any message for him from Stuart. But no, all were what they appeared to be, and whist was the only thing in which they were interested.

Passepartout had informed Fogg that Fix was aboard. Fix, he said, claimed to be an agent for the P & O and was going to Bombay on business. This could be true. But what was his business? Assassinating the two, arranging for their abduction, or what? Neither were aware yet that Fogg was wanted by the law. Fogg was still puzzling over the clipping given him by the beggar woman. He would have to find some means to clarify this, but at the moment he did not know how. He could have sent a message to Stuart at Suez or Aden, where the ship also stopped en route to Bombay. It was certain, however, that Fix would find out to whom Fogg had cabled, and this would not be allowed to happen.

Fogg had a quiet talk with his valet. He quoted the newspaper article from memory. Passepartout suddenly perceived the likeness between Mr. Fogg and the description of the thief. Why Fogg, for whom the unforeseen did not exist, had not seen this before is inexplicable. The only answer is that it was unthinkable to him that anybody could associate him with anything dishonest. Though he was an Eridanean, he was also an English gentleman. Yet it was he who had pointed out to his Reform Club whist partners that the robber was no robber but a gentleman.

"What a coincidence!" Passepartout said. "Who would have thought of such a thing occurring? And especially at this time?"

Fogg was suddenly cured of his blindness. Now that he could perceive the facts un-shrouded by his egotism, he saw exactly what had happened. But Passepartout still thought that it was only an unlucky chance.

"No," Fogg said, "far from it. This has been brought about by you-know-whom. One of them was made up to look like me and sent out to steal the money. If we had not left so abruptly, I would now be in jail. Stuart saw what was going on, though I cannot understand why he did not warn me sooner."

"Perhaps he only began to think about it after the subject was brought up at the Reform," Passepartout said. "He had no time to get a message to us at our house. In any event, it would have aroused the curiosity of you-know-whom if a message had been delivered to you. So he chose the beggar woman, who may or may not be one of us. But then why did he himself not deliver the clipping when he said good-bye to us at the station?"

"Because Flanagan, Fallentin, and Ralph were also there. They seem to be innocents, that is, not you-know-whom, but he did not want to take a chance."

"But what could a mere clipping tell you?"

"He knew that I would soon see the connection. I should have known it immediately. But my pride prevented it. And though the description does fit me, in general that is, it is vague in particulars."

"What will we do?"

"Proceed as planned," Mr. Fogg calmly replied.

"But if you are arrested at Bombay?"

"All taken care of."

Passepartout did not ask him what his plans were. He would only have received a cold stare and rightly so. If he were to fall into the hands of the enemy, the less he knew the better. Nevertheless, Fogg did tell Passepartout to encourage the drinking in the bar with Fix. Passepartout, who had a strong head for strong liquor, considering he was a Frenchman, was to pretend to have his tongue loosened by the pale ale and whiskey with which Fix was daily plying him. He was to tell Fix nothing except what he would have known if master and valet were exactly what they pretended to be.

Passepartout reported that Fix was continuing the hints he'd made during their first supposedly chance meeting on the *Mongolia*. These were that Fogg's trip was a blind for some other mission, possibly diplomatic. Fix also kept urging the Frenchman to adjust his watch to the sun. Fogg told Passepartout to shadow Fix to determine if he was communicating with anybody.

CHAPTER X

IN WHICH PASSEPARTOUT IS TOO LUCKY
IN LOSING ONLY HIS SHOES

No one is ignorant that India, that great reversed triangle, the base of which is towards the North, and its apex to the South—contains a superficies of fourteen hundred thousand square miles, over which is very unequally spread a population of one hundred and eighty million souls. The British Government exercises a direct rule over a certain part of this vast country. It has a Governor-General at Calcutta, Governors at Madras, Bombay, in Bengal, and a Lieutenant-Governor at Agra.

But British India, properly so called, only contains a superficies of seven hundred thousand square miles, and a population of one hundred to one hundred and ten million souls. A considerable extent of territory, therefore, is still independent of the Queen's authority, and, in fact, Hindu independence still exists under the ferocious and absolute rule of certain Rajahs in the interior.

Since 1756—at which period the first English establishment was formed, on soil now occupied by the town of Madras—until the year of the great Sepoy rebellion, the celebrated East India Company was all powerful. Little by little, it had annexed province after province, purchasing them from Rajahs, to whom it paid, or promised to pay, a mere nominal income; it appointed its Governor-General, and all its servants, both civil and military; but at this moment its existence has passed away, and the British possessions in India are held direct by the Crown.

The aspect of the country, as well as its manners, the divisions of race in the peninsula, have a daily tendency to change. In former days, one availed oneself of the old means of transport, on foot, on horseback, in palanquins, coaches, even on men's shoulders; now great steamboats ply on the Indus and the Ganges, while a railway, crossing India at its broadest part, with branch lines joining it from several points, brings Bombay within three days' journey of Calcutta.

This line does not follow a direct course across India. The distance between these two places as a bird can fly, is not more than a thousand or eleven hundred miles, and even moderately fast trains would not require three days to accomplish that distance; but it is increased one-third at least by the circuitous route followed by the railway, in going so far north as Allahabad.

This is an outline of the course taken by the great Indian Peninsula Railway. On leaving the Island of Bombay, it passes through Salcette, reaching the mainland opposite Tamiat, goes over the chain of the Western Ghauts, keeps northward as far as Burhampore, skirts along the nearly independent territory of Bundelkund, up to Allahabad, then bends to the east, and meets the Ganges at Benares; leaving it there, it turns to the south-east by Burdivan, and the French town of Chandernagore, whence it runs in a straight line till it reaches Calcutta.

It was half-past four in the afternoon when the passengers disembarked from the *Mongolia* at Bombay, and the train was to leave for Calcutta punctually at eight.

Mr. Fogg, therefore, took leave of his whist-playing friends, left the steamer, gave his servant directions to make certain purchases, desired him to be at the station before eight, and then walked with his regular step towards the passport office.

As for seeing the wonders of Bombay, he never gave them a thought, neither the Residency, nor the magnificent library, nor the fortifications, nor the docks, nor the cotton market, nor bazaars, nor mosques, nor synagogues, nor the Armenian churches, nor the splendid pagoda on Malabar Hill, with its two polygonal towers. He neither visited the masterpieces of Elephanta, nor its mysterious subterranean vaults, hidden to the south-east of the roads, nor the grottoes of Kanheria in the island of Salcette, considered to be the finest remains of Buddhist architecture.

He saw none of these things. When he left the passport office, Phileas Fogg betook himself quietly to the station, and ordered his dinner. Among other dishes the proprietor of the restaurant particularly recommended a native rabbit *"en gibolette."*

Phileas ordered the *"gibolette"* and tasted it, but in spite of its highly spiced sauce he thought it detestable.

He rang for the head waiter.

"Sir," said he, looking him full in the face, "do you call that rabbit?"

"Yes, my lord," replied the rascal, quite unabashed, "jungle rabbit."

"Did not that rabbit mew when it was shot?"

"Mew! my lord; how? what?"

"Waiter," said Mr. Fogg, coldly, "do not swear, but remember this, in former years in India cats were considered sacred animals; those were good times, indeed."

"For the cats, my lord?"

"And for travellers too, perhaps."

Having made these observations, Mr. Fogg continued his dinner.

Very soon after Mr. Fogg had landed Fix quitted the *Mongolia*, and hurried off to the chief of the Bombay police, told him what he was and what his object was with regard to the party suspected. Had the warrant for his arrest arrived at Bombay? No, and, in fact, as the warrant left London later than Fogg, it could not possibly have arrived yet.

Fix was rather disconcerted—he tried to persuade the police inspector to authorize Fogg's arrest. This the inspector declined doing. It was in the department of the metropolitan police which alone could give such an order. This strictness of principle and respect for the law is quite in accordance with English habits, which, in all that regards the liberty of the subject, admit no compromise.

Fix gave up the point and made up his mind to wait for the warrant. But he was determined not to lose sight of his thief as long as he remained in Bombay—he had not the least doubt that Fogg would make some stay there. And we know that such was Passepartout's opinion, which would give the warrant time to reach him.

But judging from his master's last orders as he left the *Mongolia*, the valet soon found that he would make no longer stay at Bombay than at Paris and Suez, that the journey would not end there, but be continued as far as Calcutta and perhaps farther. He began to think the story of the bet might perhaps be true, and, nothing occurring to prevent it, he whose object it was to live quietly at home might find himself making the tour of the world in eighty days.

In the meantime, having bought some shirts and stockings, he took a walk through the streets of Bombay. There was a great crowd of Europeans of every country, Persians with their pointed caps, Burmese with their circular turbans, Scinds with square caps, Armenians in long robes, and Parsees in black mitres. It happened to be a Parsee or Guebre festival, direct descendants of the followers of Zoroaster, who are the most industrious, most civilized, most intelligent, strictest of Hindus—a sect to which in these days all the wealthy native merchants in Bombay belong. That day they were celebrating a sort of religious carnival, with spectacles and processions, in which bayaderes in pink gauze robes, embroidered in gold and silver, danced gracefully but modestly to the music of stringed instruments and native drums.

Unfortunately for his master's interest, the successful

issue of whose journey was thereby seriously compromised, Passepartout's curiosity led him farther than was prudent.

After standing for some time looking at the Parsee procession, Passepartout turned his steps towards the station, when, as he passed the wonderful pagoda on Malabar Hill, it unfortunately occurred to him that he should like to see the interior. On two points he was ignorant; first, that there are certain Hindu temples, the entrance to which is strictly forbidden to Christians, and, secondly, that even the faithful are not allowed to visit them without leaving their shoes at the door. It is as well to observe that the British Government, from motives of sound policy, respects and insists on the religion of the natives being respected even in its most trifling details, and severely punishes any one who in any way infringes its observance.

Passepartout, far from thinking he was doing wrong in his quality of simple traveller, was admiring the glittering splendour of Brahminical decoration in the interior, when he suddenly found himself on his back on the pavement. Three priests, with fury in their looks, rushed upon him, tore off his shoes and stockings, and began to belabour him, yelling at the same time with all their might.

The Frenchman was strong and active; he was soon on his legs again, and with a blow and a kick he knocked down two of his antagonists, who were encumbered in their long robes, and rushed out of the pagoda as fast as he could, leaving the third Hindu, who had followed him, calling on the crowd for assistance as he did so, far behind.

Passepartout reached the station at five minutes to eight, without his hat, bare-footed, having lost the bundle containing his purchases, only a few moments before the train left.

Fix was there. Having followed Mr. Fogg to the station, he saw that his man was about to leave Bombay; he immediately decided on following him to Calcutta, and farther, if necessary. Passepartout did not notice Fix, who kept in the dark, but Fix could overhear him telling his master, in a few words, what had happened to him.

"I hope that will not occur again," was all that Phileas Fogg replied, as he took his seat in one of the carriages.

Poor Passepartout, without shoes or stockings, and very disconcerted, took his seat in silence.

Fix was about to get into another carriage when an idea came into his head, and made him suddenly change his plan of action.

"No," said he to himself, "I shall stay here. An offence committed on Indian soil—I am sure of my man now."

The locomotive gave a shrill scream from its steam whistle, and the train disappeared in the darkness of the night.

THE OTHER LOG OF PHILEAS FOGG

At thirty minutes after four in the afternoon, the two world travelers stepped onto the soil of Bombay. Verne says that Fogg gave his servant some errands to do after telling him he must be at the railroad station at eight that evening. And then, with his clockwork gait, he proceeded to the passport office. He exhibited no curiosity whatever about the architectural wonders of this jewel of India. This was to be expected from his character. But it probably was also due to the fact that he had seen them before and more than once. Verne reports a strange incident in the restaurant of the railroad station. Fogg ordered a *gibelotte* of "native rabbit" which the proprietor highly recommended. Tasting it, he rang for the owner. Staring coldly, he said, "Is this rabbit, sir?"

"Yes, my lord. Jungle rabbit."

"And this rabbit didn't mew when he was killed?"

The owner protested at length.

Fogg said, "Remember this. Cats were once considered to be sacred in India. That was a good time."

"For the cats, my lord?"

"Perhaps for the travelers as well."

By which we know that Fogg was not altogether without a certain dry wit. But by this curious conversation Fogg had determined that the proprietor was an Eridanean and that he had seen nothing suspicious to report. There had been no doubt in Fogg's mind, or in his tongue, that the animal was what it was claimed to be. If the owner had said, "For the rabbits, my lord?" instead of, "For the cats, my lord?" Fogg would have known that the owner had something important to impart.

Fogg's own final statement signified that he had nothing else to say and that all was well as far as he knew.

This was not the first time this had occurred. When Fogg was a new member of the Reform Club, a waiter had brought a rabbit instead of the beef he always had for dinner. During the course of the conversation—kept subdued because he did not wish the waiter to get fired—Mr. Fogg had received instructions. Stuart had not been able to deliver a message via the cards because of urgent business elsewhere. The same mix-up with rabbits had taken place twice more but at widely separated intervals of time. After all, if rabbit was mistakenly brought to him too often, some Capellean might get suspicious.

It was not too long after the restaurant incident that another and unfortunate incident occurred. Passepartout, though an Eridanean, was also human. He allowed his curiosity to lead him into the splendidly pagan pagoda of Malabar Hill. He was unaware that Christians were forbidden to enter this holy place. Not only the Brahmin but the British law prohibited this desecration. Passepartout was forced to knock down several priests while they were beating him and tearing off his shoes. The latter act was motivated by the injunction against anyone, even the faithful, wearing footgear in the temple. Lacking these, and also lacking the package of shoes and shirts he'd purchased, Passepartout fled. Fix overheard the valet explain to his master what had happened.

Fix had been about to follow them on the train, but this changed his mind. Though the warrant from London had not yet arrived, he could see to it that the two were arrested for an offense committed in India. He stayed behind to inform the authorities of the offenders' identity.

CHAPTER XI

PHILEAS FOGG PAYS VERY DEAR FOR A RIDE

The train had started at its appointed time; there were officers, civil functionaries, indigo planters, and opium dealers, whose business took them to the eastern side of the peninsula.

Passepartout was in the same compartment as his master; a third traveller sat in the opposite corner.

It was Brigadier-General Sir Francis Cromarty, one of Mr. Fogg's partners at whist on the passage from Suez to Bombay, who was about to rejoin his command in their cantonments near Benares. Sir Francis Cromarty was tall and fair, about fifty years of age; he had distinguished himself very much in the recent mutiny, and really deserved to be considered a native of the country. He had lived in India from early youth, and only made few and short visits to his native soil; he was a man of education, very capable of giving Mr. Fogg any information on the manners, history, and political organization of India, had that gentleman been likely to make any inquiry on the subject. But Fogg never asked him a question. He was not on his travels, he was merely describing a circle. It was a solid body performing a circle round the globe according to the laws of mechanical action. At that moment he was calculating the number of hours expended since he had left London, and he might have rubbed his hands with satisfaction had he been given to exerting himself so unnecessarily.

Sir Francis was not long in discovering that his fellow traveller was an original, before he had played a couple of rubbers with him. He was therefore justified in doubting whether the heart of man could beat within such a cold exterior, and whether Phileas Fogg had a soul susceptible of feeling the beauties of nature, or of comprehending a moral duty. Of all the characters the brigadier had ever met none were to be compared to this specimen of the exact sciences.

Phileas Fogg had not concealed his intention of making the tour of the world from Sir Francis Cromarty, nor the circumstances under which he started. The brigadier only saw in the affair of the bet an instance of eccentricity, without aim, and which was entirely without any beneficial object which ought to inspire a sensible man. At the rate at which this strange character was going, he was of no advantage either to himself or others.

An hour after leaving Bombay the train had passed the viaducts between Salcette and the mainland. At Callyan station they left the branch which runs to the south-east by Kandallah and Poonah, and at Pauwell they entered the passes of the western Ghauts with their bases of trapp and basalt, and whose highest peaks are thickly covered with wood.

From time to time Sir Francis Cromarty and Phileas Fogg exchanged a few words, and just then the brigadier observed—

"A few years ago, Mr. Fogg, you would have been delayed in a manner which would have seriously compromised your success."

"How so, Sir Francis?"

"Because, the rail ceased at the base of these mountains, and travellers crossed the mountains to Kandallah station either in palanquins or on ponies."

"This delay would not in any way have interfered with my programme," replied Mr. Fogg. "I had provided for encountering certain obstacles."

"Nevertheless, Mr. Fogg, that affair of your servant might have caused you some trouble."

Passepartout, with his feet wrapped up in his travelling rug, was fast asleep, and little did he dream they were talking about him.

"The British Government is, with great reason, very severe on this sort of offence," continued Sir Francis Cromarty. "It is particularly careful that the religious observances of the Hindus should be respected, and if your servant had been taken—"

"Well, and if he had been taken, Sir Francis," replied Mr. Fogg, "he would have been punished, and he could easily have returned to Europe. I do not see how such an affair could have delayed his master."

Thereupon the conversation dropped. In the night the train crossed the Ghauts, passed Nassik, and the next, the 21st of October, ran over the rather flat country of the Khandeish—a well cultivated soil, sprinkled with villages, in which the minaret of the pagoda took the place of the spire of the village church at home. This fertile district was irrigated by numerous small streams, most of them tributaries to the Godavery.

Passepartout woke up, and when he looked out he could hardly believe he was travelling through India on the Peninsula Railway. It seemed so impossible, yet nothing was more real. The locomotive, driven by an English engineer, and fed with English coals, vomited its smoke over cotton, coffee, nutmeg, clove, and red pepper plantations. The steam curled round clumps of palm trees, through which appeared picturesque bungalows, ruins of monasteries, called viharis, and wonderful temples enriched by the inexhaustible richness of Indian architecture. Then they came on endless plains, or jungles, which still contained tigers and serpents, to be put to flight by the scream of the engine; and at last forests, through which the line was cut, still the haunts of elephants, who, with pensive eyes, watched the headlong course of the train.

In the morning, beyond Malligaum station, the travellers found themselves in the accursed district so often the scene of the murderous exploits of the followers of the goddess Kali. Ellora and its admired pagodas were at no distance, and the celebrated Aurungabad, the capital of the ferocious conqueror, Aurungzebe, now only the chief town of one of the detached provinces of the Nizam's territory. Over this country Feringhea, the head of the Thugs, once ruled. These assassins strangled victims of every age, in honour of their goddess, Death, without blood spilling, and for a long time there was hardly a likely spot which did not conceal a corpse. The exertions of the English Government have greatly diminished the number of these murders, but this hideous association still exists and still finds victims.

At half-past twelve the train stopped at Burhampore station, and Passepartout was able to buy a pair of slippers, embroidered with imitation pearls, but very dear, which he put on with great satisfaction.

They had a hasty breakfast, and started again for Assurghur, after skirting the bank of the Taptee, a small river flowing into the gulf of Cambay, near Surat.

Until his arrival in Bombay Passepartout had allowed himself to cherish the expectation that there they would stop. But now that he was hurrying across India as fast as steam could drive him, he began to think differently. The natural propensity of his youth returned, he believed his master was quite serious in his plans, he believed in the story of the bet, and consequently of the journey round the world, and the space of time in which it was to be done. He was already growing uneasy at the possibility of delay, or of accidents which might happen on their way. He felt himself interested in the bet, and trembled when he thought what a risk he had run of causing his master to lose it by his foolish curiosity the evening before. He was less phlegmatic and more restless than Mr. Fogg. He counted the days lost over and over again, cursed the train every time it stopped, and privately blamed Mr. Fogg for not bribing the engineer. He did not know that while it was possible on board a steamer it was not to be done with a train, the speed of which is regularly timed.

Towards evening they were in the passes at the Subpoar hills which separate Khandeish from Bundelkund. The next day Sir Francis Cromarty, having asked Passepartout what the time was, the latter, looking at his watch, said it was three P.M. This famous watch, keeping Greenwich time, being now some seventy-seven degrees westward, was about four hours too slow.

Sir Francis corrected Passepartout's time, making the same remark to him which Fix had done. He endeavoured to make him understand that it was necessary to regulate his watch in every new meridian, as he was continually travelling eastward, that is, towards the sun, and the days were shorter by four minutes for every degree they went. Whether the obstinate fellow understood or not the general's observations, he persisted in not altering his watch, which he kept at London time. It was only an innocent delusion and could hurt no one.

At eight in the morning, about fifteen miles beyond Rothal station, the train stopped in the middle of a large clearing, bordered by several bungalows and workmen's cabins. The guard passed along the carriages, calling out, "Passengers alight here!"

Phileas Fogg looked at Sir Francis Cromarty, who did not seem to understand why they thus came to a stop in a tamarind and khajour forest.

Passepartout, equally surprised, jumped out of the carriage, and soon returned, saying—

"Sir, there is no line any farther."

"What do you mean?" asked Sir Francis.

"I mean to say the train goes no farther."

The brigadier immediately left the carriage, followed by Fogg, with great deliberation. They both inquired of the guard why they stopped.

"Where are we?" asked Sir Francis.

"At Kholby village," was the reply.

"Do we stop here?"

"Of course. The line is not finished."

"What do you mean? not finished!"

"No, there is still a distance of fifty miles to complete from this place to Allahabad, where the line goes on again."

"But in the papers it was stated the line was open the whole distance."

"All I can say, sir, is that the papers made a mistake."

"And you issue tickets from Bombay to Calcutta!" returned Sir Francis Cromarty, who began to grow angry.

"Certainly we do, but travellers know very well they must find means of conveyance for themselves from Kholby to Allahabad."

Sir Francis was furious. Passepartout wanted to knock the guard down, who after all was not to blame. He did not like to look at his master.

"Sir Francis," said Fogg, quietly, "if you please, we will consult what measures to take to reach Allahabad."

"Mr. Fogg, this question of delay must prejudice your interests very much."

"No, Sir Francis, I had anticipated it."

"What, did you know the line was—"

"Not at all, but I was quite aware that sooner or later some obstacle or other must present itself. Now, hitherto nothing has been lost. I am two days beforehand as yet. A steamer leaves Calcutta for Hong-kong on the 25th, at 12 o'clock. This is only the 22nd, and we shall be at Calcutta in time yet."

There was nothing to be said to such a confident reply as this.

It was only too true that the works on the line stopped where they were. Newspapers are like certain watches, which persist in going too fast, and they had been premature in announcing the opening of the line. Most of the passengers were aware of this break in the railway, and on leaving the carriages they had taken possession of all modes of conveyance the village could furnish them with, four-wheeled polikaries, carts drawn by zebu, carriages resembling pagodas on wheels, palanquins, ponies, &c.

Thus it was that Sir Francis Cromarty and Mr. Fogg made a fruitless search through the village by means of transport to Allahabad.

"I shall walk," said Phileas Fogg.

Passepartout, who had now rejoined his master, made a wry face as he looked at his magnificent, but, for that purpose, useless Indian slippers. Fortunately he too had been making inquiries, and after some hesitation—

"Sir," said he, "I think I have found a way to get on."

"What?"

"An elephant, belonging to a native, lodging close by."

"Let us go and look at the elephant," replied Mr. Fogg.

Five minutes later Phileas Fogg, Sir Francis Cromarty, and Passepartout arrived at a hut, near which was a high enclosure of palisades. In the hut was an Indian, and in the enclosure an elephant. At their own request the Indian admitted Mr. Fogg and his two companions within the enclosure.

There they found themselves in the presence of the elephant, only half tamed, for its owner had trained it, not as a beast of burden, but to fight. With this object he had begun to change the animal's naturally mild disposition by degrees by feeding him for three months on sugar and butter. Such a mode of training an animal to fight does not seem very likely to lead to the result of rendering it ferocious, but it is nevertheless successfully employed by those who train fighting elephants. Fortunately for Mr. Fogg, they had only just begun this *régime* with the animal in question and his temper was as yet none the worse. Kiouni—so the beast was called—would, like all his race, travel tolerably quickly for some time, and as nothing else was to be found, Mr. Fogg determined to avail himself of him. But elephants are dear in India, where they are getting scarce. The males, which are the only ones which are used for fighting in the arena, are in very great request. In a domestic state they rarely breed, so that they are only to be had by trapping them. For this reason the natives take the greatest care of them, and

125

when Mr. Fogg proposed to hire him the Indian positively refused.

Fogg, however, pressed his offer, and told the Indian he would give him ten pounds an hour for the use of him—no, twenty pounds—no, forty pounds! Still refused. Passepartout was in a great state of excitement at each advance. But the Indian was not to be tempted.

Nevertheless, it was a tempting offer. Supposing the animal was fifteen hours on the journey to Allahabad, he would have earned six hundred pounds for his owner.

Without becoming in any degree excited, Phileas Fogg very deliberately proposed to give the Indian one thousand pounds for his animal.

The native refused to sell him! Perhaps the rascal thought he should make a better bargain still.

Sir Francis Cromarty took Mr. Fogg aside, and begged him to reflect before he went any farther. Phileas Fogg replied he was not in the habit of acting without due reflection, and that as it was a question of winning twenty thousand pounds, the elephant was absolutely necessary. He meant to have him if he paid twenty times his value for him.

Mr. Fogg returned to the Indian, whose quick little eyes, lighted up by greed, let him see it was only a question of price. Fogg made him successive offers of one thousand two hundred pounds, then one thousand five hundred pounds, then one thousand eight hundred pounds, and at last two thousand pounds! at which last offer the Indian gave way.

Passepartout's red face was pale with emotion.

"By my slippers!" cried Passepartout, "this is putting a high price on an elephant!"

This affair concluded, the next question was where to find a driver. A young Parsee, with an intelligent face, offered his services, which Mr. Fogg accepted, and promised him a liberal recompense, which could not fail to stimulate his zeal.

The elephant was brought out and equipped at once. The Parsee understood the duty of a mahout or cornac. He covered the elephant's back with a large pad, and arranged a couple of open baskets, one on each side, a not particularly comfortable mode of travelling.

Phileas Fogg paid the Indian in bank notes, which were taken from the famous bag. It seemed as if they were torn from Passepartout's bowels.

Then Mr. Fogg proposed to Sir Francis to go on with him to Allahabad; and the general accepted his offer. A traveller the more could make no difference to this enormous beast. They provided themselves with provisions at Kholby. Sir Francis Cromarty got into one of the baskets, and Mr. Fogg into the other. Passepartout sat on the pad, between his master and the brigadier-general. The Parsee perched himself on the animal's neck, and at nine o'clock the animal left the village, and took the shortest way through a dense palm forest.

THE OTHER LOG OF PHILEAS FOGG

The two got into a carriage with Sir Francis Cromarty, the brigadier-general who had played whist with Fogg on the *Mongolia*. This looked suspicious, but if Sir Francis was either Capellean or Eridanean, Fogg did not record it. Further events validate that he was what Verne says he was. Sir Francis had observed the eccentricity of his companion and wondered if a human heart did really beat beneath that cold exterior. Also, having learned from Fogg about the bet, he considered their journey to be useless and nonsensical. Of course, he had no way of knowing that Fogg was traveling to save the world, not just to girdle it.

At eight o'clock the next evening, the train stopped some fifteen miles beyond Rothal. The conductor shouted that all passengers should get off, an announcement which amazed the three. Passepartout, sent out to inquire about it, returned alarmed. They had stopped here because the railway ended here. A further inquiry revealed a disturbing situation. No one had bothered to inform them that, contrary to what the London papers said, one could not ride the rails from Kholby to Allahabad.

Sir Francis was angry. Fogg was unperturbed. Very well. All was foreseen. Fogg knew that, sooner or later, some obstacle or other would present itself. Due to the speediness of the trip so far, Fogg had gained two days. At noon on the twenty-fifth, a ship would leave Calcutta for Hong Kong. That day was the twenty-second. They had almost three days to get to Calcutta. That they might have to go on foot for seventy miles or more through jungle and over mountain was not something to worry about—for Fogg.

The restless, ever curious, Frenchman, having investigated possible means of conveyance on his own, returned with good news. They could continue on an elephant!

They proceeded to a nearby hut where they were introduced to a Hindu. Verne says that Fogg talked directly to the native. This means that the Hindu could speak some English or Fogg used the local dialect of these Khandesh people. Since Sir Francis might have wondered how he, supposedly a stranger to India, could have mastered this, Fogg must have refrained. Possibly the general did the interpreting and Verne did not bother to note this. In any event, there was no language difficulty.

Yes, the Hindu had an elephant. His name was Kiouni. But Kiouni was not for sale or hire. He was very valuable; he was being trained to be a war elephant.

Mr. Fogg offered ten pounds an hour for the use of the animal. No? Twenty? No? Forty?

Would Kiouni be for sale for a thousand pounds?

At this point, Sir Francis took Fogg to one side. He begged him not to ruin himself. Fogg coldly replied that he never acted rashly. He would pay twenty times what the beast was worth if need be.

Twelve hundred?

No?

Fifteen hundred?

No?

Eighteen hundred pounds?

No?

When Fogg offered two thousand pounds, Passepartout almost fainted. He could hear the money in the bag boiling away.

Two thousand?

Yes!

The Indian was afraid to ask for more because he might lose it all. The sum would enable him not only to live comfortably the rest of his life but would make him the biggest man in his community.

None of the three Europeans knew how to ride an elephant nor how to keep from getting lost if they could. A young and intelligent man of the Parsi faith then offered his services. Fogg quickly accepted this, promising a large sum in payment. An hour after they arrived, the three Europeans, with the Parsi, rode off. Sir Francis and Fogg sat on each side of the howdah; Passepartout straddled the saddlecloth between them; the mahout rode on the beast's neck.

Their guide assured them that if they went directly through the jungle, they could lop twenty miles off the journey. Passepartout went pale, because this meant entering the territory of the rajah of Bundelcund. British law did not extend into it, and if the rajah were to discover that they were within, they would be in for it. He stroked the watch.

Fogg did not hesitate in ordering the shortcut taken.

CHAPTER XII

IN WHICH PHILEAS FOGG AND HIS COMPANIONS VENTURE TO CROSS AN INDIAN FOREST, AND WHAT CAME OF IT

Their guide, in order to shorten the distance they had to travel, left the line of the unfinished railway on their right. This line, owing to the capricious turns in the Vindhyan hills, was not the shortest road, which it was materially to Phileas Fogg's interest to take. The Parsee, being well acquainted with all the roads and paths in the country, fancied he could cut off about twenty miles by going straight through the forest, and they trusted to him.

Phileas Fogg and Sir Francis Cromarty, sitting buried up to the neck in their panniers, were terribly shaken by the elephant's rough paces whenever his mahout pressed him on; but they submitted to their lot with true British phlegm, holding very little conversation, being unable to see one another in their actual position.

Passepartout, being seated on the animal's back, was shaken worse than either, and took care to follow his master's advice not to talk, for he might easily have bitten his tongue. At one moment he was jolted on to the elephant's neck, at another he nearly slipped off over his tail, like a clown on a spring board; but he cut his jokes all the same, and from time to time took a piece of sugar out of his bag which the intelligent beast took with his trunk without breaking his regular trot.

After moving forward for a couple of hours, the driver stopped the elephant and gave him an hour's rest, and fed him on branches and shrubs, after having watered him at a neighbouring tank. Sir Francis was not sorry to stop, he was very much shaken. Mr. Fogg seemed as fresh as if he had just left his bed.

"He must be made of iron!" said the brigadier, looking at him with wonder.

"Of wrought iron," replied Passepartout, who was busy preparing a hasty breakfast.

At twelve the Parsee proposed starting. The country soon assumed a very wild appearance—tamarinds and dwarf palms succeeded the lofty forest trees, then extensive sandy plains, with a few stunted shrubs and studded with great blocks of syenite. All this part of upper Bundelkund is very little frequented by travellers, and inhabited by a fanatical population. The English rule has not been able to establish itself completely in a territory still subjected to the influence of its rajahs, who in their inaccessible retreats among the Vindhyan hills are almost out of reach.

They often perceived bands of wild-looking Indians who did not conceal their anger when they saw the elephant pass by. But the Parsee avoided them as much as possible, thinking a meeting with them would only end ill. They saw very few animals the whole of that day, with the exception of a few monkeys, whose grimaces and tricks amused Passepartout exceedingly.

One question troubled him much. What would Mr. Fogg do with the elephant when they got to Allahabad station? It was impossible to take him with them, for his carriage by rail, added to his original cost, would amount to a ruinous sum of money. Would he sell him, or turn him loose? the good-tempered animal deserved to be considered. Suppose Mr. Fogg was to make a present of him to himself, Passepartout, he would be very much embarrassed what to do with him. These questions preoccupied his mind for some time. At eight in the evening they had crossed the principal of the Vindhyan chain, and the travellers halted at a ruined bungalow at the foot of the other slope.

They had got over about twenty-five miles that day, and they had only as many more to do to reach Allahabad station.

The night was cold. The Parsee lighted a fire in the bungalow, the warmth for which they were very grateful. Their supper consisted of provisions purchased at Kholby, and the travellers, as hungry and wayworn men would be, after a brief effort at conversation, slept soundly. Their guide kept watch, close by Kiouni, who slept on his legs, leaning against a tree.

Nothing occurred to disturb them during the night; silence was occasionally broken by the snarl of a panther, or the shrill cry of a monkey. But the more savage animals made no attempt to disturb the occupants of the bungalow. Sir Francis Cromarty slept as only an old soldier, thoroughly tired out, can sleep. Passepartout's sleep was broken from the previous day's jolting, which he could not shake off. As for Mr. Fogg, he slept as soundly as if he had been in his own house in Savile Row.

They set out again at six the next morning. Their guide hoped to reach Allahabad in the course of the evening; if so, Mr. Fogg would only lose a fraction of the forty-eight hours gained since the beginning of his journey.

They were descending the last slopes of the Vindhyan range, and Kiouni had resumed his trot. About twelve the guide turned away from a small place called Kallander, on the river Cani, one of the Ganges' tributaries. He always avoided inhabited places, feeling himself in greater safety in the desert district which first indicates the basin of the great river. Allahabad station was only about twelve miles in a north-easterly direction. They halted under a clump of bananas, the fruit of which, as wholesome as bread and as rich as cream, as travellers tell us, was highly appreciated.

At two their guide entered a very dense forest, through which they would have to make their way for several miles.

He preferred the cover of the woods. Until then they had met with nothing unpleasant, and their journey seemed about to terminate without any accident, when the elephant, after showing signs of restlessness, came to a sudden stop.

It was then about four P.M.

"What is the matter?" asked Sir Francis, putting his head out of his pannier.

"I cannot say, general," replied the Parsee, listening attentively as he spoke to a confused murmur coming through the thick branches.

It soon became more distinct. It might have been a distant concert of brass instruments and human voices.

Passepartout was all ears and eyes. Mr. Fogg waited patiently without saying a word.

The Parsee sprang down, fastened his elephant to a tree, and disappeared in the thicket. In a few minutes he returned, and told them that a Brahminical procession was coming their way, and they had better avoid being seen; he, therefore, unfastened the elephant and led him into some thick cover, advising the others not to get down. He kept himself ready to mount on a moment's notice, if necessary. But he hoped the procession of votaries would pass without seeing them, for they were quite concealed by the dense cover in which they found themselves.

The discordant noise of voices and instruments came nearer, and they could distinguish monotonous chanting, accompanied by drums and cymbals.

The head of the procession soon appeared under the trees about fifty paces from the spot where Mr. Fogg and his friends were hidden. They could easily distinguish the strange individuals who were the actors in this religious ceremony.

First came the priests with mitres on their heads, and wearing long robes covered with tinsel. They were surrounded by men, women and children, who sang a sort of dismal psalm, broken at regular intervals by drums and cymbals. Following them came a hideous figure, seated on a car with high wheels, the felloes and spokes of which represented serpents, and drawn by two pairs of richly-harnessed zebu.

This figure had four arms, the body was painted a dull red, staring eyes, dishevelled hair, the tongue hanging out of its mouth, and its lips stained with henna and betel. It wore a necklace of skulls, and round its waist a belt of severed hands. It stood upright on the body of a headless giant.

Sir Francis recognized the figure.

"The goddess Kali," he muttered; "the divinity of love and death."

"Of death it may be," whispered Passepartout, "but never of love. What a hideous old woman."

The Parsee motioned him to be silent. A group of old fakirs striped with ochre, and covered with gashes whence blood was dropping, were dancing and making wild gestures round the figure; striped devotees, who on occasion of very great Hindu ceremonies cast themselves under the wheels of the car of Juggernaut. After them came some Brahmins in most sumptuous oriental costumes, supporting a woman who was quite unable to support herself. The woman was young and fair as a European. Her head, neck, shoulders, ears, arms, hands and toes, were loaded with jewels, necklaces, bracelets, ear and finger rings; a tunic of gold tissue, covered with a light muslin, showed the outline of her figure. Immediately behind this young woman—and offering a violent contrast to her—came guards armed with drawn sabres thrust into their waistbands, and long Turkish pistols; they bore a palanquin containing a dead body.

It was that of an old man in a rajah's robes, wearing as in life a turban embroidered in pearls, a robe of silk and golden tissue, a cashmere shawl round his waist, and the splendid arms of an Indian prince by his side.

Musicians and an after-guard of fanatics, whose shouts sometimes drowned the deafening clang of the instruments, closed the *cortège*.

Sir Francis Cromarty regarded all this pomp with an expression of sadness, and then turning to the guide, said —

"A Suttee."

The Parsee nodded, and put his fingers to his lips. The long procession wound slowly through the trees, and its last ranks soon disappeared in the depths of the forest. By degrees, too, the singing ceased; there were a few distant cries audible, and then all was still.

Phileas Fogg had heard the word uttered by Sir Francis, and as soon as the procession was out of sight —

"What is a Suttee?" asked he.

"A Suttee, Mr. Fogg, is a human sacrifice, but a voluntary one. That woman whom you have just seen will be burnt tomorrow soon after daybreak."

"The villains!" cried Passepartout, unable to check a cry of indignation.

"Whose body was it?" said Mr. Fogg.

"That of the prince, her husband," replied the guide, "an independent rajah of Bundelkund."

"What!" returned Phileas Fogg, without the slightest trace of emotion apparent in his voice, "do these barbarous customs still exist in India, and have the English not been able to put a stop to them?"

"In the greater part of India," replied Sir Francis Cromarty, "these sacrifices are no longer performed, but we have no influence over the more savage districts, and especially here in Bundelkund. The northern side of the Vindhyan range is the scene of incessant murder and robbery."

"Poor creature!" exclaimed Passepartout, "did you say burnt alive?"

"Yes," said Sir Francis, "burnt alive, and if she were not you cannot conceive to what a wretched state of existence her own relatives could condemn her. They would shave her head, feed her on a few handsful of rice, they would shun her, and consider her as some foul creature, and she would die in a corner like a mangy dog. The prospect of such an existence often impelled these poor creatures to make this sacrifice, much more than love or fanaticism. Occasionally, however, the sacrifice is really voluntary, and the active intervention of Government is required to prevent it. A few years since, when I was quartered in Bombay, a young widow came to the governor and asked his permission to burn herself with her husband's body. As you may suppose the governor refused to grant it. The widow left the town, took refuge with some independent rajah, and performed the sacrifice."

While Sir Francis was telling this story, the guide shook his head several times, and when he had concluded —

"The sacrifice at to-morrow's dawn is no voluntary sacrifice," said he.

"How do you know?"

"Every one in Bundelkund is acquainted with the story," replied the guide.

"But this poor creature seemed to make no resistance," observed Sir Francis.

"Because she had been stupefied with bhang and opium."

"Whither are they now taking her?"

"To the pagoda of Pillaji, about two miles from this. There she is to pass the night till the appointed hour."

"Which will be —"

"Tomorrow at daylight."

After this reply the guide led the elephant out of the cover, and clambered up on his neck, but just as he was about to give the usual signal to move on, Mr. Fogg stopped him, and turning to Sir Francis Cromarty —

"Suppose we were to rescue that woman?" said he.

"Rescue that woman, Mr. Fogg!" cried the brigadier-general.

"I have still twelve hours to spare, I can devote them to that object."

"Why, you can feel!" said Sir Francis Cromarty.

"Sometimes, when I can afford the time," quietly replied Phileas Fogg.

THE OTHER LOG OF PHILEAS FOGG

At noon they had left the dense jungle for a country covered with copses of date trees and dwarf-palms. The pachyderm's long legs soon left this behind, and they were on great arid plains on which were sickly-looking shrubs and huge blocks of syenite. This stone, Fogg informed Sir Francis, was an igneous rock largely composed of feldspar. It derived its scientific name from the ancient Egyptian city of Syene, where it was found in large quantities.

Sir Francis merely grunted in reply. He was hanging onto the side of the howdah, which moved up and down with a motion like a small boat's in a choppy sea. Passepartout also found the motion upsetting and sickening. He had no inclination to meditate on what would happen if they encountered Bundelcundians. If he had, he might have wished that the meeting would be fatal, since he would rather die than continue this ride, and would soon do so anyway if it did not cease. Then they did see some natives, and these gestured threateningly. The Parsi, however, urged the beast to a faster speed, and the Hindus did not try to pursue them.

By eight that evening, they had crossed the principal chain of the Vindhya Mountains. They stopped at a ruined bungalow to rest in it for the night. The elephant had carried them for twenty-five miles, twice as fast as they could have gone on foot in this rough country. Allahabad now lay only another twenty-five miles away.

Verne says that the Parsi built a fire against the cold night and that they then ate the provisions they had brought from Kholby. This is confirmed by Fogg's secret log. They resumed, as Verne says, at six o'clock next morning. But Verne's account of the time intervening is not at all accurate. The guide, according to Verne, watched the sleeping elephant. Sir Francis slept heavily. Passepartout dreamed uneasily of the jolting journey. Fogg slept as peacefully as if he were in bed in No. 7, Savile Row.

This is not a likely picture. Anybody who has for the first time in a long time ridden all day on a horse would know how sore they would be and how hard sleep would come. Magnify the soreness and fatigue by a third and add to that the inevitable distress occasioned by eating the food of tropical jungle aborigines, and you have an excellent idea of their state. The truth, as revealed in the other log, is as follows.

Though their trip had been speedy, it had not been nonstop. All three Europeans had frequently required the Parsi to halt the elephant while they dashed into the bushes. Toward the end of the day even the imperturbable Fogg looked pale. Before they went to bed, master and servant stepped out into the thick jungle to perform certain bodily functions they felt almost too weak to perform. Fogg listened serenely, if sympathetically, to Passepartout's groans, moans, and complaints until they were finished with their duties—or hoped they were.

He said, "Have you been checking your watch, as I impressed on you that you should?"

"But certainly . . ."

"And?"

"And nothing! No signals of any kind! Which is indeed fortunate! If there had been, then we would be certain that that pig of a rajah . . ."

"Speak more quietly," Fogg said. "It would be easy for someone to approach unnoticed in this dense forest."

"Pardon, sir, but it is possible that I did not hear the tiny gong which announces that another . . ."

"Do not use that word."

". . . another, er, watch, is activated and broadcasting. The noise made by the beast's motion and the creaking of the howdah, not to mention our groans, made it difficult to hear."

"It's quiet enough now."

"Except for the screaming and chattering of those monkeys and the yelling of those birds. And the Parsi says that we will hear leopards and tigers tonight."

"It will be quiet enough in the bungalow," Fogg said. "You will keep the watch beside your ear tonight."

"But certainly! I had planned to do just that. And if the signal comes?"

"We will answer it."

"Name of a pig!"

"In our own fashion," Fogg said. "However, there is one way we can assure that it is sent."

"Assure it?" Passepartout said. He had been pale before: now he looked as white as one of the demons in the legends of the Hindus.

"There is no need to repeat myself. When the others have gone to sleep, you will set it on *transmit*."

Passepartout's eyes swelled like a pouter pigeon's chest.

"But why? We will be instantly whisked . . ."

"I am not finished. You will do this very briefly. Flick it off and on and then wait. If, in ten minutes, there is no indication that another device is on, you will repeat the *transmit*. For a half-second only. You will repeat this pattern for two hours, after which I will take over."

"What do you plan? What could we do if we did get a signal?"

"That is arranged," Fogg said. "If you get a signal before your two hours are up, wake me at once."

Passepartout did not like the idea of having to stay awake when he was so tired. He discovered, however, that he would not have been able to sleep in any event. His muscles felt as if they were ropes which had been used to lift heavy stones all day; his bones, it seemed to him, had been twisted as if someone had been trying to make corkscrews out of them. His nerves were like harp strings which vibrated to every sound as if they were sounded by ghostly hands. The sudden maniacal laughter of birds, the screaming of some large animal far-off—a leopard?—and a distant roar—a tiger?—made him jump as if Fogg had kicked him. Soft slitherings and rustlings in the thatch of the ceiling did not contribute to his relaxation. And the apprehension with which Fogg's unknown plans filled him built up like dough in an oven.

He heard the Englishman's regular breathing and wondered how he could go to sleep so soundly and so quickly. Sir Francis was quietly groaning and turning every few minutes; evidently, he was finding it difficult to drop off. What if the brigadier-general were still awake when, or if, a signal came?

After a while, unable to lie still, the Frenchman arose and stepped outside the bungalow. The moon had risen and was shedding an effulgent light on the hillside. The vast bulk of Kiouni and the small body of the mahout-guide were black under the shade of a giant tree about twenty yards away.

A loud cracking made him leap a few inches off the ground. His heart accelerated. Were the thuggees approaching through the bush with their garrots in hand, intending to strangle the foreigners and so sacrifice them to the goddess Kali without the spilling of blood? Was a wild elephant coming toward them with a vast malice in its vast heart? Was a herd of the dangerous wild buffalo or savage wild pig about to attack them?

Passepartout sighed, and his tired heart beat more slowly. No, it was only Kiouni tearing off a branch of the tree to feed his huge stomach. He munched while his belly rumbled as if it were a distant but mighty cataract.

Verne says that Kiouni slept all night, forgetting that the poor beast had been traveling all day and had had nothing to eat. Kiouni needed sleep, but needed food more, since an elephant requires several hundreds of pounds of forage a day to maintain his strength. Kiouni had gone to sleep, standing up, for several hours after arriving. Now hunger pangs had awakened him, and he was eating, indifferent to the noise he was making or its possible interference with the sleep of the humans.

Though the mountain air at night was cold, Passepartout perspired heavily. *Mon dieu!* he thought. What could they do if they were transported into the heart of the rajah's palace? Their only weapons—pitifully tiny—were the jackknives he and Fogg carried. And would not the rajah be prepared for them? Would he not have many of his soldiers lined up around the distorter, all armed with rifles and swords? Would not he, Passepartout, and his mad master be helpless to resist capture or slaying? Far better to be killed at once. To fall into the hands of a Capellean meant days of the most terrible torture. Ah, if he did not quit perspiring he would catch a cold which would quickly transform itself into a fatal pneumonia.

Look! The Parsi, who had said he would stand watch over his beast, had lain down on the ground and was even now snoring so loudly that he could be heard through the elephant's stomach stormings. Wretched creature! Had he no sense of duty? How could the Parsi sleep while he, Passepartout, suffered? Was all the world asleep except for the sinister predators of the jungle, the voracious Kiouni, and himself?

He held the watch up to his ear and listened. It emanated nothing but its steady ticking, measuring Time, the shadow of Eternity, while Passepartout and the universe grew older. But the universe, though doomed to die eventually, would be here a long long time after Passepartout had become dust and less than dust. Dust which a tree would draw up within its woody body and which some elephant would strip off and digest in its stomach and then eject and which the ground, not to mention some bugs and birds, would eat and then eject. So Passepartout, in a million dissociations, would go through eternity being taken in and driven out, though, thank God, unconscious of all the indignities and nastinesses. Unless the Hindus were correct and he, as Passepartout, a whole, would be reincarnated again and again.

Yet he could live in his body for a thousand years if he escaped accident, homicide, or—here he crossed himself, since though an Eridanean he was also a devout Catholic—he killed himself. Why throw away a millennium by allowing himself to be sucked into the trap assuredly set by the rajah of Bundelcund? Was this not suicide, and was not suicide unforgivable? Would Fogg agree to this reasoning, this inescapable logic, if it were set before him?

Alas, he would not!

But perhaps the rajah had no intention of sending out a distorter wave. Perhaps he was sensible and was snoozing away at this very moment, no doubt in the soft arms and on the soft breasts of some beautiful houri or whatever the Hindus called their wives. That would be much more rational than sitting up late at night and sending out signals. But men, alas, were not always—or, in fact, were seldom—rational.

As if to affirm this conclusion, the watch emitted a ringing sound.

Passepartout jumped again, and his heart thumped as if it were a trampoline on which fear was performing. The dreaded had indeed happened!

For a second, Passepartout thought of keeping the news to himself. But, despite his terrors, he was a courageous man, and it was his duty to inform the Englishman. First, though, he must send the return signal.

As soon as the ringing stopped, he pushed down on the stem of the watch and quickly twisted it one hundred and eighty degrees to the right and then set the hands on the prescribed numbers. Immediately after, he returned the hands to the correct time—his correct time, anyway—and returned the stem to its original position. Then he hurried into the bungalow to wake Fogg up.

Fogg awoke easily and was on his feet at once. After listening to Passepartout's excited whisperings, he said, "Very well. Now, here is what we shall do."

Passepartout had been as pale as moonlight on still waters. Now his skin looked like that moonlight after it had been passed through a bleach. But when Fogg was through talking, Passepartout obeyed at once. His first task was made easier because the Parsi was still sleeping soundly and soundly. His snores were terrible enough to frighten off a tiger. Passepartout led Kiouni away. When they were half a mile down the southern slope of the mountain, the two men climbed up the rope ladder and rode him the rest of the way. Kiouni did not like being taken away from his feeding, but he did not trumpet. He went slowly because his eyes could not pick out obstacles easily in the moonlight. Also, he had to be careful about stepping into holes. The weight of the beasts is such that even a four-inch misstep may break their legs.

About an hour later, the two were at a distance which Fogg judged sufficient. Passepartout dismounted; Fogg remained on the elephant.

"But will not Sir Francis and the guide be able to hear the sounds even from here?" Passepartout said.

"Possibly," Fogg said. "However, the mountain itself and much forest is between us. They should deaden the sounds. They may believe they are hearing a distant temple bell. In any event, there is nothing they can do about it. When we return, we shall tell them that the elephant ran away and we went after it."

Passepartout shivered. "*When* we return . . . !"

It would be more realistic to say "if," not "when." Nevertheless, he admired the optimism of the Englishman and deeply hoped that it was not ill-founded.

During the journey, Passepartout had three times swiftly adjusted the watch to send out signals. The received signals were now coming every twenty seconds.

"Set it so it will go on *transmit* in five minutes from now," Fogg said. "But make sure that its field is wide enough, since it must include Kiouni. And make sure that it will automatically go on *receive* five minutes after its transmit mode is terminated."

Passepartout, his teeth chattering, opened the back cover of the watch and set it as directed, turning three tiny knobs. He placed the watch in a small hole he had dug in the ground with his knife. It was necessary that the device be below the ground level of those to be teleported. Also, the hole would keep the elephant from accidentally stepping on it if he should move, though Passepartout hoped that the beast would stand still. If he did take too many steps in any direction, he and his riders might find themselves cut in half.

He scrambled back up the rope ladder and pulled up the rope after him. He coiled it on the floor below one of the howdah seats. Mr. Fogg was already sitting on the neck of the beast. He had closely observed the command words and hand and touch signals used by the mahout. He used them now as if he had been in the profession for years. So far, the animal had obeyed him. Would it continue to do so when it suddenly found itself elsewhere and surrounded by hostile humans?

Passepartout, unable to consult his watch, mentally counted off the seconds. He was sitting on the saddle between the howdah seats, his unfolded jackknife in his hand. He felt pathetically helpless, and he wondered what the nine hundred and sixty years of life that he was throwing away would have been like. Ah, to see what 2842 A.D. held for him! Or even 1972! When the Eridaneans had exterminated the verminous Capelleans, then they could change the world. Would it take more than a hundred years? Would not Earth be a paradise, a veritable Utopia, with all war, crime, poverty, disease, and hatred wiped out forever? Why should he be denied the fruits of his labor because of this madman whose placid back was now before him?

But if a cause is to win, it must do so over the bodies of martyrs, as someone, probably an Englishman, had once said. It was his misfortune to be one of those martyrs. Still, a martyr should not sacrifice himself unless the cause could profit by it. There would be no profit to anybody tonight except the rajah of Bundelcund.

Yet, had not Fogg said that, for him, the unforeseen did not exist?

But what if he had foreseen that the rajah would die but they would die too?

No, Fogg was a gentleman, and he did have a kind heart. He would not ask his servant, and his colleague, to be killed also. Not unless it was necessary, Passepartout thought, his heart drooping now like a flag on a breezeless day. But what could they do with only small knives against rifles and spears?

"Ah, *mon* . . ."

And they were there ". . . *Dieu!*"

Fogg had not been as blind as Passepartout had thought. A spy had long ago managed to report where and in what manner the distorter was located and guarded. Fogg had not told Passepartout about this simply because he was not sure that the situation had not changed since the report. It would not do to have Passepartout all set for one environment and suddenly be faced with the unexpected. It might throw him too much off balance. The poor fellow was in a state of terror as it was. Indeed, Fogg would have left him behind if he had not been sure that Passepartout would be thoroughly capable once the action began. No genuine coward would have survived to the age of forty in this secret war. Nor would Stuart have entrusted his mission to anybody who had not proved himself many times over. To fear is not to lack courage.

His main concern was the behavior of Kiouni. His training as a war elephant was only half-completed. Even a seasoned old veteran might go into hysterics.

The transit was made instantaneously. There was no sense whatsoever of passage through time or distance. Their ears were battered with a great clanging as if they were standing a few inches below a bell as large as the bungalow. Its sound was shattering, and Fogg and his aide, though holding the jackknives with their fingers, had to thrust the ends of their thumbs into their ears.

Kiouni bolted; his trunk was raised and he was, seemingly, shrilling panic through it. He could not be heard above the hideous clanging, which, as always, tolled nine times. This auditory phenomenon accompanied the operation of a distorter at both the receiving and transmitting ends. The site of the watch they had left behind would be loud with nine clangs, loud enough to carry faintly to Sir Francis and the Parsi even with some miles of mountain and forest deadening it.

The theory accounting for the noises was that the distortion of the space in the area around the devices caused a condensation and bending of the electromagnetic field of the Earth itself. The return to a normal state resulted in atmospheric disturbance and consequent clangings. This theory was disputed, but it did not matter what made the noises. They were unavoidable and, unfortunately, acted as an alarm.

Fogg saw at a glance that the rajah had not moved the distorter since the report. Its location was something that only a fiend would dream up.

They were in a vast room lit by thousands of gas jets. It soared perhaps six stories, ending in a great white dome. The room itself was circular with a diameter of perhaps two hundred yards. Its circumference was set with over three hundred tall and narrow archways—a quick estimate—with a mosaic walk about ten feet wide inside it. This ran completely around the chamber. The walk was set about an inch above the level of the great pool that constituted most of the surface level of the place. The floor was mostly a body of water, and in its center was a circular islet of smooth red marble. This had a diameter of forty feet. Kiouni and his riders had appeared in its exact center, though they did not stay there long.

Kiouni had begun running madly almost at once around and around the edge of the islet. Elephants are splendid swimmers, but even in his panic he had not cared to plunge into the water. The reason, Fogg perceived as he rode around and around, was the large number of large crocodiles in the pool.

Fogg set himself to calming the beast. While engaged in this seemingly hopeless business, he felt a tap on his shoulder. He looked back and then upward. Passepartout was pointing at the ceiling. Fogg saw a square of blackness appearing in the center of the white dome. From it, suspended on a cable, a car was descending. Six dark faces topped by white turbans stared over the sides of the car.

Fogg looked at the archways around the walk. They were still empty.

Passepartout then pointed at the center of the islet. He indicated what they had missed before because the bulk of the elephant had been between the rajah's distorter and the two men, and both had been too occupied since to look for it.

The device must have been set in the circular depression in the center of the islet. Certainly, it had not just been placed in the hole so the newcomer merely had to stoop over to pick it up. It would be placed within a defense of some kind. What alarmed Passepartout was that the distorter, contained in a watch, was disappearing. It had been placed on top of a cylinder set about an inch below the level of the islet's surface. Now the cylinder was sinking swiftly into the shaft.

The islet must be hollow with a room beneath the surface. Men below were operating the machinery which raised and lowered the cylinder of stone. They would remove the device from the top of the cylinder and take it to a safe place. Then the rajah's men would take care of the intruders.

Kiouni had not slowed down in his circular dash. There was no more time for endeavoring to control him. Fogg gestured at Passepartout to take his place, and he rolled off the neck of the beast. His agility would have drawn applause from the professional acrobat, Passepartout, under different circumstances. But the Frenchman was too busy hanging on.

As Fogg slid down the gray wrinkled side, he pushed himself away, landed facing the elephant's side, fell back, but kept on walking backwards and so saved himself a hard fall on the marble. Whirling then, he yanked from a vest pocket a watch, twisted its stem, looked down into the hole, and dropped the watch. From first to last, despite his swiftness, he managed to perform with an air of unhurriedness, of perfect aplomb.

The men above him and the men below may have, undoubtedly did, cry out. He could not have heard them since his ears were still ringing. But he did look up and saw, not unexpectedly, that five in the car were brandishing sabers and one was holding a rifle. This looked like a modern rifle, perhaps the Mauser adopted by the Prussian army only the year before. Those in the car could see that the invaders had no firearms. Since no smoke had resulted from his dropping of an object into the shaft, they must have believed that, if it were a bomb, it had failed to go off. Possibly, they had not seen him drop the watch, since his body had been between them and the shaft. Nor would they believe they had to shoot the intruders; they were trapped. They could take their time, dispose of the elephant if it failed to calm down, and overpower the men. Meanwhile, the rajah would have retrieved the distorter in the room.

Fogg believed that the rajah was down there, since it was unlikely that he would allow anyone but himself to handle the invaluable device. In fact, Fogg was certain that there was only one man below, the rajah. The fewer who saw the distorter, the better. It would be, in the eyes of the Hindus, a magical device, one that many would do anything to possess.

Mr. Fogg turned, having extracted and set another watch. With a smooth motion, he tossed it upward into the car, which was now about two and a half stories above the islet. The actions of those he could see became very agitated. Two dived out of the car into the pool. The car disappeared in a spurt of flame surrounded by smoke. The blast was dimly heard by the two men and Kiouni, but they felt it as if it were a giant hand slapping them. Bits of thin steel and flesh and bone rained over them.

Fogg was knocked off his feet. Passepartout came tumbling off Kiouni's neck. The elephant whirled and began running in the opposite direction along the edge of the islet. Passepartout fell without injury, rolling on the floor and coming up on his feet as if at the end of an act. His hair was wilder than ever, and his blue eyes were huge. Fogg returned to the hole in the center while smoke from the explosion, blown downward at first, rose around him. He knelt down and looked into the shaft. The watch case, for it had contained no watch, could be set to explode its contents or to convert them into a gas. This would be expelled at a high rate of speed to fill any small chamber. Its effect dissipated almost immediately so that he did not have to fear breathing the air coming up from the shaft.

Mr. Fogg's face kept its serenity, but his log records his astonishment and alarm at what he saw. The cylinder had continued to sink into the shaft in the floor of the room below. Even as he watched, it stopped with its top about three feet above the floor. Beside it lay a short, stocky dark-skinned man dressed in gorgeous garments. His wrists and fingers were covered with bracelets and rings bearing pearls and jewels that only a very rich rajah could afford. His hair and beard were gray, and his hook-nosed face was wrinkled. Fogg knew that the gray and the wrinkles were only makeup. Rajah Dakkar of Bundelcund had not wanted his agelessness to be rumored about. Such a story would have brought him to the attention of the Eridaneans far sooner than it had, and the British might have become aggressive if they thought he had a secret for prolonging life.

The rajah had opened the lid of the cylinder before it had stopped sinking. If it had not been for the anesthetic gas, he would have been out of the room by now with the distorter. But the device, encased in a big golden-plated watch with several inset diamonds, lay nine feet directly below Fogg. He only had to remove from around his waist the magnet and the long thin silken cord to which it was attached and to drop it straight down. The gold covering would not be affected, but the steel plates and the steel works within would be sufficiently magnetized. And then he could pull the treasured object up by the cord.

But a man was standing by the marble cylinder and reaching out for the device. Something stopped him, perhaps a sense which told him that he was being observed. He looked upward. Fogg did not cry out, though how even he kept his self-control is difficult to understand. He knew the man. His beard was gone, and the eyes were no longer black but a dark gray. Fogg might not have recognized him now if it had not been for the extraordinary width between the eyes.

The man was now wearing the uniform of an officer of Her Majesty's Indian Sappers, which accounted in part for Fogg's failure to recognize at once that he had seen him only recently. Once the effect of the uniform passed, Fogg saw the resemblance between him and the man he had seen standing in the doorway near the Reform Club. Yes, it was he. The man he had served under, the man in the doorway, the man now about to take the distorter were the same. But how had he arrived ahead of Fogg? Had he come via a distorter?

The man mouthed one word, faintly.

"Fogg!"

So, he did not recognize Fogg as a former member of his crew. If he had known, would he not have wanted to let Fogg be aware that he had penetrated his disguise?

Fogg uttered the man's name softly.

"Captain Nemo!"

Fogg records in his secret notebook many things that were puzzling about this man's presence, though he had no time to think of them then. Why was he, a Capellean of good standing as far as Fogg knew, with the traitor rajah? Or had he talked Dakkar into believing that he himself had become a traitor? How had he gotten here? Why had he not been overcome by the gas?

The last could be accounted for by a quickness in running out of the room when the watch fell. Or perhaps he had been outside and had just entered.

Fogg let the magnet fall down the shaft onto the watch. Nemo had no weapons; his holster was empty. Doubtless, the rajah permitted no one except the most trusted guards to be armed in his presence. Nemo, acting on his reflexes, shot his hand toward the nonexistent gun, realized the situation, cried out—Fogg heard it faintly—and dodged away. Fogg could no longer see him. But if he believed that the watch was another bomb, gas or explosive, he would leave the room and perhaps slam the door behind him. Yes, there was a muffled slamming noise. But he might come back at once. He might be behind armed men whom he'd send into the room to determine if the watch case held anything deadly. Or, quick thinker that he was, he might perceive the significance of the cord attached to the case, guess it held only a magnet, and would come charging back in with a gun.

He would also be sending armed men into the huge room. Fogg was surprised that none had appeared by now; at any moment he expected to hear the explosions of rifles. He glanced up and looked around. No figures were emerging from the archways. So, the rajah had wanted as few people as possible to be near the distorter. He had had faith that a few men in the car above and he and Nemo below could take care of the Eridaneans.

But the soldiers would soon be here.

Now another distraction occurred. Passepartout was pulling one of the men out of the water who had dived out of the car. He was doing it with all possible speed to get out of the way of Kiouni, still racing along the perimeter. The explosions had frightened the huge saurians in the water long enough for one man to get away. The other had not been so lucky. Some crocodile, quicker to recover than the others, had seized him. Only the roiling of the water as the crocodile turned over and over, trying to tear a leg or arm off, showed where the man was.

Fogg had not time to shout at Passepartout to abandon the man if the elephant came around too fast. He turned his attention back to the shaft, lifted the magnet again, swung it a little to one side, and dropped it. This time it fell squarely on the rajah's watch, and Fogg drew it up swiftly.

Before he had gotten it out of the hole, he saw the face of the rajah, now recovered, directly below him. It was contorted with rage, and he held in his hand a Colt revolver. He pointed it upward. Fogg could either drop the device and fall back out of the way or be shot. In fact, even if he dropped it, he might not get away in time.

The rajah's face passed from rage to triumph. Fogg decided that he would have to try to dodge. If he continued to draw up the device, he would be shot anyway. His only chance, not a very good one, was to throw himself to one side at the same time yanking up on the cord. If he did not get the distorter away from the rajah, then he was stuck here. And he would be stuck later in various unpleasant ways.

The rajah cried out in English for him not to move or he would get a bullet between his eyes.

Fogg wondered how the rajah knew he was an Englishman. He also wondered if the rajah's reputation as a marksman was deserved. Next to a certain Captain Moran of the Indian Army, the rajah was supposed to be the best hunter in India.

He had just made up his mind to throw himself to one side, since death was better than being captured alive in any event. A shadow fell on him. Something half-dark and half-glittering sped down the shaft. As if it had sprung out of some hidden magician's compartment on his body, the handle of a knife was sticking out of the rajah's throat. He had had to lean backwards to point the gun up and so had left his throat exposed.

Dakkar's eyes glazed, and he crumpled. As his revolver hit the floor, it discharged. There was a shout, and a soldier fell into view face down. He must have been struck by the ricocheting bullet.

Fogg serenely pulled the magnet and device up, turned the magnet off by pressing the stem on the watch case which held it, pocketed the case, reset the magnet, and lowered it down the shaft again. He then proceeded to draw up the revolver.

"Where did you get that throwing knife?" he said.

"From a man whom I rescued from the crocodiles," Passepartout said. "Alas, not reptiles but a pachyderm was what he should have feared."

He pointed at a gruesome object, what was left after Kiouni had found him lying in his path. The beast had stopped running now, but it was still trumpeting, and its eyes looked dangerous. Its feet and trunk and tusks were splashed with blood.

"Splendid," Fogg said, and Passepartout smiled with pleasure.

"I learned more in the circus than just to tumble and to walk a high wire, sir."

"Obviously."

"So what now, sir, if I may presume?"

"There is a very dangerous man in the palace," Fogg said. "If he were in London, he would be the most dangerous man there. Or anywhere. He should be killed, but that is impossible now. Indeed, if we do not make an expeditious retreat, we shall be the ones to suffer death. Still . . ."

"Yes, sir?"

"Never mind. We must not test probabilities too far. Ah, I see the soldiers are coming through the archways. Get up on the elephant quickly."

"Without a rope ladder, sir? Besides, he does not look as if he would give permission, ladder or not."

"If he will not give permission, we leave without him."

Fogg removed another watch from his pocket. He set it and placed the magnet between it and the distorter. The three were now bound together by the magnetic field. He lowered the trio into the shaft a few inches. He had nothing to put on the cord to keep the three objects from slipping further except the body of the trampled man. He did not have time to drag the corpse to the shaft and place it on the cord. The first fire from the guns of the soldiers was ringing in the dome. Fortunately, the Bundelcundians were excited and were, probably, poor marksmen to begin with, as were many of the ill-trained natives of that day. Moreover, only five had rifles; the rest were equipped with matchlock muzzle loaders, unrifled weapons with not much accuracy. But as soon as enough came in, the volume of fire would ensure their hitting their target. The elephant, big as he was, would be hit even if no one was firing at him. Wounded, he might turn on the two men, who would have no place to go except into the pool.

Fogg shot three bullets from the rajah's revolver as cooly as if he were on the firing range. Three soldiers dropped. The others ran behind the scanty shelter of the archways. Fogg removed the last of his watches and hurled it. This struck just beyond the edge of the walk, skittered across it toward an archway, and stopped. It began whirling and emitting a thick smoke. This quickly spread over the walk on that side of the room and out across the lake. The winds were blowing it from the archways, helped by the draft created by the opened trapdoor in the top of the dome. Cries of fear and a number of loud coughs came through the smoke.

Still holding onto the end of the cord, Fogg approached the swaying beast. He started to speak softly the loving words he had learned from the mahout, then realized that the beast could not hear these. He spoke more loudly while he held one hand out to the beast. It watched him with rolling eyes, but Fogg's composure and the lack of fear-scent steadied Kiouni. Fogg had thrust all disturbing emotions into another circuit of his mind—he would pay heavily for it later—and was as cool and unafraid as he looked. The elephant allowed him to get close and lowered his trunk to feel along his clothes. Passepartout got to the extreme other side of the islet, crouched, and then ran straight toward the animal's tail and pulled himself on up and over onto the animal's back. Fortunately, he managed to get hold of the howdah before the startled beast began running around again. Fogg had hurled himself to one side just in time and then he stood near the shaft and began trying to quiet Kiouni down again.

The Frenchman threw out the rope ladder, which trailed along a few inches on the floor. He got onto the beast's neck and did his best to imitate the Parsi. This, with Fogg's renewed words, brought Kiouni to a standstill. By then, some of the soldiers had run out from the cloud to the far side of the pool and begun firing. Even so, the smoke hindered them.

Fogg climbed up the ladder quickly and drew the rope after him. Kiouni was urged toward the shaft, finally coming to another stop a few feet from it. This was as close as Fogg dared get him, since soldiers might now be in the chamber below. He was not certain that this was close enough, but he must take the chance.

"Transmit, for the love of God! And of Passepartout!" the Frenchman cried. "Transmit! Transmit!"

A shout came from above. Passepartout looked upward, and his eyes rolled.

"Mother of Mercy! They will shoot straight down! They cannot . . ."

His words were beaten into thin sheets by the terrible nine clangings. And they were deaf again, though happy. At least, Passepartout smiled. The expression of Fogg, holding to the cord minus its load, did not change. A second later, both were busy hanging onto Kiouni. It took half an hour to get the nerve-shattered animal back to the buried distorter.

Arriving at the desired spot, Passepartout descended from the elephant, dug up his watch, cleaned its surface, and reattached it to his old watch chain.

On the slow journey back up the slope, Passepartout said, "Sir, is it permitted to ask a question?"

"Certainly," Fogg said, "though the answer may not be permitted."

"One certainly carried an unusual number of unusual watches."

"That is an observation, not a question."

"But where are these deadly watches obtained? I have seen nothing to indicate their existence. No one could have slipped them to you en route, surely?"

"They were originally in my bureau in my house. A man who runs his life by the watch would not seem out of character if he had some spare chronometers."

"But how did you, sir, get them past my eyes? I am not altogether dull-eyed."

"They were in my vest from the beginning."

"Ah! And if a prying Capellean had found them and opened them for examination?"

"The first one to be tampered with would have blown up in his face."

"But, sir, I might have found one and, being curious . . ."

"Then you would have discovered that there are certain things into which you should not pry."

Passepartout was silent for a while. He wiped the sweat off his face and said, "And the rajah's distorter? Was that a bomb you attached to it?"

"Set to go off when we were transmitted."

Passepartout exclaimed with delight.

"And now we will return to London? We have killed a major Capellean and destroyed their distorter."

"That is the third question, and you stated that you had only one in mind."

There was another silence. A leopard screamed in the distance. Mr. Fogg said, "We will not return. The bet has not been canceled."

"And this dangerous man of whom you spoke?"

"He is the one I told you to watch for while we were on the *Mongolia*. And there are no more watches."

Passepartout wished to ask more questions but was deterred by Fogg's tone of finality.

When they returned to the bungalow, they found the Parsi still snoring beneath the tree and Sir Francis in the same position in which they had left him. They restored Kiouni to his spot beneath the tree where the beast, half-asleep, began ripping off branches and stuffing them into his mouth. Fogg and Passepartout crept into the bungalow, lay down, and this time both slipped away.

Two hours later, they were awakened by the Parsi. Mr. Fogg asked him if he was tired because of standing watch all night. The Parsi replied that he did not feel in the least fatigued. He could go for several days without a wink of sleep. Mr. Fogg, of course, made no comment.

At six o'clock, two refreshed and two tired men crawled onto the elephant. Kiouni, despite lack of food and sleep, seemed to have vast reservoirs of strength. He went almost as speedily as the day before. Nevertheless, the guide remarked about the beast's tendency to shy at any sudden movements of the brush or the animals in it. And they had to pause for half an hour to allow Kiouni to eat and so quell some of the rumblings in his stomach.

They passed down the lower branches of the Vindhya Mountains and near noon went by a village on the Kani River, a branch of the great Ganges. The mahout steered Kiouni away from habitations for safety's sake. Mr. Fogg agreed privately with this decision. The dead rajah's men would be out looking for them. There was no reason to trouble the Parsi and the general with the story of last night, which, in any event, they would not have believed.

When Allahabad was twelve miles away, they stopped by some banana trees to refresh themselves and Kiouni. Around two, they plunged into another dense jungle. Passepartout was happy that they were so hidden in this but was apprehensive about their nearness to the capital city of Bundelcund. Two hours later, they were still in the dense forest, though the Parsi said that they would soon be out. Passepartout was about to ask him how soon was soon when the beast suddenly stopped.

"What the devil now?" Sir Francis said, sticking his head out of the howdah.

"I do not know, sir," the Parsi said.

They heard voices, as of many people, coming through the jungle. After a few minutes, they could distinguish both voices and musical instruments of brass and wood. The Parsi descended, tied Kiouni to a tree, and wriggled away through the bush. In a moment, he returned.

"A procession of Brahmins approaches. We must hide."

He untied the rope from the tree and led the animal with its riders into the green thickness. From their vantage, the three on Kiouni could see the procession. First came priests, then many men, women, and children. The crowd was singing a sad chant intermingled with the beat of tambourines and the clash of cymbals and the wailing of pipes and the strumming of various stringed instruments. After the crowd came a large car with huge wheels drawn by four zebu.

Sir Francis, seeing the hideous statue in the car, whispered to the others, "It's Kali, the goddess of love and death."

"Perhaps she is of death," Passepartout said. "But of love? That old hag? Never!"

The Parsi gestured for silence.

A mob of long-bearded and naked old fakirs were dancing wildly around the idol and cutting themselves with knives.

After them came more Brahmins. They led a young woman who did not seem to be a voluntary member of the parade. Despite her dull expression and dragging steps, she was beautiful. Her hair was black, and her eyes were brown, but her skin was as free of pigment as any Yorkshireman's. She wore a gold-edged tunic and a light muslin robe which clung to a splendid figure. Bracelets, rings, and earrings set with jewels of many kinds loaded her down.

Accompanying her were men evidently charged with seeing that she did not run away. These carried sabers and long decorated pistols. Four of them also carried a palanquin on which lay a richly dressed corpse.

Fogg said nothing. Passepartout hissed with astonishment. The body was that of the rajah of Bundelcund.

Behind it were musicians and more dancing bloodied fakirs.

Sir Francis, looking sorrowful, said, "It's a suttee."

When the parade had passed, Fogg said, "What is a suttee?"

This seems a strange thing for the highly knowledgeable Fogg to ask. Perhaps Verne inserted this question to give Sir Francis a chance to enlighten the reader.

"A suttee is a voluntary human sacrifice. The woman you've just seen will be burned at dawn tomorrow."

"Oh, the scoundrels!" Passepartout cried.

"And the corpse?" Mr. Fogg asked.

"It is that of her husband, an independent rajah of Bundelcund."

Fogg said, emotionlessly, "Is it possible that these barbarous customs still exist in India? Why haven't we put a stop to them?"

"They have been terminated in most of India. But we have no power in the savage areas and especially in Bundelcund. The whole district north of the Vindhyas is the theater of unceasing murders and pillage."

"The miserable woman!" Passepartout said. "Burned alive!"

Sir Francis explained that if a widow somehow got out of the sacrifice, she would be treated with utmost contempt by her relatives, indeed, by all who knew of her refusal to become ashes with her husband. She would have to shave her head and exist on the scantiest of food. She would be less than a pariah, because even a pariah had his own kind to associate with. Eventually, she would die of shame and heartbreak.

Sir Francis did not know that this was not exactly the case with this poor woman. If she could have escaped from Bundelcund, she would have gone to live with her relatives in far-off Bombay. These were Parsis who did not hold with suttee. This sect, descended from Persian fire worshippers whose prophet was Zoroaster, had customs as different from the Hindus as those of the Orthodox Jews from their Gentile neighbors.

The Parsi did not agree with Sir Francis.

"The sacrifice is not willing," he said.

"How do you know that?"

"Everybody knows about this affair in Bundelcund."

This statement is another of the many puzzlers in *Around the World in Eighty Days*. The Parsi lived only thirty miles from the borders of Bundelcund. Yet, what with the mountains, the jungle, and the isolation of his small village, he might as well have lived three hundred miles away. The Bundelcundians were hostile to his people and were not likely to exchange news with him through the so-called grapevine, even if it existed. And how would he know that the rajah had died? He had spoken to no one except the three Europeans since the journey started, and the rajah had died only the night before. Yet Verne says he knew all about it.

The truth seems to be that none of the travelers could possibly have known about the situation if Verne's story were as he reported it. Fogg and Passepartout knew, of course, that the rajah was dead. But they could not say so, and Verne was unaware of what had really happened that night.

However, the Parsi did say that the rajah's widow was drugged with fumes of hemp and opium. This would have indicated to him that she had been put into a state wherein she would not disgrace herself or the community by resisting.

This is what happened. Verne, like every good novelist, had inserted some remarks of a purely fictional character to inform the reader swiftly about what was going on.

Still, would the impulse to save the woman from this horrible rite have been strong enough for Fogg to act on it? Why should he have endangered his all-important mission and the wager to attempt a seemingly hopeless rescue? Was it just humanity that caused him to interfere? Perhaps it was. Perhaps there was also the fact, unrecorded by anyone, that Fogg fell in love at first sight with the beautiful woman. But the log reveals that there was another, and no doubt stronger, motive. An Eridanean had been planted in the heart of the rajah's palace. This was the one who had slipped out a description of the domed room in which the rajah kept his distorter. She, for this Eridanean was female, had gotten as close to the rajah as it was possible for anyone to get. Her beauty and charm enabled her to attract the rajah's attention easily, and from this to marriage was another easy step.

Fogg had been told all this a long time ago by Stuart via a whist game. This is why, just as the journey was about to be resumed, Fogg said, "Suppose we save this woman?"

Sir Francis exclaimed, "What, save this woman, Mr. Fogg?"

"I have twelve hours to spare. I can devote them to this."

"Why," Sir Francis said, "you *are* a man of heart!"

"Sometimes, when I have the time," Fogg replied.

CHAPTER XIII

IN WHICH PASSEPARTOUT PROVES ONCE MORE
THAT FORTUNE FAVOURS THE BRAVE

The idea was a bold one, surrounded by obstacles, and possibly impracticable. Mr. Fogg was about to risk his life, or at all events his liberty, and consequently the success of his undertaking, but he never hesitated for a moment. In Sir Francis Cromarty he had a valuable ally.

As for Passepartout, he was quite ready for anything he was told to do. His master's idea had raised him in his opinion. He felt there was really a heart under that icy exterior. He began to love Phileas Fogg.

But the guide was a difficulty—what share would he take in the business? might he not be inclined to take part with the natives? if he would not assist them, could they count on his neutrality? Sir Francis Cromarty put the question to him very frankly.

"General," replied the guide, "I am a Parsee, and that woman is a Parsee; command me!"

"Very good, guide," said Mr. Fogg.

"But you must know," continued the Parsee, "we not only risk our lives, but the most horrible torments if we are taken. So you must make up your minds."

"They are made up," returned Fogg. "I think we had better wait till night before we attempt anything."

"I think so, too," replied the guide.

The worthy Hindu then gave them an account of the victim. She was a celebrated native beauty of Parsee extraction, daughter of a wealthy Bombay merchant. She had there received an English education, and from her manners and instruction she might have been taken for an European. Her name was Aouda. Left an orphan, she was married against her will to this old rajah in Bundelkund, and was a widow in three months. Knowing the fate which awaited her she made her escape, was soon retaken, and the rajah's relations, who were devoted to her death, from which there seemed to be no escape. This story would only confirm Mr. Fogg and his friends in their generous intentions. It was arranged that the guide should take the elephant as near as he could to the pagoda of Pillaji.

Half an hour afterwards they stopped in a thicket, about a hundred yards from the temple, which they could not see, but they could distinctly hear the yells of the devotees.

They then discussed how they could get at the victim. Their guide was well acquainted with the temple in which he expected the young woman was confined. Would it be practicable to get in by one of its doors when the whole band would be plunged in a drunken sleep, or would it be necessary to make a hole in the wall? This they could only decide on the spot. There was no doubt she must be carried off that very night, and not when the victim was led to her doom at daybreak—no human intervention could save her then.

Mr. Fogg and his companions waited until nightfall. As soon as it was dark, about six o'clock, they determined to reconnoitre the pagoda. The last cries of the fakirs had just ceased. According to their usual custom the natives were intoxicating themselves with bhang, liquid opium mixed with a decoction of hemp, and it might be possible to steal through them into the temple.

The Parsee, leading Mr. Fogg, Sir Francis Cromarty, and Passepartout, noiselessly crept through the forest. After crawling for ten minutes through the bushes they reached the bank of a small stream, and there, by the light of torches, they could see a pile of wood. It was the pyre of sandal wood, soaked in perfumed oil, on which lay the embalmed corpse of the rajah, which was to be burned with his wife. The pagoda was a hundred yards distant; they could see its minarets rising above the shade of the trees.

"Come," whispered the guide.

He crept more cautiously still through the high grass, followed in silence by his companions. The surrounding silence was only broken by the murmur of the wind through the trees.

The guide soon stopped at the end of a cleared space, lighted by a few resin torches. The ground was covered by groups of natives in their drunken sleep. It looked like a field of battle covered with dead bodies. Men, women and children all confounded together. A few drunkards here and there were still restless.

In the background the temple of Pillaji could be seen indistinctly.

But to the great disappointment of their guide the rajah's guards, lighted by torches, mounted guard with drawn swords at the doors—and it was probable that the priests were also on the watch, inside.

The Parsee advanced no further, but led his companions back as he saw the impossibility of forcing an entrance into the temple.

Phileas Fogg and Sir Francis Cromarty, who saw there was nothing to be done in that direction, halted and consulted how they should proceed.

"Let us wait," suggested the general, "it is only eight o'clock now, and it is possible the guards may go to sleep soon."

"It is possible they may," said the Parsee.

Phileas Fogg and his companions stretched themselves out at the foot of a tree and waited.

The time seemed very long. Their guide left them and went to watch the border of the wood; the rajah's guards were still at their posts, and a dim light was visible through the windows of the temple. Thus they waited till midnight without any change in the situation. The same watch was kept. It was clear that they could not reckon on the sleepiness of the sentries; they had probably abstained from the intoxicating bhang. They must adopt a different plan and make an opening in the wall of the temple. It remained for them to ascertain whether the priests watched their victim within the temple as carefully as the guards did without.

A few more words, and the guide announced he was ready to move. Mr. Fogg, Sir Francis, and Passepartout followed him. They made a detour in order to get well in the rear of the pagoda.

About half-past twelve they reached the wall without having met any one. On this side were no guards, for there were neither doors nor windows. The night was dark; the moon, in her last quarter, scarcely rose above the horizon, and was obscured by clouds, while the height of the trees deepened the gloom.

But it was not enough to find the wall, they had to make an opening in it, and to do this, Fogg and his friends had only their pocket knives. Very fortunately the walls of the temple were built of wood and brick, which he easily forced. After the removal of one brick the others would easily give way. They set to work, making as little noise as they could. The Parsee on one side, and Passepartout on the other began to loosen the bricks so as to make an opening two feet wide. They were getting on with their work when a cry was heard inside the temple, to which other cries outside responded. Passepartout and the guide ceased working. Had they been surprised? had the alarm been given? Common prudence suggested a retreat, which they made at the same time as Sir Francis and Mr. Fogg. They once more kept under cover of the wood until the alarm, if there had been one, had passed over, and ready to recommence operations when such would be the case.

But — most unluckily — guards appeared at the rear of the

temple and took up a position which effectually prevented any approach.

It would be difficult to describe the disappointment of these four men thus stopped in their operations. Now that they could not reach the victim how could they save her? Sir Francis Cromarty groaned, Passepartout was beside himself, and their guide could hardly control his emotion. Fogg waited in quiet without the least display of feeling.

"We have nothing to do now but retreat," whispered Sir Francis.

"Nothing more," said the guide.

"Wait a moment," said Fogg. "I am only due at Allahabad tomorrow before noon."

"But what do you hope to do?" replied Sir Francis. "It will be day in an hour or two, and—"

"The chance we have just lost may offer itself again at the last moment."

The brigadier wished he could read in Fogg's eyes what he was thinking of. Was he meditating making a rush and snatching the young woman from her executioners at the very moment of the sacrifice?

It would have been folly, and how could any one suppose Fogg so foolish.

Nevertheless, Sir Francis agreed to wait till the last moment to see the catastrophe of this dreadful scene. The guide would not allow his companions to remain where they had taken refuge, but brought them back to the rear of the clearing, whence, hidden by a clump of trees, they could watch the groups of sleepers. All this time Passepartout, perched on the lower branches of a tree, was working out an idea which had flashed across his mind, and remained fixed in his head.

He began by saying, "What madness!" and now he repeated to himself, "Why not? it is the only chance, and with such brutes as these—"

At all events, Passepartout gave no other utterance to his idea, but slipped down like a snake by the lower branches of the tree, which almost touched the ground. Time went slowly by, and soon a few gleams of light announced the approach of day, but it was still very dark.

The moment came. It seemed the hour of resurrection for the sleeping crowd. The groups became animated. The beating of the tamtams recommenced; shouts and singing began again. The hour had come for the poor wretch to die. The doors of the pagoda were thrown back, and a bright light escaped from the interior.

Mr. Fogg and Sir Francis could perceive the victim from the bright light thrown upon her, dragged on by two priests. It seemed to them that the poor creature, shaking off the stupor of intoxication, tried, from a last instinct of self-preservation, to escape from her murderers. The heart of Sir Francis beat faster in his bosom, and grasping Phileas Fogg's hand convulsively in his own, he felt that hand held an open knife.

At that moment the crowd opened—the young woman had relapsed into the torpor produced by the fumes of opium. She passed through the ranks of fakirs, who escorted her with religious shouts and exclamations.

Phileas Fogg and his companions mixed with the last of the crowd and followed her.

In a couple of minutes they came to the river's bank, and halted at less than fifty yards from the pile on which lay the rajah's body. In the semi-obscurity they could see the victim lying helpless and motionless by the body of her husband.

A torch was then applied to the pyre, and the wood, soaked with oil, instantly caught fire.

At that moment Sir Francis Cromarty and the guide seized upon Phileas Fogg, who with generous madness was about to rush toward the funeral pile. But Phileas Fogg shook them off, when a sudden change of scene took place. A cry of terror arose. The whole crowd in a state of terror threw themselves with their faces to the earth. The old rajah then was not dead, for they saw him suddenly arise like a spectre, lift the young woman in his arms, and descend from the pile amidst clouds of smoke which gave him a ghost-like appearance.

Fakirs, guards, and priests, struck with dread, lay there with their faces to the earth, not daring to raise their eyes or look on such a miracle.

The inanimate victim lay in the strong arms of him who bore her as if she was no burden to them. Mr. Fogg and Sir Francis were still standing. The Parsee had bowed his head, and doubtless Passepartout was no less wonder-struck.

The resuscitated rajah came close to where Sir Francis and Mr. Fogg were standing, and briefly said, "Let us be off." It was Passepartout himself who had crept up to the pyre through the thick smoke! It was Passepartout who, profiting by the gloom still pervading the scene, had snatched the young woman from death! It was Passepartout who, playing his part with happy audacity, made his way through the terrified crowd.

In a moment they all four disappeared in the wood, and the elephant carried them quickly off. But shouts and yells, and even a ball, which went through Mr. Fogg's hat, told them their plot had been discovered.

For, now the body of the old rajah was seen distinctly on the flaming pyre, the priests had recovered from their consternation, and understood that a rescue had been effected.

They rushed after the fugitives into the forest. The guards followed them; they fired upon them, but the rescuers speeded rapidly on, and in a few moments were out of reach of balls or arrows.

THE OTHER LOG OF PHILEAS FOGG

Sir Francis must have wondered about this man whose emotions could apparently be turned on or off as if they ran through a spigot. What he did not know, of course, was that Fogg could not decide whether or not he would have a certain emotion or not. The emotion came, willy-nilly, but he could shunt it aside, store it in a neural circuit where the emotional charge ran around and around the track, like a current in today's superconductive circuit. But he could not kill the emotion, because it would not die. Sooner or later, he had to pay for the storage, and he would pay double or treble the bill by the time he released it.

The two other Europeans were all for this idea. But what about the Parsi guide? He could not be expected to risk his life, but he might agree to stay behind and wait for them. Even this would be dangerous for him.

He answered that he was a Parsi and that the woman was a Parsi. He was in this with them all the way.

Verne says that the Parsi knew all about her. Probably, Verne got this from Fogg's public log and inserted the informational conversation about her in the Parsi's mouth for the benefit of the reader. In any event, we know that she was a famous beauty, the daughter of a wealthy merchant of Bombay. If she were that famous, then the Parsi may have heard about her after all. Travelers coming through his remote village may have gossiped about her.

The woman's name was Aouda Jejeebhoy, and she had been educated in an English school in Bombay. This, plus her light skin, enabled her to pass as a European. She was related to the wealthy Parsi who had been created a baronet by the queen. He was Sir Jametsee Jejeebhoy, whom the curious reader may find listed, with some biographical details, in Burke's *Peerage*.

The Parsi said that after her parents had died, she had been forced to marry the rajah.

(This, of course, was what the rajah and the public believed. She had succeeded in making it look as if she were a victim. If she had been eager to marry him, she would have aroused his suspicions.)

The Parsi, however, was right in saying that she had fled as soon as the rajah died but had been captured and returned to the capital city. The rajah's relatives were insistent that she perform the suttee, since they did not wish her to inherit the rajah's wealth.

This was probably true, Fogg thought. If Nemo had found out, or even suspected, that she was an Eridanean, he would have saved her from the suttee. She would be too valuable as a source of information for him to allow her to be wasted on the funeral pyre. But it was possible that Nemo no longer had any influence in Bundelcund and was helpless to prevent her—to him—too-early death.

The Parsi guided the travelers to the temple of Pillaji, where the distressing ceremony was to take place. Thirty minutes later, they were hidden in a dense copse about one hundred and sixty-seven yards from the Brahmin temple. Kiouni made much noise by tearing off branches and eating them, but this could not be helped. The beast was very hungry, and any efforts to stop him might result in his making even more noise. Fortunately, the distance from the crowd, the uproar it was making, and the thick vegetation that surrounded the travelers would keep the Bundelcundians from noticing the sounds the elephant was making.

Fogg questioned the guide about the layout of the area around the temple, its interior design, and the behavior of the Hindus at such occasions. Verne says that the Parsi was familiar with the temple. But why would a Parsi ever have gone into a Hindu temple, especially one in hostile territory? Perhaps, being intelligent, and hence curious, the Parsi had picked up his knowledge by questioning various Hindus of his village, or travelers, who had worshipped there. The Pillaji temple seems to have been a famous one.

The party waited in the copse until night fell. Meanwhile, they were still apprehensive about being discovered. Kiouni had not stopped feeding, and now and then children wandered off from the crowd and came close to the hiding place. Once, three ten-year-olds, playing some sort of hide and seek, started toward the copse. They were quite close when the mother of one came after them. Kiouni was stuffing some broken branches into his mouth at that time, so there was no snapping and cracking of wood to attract her. Also, the wind was blowing toward the travelers and helped to carry the noise away from the crowd.

Even so, they had some anxious moments.

As the sun set, the noise of the mob began to die. Kiouni had by then stripped half of the trees, but, his belly full, was now dozing. The celebrators were not only worn out; they were sleepy from the effects of liquid opium mixed with hemp. This use of such drugs and some other features of Verne's description of them indicate that the Bundelcundians did not belong to a conventional sect of Hinduism. The Bundelcundians were, after all, devotees of Kali and undoubtedly considered unorthodox even by other branches of this particular worship. There were elements of a pre-Hindu religion in the Bundelcundian religion, probably adopted from the original inhabitants, the small dark peoples who now survived only in the mountain jungles.

Fogg's record validates Verne's description, so we can accept it as true that these Kalians did indeed use opium and other drugs.

After dark, the Parsi stole out to observe the situation at close range. He found that all the mob were lying in a stupor, children included. The unfortunate exceptions were the priests and the guards, alert within the temple. Fogg, hearing this, was unperturbed. They would wait on the chance that the people in the temple might go to sleep later.

At midnight, it became apparent that the guards intended to stay up all night. Fogg gave an order, and the travelers went out into a night which lacked a moon, since it was covered by heavy clouds. They stopped at the rear wall of the temple and began chipping away with their pocketknives. Fortunately, after one brick had been removed, the others came out without much labor. Once, they had to retreat into the woods because the guards were disturbed by a cry. This caused Sir Francis and the Parsi to argue that they should give up their rescue attempt. Whatever had caused the cry, the guards would now be even more vigilant. And daylight would soon come.

Fogg replied that he wished to stay until all hope was gone. Something might happen to their advantage.

Passepartout, watching from the branches of a tree, had a sudden inspiration. Without a word to the others, he got down off the tree and slipped off. His act was motivated only by humanity. He had no idea at that time that the woman was a fellow Eridanean.

At dawn, Aouda Jejeebhoy was brought out of the temple. The crowd recovered from its stupor, and the voices and the music became as loud as before. Aouda struggled until she was held over burning hemp and opium and forced to breathe. Sir Francis, greatly moved by this pitiful scene, grabbed Fogg's hand and found in it an open knife. But Fogg did not rush into the crowd brandishing the knife in a vain effort to save her. Verne says that, at this point, Fogg and the other two men mingled in the rear ranks of the crowd and followed it to the pyre. This is obviously not true, since they would have been noticed at once and set upon. In actuality, they remained at some distance and took care to hide behind bushes.

Verne fails to say what Fogg thought of Passepartout's unauthorized disappearance. Fogg records that he had assumed that the Frenchman was still up in the tree posted as their lookout.

The three men saw the now senseless woman placed beside the corpse. They saw the oil-soaked wood of the pyre being ignited with a torch. Fogg seems to have lost his self-control. He was about to dash through the crowd when Sir Francis and the Parsi grabbed him. Despite their efforts, he broke free and was about to launch himself again when something unexpected and terrifying happened. The whole crowd, screaming with terror, threw itself on its face and cowered.

The dead rajah had sat up, gotten to his feet, lifted Aouda in his arms, and was now coming down from the pyre. Smoke flowered about him as if he were a devil carrying a poor lost soul through the fires of Hell. He walked through the prostrate mob straight to the party in the rear, all of whom had come out from their concealment.

The reanimated rajah, as everybody knows, was Passepartout. In the darkness, while the crowd slept, he had stripped the corpse, buried it under sticks of wood, put on its clothes, and then lain down in the posture and place of the dead man. In fact, the dead rajah was directly below.

A few moments later, Kiouni, aroused from his sleep, bearing five on his back now, was tearing along as if he fully understood the necessity for a speedy departure. Cries and gunshots sounded behind him, and a bullet pierced Mr. Fogg's hat. The fire had by then exposed the naked body of the rajah. The worshippers of Kali at once understood not only that they had been duped but in what manner. Inasmuch as they had no elephants or horses at hand, they were soon hopelessly outdistanced.

CHAPTER XIV

IN WHICH PHILEAS FOGG TRAVELS THE WHOLE LENGTH
OF THE BEAUTIFUL VALLEY OF THE GANGES WITHOUT
THINKING OF LOOKING AT IT

The abduction had been carried out happily, and for an hour Passepartout smiled at his successful trick. Sir Francis Cromarty had shaken hands with him, and Mr. Fogg had said "Very well," which, in that gentleman's mouth, was equivalent to an expression of very great approbation, to which Passepartout replied that all the credit of the affair belonged to his master. His was only a droll idea, and he could not help laughing when he thought that he, Passepartout, once an acrobat, ex-sergeant in the fire-brigade, had been the widower of a charming woman, and an old embalmed rajah.

As for the young Hindu, she was still unconscious of what had happened to her; wrapped up in rugs and blankets, she was now reposing in one of the panniers. The elephant, under the safe guidance of the Parsee, was rapidly traversing the forest. After they had left the pagoda of Pillaji an hour, they came upon an extensive plain. At seven they halted, the woman was still in a complete state of prostration. The guide administered to her a little brandy-and-water, but the state of stupor in which she remained must have lasted some time longer.

Sir Francis Cromarty, who was well acquainted with the

intoxicating effects of bhang, was not at all uneasy on her account.

But if the young native's recovery caused the brigadier no uneasiness, what would be her fate eventually disquieted him much. He told Phileas Fogg frankly that if Aouda remained in India, she would inevitably fall into the hands of her assassins again. These devotees existed all over the peninsula, and in spite of the British police they would be sure to succeed in obtaining possession of their victim, either in the Madras, Bombay, or Calcutta presidency, and Sir Francis quoted a case which had recently happened, in support of his opinion. He thought her only chance of safety consisted in leaving India as soon as possible. Phileas Fogg replied he would think over what Sir Francis had said, and would reflect on what ought to be done in the matter.

At ten the guide announced their arrival at Allahabad station; there the broken line was resumed, and the trains ran from Allahabad to Calcutta in less than twenty-four hours. Thus Phileas Fogg would arrive in time to take the steamer which only left the following day, October the 25th, at noon, for Hong-kong.

The young woman was taken to an apartment at the station. Passepartout was despatched to purchase for her dresses, shawls, furs, and whatever articles of toilette she needed, for which his master gave him *carte blanche*.

Passepartout set off directly, and perambulated the streets of Allahabad, which is, from its name, the "city of God," and one of the most venerated in India, for it is built at the junction of two holy rivers, the Ganges, and the Jumna, the waters of which attract pilgrims from all parts of the peninsula. It is well known that according to the Ramayana legends the Ganges takes its rise in Heaven, whence, thanks to Brahma, it flows down upon the earth.

While engaging in making his purchases, Passepartout had a good look at the town, which was once defended by a magnificent fort, now a State prison. This city, once so industrious and commercial, could now boast neither industry nor commerce.

Passepartout vainly looked for such a shop as he could have found in Regent Street, near Farmer & Co. He could only find at a store that sold old clothes, the articles he required—a dress of Scotch check, a cloak, and an otter skin pelisse, for which he paid seventy-five pounds, and then returned in triumph to the station.

Aouda was beginning to come to her senses, the influence of the drugs administered to her by the priest was gradually diminishing, and her beautiful eyes were regaining all their Indian softness.

When the royal poet Uçaf Uddaul celebrates the charms of the Queen of Ahmenagara, he does it in the following terms;—

"Her glossy locks, evenly parted, encircle the harmonious contours of her white and delicate cheeks, brilliant in their smoothness and freshness; her ebon eyebrows have the shape and power of the bow of Kama, god of love, and beneath her long and silken lashes, in the dark pupil of her large, clear eye, is reflected, as in the holy lakes of the Himalaya, the purest of celestial light; her teeth, fine, even, and white, glisten between her smiling lips, like drops of dew in the half-blown flower of the pomegranate; her delicately curved ears, her pink hands, her little feet, arched and tender, as the buds of the lotus, shine with the brilliancy of Ceylon's finest pearls, and Golconda's brightest diamonds; her slender and supple waist, which one hand could span, displays the richness of her bust, where youth in bloom sets forth its most perfect treasures, and under the silken folds of her tunic she seems to have been modelled in silver, by the divine hand of Vicvacarma, the immortal sculptor."

Making an allowance for a poet's exaggeration, it is quite enough to say that Aouda was a very charming person, as the expression is usually understood in Europe. She spoke English perfectly, and the guide had only said what was true when he affirmed that education had quite transformed the young Parsee.

But now the train was about to leave the station of Allahabad. The Parsee was waiting. Mr. Fogg paid him the stipulated price of his services, without adding thereto a farthing. This rather surprised Passepartout, who was well aware how much his master was indebted to the guide's devotion. In fact, the Parsee had voluntarily risked his life in the Pillaji affair, and if at any time the Hindus found it out, he would have some difficulty in escaping their revenge.

And then there was the question of Kiouni. What was to be done with an animal which had cost such a price?

But Phileas Fogg had already resolved what to do in that case.

"Parsee," said he to the guide, "you have been to me a good and a devoted servant. I have paid you for your services, but not for your devotion. Will you accept the elephant? if so, he is yours."

The eyes of the guide began to glisten.

"Your honour bestows a fortune on me," cried he.

"Take him then, guide," replied Mr. Fogg, "and I shall still be your debtor."

"That's right," cried Passepartout, "take him, my friend. Kiouni is a good and brave beast."

And going up to the elephant he gave him some lumps of sugar, saying—

"Take it, Kiouni, take it."

The elephant gave a grunt of satisfaction, and then taking Passepartout by the waist-belt, he raised him in his trunk above his head. Passepartout, in no way frightened, caressed the animal, who set him gently on the ground again.

Shortly afterwards, Phileas Fogg, Sir Francis Cromarty, and Passepartout were installed in a comfortable carriage, in which Aouda occupied the best seat, and were hurrying along at full speed to Benares.

About eighty miles separated this town from Allahabad, and the distance was done in two hours.

During the journey the young woman recovered herself completely, and the soporific effects of bhang passed off.

What was her astonishment to find herself in a railway carriage, dressed in European clothes, among travellers who were absolutely unknown to her.

Her companions were lavish in their attentions to her, and then the brigadier-general told her the whole story; how Phileas Fogg had not hesitated to risk his life to save hers, and the result of Passepartout's bold idea, and the end of the adventure.

Mr. Fogg allowed him to speak without uttering a word. Passepartout modestly remarked, "It was not worth talking about."

Aouda feelingly thanked her deliverers, more by tears than in words; her beautiful eyes expressed her gratitude better than her lips. Then, as her thoughts dwelt again on the scene of the suttee, and she still looked on that soil of India where so much danger still awaited her, she shuddered with fear.

Phileas Fogg understood what was passing through her mind. To reassure her, he proposed, though in his coldest manner, to take care of her to Hong-kong, where she could remain until this affair was forgotten. Aouda gratefully accepted this offer. One of her relations, a Parsee, and one of the principal merchants of the place, was living in that town, which is in every respect English, except that it is built on a spot on the coast of China.

At half-past twelve the train stopped at Benares station. The legends of the Brahmins assert that this city occupies the site of the ancient city of Casi, which was once suspended, like Mahomet's tomb, between heaven and earth. But in these more literal days, Benares, the Athens of India, now rests very prosaically on the ground, and Passepartout was able to catch a glimpse of its brick houses, and its huts of clay, which gave it a most desolate look, with nothing remarkable about it.

Here Sir Francis Cromarty left them.

The troops he commanded were encamped some miles to the north of the town. So the brigadier-general took leave of Phileas Fogg, wished him success, and expressed a hope he would continue his journey in a less original but more profitable manner than he began it. Mr. Fogg just slightly pressed his companion's hand. Aouda's farewell was more affectionate. She could never forget how much she was indebted to Sir Francis. The brigadier-general then shook Passepartout heartily by the hand, who, very much affected, asked when and how he could show his devotion to him— and so they parted.

On leaving Benares, the railway for some distance runs along the valley of the Ganges. Through the carriage windows they could see the varied landscape of Behar, mountains covered with verdure, fields of barley, maize, and wheat, rivers and tanks, the abode of alligators, well and prosperous-looking villages, and green forests. Elephants and zebu came and bathed in the sacred river, and, though the season was far advanced, and the water was now cold, bands of Hindus of both sexes piously performed their ablutions in its holy waters. These are the faithful followers of Brahma, who was incarnate in these three personages— Vishnu, the solar divinity, Shiva, the divine personification of natural force, and Brahma, the supreme head of priests and legislators. But with what eyes must Brahma, Shiva, and Vishnu regard now Anglicised India, when a steamer passes along, puffing, and troubling the sacred waters of the Ganges, frightening the gulls that fly across them, the turtle swarming on its banks, and its worshippers stretched along its shores? This panorama passed like a flash of lightning before them, and its details were often hidden from sight by a cloud of steam. The travellers could hardly catch a sight of the fort of Chunar, twenty miles to the southeast of Benares, the ancient fortress of the rajahs of Behar. Ghazepore, and its celebrated factories of rose-water; Lord Cornwallis's tomb, which stands on the left bank of the Ganges; the fortified town of Buxar; Ratna, a large manufacturing and commercial city, which is the principal opium market in India; Monglier, a more than European city, English, after the fashion of Manchester and Birmingham, celebrated for its iron foundries, its cutlery and swords, &c., whose lofty chimneys defile Brahma's sky with the blackest smoke—a terrible blow to the land of romance.

Then night came, and through the howls of tigers, bears, and wolves, flying before the locomotive, the train sped on, and nothing was seen of the wonders of Bengal, Golconda, nor Gour in ruins, nor Moorshedabad, formerly its capital, nor Burdovan, nor Hooghly, nor the French town of Chandernagore, where Passepartout would have been delighted to see the flag of his country fluttering in the wind.

At last they reached Calcutta at seven in the morning. The steamer did not leave for Hong-kong till noon, so Phileas Fogg had five hours before him. According to the itinerary of his journey, as arranged beforehand, he was due in the capital of India the 25th of October, three-and-twenty days after leaving London, and he was there the day named; thus he had neither gained nor lost. Unfortunately he had lost, as we know, in crossing the Indian Peninsula, the two days he had gained between London and Bombay. But we must conclude Phileas Fogg did not regret them.

THE OTHER LOG OF PHILEAS FOGG

Passepartout was delighted with his exploit. Sir Francis shook his hand. Fogg said, "Well done," though he must have thought that the valet, who was, after all, under his command, should have consulted him before acting. He was, however, eminently pragmatic. And it was the Eridanean custom to act independently if the situation required.

Sir Francis told Fogg that the woman would never be safe in India again. The fanatics of Kali would track her down and strangle her.

At Allahabad, the young woman waited in a room in the railroad station while Passepartout purchased suitable clothes for her. Though Verne does not say so, he must have bought clothes for himself, too. When he entered Allahabad, he was still wearing the garments he had taken from the rajah. His own had been burned in the pyre.

On the train to Benares, Aouda fully recovered. She was

astonished, of course, since she had expected to awaken in the Parsi Heaven. Fogg made no mention at this time of their Eridanean connections. He pretended to her to be what the world thought him, an overly eccentric English gentleman. He did offer to take her with him as far as Hong Kong. There, it seemed, she had a Parsi cousin who was a rich merchant.

At Benares, Sir Francis, who had to rejoin his brigade, bade them a fond farewell. He said that he would never forget their adventure, and neither Fogg nor Passepartout enlightened him on the one that he had missed.

On the twenty-fifth of October, exactly on schedule, the party arrived at Calcutta. The two days gained on the trip from London to Bombay had been lost during the journey across India. Verne says that it is to be supposed that Fogg did not regret the loss. He spoke more truly than he knew.

CHAPTER XV

IN WHICH THE BAG OF NOTES IS AGAIN LIGHTENED
OF SOME THOUSANDS OF POUNDS

The train stopped at the station. Passepartout was the first to descend, and was followed by Mr. Fogg, who aided his young companion out of the carriage. Phileas Fogg intended to go direct to the steamer for Hong-kong, in order to settle Aouda there in comfort, as he did not intend to leave her as long as she remained in a country where her safety was doubtful.

Just as Mr. Fogg was about to leave the station a policeman came up to him, and said—

"Mr. Phileas Fogg, I believe?"

"I am Mr. Phileas Fogg."

"Is this man your servant?" asked the policeman, pointing to Passepartout.

"Yes."

"Be so kind as to follow me, both of you."

Mr. Fogg could not help a movement of surprise. This police agent represented the law, and in the eyes of every Englishman the law is paramount. Passepartout, with his French habits, wanted to argue the question, but the policeman tapped him with his staff, and Phileas Fogg made him a sign to follow.

"This young lady can accompany us, I suppose?" asked Mr. Fogg.

"She can," replied the policeman, who then led Mr. Fogg, Aouda, and Passepartout to a palki-ghari, a four-wheeled carriage holding four persons, and drawn by two horses. They started. No one spoke during the drive, which lasted about twenty minutes.

The carriage traversed the northen part of the city, with its narrow streets of cabins, in which a filthy, ragged, cosmopolitan population swarmed, then through the European part of the city, with its brick houses, shaded by cocoa-nut trees, and bristling with masts, and about which, though it was yet early, people were riding or driving in elegant equipages.

The palki-ghari stopped before a plain-looking house, but which was not intended for domestic use. The policeman made his prisoners get down—one can in truth call them so—and showed them into a room with barred windows, saying as he did so—

"At half-past eight you will appear before Judge Obadiah."

Then he withdrew, and shut the door after him.

"What have they shut us in here for?" cried Passepartout, dropping into a chair.

Aouda turned to Mr. Fogg, and said, as she vainly strove to conceal her emotion—

"Leave me, sir, leave me! You are followed on my account. It is because you saved me."

Phileas Fogg only replied it was not possible. Prosecute them on account of a suttee! Most unlikely. How could the plaintiffs in such a suit present themselves in court? There must be some mistake. Mr. Fogg added that under no circumstances would he give up the young woman, but that he should take her with him to Hong-kong.

"But the boat leaves at twelve!" cried Passepartout.

"We shall be on board before twelve," said the gentleman, quietly.

This was said with such an air of conviction that Passepartout could not help saying to himself—

"*Parbleu*, that is a certainty, before twelve we shall be on board!" But he did not feel very confident, nevertheless.

At half-past eight the door was opened, the policeman reappeared, and conducted his prisoners into an adjoining apartment. It was a court of law, and there was a numerous auditory, consisting of Europeans and natives. Mr. Fogg, Aouda, and Passepartout sat down on a bench opposite the seats reserved for the magistrate and his clerk.

The magistrate, Judge Obadiah, followed them, accompanied by his clerk. He was a fat, round man. He took a wig down from a hook and clapped it on his head.

"The first case!" he cried.

Then putting his hand to his head he called out—

"This is not my wig."

"No, sir, it is mine," replied the clerk.

"My dear Mr. Oysterpuff, how can a judge decide rightly when he wears his clerk's wig?"

Wigs were exchanged. While this was going on Passepartout was boiling over with impatience, for the hands of the clock over the magistrate's head seemed to go terribly fast.

"The first case!" cried Obadiah once more.

"Phileas Fogg!" called out the clerk Oysterpuff.

"Here," replied Mr. Fogg.

"Passepartout!"

"Here," replied Passepartout.

"Very well," said the magistrate. "Accused, for the last two days the Bombay trains have been watched on your account."

"But what are we accused of?" cried out Passepartout, angrily.

"You are about to learn," replied the judge.

"Sir," observed Mr. Fogg, "I am a British citizen, and I have a right—"

"Have you anything to complain of?" asked Obadiah.

"Nothing."

"Very well; let the complainants come forward."

At the magistrate's order a door opened, and the Hindu priests were shown in by the usher of the court.

"That must be the truth," murmured Passepartout; "those are the rascals who wanted to burn our young lady."

The priests stood up in front of the magistrate, and the clerk read out an accusation of sacrilege brought against a certain Mr. Fogg and his servant, who were accused of violating the sanctity of a place consecrated to the worship of Brahma.

"You hear?" said the magistrate.

"Yes, sir," replied Mr. Fogg, looking at his watch, "and I confess it."

"Ah, you confess it?"

"Yes; and now let these three priests, in their turn, confess what they were about to do at the pagoda of Pillaji."

The priests looked at one another. They did not seem to understand the defendant's words.

"Yes!" cried Passepartout, impetuously; "at that temple of Pillaji, before which they were on the point of burning their victim."

Fresh astonishment on the part of the priests and the magistrate.

"What victim?" asked he. "Burn whom? What, in the middle of Bombay?"

"Bombay!" cried Passepartout.

"Yes, Bombay; we are not talking about the pagoda of Pillaji, but of the pagoda on Malabar Hill, at Bombay."

"And, as evidence against one of the accused, here are the guilty person's shoes," said the clerk, laying the articles in question on the desk before him.

"My shoes!" cried Passepartout, who was so surprised that he could not help making this involuntary admission.

The confusion of master and servant may be imagined. They had forgotten the affair of the temple at Bombay, which had brought them before the magistrate at Calcutta.

Fix soon saw how he could turn that awkward affair to his own advantage. Delaying his own departure twelve hours, he made himself the advocate of the native priests. He promised them ample damages, knowing how strict the Government was in all such offences; then he took them with him in pursuit of the desecrator. But in consequence of the time lost in rescuing the young widow, Fix and the priests arrived in Calcutta before Phileas Fogg and his servant. He began to think his man had stopped at one of the stations on the line, and had taken refuge in the northern provinces. For twenty-four hours Fix watched the station in a state of great anxiety. What was his satisfaction when, that very morning, he saw him get out of the carriage, accompanied, it is true, by a young woman, for whose presence he could not account. He immediately sent a policeman after him, and this is why Mr. Fogg, Passepartout, and the Bundelkund rajah's widow found themselves brought before Judge Obadiah.

And if Passepartout had been less preoccupied he might have seen the detective in a corner watching the proceedings with the liveliest interest, for at Calcutta, as at Bombay and Suez, there was no warrant forthcoming. However, the magistrate had caught at the acknowledgment which escaped from Passepartout, who would have given all he was worth to recall so imprudent an admission.

"The facts are not denied?" said the judge.

"Not denied!" coolly replied Fogg.

"Inasmuch as the law of England protects in an equal degree all professions of faith existing among the populations of India; and the offence being acknowledged by the individual, Passepartout, proved to have desecrated the pagoda of Malabar Hill with his presence on the 20th day of October, the said Passepartout is condemned to fifteen days in prison and a fine of three hundred pounds."

"Three hundred pounds!" cried Passepartout, who had only noticed the amount of the fine.

"Silence!" croaked the usher.

"And," added Judge Obadiah, "as there is no positive proof of connivance between master and servant, nevertheless the former being responsible for the actions of his paid domestic, the said Phileas Fogg is condemned to a week's imprisonment and a fine of one hundred and fifty pounds. Clerk, call the next case!"

Fix, in his corner, was inexpressibly delighted, for Phileas Fogg detained in Calcutta for a week, gave more than the time required for the warrant to arrive.

Passepartout was disconsolate. This decision was his master's ruin. A bet of twenty thousand pounds lost, and all because he must go loitering about in that cursed pagoda, where he had no business whatever. Phileas Fogg, who had just as much control over himself as if the sentence did not regard him in the least, had not even raised his brow. But just as the clerk was about to call on the next case, he rose and said—

"I put in bail."

"You have a right to do so," said the judge.

Fix felt a chill run down his back, but his courage returned when he heard the judge say, as Phileas Fogg and his servant were strangers, he should require bail for each of them, in the sum of one thousand pounds.

Thus, if he could not reverse the sentence of the magistrate, this affair would cost Mr. Fogg two thousand pounds.

"Here is the money," said he, and he took a bundle of notes out of Passepartout's bag, and laid it on the clerk's desk.

"This sum will be returned to you when you come out of prison, in the meantime you are free on bail."

"Come," said Mr. Fogg to his servant.

"But they ought to give me back my shoes," cried Passepartout in a rage.

His shoes were handed to him.

"They have cost dear indeed," he muttered, "more than one thousand pounds each of them, and they always hurt me!"

Passepartout was quite humbled, and he followed Mr. Fogg, who had offered his arm to Aouda. Fix was in hopes his thief would never make up his mind to lose two thousand pounds, but that he would rather go to prison for a week, so he followed Mr. Fogg.

Mr. Fogg took a carriage and got into it with Aouda and Passepartout. Fix hurried after it, which soon stopped on one of the quays.

The *Rangoon* was lying out in the river about half a mile off, with her Blue Peter flying. It was striking eleven. Mr. Fogg had an hour before him. Fix watched him leave the vehicle and get into a boat with Aouda and his servant. The detective stamped with rage.

"The scoundrel!" he cried; "the scoundrel! he's off. Two thousand pounds thrown away. Extravagant as a thief! All, I will follow him all over the world if necessary, but at the rate he goes all the stolen money will go too."

The detective was justified in making that reflection. In fact, since they left London, what with travelling expenses, bribes, price of elephant and fines, and money deposited as bail, Phileas Fogg had already run through more than five thousand pounds, and the percentage of the sum recovered to be paid to the detective was still growing daily less.

THE OTHER LOG OF PHILEAS FOGG

As they left the railway station, a policeman politely asked the two men to follow him. Aouda accompanied them to the police station. There they were held for trial, which would begin at 8:30 that morning. They were not told why they were detained, which seems strange since British law required that they be so informed. Aouda said that it was because of their interference with the suttee. Fogg replied that that was highly improbable. Who would dare complain to the authorities? Whatever happened, he would not desert Aouda. He would go with her to Hong Kong.

Passepartout, wiping the perspiration from his forehead, cried, "But the steamer leaves at noon!"

"We shall be on board at noon," Fogg said.

At the stipulated time, the three were brought into the courtroom. Here they discovered the nature of the charges brought against them. It was not the affair at the temple of Pillaji which had caused their arrest. It was that at the temple of Malabar Hill in Bombay.

Fix, whom we last saw in Bombay, had traveled with the three priests to Calcutta. Because Fogg and party were delayed in the rescue of Aouda, Fix and party had beaten them to Calcutta. There they had complained to the British authorities of Passepartout's desecration of the temple. Fix, who had paid their passage, had also promised them that they would collect a large sum in damages. On seeing Fogg and party arrive, he had gotten a policeman to detain them.

Sitting inconspicuously in the crowd in a corner, Fix observed the trial. He was delighted at the sentence. Passepartout was fined three hundred pounds and given fifteen days in jail. Since Fogg, as master, was responsible for his servant, he was sentenced to seven days in jail and fined one hundred and fifty pounds.

Fix knew that there was now time for the warrant to arrive. And while Fogg was on his way back to England as Fix's prisoner, many things could—and would—happen to Fogg.

Mr. Fogg, however, claimed his right to bail. Fix became cold at this point but warmed up when he heard that bail would cost each prisoner a thousand pounds. Then he became cold again when Fogg paid the amount from his carpetbag.

Passepartout insisted that the shoes left behind in the temple be returned to him. They were, whereon he complained that they not only had cost a thousand pounds apiece, they pinched his feet.

Fix, hoping that Fogg would never leave two thousand pounds behind him, shadowed him. To his consternation, he saw the party board a small boat and head for the steamer *Rangoon*. There was nothing he could do except follow them to Hong Kong. So far, he thought, he had certainly failed to "fix" them. He did succeed in getting onto the *Rangoon* without being seen by the Frenchman. But first he left orders that the warrant, when it arrived, should be forwarded to Hong Kong.

CHAPTER XVI
IN WHICH FIX DOES NOT SEEM TO UNDERSTAND
WHAT IS SAID TO HIM

The *Rangoon*, one of the Peninsular and Oriental Company's steamers in the Japan and China seas, was an iron screw vessel of about eighteen hundred tons, and four hundred horse-power, nominal. It was as fast as the *Mongolia*, but not so comfortable. And Aouda consequently was not quite as comfortable as Phileas Fogg desired. After all it was only a passage of three thousand five hundred miles, about eleven or twelve days, and the young widow was not very difficult to please.

During the first days of their voyage, Aouda had the opportunity of becoming better acquainted with Phileas Fogg,—and continually expressed the liveliest gratitude to him. That phlegmatic person apparently listened to her without showing the slightest emotion, either in word or manner. He was attentive that she should want for nothing. At certain hours he presented himself, if not to talk, at least to listen to her. He was strictly polite in every respect, but with the ease of an automaton whose movements had been arranged for that purpose. Aouda hardly knew what to think of him, but after all she owed her life to him, and Passepartout had in some measure prepared her for that gentleman's eccentricity—he had told her of the bet he had made to go round the world. Aouda smiled; but her preserver lost nothing because she regarded him through the medium of her gratitude.

Aouda confirmed the Parsee's account of her affecting history. She did really belong to that race which takes high rank among the natives. Many Parsee merchants have made fortunes in Indian cotton. The relation she hoped to find at Hong-kong was a cousin of Sir James Jejeebhoy who lived at Bombay, and had been created a Baronet by the Home Government. Was she likely to find with him refuge and assistance? She could not say, and then Mr. Fogg used to tell her not to be uneasy, for it would come mathematically right at last—that was his expression.

Could the young woman understand that expression? One cannot say. She used to fix her large eyes, clear as the sacred lakes of the Himalaya, on the intractable Fogg, but he did not seem inclined to throw himself into the said lake.

The first part of the *Rangoon*'s passage was favourable. The *Rangoon* soon sighted the great Andaman, the largest of the group, which is recognized at a great distance by sailors from its picturesque mountain called the Saddleback, about two thousand four hundred feet high.

They passed near the shore, but the Ragusans would not show themselves. This island panorama was superb— vast forests of palms, arecas, bamboos, nutmeg trees, teak trees, gigantic mimosas, and tree ferns covered the foreground; behind was the elegant profile of the mountain ranges—thousands of those precious swallows swarmed along the coast, their nests being one of the most highly-esteemed dishes in the celestial empire. But the varied scenes afforded by the Andaman Isles were soon left behind, and the *Rangoon* was fast approaching the Straits of Malacca, through which she would pass into the China seas.

But what was Detective Fix about, so unluckily made a party to this voyage round the globe? On quitting Calcutta, after leaving instructions that the warrant, if it came, should be forwarded to Hong-kong, he contrived to get on board the *Rangoon* unseen by Passepartout, and he hoped to conceal his presence on board from him until the steamer arrived, for it would have been very difficult to explain his presence there without rousing Passepartout's suspicions, who believed he was still at Bombay. But he was brought to renew his acquaintance with him by the mere force of circumstances, and so it happened.

All the "detective's" hopes and wishes were now centred on one spot, Hong-kong, for the steamer stopped too short a time at Singapore for him to take any steps there. It was at Hong-kong, then, that he hoped to arrest the thief, or he was lost to him, he might say, for good.

Hong-kong was English territory, but the last he would touch at. Beyond, China, Japan, America, all offered a nearly sure asylum to Mr. Fogg. At Hong-kong, if he found the warrant of arrest, which was no doubt following him, Fix could arrest Fogg and hand him over to the local police. But beyond Hong-kong a warrant was useless; the Extradition Act must be appealed to, consequently delays and all manner of difficulties, by which the rascal would profit and eventually escape. If he failed in his object at Hong-kong it would be, if not impossible, at least very difficult, to bring it to a successful issue.

"Now," Fix used to say to himself in the long tedious hours he passed alone in his cabin, "either the warrant is at Hong-kong, and I arrest my man, or it is not; and this time, come what may, I must prevent his going on. I failed at Bombay, I failed at Calcutta! if I fail again at Hong-kong my reputation is lost; cost what it may, I must succeed. But what course can I adopt to delay the departure of this cursed Fogg, if need be?"

As a last resource Fix decided on telling everything to Passepartout, in making him understand what sort of a master he had, whose accomplice he certainly was not. Passepartout, on hearing this, might fear being implicated in the robbery, and would take Fix's side in the matter. But it was a hazardous experiment, and could only be put in execution if everything else failed. One word from Passepartout, and his master would compromise the whole affair beyond redemption.

Thus the police agent was extremely embarrassed when Aouda's presence on board the *Rangoon*, in company with Phileas Fogg, opened a new field for reflection.

Who was this woman? what combination of circumstances had brought her into Fogg's company? It was evident they had met somewhere between Bombay and Calcutta; but where? Was it chance that had thrown Phileas Fogg and the young traveller together? Perhaps this journey across India had been undertaken by the gentleman with the object of meeting this charming young person, for she was charming. Fix had seen her at the magistrate's office in Calcutta.

One can easily understand the detective's perplexity; he began to think there was something like a criminal abduction in this affair. Yes, it must be so! this idea became fixed in his brain, and he saw directly how he could turn it to his own advantage. Married or not, the young woman had been carried away, and it might be possible to create such obstacles at Hong-kong to Mr. Fogg's further progress that money would fail to serve him. But he must not wait the arrival of the *Rangoon* at Hong-kong, for Fogg had the horrid habit of jumping from one boat into another, and before any steps could be taken he would be off.

It was therefore very important to communicate with the English authorities, and to signal the passage of the *Rangoon* before he could land. Nothing was easier than this, for the steamer stopped at Singapore, and there is telegraphic communication thence to Hong-kong.

However, before taking any steps, and to be the more certain, Fix determined to question Passepartout. He knew there would be no difficulty in making the Frenchman talk, so he decided on laying aside the incognito he had observed till then. There was no time to lose, it was now the 30th of October, and the *Rangoon* would touch at Singapore the following day.

On that day, then, Fix left his cabin, and went on deck, with the intention of meeting Passepartout first, apparently quite surprised to see him. Passepartout was in the forepart of the ship when the police agent rushed up to him, crying out—

"What, you on board the *Rangoon*?"

"Mr. Fix," returned Passepartout, really surprised to recognize his fellow traveller on the *Mongolia*. "Why, I left you at Bombay, and now I find you on the way to Hong-kong! Why, you must be going round the world too."

"No, no," replied Fix, "and I think I shall remain at Hong-kong—at least, for a few days."

"Ah," said Passepartout, who seemed rather struck at something. "But how is it I have never once seen you since we left Calcutta?"

"Well, I have been ill, rather sea-sick, so I remained below. The Bay of Bengal has not treated me as well as the Indian Ocean. And how is your master, Mr. Phileas Fogg?"

"Perfectly well, and as punctual as ever, keeping his time exactly. By-the-by, Mr. Fix, you must know we have a young lady with us."

"A young lady!" replied the detective, affecting not to understand what Passepartout meant.

He was soon master of the whole story. Passepartout told him what had happened to him in the pagoda at Bombay, the purchase of the elephant for two thousand pounds, Aouda's rescue, their being sentenced to fine and imprisonment at the Calcutta police-office, and their release on bail.

Fix, though well knowing all the last part of this story, affected entire ignorance. Passepartout quite enjoyed relating their adventures to a hearer who seemed to take so much interest in them.

"But, after all," said Fix, "does your master intend to carry this young lady back to Europe with him?"

"No, Mr. Fix, certainly not. We are only going to put her under the care of one of her relations, a wealthy merchant at Hong-kong."

"Nothing to be done here," said the detective, dissimulating his disgust. "Mr. Passepartout, let me offer you a glass of gin."

"With pleasure, Mr. Fix; we ought to have a glass to our meeting on board the *Rangoon*."

THE OTHER LOG OF PHILEAS FOGG

Fix stayed in his cabin as much as possible. While there, he considered the addition to the party. Where had she come from? Who was she? Was she an Eridanean? The latter seemed more probable, since Fix could not conceive of the coldly inhuman, or inhumanly cold, Fogg taking a mistress.

Suffering from cabin-fever, and convinced that Passepartout might give him more information, Fix left his quarters. This was on the thirtieth of October; the next day, the *Rangoon* would stop briefly at Singapore.

Fix located the Frenchman, who was promenading on the first-class forward deck. Pretending to be surprised at finding him aboard, Fix greeted him. He explained to Passepartout that unexpected business at Hong Kong was responsible for his being on the ship. He had not been on deck before because seasickness had kept him in bed. He expressed astonishment on hearing from the Frenchman that a young lady was now with Mr. Fogg—though in a separate cabin, of course. Passepartout told the story of the rescue, their flight, their trial, and the bail. The woman, Fix discovered, was to be left at Hong Kong with a relative.

Fix, hearing this, thought that perhaps she was not an enemy after all. Disappointed, he gave up his plan to get Fogg arrested at Hong Kong on a morals charge. Fogg's behavior toward Aouda was, according to Passepartout, irreproachable.

Fix invited Passepartout to have a drink of gin on him. Perhaps this time the Frenchman would drink enough to unlock the door of his discretion.

Later, Passepartout, having sent Fix reeling home to his cabin, reported to Fogg. This fellow, Fix, was undoubtedly trailing them. Whether he was just a detective or a Capellean remained to be seen.

CHAPTER XVII
WHICH RELATES TO MUCH THAT TOOK PLACE DURING
THE PASSAGE FROM SINGAPORE TO HONG-KONG

From that day forward Passepartout and the detective very often met, but Fix was very reserved towards his companion, and never tried to make him talk. He only saw Mr. Fogg once or twice, for the latter spent most of his time in the saloon of the *Rangoon*, either with Aouda, or playing at whist as usual.

But Passepartout had begun to reflect very curiously on the singular chance which had once more thrown Mr. Fix in his master's way, and, in fact, less than that might have surprised him. This very polite, and certainly very obliging gentleman, whom they met first at Suez, who goes on board the *Mongolia*, leaves her at Bombay, where he intended to remain, then he turns up again on board the *Rangoon*, on his way to Hong-kong; in a word, following Mr. Fogg's route step by step. It surely required some consideration. It was, to say the least, a strange coincidence. What could be Fix's object? Passepartout was ready to risk his slippers—he had taken great care of them—that Fix would leave Hong-kong the same time they did, and probably by the same steamer.

Passepartout might have spent years in reflecting before he would ever have guessed that Phileas Fogg was followed as a criminal round the world. But as it is in the nature of men to find an explanation for anything, this is how Passepartout, in a sudden fit of inspiration, accounted for the constant presence of Mr. Fix, and in truth his interpretation of it was very plausible. Fix was and could only be some agent sent by the Reform Club to follow the steps of Mr. Fogg, in order to prove that the voyage had been accomplished according to the course originally agreed upon.

"That is clear," said the honest fellow, quite in admiration of his own acuteness; "he is a spy, sent out not to lose sight of us, by those gentlemen. This is not very dignified on their part. Mr. Fogg is so straightforward and honourable — to have him watched by a paid agent! Ah, you Reform Club gentlemen, this shall cost you dear!"

Though Passepartout was delighted at his discovery, he made up his mind not to say anything about it to his master, lest he should very justly feel hurt at the distrust his adversaries exhibited. But he resolved to chaff Fix the first opportunity with allusions which might mean nothing.

On Wednesday, October the 30th, in the afternoon, the *Rangoon* entered the Straits of Malacca, which separate the peninsula of that name from Sumatra. Small, steep, and picturesque mountainous islands prevented the passengers from having a view of the chief island.

The next day, at four in the morning, the *Rangoon*, having gained half a day on her regular time, stopped at Singapore to coal.

Phileas Fogg set down this gain in his journal, and this time he went ashore, accompanying Aouda, who had expressed a wish to take a walk on land.

Fix, to whom every action of Fogg seemed fraught with suspicion, followed him unperceived. As for Passepartout, who laughed in his sleeve at Fix's manœuvres, he went to make his usual purchases.

A light carriage, drawn by a pair of New Holland horses, conveyed Aouda and Mr. Fogg through groups of palm trees and clove bushes, where thickets of pepper plants take the place of thorn hedges in European scenery, sage bushes and lofty ferns gave variety to the aspect of this tropical region. There was no want of monkeys in the woods, nor, perhaps, of tigers in the jungle. If any one should express surprise that in a comparatively small island such savage beasts were not entirely destroyed, it may be replied that they swim across from the Malacca shore.

After driving about the country for two hours, Aouda and her companion—who looked at things, but saw them not—returned to the town, a collection of heavy, tumble-down houses, surrounded by beautiful gardens, in which pines, mangoes, and all the finest fruits in the world grew in abundance.

At ten they returned to the steamer, having been unconsciously followed all the time by the police agent, who had also been put to the expense of a carriage.

Passepartout was waiting for them on the *Rangoon's* deck. He had bought several dozen mangoes for them, as large as good sized apples, and which *gourmands* appreciate highly. Passepartout was very happy to offer some to Aouda, who gracefully thanked him for them.

At eleven the *Rangoon*, having completed coaling, cast off from her moorings, and in a few hours the passengers had lost sight of the highlands of Malacca, in whose forests the finest tigers in the world seek shelter.

About thirteen hundred miles separate Singapore from the island of Hong-kong, which is a small English settlement on the coast of China. Phileas Fogg had six days to allow for the passage thither, in order to catch the steamer which ought to leave for Yokohama, one of the principal Japanese ports, on the 6th of November.

The *Rangoon* had a full cargo. Many passengers had embarked at Singapore—Hindus, Cingalese, Chinese, Malays, and Portuguese—who were principally second class passengers.

The weather, which had been hitherto fine, changed with the moon's last quarter. There was a heavy sea; sometimes it blew very hard, but, fortunately for the steamer, from the south-east, which was much in her favour. Whenever it was possible the captain made one of his sails—the *Rangoon* being brig-rigged, was often under her two topsails and spanker—and she made great progress, under steam and sail, along the coasts of Aumam and Cochin China. But the *Rangoon* was more to blame than the sea, and the passengers, the greater number of whom were sea-sick, had to thank that vessel for it. For there is an important fault in the build of the company's ships which ply in the China seas. Their draught of water, compared with their carrying power, has been badly calculated, and consequently they are not sufficiently able to stand a heavy sea; therefore, in bad weather it was necessary to take greater precautions, and sometimes to work under a smaller pressure of steam. This was a loss of time which did not seem to affect Phileas Fogg in any way, but which irritated Passepartout excessively. On such occasions he would accuse the captain, the engineer, the company, and abuse every one connected with them. Perhaps the remembrance of the gas-burner, which remained still alight at his expense in Savile Row, was one cause of his impatience.

"You seem very anxious to arrive at Hong-kong," the detective remarked one day.

"Very," replied Passepartout.

"Do you think Mr. Fogg in a hurry to catch the steamer for Yokohama?"

"In a very great hurry."

"Do you still believe in this extraordinary trip round the world?"

"Certainly I do! Don't you, Mr. Fix?"

"No, not I."

"Cunning fellow!" replied Passepartout, winking his eye.

This expression set the police-agent reflecting again. It made him very uneasy, and he could not tell why. Had the Frenchman found him out? He did not know what to think. But how could Passepartout see through his position as detective, the secret of which was known only to himself?

And when Passepartout talked in that manner he surely meant more than he said.

It happened one day that the good fellow went farther still; he could not help himself, he could not hold his tongue.

"Tell me, Mr. Fix," said he, to his companion, slily, "shall we have the misfortune to lose your company when we arrive at Hong-kong?"

"Why," replied Fix, rather puzzled, "I don't exactly know. Perhaps—"

"Ah," said Passepartout, "if you were to go on with us I should be so pleased. See here, an agent of the Peninsular and Oriental Company could not stop on the road! You were only going to Bombay, and now you are almost in China! America is no great distance, and it is only a step from America to Europe."

Fix looked hard at the speaker, whose face expressed nothing but good-humour, and turned it off with a laugh. But the latter went on to ask him if "that occupation paid him well?"

"Yes, and no," replied Fix, without hesitation. "Sometimes I do very well, sometimes the reverse. But you must understand I do not travel at my own expense."

"Oh, no, of course not, I am sure of that," replied Passepartout, laughing again.

When the conversation ceased, Fix retired to his cabin and began to think. He was evidently found out. By some means or other the Frenchman had seen through his disguise. But had he told his master? What part was he taking now? Was he an accomplice or not? Was the affair found out, and the whole thing a failure? The police agent passed many a troubled hour, sometimes believing all was lost, sometimes hoping that Fogg knew nothing about him; in fact, quite at a loss how to act.

At last he became easier in his mind, and he resolved to open his heart to Passepartout. If he did not find himself in a position to arrest Fogg at Hong-kong, and if Fogg showed any intention of leaving English territory for good, he, Fix, would tell Passepartout everything. Now, either the servant was his master's accomplice—and then he must know all about it, and then the game must be up for good—or the servant had nothing to do with the robbery, and then it would be to his advantage to abandon the thief.

Such were the relations then existing between these two men, while Phileas Fogg soared above them with majestic indifference to them and their devices. He was passing in his own circle round the world, without troubling himself about the lesser stars which were gravitating round him.

And yet, there was close to him—according to the expression of astronomers—a disturbing star, which ought to produce certain influences on that gentleman's heart. But no—Aouda's charms seemed to have no influence at all, to Passepartout's great surprise, and the disturbing effects, if any, would have been as difficult to calculate as those of Uranus, which led to the discovery of Neptune.

Yes, it was an every-day's wonder for Passepartout, who could read in the young woman's eyes her feelings of gratitude to his master. Certainly, Phileas Fogg had just enough heart to act like a hero, but not like a lover. As to the feelings which the chances of the voyage might have aroused in him, there was not a symptom of them. But Passepartout was living in a continual fright. One day, as he was leaning over the rail of the engine room, and looking at the powerful engine as it worked, a sudden pitch of the vessel raised the screw out of the water. The steam escaped in consequence from the valves, which put the poor fellow in a rage.

"There is not half steam enough!" cried he. "We are not moving ahead at all! Just like these English! If this was an American vessel, we might blow up, perhaps, but we should go much faster!"

THE OTHER LOG OF PHILEAS FOGG

Not much happened at Singapore, according to Verne. While the *Rangoon* coaled up, Fogg and Aouda took a long drive through the city and the surrounding country. Fix shadowed them so skillfully that they did not observe him. Passepartout, however, had shadowed Fix for a while, saw whom he was following, and went off to carry out some errands. At eleven o'clock, a half an hour ahead of time, the ship left the English-founded colony.

When Fix returned to his cabin, he discovered waiting in it a man whom he had met once before. We know this because it is recorded in Fogg's secret log, though he was not aware of the meeting until much later.

The man was sitting in a chair, his long well-muscled legs extended straight out, the posterior edges of the heels of his expensive boots on the deck. Though he was about forty years of age, he had the physique of an athlete of twenty-five. His waist was narrow; his chest was broad and deep; his shoulders were wide. His nose was long and straight. His mouth was thin. His chin jutted out. His forehead was high and bulging. His eyes were a pale gray and set so far apart that they could cover one hundred and eighty degrees. He was smoking a long thin cigar the make and aroma of which Fix could not identify. It had a certain salty tang to it.

"Sit down, Fix," the intruder said in Capellean. "Do you have anything of interest to report?"

Fix sat down as if he could not obey the man fast enough. His nervousness became even more manifest as he told what had happened from the day he met the *Mongolia* at Suez. While he talked, he could not keep from wondering if his guest was one of the Old Ones or an adopted human. Those widespread eyes and the superhuman and chilly intelligence in them! But he dared not ask. In any event, it made no difference. He was under the orders of this person, man or alien. And he was a deadly person. An utter lack of compassion emanated from him in an almost visible aura, if a negative quality could be said to radiate.

At the end of Fix's lengthy account, the man straightened up in the chair. "You will continue to follow him, all the way back to London, if need be. And continue to make friends with this Passepartout. He is undoubtedly an Eridanean. That watch which he refuses to adjust to the sun sounds suspicious. It may contain a distorter. One of them is carrying a distorter."

This man was the one whom Fogg had called Nemo when he had seen him in the rajah's palace. Nemo knew that Passepartout was Fogg's accomplice. He had not seen him during the raid, but the soldiers in the dome had described the Frenchman. That he did not bother to tell Fix this was a mistake due to his arrogance. Fix was only an underling and a not very competent one at that in his opinion. Why should he tell Fix that he knew for certain that Passepartout was Eridanean? He had stated that the Frenchman was Eridanean and that should be enough for Fix.

That, however, was not enough for Fix. He assumed that the man's statement was based on suspicions only. As far as he was concerned, Passepartout could be just a human.

Fix had some questions and some suggestions, but he did not voice them. This man was evidently one who gave orders and did not care to have them questioned. Fix would be glad when he left.

"Both Fogg and Passepartout," the man said, "are aware that you are probably not just a detective. I don't know why they haven't killed you or tried to extract data from you. They must know that you may try to eliminate them at any moment and that you can easily do so. Still, they may be waiting to act until their plans develop further. They are iron-nerved, intrepid, and intelligent—for Eridaneans. As I have good reason to know."

He puffed on his cigar for a while. Fix wished he would tell him just why he had such good reason to know. He also thought that he had identified at least one of the elements in the odor of the tobacco. Seaweed? But, if so, it was a fine seaweed, for the smoke was certainly pleasant enough, even to a non-smoker.

The man, as if reading his mind, said, "This is the next to last cigar. Then I go back to the more easily procured."

He puffed again and said, "I think I'll save it for a special occasion. Such as the demise of Fogg, who, by the way, has something familiar about him. Where have I seen him before?"

Fix sweated even more heavily. If a superior talked too much to an inferior, it could mean that he no longer cared if the underling knew too much. The underling would soon be dead. But what had he done? Where had he failed? He had carried out all orders, and it was not his fault that London had not sent the warrant.

The man, whose expression had been unrelieved by any sign of emotion, unless coldness is one, now smiled.

"I can't tell you what is going on. But I can tell you that never have affairs looked so good for us. There is a very important operation, perhaps the most important in our history, going on right now that will undoubtedly bring an end to our war with the Eridaneans."

Fix sat up. "Incredible!"

"Not if I say so," the man said,

"Pardon me, sir. But an end!"

"Yes, an end."

"But they would never make peace with us!"

The man quit smiling.

"You think strangely, perhaps too strangely. Did you really imagine that we would make a treaty with those demons? Or"—he stabbed the cigar as if it were a knife—"do you *hope* that we will? Peace will be declared only when every Eridanean is peaceful. That is, with the peace of death."

"Pardon me," Fix stammered, the sweat running down into his eyes. "I was so taken aback by your news!"

"Yes? Well, this near-total isolation, this secrecy, this non-communication, is correct for soldiers in the field. But it has had a deleterious effect, too. How can you keep a community of interests, a secret nation, together if the members lose their sense of community, of communion, of commonness, as it were?

"The truth is that if it weren't for one thing both Eridanean and Capellean would have become extinct long ago. Most of the Old Ones are dead. Even they, with one or two possible exceptions, are second or third generation. All the females of the Old Ones have been killed during the war or are sterile. Some trace element necessary for conception seems to be lacking in the soil of Earth. This is no secret, so don't look so surprised. The original ships only contained five females apiece, and both we and our enemies chose the females as the prime target in our war. But you know this. Or has this secrecy been carried so far that no one has told you?"

Fix thought that the man, however hard he looked on the surface, and doubtless was, was still human. He was "visiting," trying to re-establish some sense of being Capellean. On the other hand, he might just be testing him or softening him up for something unpleasant.

Fix felt lonely only because he had been away from home so long and was in a country he did not like at all. In London, he had a wife (a Capellean, of course) and three children. The children had been conditioned from the time they started to talk. They were now listening to stories from him and his wife of far-off planets and space flight and galactic war. They thought these were fairy tales now, but in a few years they would, if they passed certain tests, be admitted into the blood brotherhood. An Old One would contribute some of his blood to be mingled in their veins.

Fix loved his wife and children. He liked to come home to them after a hard day or night of tracking down criminals, arresting them, and occasionally beating them up in the interrogation cells. Only, of course, if he was absolutely certain they were guilty and they had committed some terrible crime such as murder, child abuse, or sodomy. If the mundane life of a policeman got dull, and it often did, it was relieved enough by the sudden secret codes, the esoteric messages, the missions against the evil Eridaneans. But he liked his missions to be on home soil. After all, he was English.

"Two things only have kept us from disintegrating," the man was saying. "One, fear of death if we should defect. Two, the strongest by far, is the possibility of living for a thousand years. Most men and women would sell their souls—if they had any—for this gift. But, of course, being brought up as a Capellean or Eridanean is the glue that holds us together. And we do have ideals. We do intend, once the enemy is out of the way, to steer the world into peace, prosperity, freedom from disease and pain, and brotherhood."

He puffed again, sending out thick green stormclouds, smiled like lightning, and said, "This world will be ruled by the only ones who have the ancient knowledge to do it. Us. And our grandchildren may be among the aristocracy, Fix."

"Yes, sir."

"In any event, you are now forty years old and won't become any older, physiologically speaking, for about eight hundred to nine hundred years. But you can be killed, Fix. And our enemies want to kill you. So we must kill them first. Isn't that right?"

"Yes, sir."

"But it is better to take them alive first so we can find out who the others are and so catch them, too."

"Yes, sir."

"So you will play your role. And Fogg and Passepartout will play theirs until we lower the curtain on them. Meantime, what are your thoughts on this woman?"

"Possibly an Eridanean," Fix said.

Since Nemo's conversation indicated an uncertainty about Aouda's true identity, it may safely be presumed that he had never seen her before. The rajah of Bundelcund had evidently kept her hidden in his seraglio, and Nemo had left Bundelcund immediately after the rajah's death.

"It seems unlikely," he said, "that the two Eridaneans would have risked their lives for anyone besides another of their kind."

"I don't know about that, sir, if I may be so bold," Fix said. "That Fogg is a strange one. No fear there, if I may say so, sir. And he is an Englishman, sir."

"Would you have rescued her?"

"Yes, sir. As an Englishman, sir. As a Capellean, no, sir, not unless I had orders to do so."

"And which do you think is the most human action, Fix?" the man said with a hint of a sneer.

"Most human, sir?"

Fix was silent for a moment, then smiled.

"Being human, sir, if I do say so myself, and capable of both of the actions you mentioned, I'd say neither is more human than the other. As for a question of heart, sir, what is the word for that . . . cumpass . . . ?"

"Compassion, Fix. I can quote you its dictionary definition, as I can every word in the dictionary and in the *Encyclopedia Brittanica* of 1871."

But I doubt if you really *know* the word, Fix thought. The word is the shadow, but what about the substance? His mind knows, but it's not connected to his heart. And that's where the only knowing worth knowing is.

What the man had said about the millennium medicine, as Fix called it, made sense, though. He wanted to live for a thousand years. He wanted desperately for his children to share in that long life. But there was a chance that at least one of his children might not be permitted to do so. If the chiefs decided that the child was too emotionally unstable, that he or she might blab to the world, then that child would share neither in the Blood or the elixir. And his little Annie, his beloved little Annie, showed signs of instability.

The man suddenly stood up. He was very tall, at least six feet five inches tall. And, now that Fix considered it, under that cultured English voice was the faintest of brogues. Was this man of Irish descent?

"I shall be out of sight," the man said. "But I shall be close. When the time is ripe, you'll hear from me. Meanwhile, play your part. And delay Fogg as much as possible without being obvious about it. Let's hope that the warrant will be waiting for you in Hong Kong. If it is, we'll attempt to keep him from arriving in America on time or at all."

No greetings. No good-byes. He walked out boldly, though he shut the door softly enough.

Mr. Fix said, "Whew!" He pulled out a handkerchief to wipe his face. He felt as if a tiger had decided not to eat him after all. The room reeked of the essence of predator. It was nothing he could smell, or anybody could smell, unless he had that extra set of nerves in his nose. Just as he had boasted to the British consul that he could smell a criminal, just so he could smell the human tiger in a human. In this case, the man stank of both criminal and tiger. Fix would have felt sorry for Fogg and Passepartout if they had not been Eridaneans. And, even so, but no, he must never feel like that. He must never think of the enemy as anything but vermin and deadly vermin at that.

Still, he was glad that man with the widely spaced gray eyes had not ordered him to assassinate the two.

CHAPTER XVIII

IN WHICH PHILEAS FOGG, PASSEPARTOUT, AND FIX
GO EACH ABOUT HIS OWN BUSINESS

The weather was bad during the last days of the voyage. The wind was high, and as it blew from the north-west it was much against their vessel. The *Rangoon*, not being a stiff ship, rolled considerably, and the passengers had enough of those long rolling seas, raised by the westerly wind. During the 3rd and 4th of November there was a storm; the squall caused a heavy sea, the *Rangoon* was compelled to lie to for half a day, just keeping herself head to wind by her screw. All her canvas was taken in, and even the weight of her spars made her labour in the sea.

Her speed was consequently much diminished, and it was probable that she would be twenty-four hours behind her regular time at Hong-kong, perhaps more, unless the weather moderated.

Phileas Fogg looked at the raging sea unmoved as usual; though it seemed to struggle to delay his progress, his forehead was not for an instant clouded, although a delay of twenty-four hours would compromise him seriously, by causing him to miss the steamer for Yokohama. But this man of nerve felt neither impatient nor annoyed. It seemed as if this stormy weather made part of his programme, and had been anticipated. Aouda, when discussing the question with her companion, found him as calm as ever.

But Fix did not look at it in the same light. The storm was all in his favour. His satisfaction would have been all the greater had the *Rangoon* been obliged to run before it. All these delays were in his favour, for they would compel Mr. Fogg to remain some days at Hong-kong. Thus the elements battled in his cause; he had certainly been sea-sick, but that mattered little, and while his body was suffering horribly, his mind experienced the greatest satisfaction.

But Passepartout could not conceal his disgust during this period of trial. Till then they had got on so well, land and water seemed subservient to his master. Steamers and railways obeyed him. Steam and wind united in causing him to have a prosperous voyage. Had the hour of disappointment come at last? Passepartout was as much depressed as if the twenty thousand pounds were to come out of his own pocket. Poor fellow! Fix carefully dissembled his own satisfaction, and he was right in doing so, for if Passepartout had only guessed how pleased Fix secretly felt, he would have had a bad time of it with Passepartout.

Passepartout remained on deck all the time the squall lasted, he could not stay below; he went aloft and astonished the crew by his activity; he questioned the captain, the officers, and the sailors, who could not help laughing to see him so anxious. He wanted to know exactly how long the storm would last. They told him to consult the barometer, which would not rise. Passepartout shook the barometer, but neither shaking nor abuse could make the instrument rise as he wished.

At last the bad weather blew itself out, the sea went down considerably on the 4th, the wind veered round to the southward, in their favour.

Passepartout regained his serenity as the weather changed. Main and top sails were set, and the *Rangoon* soon went on her way as fast as ever.

But the time they had lost was not to be recovered, and land was only sighted at five on the morning of the 6th. Phileas Fogg had calculated the steamer's arrival for the 5th.

Now it only arrived on the 6th, consequently he was twenty-four hours behindhand, and he had missed his passage to Yokohama.

At six the pilot boarded the *Rangoon*, and took his place on the bridge in order to take the ship through the difficult channels up to Hong-kong.

Passepartout longed to ask him if the steamer for Yokohama had left. But he dared not do it, and preferred to nourish just the faintest hope until the last moment. He had confided his anxiety to Fix, who affected to console him by saying Mr. Fogg would be in time for the next boat, which made Passepartout very angry indeed.

But if Passepartout would not risk asking the pilot, Mr. Fogg, after having consulted his *Bradshaw's*, quietly inquired of the pilot if he knew when the steamer left for Yokohama.

"Tomorrow morning at high water," replied the pilot.

"Ah," said Mr. Fogg, not at all surprised.

Passepartout who was standing by would have embraced him, while Fix felt equally inclined to wring his neck.

"What is the steamer's name?" asked Mr. Fogg.

"The *Carnatic*."

"Ought she not to have left yesterday?"

"Yes, but there was something to be done to one of her boilers and her departure was delayed until to-morrow."

"Thank you," said Mr. Fogg, who stalked below to the saloon of the *Rangoon*.

Passepartout shook the pilot hastily by the hand and exclaimed, "Pilot, you are a very good fellow!"

The latter was, and is, probably, still ignorant why his answers gave so much satisfaction; he remained on the bridge, and directed the steamer's course through the flotilla of junks, tankas, fishing boats, and vessels of every description which crowded the harbour of Hong-kong.

At one the *Rangoon* was alongside the quay and the passengers were going ashore. In this instance chance had wonderfully favoured Phileas Fogg—had the *Carnatic* not been delayed on account of her boilers she would have left the 5th of November, and those bound to Japan would have been delayed a week. Mr. Fogg had now lost twenty-four hours it is true, but that loss of time would not necessarily endanger the remainder of his journey. In fact, the steamer which crosses the Pacific from Yokohama to San Francisco was in direct communication with that from Hong-kong, and it could not sail before the latter's arrival. The twenty-four hours lost at Yokohama might possibly be made up during the passage of twenty-two days across the Pacific. Thus, Phileas Fogg was within twenty-four hours of his time, five-and-thirty days after leaving London.

The *Carnatic* was advertised to leave the next morning at nine, so Mr. Fogg had sixteen hours before him to attend to his, or rather to Aouda's affairs. On landing he gave the young lady his arm, and put her into a palanquin. The bearers recommended the Club Hotel, and thither he went, followed by Passepartout.

A room was engaged for Aouda, and Phileas Fogg saw that she was well attended to. Then he told her he should go and make inquiries for the relation into whose care she was to be committed at Hong-kong. At the same time he gave Passepartout orders to remain at the hotel until his return, that Aouda might not be alone. He went to the Exchange, where he thought the cousin of Sir James Jejeebhoy would not fail to be known, being one of the wealthiest merchants in the town.

The shipbroker he addressed was well acquainted with the Parsee merchant. But he had left China two years and more; having made a large fortune he had settled in Europe, it was believed in Holland, which was explained by the fact that his business connection had chiefly been with that country.

Phileas Fogg returned to the Club Hotel; he immediately presented himself to Aouda with the intelligence that the honourable Mr. Jejeebhoy was not resident in Hong-kong, but probably in Holland, to which at first Aouda made no reply. She passed her hand across her eyes, and for some moments remained in reflection. Then she said very gently—

"What do you advise me to do, Mr. Fogg?"

"It is very plain," replied he; "go to England."
"But I cannot, perhaps, any longer—"
"You do not perhaps at all. Passepartout!"
"Sir."
"Go and engage three cabins on board the *Carnatic*."

And Passepartout, who was delighted to continue his voyage in company with the young woman, who was very kind to him, immediately left the hotel on his errand.

THE OTHER LOG OF PHILEAS FOGG

The story that Verne tells of the tribulations of Fogg from this point until he was at the 180th meridian is well-known. The events of that period are briefly outlined here for those who have read the story so long ago that their memory of it is vague.

Aouda, it was evident, fell in love with Fogg. That gentleman, if he were aware of her emotion, betrayed no knowledge of it. Passepartout could not understand why Fogg did not respond to this adoration. Certainly, he would have.

A storm put the *Rangoon* twenty hours behind schedule. Fix, though rendered seasick by the tempest, had a consolation. Perhaps the delay would allow time for the warrant to arrive at Hong Kong, and he could then arrest Fogg.

There were times, though, that Fix wished that the warrant would not get there in time. Once he put the handcuffs on Fogg, he would have to participate in the abduction and torture of Fogg. No, he wouldn't. That *man* would not take him along with Fogg, since it would seem strange if he, Fix, were to disappear also. He would have to play the outraged detective who had been incompetent enough to lose a prisoner.

Fix felt better thinking about this. He did not contemplate the fact that he would be just as responsible for whatever happened to Fogg as if he himself were torturing and then murdering, no, killing him; whatever was done to him was not enough.

At last the storm subsided and with it Fix's perturbed and guilty thoughts. The *Rangoon* was a day late; Phileas Fogg seemed doomed to miss the steamer for Yokohama.

Passepartout was afraid to inquire about the Yokohama ship. Better no news than bad news. Fogg did not hesitate, however, and he received good news. The steamer had been held up for one day for repairs to a boiler. They would make it on time after all. This was indeed fortunate, not to mention an absolute necessity. If he had missed this ship, he would have had to wait a week for the next steamer. He was still twenty-four hours behind schedule, but this was not disastrous.

As he had sixteen hours to spend at Hong Kong, Fogg took advantage of it to see that Aouda was put under the protection of her cousin, Jejeebhoy. Fogg had by now ascertained that she was the Eridanean spy. But, since neither of them had orders about her, she would remain in Hong Kong until she received them. At the Exchange, Mr. Fogg inquired about her cousin. He was informed that two years had passed since Jejeebhoy, had left China. He had retired and now he was supposed to be living in Holland. Fogg returned to the Club Hotel, where he had installed Aouda in a room.

Verne says that she did not comment on this turn of events which left her alone and unprotected. Instead, she merely asked Fogg what she should do.

Serenely, he replied, "Go on to Europe."

She is supposed to have said that she could not intrude or in the least hinder him on his voyage. Fogg replied that she would be doing neither, and he sent Passepartout to obtain three cabins on the *Carnatic*.

This scene is quite in keeping with Fogg's character. But it is not quite what happened.

Fogg did not like to leave her alone in Hong Kong. He could have given her money to support herself for a while or to buy passage to England. But he did not wish to leave her exposed to poverty, to white slavers, or to the thuggees of Kali, who might come after her even in China. Moreover, the Capelleans might have identified her by now as an Eridanean, and if she were alone here, she would stand little chance of surviving. And it is likely, though he did not show it then, that he reciprocated her love. This emotion may have influenced his philosophy of rational mechanics. A rational mind has to consider all known factors, and personal emotion is certainly a part of the universe.

In any event, he told her that he doubted that she could do anything in Hong Kong for the Race. Since she had proved herself to be an exceptionally competent agent, she should accompany them. Three were stronger than two. She could keep an eye on Fix and for other Capelleans who were probably on this ship. Or, if not aboard, waiting for them in Yokohama or America.

CHAPTER XIX

IN WHICH PASSEPARTOUT TAKES TOO GREAT AN INTEREST
IN HIS MASTER, AND ITS CONSEQUENCES

Hong-kong is but a small island ceded to England in 1842 by the Treaty of Nankin. In a few years the genius for colonization of the English has founded a city there of great importance, and created a port called Victoria. This island lies at the mouth of the Canton river, and only sixty miles from the Portuguese settlement of Macao, built on the opposite shore. Hong-kong would necessarily be a successful rival to Macao in a commercial struggle, and now the greater part of the Chinese transit trade is carried by the English city. Docks, hospitals, wharfs, warehouses, a Gothic cathedral, a government house, macadamized streets, everything contributes to make one think that some town from Kent or Surrey had fallen through the bowels of the earth to reappear at this point in China, nearly at the Antipodes.

Passepartout walked off to Port Victoria with his hands in his pockets looking at the palanquins, wheelbarrows drawn by kites, still a favourite amusement in the celestial empire, and the crowd of Chinese, Japanese, and Europeans which thronged the streets. He met with something of Bombay, Calcutta, and Singapore as he walked along—there seems to be a line of English towns all round the world.

Passepartout reached the port at last. There he found a

crowd of vessels of all nations, English, French, American, Dutch, vessels of war, merchantmen, Japanese and Chinese junks, sampans, tankas, and even flower-boats, like so many floating parterres. As he walked along, Passepartout noticed a certain number of natives of great age dressed in yellow. On going to a native barber to be shaved, he learnt that these old men were all above eighty years old, and at that age they were allowed to wear yellow, the imperial colour. Passepartout thought it very funny, although he did not know exactly why.

Having been shaved he betook himself to the company's wharf, where the *Carnatic* was lying, and there he saw Fix walking up and down, which did not in the least surprise him. But the police agent looked excessively disappointed.

"Ha," thought Passepartout, "things don't look well for the Reform Club gentlemen;" so he smiled as he accosted Fix, without noticing his companion's air of vexation.

Now the police agent had very good reason for cursing his bad luck. No warrant! It was evident it was following him, and could only reach him if he stopped some days where he then was, and as Hong-kong was the last spot of English territory on his route, Mr. Fogg would certainly slip through his fingers if he did not succeed in delaying him.

"Well, Mr. Fix, have you decided on going with us to America?" asked Passepartout.

"Yes," said Fix from between his teeth.

"Good," cried Passepartout shouting with laughter, "I knew you never could leave us—come, and engage your berth." So they both went to the steamboat office and engaged cabins for four persons. But the clerk informed them that as the repairs of the *Carnatic* were completed, she would start that same evening at eight instead of the next morning as advertised.

"Very good, that will suit my master very well," said Passepartout. "I will go and tell him."

Then it was Fix made up his mind to a decisive step. He determined to tell Passepartout everything. It was the only chance left for him to keep Phileas Fogg for some days at Hong-kong.

When they left the office Fix invited his companion to have something to drink at a public-house. Passepartout could spare the time—he accepted Fix's invitation.

There was a public-house on the quay. They walked into a large well-furnished room, at one end of which there was a long couch furnished with cushions, on which were several sleepers. About thirty people were drinking at small tables, some beer, ale or porter, others brandy or gin. Most of them were smoking long pipes of red clay, filled with a preparation of opium and essence of roses. From time to time a smoker fell off his chair, and the waiters would then carry him by his head and his feet to the couch and lay him down with the other sleepers. About twenty of these sots were thus laid out in the last stage of drunkenness.

Fix and Passepartout thus found themselves in an opium-smoking establishment, haunted by those wretched, cadaverous idiots to whom commercial England sells every year opium to the amount of one million four hundred thousand pounds—a sad revenue, drawn from one of the vices most fatal to humanity.

The Chinese Government has done its best to put a stop to such a state of things by very stringent laws, but in vain. This habit has descended from the wealthier class, by whom it was at first exclusively practised, to the lower classes, and now it is impossible to arrest its ravages. Opium is now smoked always and everywhere. Men and women are addicted to this deplorable passion, and once accustomed to it they cannot do without it without experiencing excruciating pain. A great smoker can smoke as many as eight pipes a day; but he dies in five years.

It was in one of these numerous dens, which swarm, even in Hong-kong, that Fix and Passepartout found themselves, with the intention of taking some refreshment. The latter was without money, but he willingly accepted the invitation of Fix, knowing he could return the compliment at any time.

They ordered two bottles of port, to which the Frenchman did ample justice, while Fix, who was more cautious, watched his companion attentively. They conversed on many subjects, especially on the fact that Fix had taken his passage in the *Carnatic*. Then Passepartout, as the bottles were empty, thought he had better go and tell his master.

Fix held him back.

"Wait a moment," said he.

"What do you mean, Mr. Fix?"

"I want to talk seriously to you."

"Seriously!" cried Passepartout; "well, we can talk seriously tomorrow. I have no time now."

"Stay," replied Fix, "it concerns your master."

At this Passepartout looked at Fix attentively. The expression on the latter's face struck him, and he sat down again.

"What have you got to say to me?" he asked.

Fix laid his hand on his companion's arm, and lowering his voice—

"You have guessed what I am," said he.

"I have, indeed," replied Passepartout, with a smile.

"Then I will tell you everything."

"Yes, now I know it already, my friend. That's good! Go on. But I must first tell you these gentlemen have gone to a useless expense."

"Useless!" said Fix; "you take it very coolly. I can see you are ignorant how large a sum it is!"

"I know very well," replied Passepartout. "It is twenty thousand pounds."

"Fifty-five thousand," returned Fix, pressing the Frenchman's hand.

"What?" cried Passepartout, "has Mr. Fogg ventured—fifty-five thousand pounds? Well, that is another reason why I should not lose a moment," added he, leaving his seat.

"Fifty-five thousand pounds," said Fix again, forcing Passepartout down in his chair, after calling for a bottle of brandy; "and if I succeed I shall get the reward of two thousand pounds. Will you take five hundred, and help me?"

"Help you! how?" cried Passepartout, whose eyes opened very wide.

"Yes, help me to detain your master for some days at Hong-kong."

"Ha!" began Passepartout, "what are you talking about? What, not content with having my master followed, and suspecting his honour, these gentlemen must try to throw obstacles in his way! I am ashamed of them!"

"What can you mean?" asked Fix.

"I mean to say it is most dishonourable. You might just as well stop Mr. Fogg and rob him at once."

"Well, that is what we have to do."

"It is a conspiracy, then!" cried Passepartout, on whom the brandy Fix had given him began to take effect, "a positive conspiracy! And gentlemen, and acquaintances, too—"

Fix began to get bewildered.

"Friends!" went on Passepartout, "members of the same club! You must know, Mr. Fix, my master is a man of honour, and when he makes a bet, he means to win it honourably."

"What do you take me for?" asked Fix, looking hard at Passepartout.

"Why, you are agent of some members of the Reform Club, sent out to check my master's journey, which is disgraceful in the extreme. For some time I guessed what you were, but I took care not to tell Mr. Fogg."

"Then he knows nothing about it," returned Fix.

"Nothing," replied Passepartout, emptying his glass once more.

The detective passed his hand across his forehead. He hesitated for a moment before he spoke. What ought he to do? Passepartout's blunder was evidently real, but it rendered his plans more difficult. It was quite clear the man meant what he said, and that he was not his master's accomplice, which Fix at one time feared he was.

"Well," thought he, "if he is not an accomplice he will help me."

Once more did the detective make up his mind how to act. Besides, he had no time to wait. At any cost Fogg must be arrested at Hong-kong.

"Listen," said Fix, abruptly; "I am not as you fancy, an agent of the Reform Club."

"Nonsense," said Passepartout, with a laugh.

"I am a police detective, sent out by the head office in London."

"You, a police agent?"

And the agent took a document from his pocketbook and handed it to his companion. It was a commission signed by the Chief of the Metropolitan Police.

Passepartout, dumb-founded, could not utter a word.

"Mr. Fogg's bet," continued Fix, "is only a pretext of which you and his companions of the Reform Club are the dupes, for it was his interest to make sure of innocent co-operation."

"Why?"

"Look here, on the 29th of last September a robbery of fifty-five thousand pounds was committed at the Bank of England by an individual whose description has been given. Now here is that description, and it agrees in every respect with that of the said Fogg."

"Nonsense!" cried Passepartout, bringing his fist with a blow down on the table, "my master is as honest a man as ever lived."

"How can you tell?" replied Fix; "you know nothing about him. You entered his service the day he left London; he left it on some foolish pretext without any luggage, and carrying with him a very large sum in bank notes! And you venture to call him an honest man!"

"Yes, so he is," replied the good fellow.

"Would you like to be arrested as his accomplice?"

Passepartout leant his head on his hands. He was afraid of looking the inspector in the face. Phileas Fogg a thief—the rescuer of Aouda—a brave and generous man a thief! And yet there were many presumptions against him.

Passepartout tried to smother the suspicions which came into his mind. He could not believe in his master's guilt.

"What would you have me do?" said he at last with an effort to the detective.

"This," replied Fix—"I have followed Mr. Fogg as far as this, but I have not yet had the warrant for his arrest, which I expect from London. You must help me to detain him at Hong-kong."

"I? How can—"

"And I will share the reward of two thousand pounds offered by the Bank of England with you."

"Never!" replied Passepartout, who tried to get up, but fell back, finding his senses and his strength alike deserting him. "Mr. Fix," he stammered, "supposing it is all true, what you have just told me—even if my master is the thief you are in search of, which I deny—look you, I am his servant—I have seen his generosity and kindness—betray him, never—not for all the gold in the world! I come from a village where we don't earn our bread in that manner."

"You refuse to help me?"

"I do."

"Then consider I have not told you anything, and now let us drink."

"Yes, let us drink."

Passepartout felt himself getting more and more intoxicated. Fix saw how necessary it was to separate him, at all hazards, from his master, and determined to get him out of the way. Several pipes of opium were lying on the table. Fix took one and put it into Passepartout's hand, who took it and put it to his lips, lighted it, took a whiff or two, and then fell back quite overcome by the effects of the narcotic.

"At all events," said Fix, seeing Passepartout unconscious, "Mr. Fogg won't hear anything about the *Carnatic* leaving this evening, and if he does go, he must go without this infernal Frenchman."

So saying, Fix paid the waiter and left the tavern.

The Other Log of Phileas Fogg

Fix, meanwhile, was despondent. The warrant had not arrived. That it would come in a few days was no solace. Hong Kong was the last piece of British territory. The Fogg party would leave that by tomorrow. If only he could find some means of detaining them long enough.

While pacing back and forth on the quay, he met Passepartout. The Frenchman smiled at him as if he knew what was going on in his mind. No doubt he did. Passepartout asked him if he had decided to go to America with them. He did not ask Fix why he would do so. Fix, gritting his teeth, said he would be on the *Carnatic*. Together, they went to the ticket office. The clerk informed them that the repairs had been made sooner than expected. The ship would leave that evening, not tomorrow.

This gave Fix an idea. He invited Passepartout to a tavern on the quay. He knew that it held an opium den and that there he might get Passepartout to smoke a pipe of opium if he got him drunk enough. Fogg might then be delayed by a search for his missing valet. While they drank, with Passepartout downing two to Fix's one, Fix revealed that he was a detective and that Fogg was the wanted bank robber. He was still not convinced that the Frenchman was an Eridanean. If he were only a valet, his sense of duty to the law might make him desert his master. That would at least save his life. Fix was convinced that, even if Passepartout were innocent, the gray-eyed man would probably order him killed. Passepartout could identify Fix as the man who'd trailed them, and the gray-eyed man would want no investigations of Fix by Eridaneans.

Besides, Fix had become rather fond of the chap. He would never have admitted this to Gray Eyes, but there it was.

The result of this sojourn in the opium den was that Passepartout passed out, and Fogg and Aouda were forced to leave without him.

CHAPTER XX

IN WHICH FIX IS BROUGHT INTO MORE DIRECT
COMMUNICATION WITH PHILEAS FOGG

While this scene was taking place, which might, perhaps, so seriously compromise his eventual success, Mr. Fogg and Aouda were walking about the streets of the English quarter. Since her consent to accompany him to Europe he had been anxious to provide her with everything necessary for so long a journey. It was all very well for a man to go round the world with only a carpet bag in his hand, a lady could not travel under such conditions. Thus it was necessary to buy clothes and other things needful for her. Mr. Fogg acquitted himself of his task with his usual calmness, and to all the young widow's excuses and protestations his invariable reply was—

"It is in the interest of my journey, it is in my programme."

Having made their purchases, Mr. Fogg and the young widow returned to the hotel and dined at the *table d'hôte*, which was sumptuously served. Then Aouda, who was rather tired, retired to her apartment, after shaking hands with her imperturbable rescuer in the English fashion.

The gentleman himself was absorbed in the *Times* and the *Illustrated London News*. If anything could have surprised him it would have been the non-appearance of his servant at bed-time. That, as he knew the steamer for Yokohama would not leave Hong-kong before the following morning, he did not think much of. The next day no Passepartout was there when Mr. Fogg rang his bell. No one can tell what passed in Mr. Fogg's mind when he was told his servant had not returned to the hotel. Mr. Fogg contented himself with taking his bag in his hand, called Aouda, and sent for a palanquin.

It was then eight o'clock, and it would be high water at half-past nine when the *Carnatic* would take advantage of it to leave.

When the palanquin came to the door of the hotel Mr. Fogg and Aouda got into it, and their luggage followed them on a wheelbarrow.

Half-an-hour later they got out on the quay, and then Mr. Fogg was told the *Carnatic* had sailed the preceding evening.

Mr. Fogg, who had expected to find both his servant and the vessel, was obliged to do without either. But no signs of disappointment were visible on his face, and as Aouda looked uneasily up at him he only observed—

"It is only an accident, madam, nothing more."

At that moment a person, who had been watching him attentively, approached him. It was Fix, the detective, who said, with a bow—

"Are you not, like myself, sir, one of the passengers by the *Rangoon*, which arrived yesterday?"

"Yes, sir," replied Mr. Fogg, coldly; "but I have not the honour—"

"Excuse me, but I expected to find your servant here."

"Do you know where he is, sir?" asked the young lady, anxiously.

"How," replied Fix, affecting to be surprised, "is he not with you?"

"No," said Aouda, "we have seen nothing of him since yesterday. He cannot have gone on board the *Carnatic* without us, surely."

"Without you, madam?" replied the police agent—"but, excuse me for asking, was it your intention to leave by the steamer?"

"Yes, sir."

"As I intended also, and I am very disappointed. The *Carnatic* having completed her repairs has left Hong-kong twelve hours sooner, without giving any one notice, and now we must wait a week for the next vessel."

As he said "a week" Fix felt his heart beat with joy. A week! Fogg detained at Hong-kong for a whole week. The warrant would have time to arrive. At last chance had declared in favour of the law's representative. Fancy, then, what a stunning blow it was for him to hear Fogg quietly remark—

"But there are other vessels in port besides the *Carnatic*, I should suppose."

And Mr. Fogg offered his arm to Aouda, and turned in the direction of the docks to look for some vessel going to sail.

Fix, dismayed, followed him; it seemed as if he was bound to him by some invisible link.

It seemed, however, that chance had really at last abandoned one it had served so well hitherto. For three hours Phileas Fogg walked about the docks, decided, if necessary, on chartering a vessel for Yokohama, but he could only find ships either loading or unloading, and which consequently could not sail at once. Fix began to hope again.

But Mr. Fogg was not to be discouraged, and he would have continued his inquiries, even had he been obliged to cross over to Macao, when he was addressed by a sailor on the wharf—

"Is your honour looking for a vessel?" said the sailor, doffing his cap.

"Have you a boat ready to sail at once?" asked Mr. Fogg.

"Yes, your honour. A pilot boat, No. 43, the fastest of them all."

"Is it very fast?"

"Eight or nine knots an hour. Would you like to see her?"

"Yes."

"Your honour would be pleased with her. Do you want to make an excursion anywhere?"

"No, a long voyage."

"A voyage?"

"Will you undertake to convey me to Yokohama?"

"Your honour is joking," said the pilot.

"Not at all. I have missed the *Carnatic*, and I must be at Yokohama by the 14th at the latest, in order to take the San Francisco steamer."

"I am very sorry," replied the sailor, "but it is impossible."

"I will give one hundred pounds a day, and a further sum of two hundred pounds if I reach Yokohama in time."

"Are you in earnest?" asked the pilot.

"Very much so," replied Mr. Fogg.

The pilot stepped aside for a moment. He looked at the sea, evidently struggling between the wish to earn such an enormous sum, and the dread of risking such a long voyage. Fix was in a state of mortal anxiety.

In the meantime Mr. Fogg had turned to Aouda.

"You are not afraid, madam, are you?"

"Not with you, Mr. Fogg."

"Well, pilot?" said Mr. Fogg.

"Well, your honour, I dare not risk either my men, or you, or myself, in so long a passage, with a little boat hardly twenty tons at this time of the year. Besides, we could never arrive in time, for it is sixteen hundred and fifty miles from Hong-kong to Yokohama."

"Only sixteen hundred," said Mr. Fogg.

"Well, there is not much difference."

Fix drew a long breath.

"But," said the pilot, "it is perhaps possible to arrange it in some other manner."

Fix was breathless again.

"How?" asked Phileas Fogg.

"By going to Nagasaki, at the extreme south of Japan, eleven hundred miles, or even to Shanghai, only eight hundred miles from Hong-kong; by that *route* we should not be obliged to keep off the coast of China, which would be a great advantage; besides, the currents would carry us northward."

"Pilot," replied Fogg, "I must catch the American steamer at Yokohama, and not at Shanghai or Nagasaki."

"Why not?" returned the pilot. "The San Francisco steamer does not sail from Yokohama. It calls at Yokohama, and at Nagasaki, but her port of departure is Shanghai."

"Are you sure of what you say?"

"Certain."

"When does the steamer leave Shanghai?"

"On the 11th, at seven in the evening, so we have four days before us. Four days, that is to say, ninety-six hours, and averaging eight miles an hour, if the wind holds good in a north-easterly direction, and there is not too much sea, we may perhaps make those eight hundred miles which lie between us and Shanghai."

"When can you start?"

"In an hour, I only want time to put stores on board and set sail."

"It is a bargain. Are you the master of the boat?"

"Yes, John Bunsby, master of the pilot boat, the *Tankadere*."

"Shall I give you something at once on account?"

"If you would not be offended—"

"Here are two hundred pounds. Sir," added Fogg, turning to Fix, "if you would like to take advantage."

"Sir," replied Fix, summing up all his courage as he did so, "I was about to ask that favour of you."

"Well, in half-an-hour we shall be on board."

"But what is to be done about that poor fellow?" asked Aouda, who was very much preoccupied at Passepartout's disappearance.

"I shall do all I possibly can for him," replied Phileas Fogg.

And while Fix, in a nervous, feverish, furious state of mind, prepared to go on board the pilot boat, they both repaired to the Hong-kong police office. There Phileas Fogg gave a description of Passepartout, and left a sufficient sum of money there to send him home. He went through the same formality at the French consulate, and the palanquin, after calling at the hotel, where they picked up their luggage, conveyed the travellers once more to the wharf.

Three o'clock had just struck. The pilot boat, No. 43, with her crew and stores on board, was ready to sail.

The *Tankadere* was a pretty little twenty-ton schooner, very sharp forward with very fine lines. She looked like a racing yacht, her shining copper, her galvanized ironwork, and her snow-white deck showed that her master, John Bunsby, understood how to keep her up. Her two masts raked a little, she carried mainsail, foresail, main and fore topsails, staysail and jib, and plenty of canvas for running before the wind. She ought to be very fast, and in fact had won several cups in matches with other pilot boats. John Bunsby and four men comprised the crew of the *Tankadere*. He was one of those hardy mariners who go on the look-out for vessels in all weathers. He was a powerfully-built man, about five-and-forty, and knew his business well.

Phileas Fogg and Aouda went on board. Fix was already there. In the after part of the schooner there was a small, square saloon, in the sides of which were sleeping bunks. There was a table in the middle, and a lamp swinging from the ceiling. All on a very small scale, but scrupulously clean.

"I regret I have nothing better to offer you," said Mr. Fogg to Fix, who bowed without replying.

The police agent felt humiliated in thus profiting by Mr. Fogg's civilities.

"He certainly is a very civil sort of a rascal—but a rascal he undoubtedly is."

At ten minutes past three they set sail. English colours were hoisted; the passengers were sitting on deck. Mr. Fogg and Aouda gave a last look on the quay to see if Passepartout would not make his appearance.

Fix was rather afraid he might; for if by any chance

the poor fellow he had used so shamefully ill had come, an explanation would have necessarily taken place, which would not have been at all to the detective's advantage. But the Frenchman did not show himself, and without doubt he was still under the stupefying influence of the narcotic.

At last the master, John Bunsby, let his foresail draw, and was soon under full sail for Shanghai.

CHAPTER XXI

IN WHICH THE MASTER OF THE "TANKADERE" RUNS GREAT
RISK OF LOSING A REWARD OF TWO HUNDRED POUNDS

This voyage of eight hundred miles, in a boat of twenty tons, at this time of the year, was a very perilous adventure. These Chinese seas are usually dangerous, exposed as they are to terrible gales of wind, especially during the equinoxes, and it was yet very early in November.

It would obviously have been to the pilot's advantage to take them to Yokohama, since he was to be paid by the day, but it would have been too imprudent to undertake such a voyage under such circumstances; and it was bold enough, not to say rash, to try to reach Shanghai. But John Bunsby believed in his *Tankadere*, which skimmed over the waters like a sea-gull, and perhaps he was not altogether wrong.

Late in the day the *Tankadere* was running down one of the channels to Hong-kong, and on all tacks she behaved admirably.

"I need not recommend you, pilot, to use all possible diligence," said Phileas Fogg, just as the schooner got into the open sea.

"Your honour may trust me," replied John Bunsby. "We are now carrying as much canvas as we ought; our topsails would not help us, but would only press her too much and stop her way."

"It is your business, pilot, not mine, and I trust to you."

Phileas Fogg stood bolt upright with his sea-legs, as they say on board, looking at the boiling waters. The young woman, sitting near the stern, felt much affected as she gazed on the darkening face of the ocean, which she was thus braving in a frail little vessel. Over her head the white sails looked like immense wings. The schooner seemed to fly through the air before the wind.

Night came on. The moon was in her first quarter, and her feeble light soon disappeared in the rising mist. Clouds already covered part of the sky.

The pilot had already lighted his side-lights—an indispensable precaution in these seas, often crowded with vessels bound for the port. Vessels not unfrequently were run down, and at the rate she was going the least shock would have sunk the schooner.

Fix was meditating forward. He kept himself as much out of the way as possible, knowing Fogg was not a great talker, and he also felt a repugnance in conversing with the man at the very moment he was accepting a service at his hands. He was also thinking of the future. He felt certain Fogg would not stop at Yokohama, but go immediately on board the San Francisco steamer in order to reach America, whose immense extent seemed to ensure him both impunity and security. Phileas Fogg's plan seemed to him as plain as possible.

Instead of embarking in England for America, like an ordinary rogue, this fellow, Fogg, had gone round three-quarters of the globe in order to gain the American continent the more securely, where he could spend the Bank's money in peace, after having thrown the police off the track. But once on the territory of the Union what was he, Fix, to do? Should he give up the pursuit of this man? No, never, and until he could obtain a warrant of extradition he would never leave him. It was his duty, and it should be done under any circumstances. One fortunate event had happened, Passepartout was no longer with his master, and after Fix's confidential communications it was of great importance that the master and servant should never meet again.

And Phileas Fogg could not help thinking about his servant who had disappeared so strangely. After much consideration, it seemed possible, in consequence of some mistake, the poor fellow might have gone on board the *Carnatic* at the last moment; such was Aouda's opinion, who deeply regretted the loss of that excellent servant to whom she was so indebted. They might, perhaps, after all fall in with him again at Yokohama, and if he had taken his passage on board the *Carnatic*, it would be easily ascertained.

Towards ten o'clock the breeze freshened. Perhaps it might have been prudent to have taken a reef down in mainsail and foresail, but the pilot, after carefully examining the sky, let her sails stand.

The *Tankadere* carried her canvas well, and drawing, for a boat of her size, a great deal of water, she could be brought under easy sail very quickly in case of a squall.

At midnight Phileas Fogg and Aouda went below. Fix had preceded them, and was stretched in one of the sleeping bunks; the pilot and his men remained on deck all night.

The next day, the 8th of November, at sunrise, the schooner had made more than a hundred miles. On throwing the log several times it showed a mean speed of between eight and nine miles. The *Tankadere* had all her sails drawing, and she was now doing her greatest rate of speed. If the wind remained in the same quarter there was every chance for her.

All that day she had kept along the coasts where the currents were in her favour. It was not more than five miles distant on her port hand, and its irregular profile was occasionally visible across the clearings. The wind came off the land, consequently there was less sea, a fortunate circumstance for the schooner, as small vessels cannot stand a rough sea, which stops them, and drowns them, to use a sea term.

At noon the breeze fell somewhat, and set in from the south-west. The pilot set his topsails, but in two hours' time he was obliged to lower them, for the wind began to rise again.

Mr. Fogg and the young widow, both of them, fortunately, proof against sea-sickness, ate their meals with a good appetite. Fix was invited to share their repasts, and was forced to accept, knowing it is as necessary to stow food in the stomach as ballast in a vessel's hold, but it vexed and annoyed him; to travel at that man's expense, and be fed on his provisions, he thought, was not very honourable. He did eat, though only enough to keep him alive, it is true, but still he did eat.

Once, however, after a meal, he thought it right to take Mr. Fogg aside, and said to him —

"Sir!"

This "sir" stuck in his throat, and it was as much as he could do not to collar the "gentleman."

"Sir, you have been extremely obliging in giving me a passage, but although my means do not admit of my going to so great an expense, yet I should wish to pay my share —"

"Do not mention it, sir, I beg," replied Mr. Fogg.

"But I must insist —"

"No, sir," repeated Fogg, in a tone which admitted of no reply, "that is carried to my account of profit and loss."

Fix bowed. He was choking, and going forward he lay down on deck, and did not say another word all day.

They were making good way, and John Bunsby was hopeful. He told Mr. Fogg several times they would reach Shanghai in time. Mr. Fogg's only answer was he supposed they would. The whole of the schooner's crew were equally anxious; the extra reward roused these fine fellows' energies. Not a sheet that was not taut, not a sail that did not stand, no mistake made at the helm; had the vessel been sailing a match she could not have been better handled.

That evening the pilot ascertained by the log they had run one hundred and twenty miles since they left Hong-kong, and Phileas Fogg had reason to hope that on his arrival at Yokohama he would have nothing to set down to loss of time in his programme. This, the first disappointment he had met with since he left London, might possibly be of no prejudice to his undertaking.

During the night, or rather in the early morning, the *Tankadere* found herself in the Fo-Kien channel, between the island of Formosa and the coast of China, and she was crossing the tropic of Cancer. The sea was very rough, and full of eddies and currents. The schooner laboured heavily. A short, chopping sea stopped her way. It was very difficult to stand on deck.

At daybreak the wind increased, with every appearance of a gale. The mercury in the barometer fell and announced a change in the atmosphere. The sea, also, began to rise in the southwest. The sun set the evening in a red mist in the midst of the phosphorescent scintillations of the ocean.

The pilot spent some time in watching the look of the sky, and muttered something indistinctly between his teeth. He took an early opportunity of saying to his passenger—

"I should like to tell your honour something."

"Tell me everything," replied Fogg.

"We are going to have a gale of wind."

"From the north or the south?" quietly asked Mr. Fogg.

"From the southward. Look there, we shall be caught in a typhoon!"

"Never mind the typhoon. If it blows from the southward it will help us on."

"Oh, if you take it in that way," replied the pilot, "I have nothing more to say."

John Bunsby's presentiment did not deceive him. At a less advanced period of the year, according to a celebrated meteorologist, the typhoon would have passed over like a luminous cascade of electric flame, but, in the winter equinox, it was to be feared it would break over them with great violence.

The pilot took every precaution possible. He close furled all the sails, and got his yards and topmasts on deck. He ran his jib-boom in. The hatches were battened down carefully, and not a drop of water could get below. A small storm jib alone was left standing, to keep the schooner before the wind. And then they waited for the squall.

John Bunsby suggested to his passengers they had better go below, but it was far from pleasant to be shut up in the cabin, almost deprived of air and light, with the motion of the vessel shaking them extremely; therefore neither Fogg nor Aouda nor even Mr. Fix, would leave the deck.

About eight o'clock, down came the storm of wind and rain. With its morsel of canvas set, the *Tankadere* was lifted like a feather by a squall of wind, the violence of which can hardly be described. It would be short of the truth if her speed was compared to four times that of a locomotive.

During the whole of that day the vessel ran before the gale, borne along by the mountainous seas, and fortunately preserving the same rate of velocity. Twenty times she was on the point of being pooped by one of those mountainous waves which seemed ready to fall on board, but the wary pilot was always ready for it. The passengers were drenched by the spray, but they could only submit.

Fix grumbled, no doubt, at his bad luck; but Aouda courageously kept her eyes on her companion, whose coolness she could but admire, and showed herself worthy to brave the storm by his side. Phileas Fogg seemed to consider the typhoon as part of his programme.

Hitherto the *Tankadere* had always kept a northerly course, but towards evening the wind veered round to the north-west. The boat, now broadside to the wind, rolled frightfully. The sea struck her with such violence that it would have terrified any one who did not know how strongly these pilot vessels are built.

At night the gale, if possible, increased. When Bunsby saw it growing dark, and no signs of a lull, he began to feel very uneasy. He thought they might bear up for some port, and consulted his crew. After a few words with them, he addressed Mr. Fogg.

"I think, your honour, we had better run for one of the ports on the coast."

"I think so, too," returned Fogg.

"Ah!" said the pilot, "which do you think best?"

"I only know of one."

"And that is?"

"Shanghai."

The pilot for a moment was at a loss to understand his meaning, or what obstinacy his answer conveyed; then he exclaimed—

"Well, your honour is right. Shanghai be it."

The *Tankadere*'s head was kept steadily to the north.

It was a dreadful night, and it was a miracle the little schooner did not founder. Twice she shipped a sea, and her decks would have been swept, if shrouds and halyards had given way. Aouda was much bruised, but she uttered no complaint. More than once Mr. Fogg had to lash her to the side, to keep her from being washed overboard.

Day broke again. The tempest still raged, but the wind went back to the south-east. This was a change for the better, and the *Tankadere* again kept her course for Shanghai.

From time to time they could make out the coast through the breaks in the mist, but not a vessel was in sight. The *Tankadere* was the only vessel at sea.

At noon there came signs of a lull, which became more confirmed as the sun set.

The short duration of the storm had been in proportion to its violence. The passengers were absolutely worn out, and were now glad of refreshment and repose.

The night was comparatively quiet. Canvas was set on the schooner and she moved fast through the water. The next day they sighted the coast, and John Bunsby was able to say they were not a hundred miles from Shanghai. A hundred miles, and one day to do them in. Mr. Fogg was due that very evening at Shanghai, if he did not want to miss the mail steamer to Yokohama. Had it not been for the typhoon they would now have been within thirty miles of their port.

The wind was much lighter, and with the sea went down. They set every sail which the schooner could carry, and at noon they were but forty-five miles from their port. Fogg had now six hours left to catch the steamer.

On board they were very much afraid it could not be done. Everyone—of course exception must be made for Phileas Fogg—felt his heart beat with impatience. The little schooner must do her nine miles an hour, and every moment the wind became lighter. The breeze was shifting from off the land.

But the vessel was so light, and her sails so light also, that not an air of wind was lost, and by the help of the current John Bunsby found himself not more than ten miles from Shanghai river, for the town itself is some twelve miles higher up the stream.

At seven they were still three miles distant. An oath escaped the pilot's lips. The extra reward of two hundred pounds was slipping through his fingers. He looked at Mr. Fogg—Mr. Fogg was as calm as ever, and yet the whole of his fortune was at that moment at stake.

That very instant a long funnel with a cloud of black smoke was visible at the water's edge. It was the American steamer leaving port at her appointed time.

"Confound her!" cried John Bunsby, giving the tiller a shove in despair.

"Signal her," said Mr. Fogg quietly.

A small trap cannon was in the *Tankadere* bow for firing signals during fogs.

It was loaded, but just as the pilot was about to apply the match—

"Set your ensign half mast," said Mr. Fogg.

This was done. It was a signal of distress, and they were in hopes the American would see it and stop for them.

"Fire!" cried Mr. Fogg.

And the boom of the little gun resounded in the air.

CHAPTER XXII

IN WHICH PASSEPARTOUT FINDS OUT THAT
EVEN AT THE ANTIPODES IT IS AS WELL TO
HAVE SOME MONEY IN ONE'S POCKET

The *Carnatic* left Hong-kong, November the 7th, at half-past six in the evening, and made the best of her way to Japan.

She carried a full cargo and several passengers. Only two after-cabins were unoccupied, they were those engaged by Mr. Fogg.

The next morning the crew forward were surprised to see a passenger with half-stupefied eyes, staggering in his walk, and with his hair in disorder, crawl out of the second-class cabin, and drop down on one of the cork cushions on deck.

This passenger was Passepartout himself, and this is what had happened to him. Soon after Fix left the smoking-shop two of the waiters had picked up Passepartout and laid him by the side of the other sleepers. But three hours afterwards the poor fellow, even in his nightmare pursued by one fixed idea, awoke, and struggled against the action of the narcotic. The thought of what he had neglected to do helped to shake off his stupor. He left the drunkard's den, and tottered along, holding on by the walls of the houses, now falling, now getting on his legs again, but continually calling out by instinct, "*Carnatic, Carnatic!*"

There was the vessel with steam up alongside the quay ready to start; he had but a few steps to go; he stumbled across the gangway, and fell down unconscious on the deck, just as the *Carnatic* cast off her hawsers.

Several sailors, well accustomed to that sort of thing, carried the poor fellow down into the second-class cabin, and he only awoke the next morning a hundred and fifty miles from the coast of China.

And this is how Passepartout found himself on the *Carnatic*'s deck, and inhaling, with all the power of his lungs, the fresh sea breeze. He had some trouble in collecting his senses, but at last he was able to recall the scene in the opium shop, the communications of Fix, &c.

"It is very clear," he said to himself, "that I was made very drunk. What will Mr. Fogg say? However, I did not miss the boat, and that is the most important thing."

Then his thoughts turned to Fix.

"As for that fellow, I hope we have got rid of him at last, and that he has not dared to follow us on board the *Carnatic* after the offer he made me. A police agent, a detective, in pursuit of my master, and accusing him of robbing the Bank of England! Mr. Fogg is as much a thief as I am a murderer."

Ought Passepartout to tell his master all these things? Would it be better for him to be acquainted with the part Fix had been playing in this business? Would it not be more advisable to wait till they arrived in London and then tell him he was a secret police agent who had followed him all round the world, and laugh at him? Yes, at least it would be better to think it over. His first duty now was to see his master and try and excuse himself for his very improper conduct.

So Passepartout got up. The sea was rough, and the vessel rolled a great deal. His legs were, as yet, not very strong, but he reached the afterpart of the ship at last.

On deck he saw no one resembling his master or Aouda.

"Good," thought he, "Aouda is not up yet, and Mr. Fogg has probably found a rubber, and, according to his usual custom —"

So thinking, Passepartout entered the saloon. Mr. Fogg was not there. He had now but one resource, which was to ask the steward which was Mr. Fogg's cabin.

The steward replied he knew no one of that name on board.

"Excuse me," said Passepartout, "the gentleman I mean is tall, quiet, does not talk much, accompanied by a young lady."

"We have no young lady on board," replied the steward. "Here is a list of the passengers, you can see for yourself."

Passepartout read over the list. His master's name was not there.

He was quite bewildered. At last an idea struck him.

"Ah, am I on board the *Carnatic*?"

"Yes, you are."

"And going to Yokohama?"

"Certainly, you are."

For a moment Passepartout was afraid he had gone on board the wrong boat. But if he was on board the *Carnatic*, it was equally certain his master was not.

Passepartout dropped into a chair; he was thunderstruck. Then he suddenly saw it all. He recollected the hour of the *Carnatic*'s departure had been altered, that he was to have told his master, and he had neglected to do so. Then it was his fault that they had missed their passage! Yes, his fault, certainly, but still more the fault of that treacherous scoundrel, who had made him drunk to separate him from his master and keep him at Hong-kong! Now he saw through the police inspector's tricks, and now Mr. Fogg was, for certain, ruined, his bet lost; he would be arrested, and, perhaps, imprisoned! Passepartout tore his hair when he thought of this. If ever Fix was in his power how he would settle accounts with him!

After the first shock of disappointment Passepartout recovered his coolness, and began to see how matters stood. He was not in a very enviable situation; he was on his road to Japan; he was sure to get there—and what then? His pockets were empty, not a shilling, not a penny piece! his passage money and his food, however, had been paid in advance, so he had five or six days before him to make up his mind what to do. Nothing need be said about how he ate for himself, Mr. Fogg and Aouda—he ate as if the Japan he was going to was a desert without food of any description.

On the 13th the *Carnatic* entered the port of Yokohama with the morning's tide.

This is an important port of call in the Pacific, where all the steamers carrying mails and passengers between North America, China, Japan, and the Malay Island coal. Yokohama is situated in the bay of Yeddo, a short distance from Yeddo, that immense city, the second capital of the Japanese Empire, formerly the residence of the Tycoon, the civil emperor, when that office existed; and the rival of Meako, the great city inhabited by the Mikado, the spiritual emperor, the descendant of the gods.

The *Carnatic* brought up at the quay near the jetty of the port and the customs warehouses, amongst numerous vessels belonging to all nations.

Passepartout went ashore on this curious soil of the sons of the sun without curiosity. He had only to take chance for his guide and wander about the streets of the town. At first he found himself quite in an European town; the houses had low fronts with verandahs, with elegant peristyles beneath them, and which covered all the space comprised between the promontory of the treaty and the river, with streets, docks, and warehouses. There, as in Hong-kong and Calcutta, was a swarm of people of all nations, Americans, English, Chinese, Dutch, dealers in anything and everything, amongst whom the Frenchman felt himself as much lost as in a tribe of Hottentots.

Passepartout had one resource, which was to ask assistance from the French or English consuls at Yokohama; but it was repugnant to him to tell his story, connected as it was with his master's, and before doing so he resolved to try to obtain assistance from some other source.

The native town in Yeddo is called Benten, the name of a goddess of the sea, who is worshipped in the neighbouring islands. There Passepartout saw beautiful groves of cedars and firs, sacred gates of a strange style of architecture, bridges buried amidst bamboos and reeds, temples sheltered by the overhanging branches of cedars a century old, places where bonzes and votaries of Confucius dwelt, and worshipped; streets without end, where multitudes of red-cheeked, rosy-complexioned children, who looked as if they had been cut out of a hand screen, were playing with short-legged dogs and tawny, tailless cats, very lazy and very caressing. In the streets there were an incessant stir and circulation; bonzes were walking along in procession, beating their monotonous tambourines; police and customs officers, with pointed hats, with japanned fronts, and wearing two swords in their waistbands; soldiers dressed in blue cotton with white stripes, and armed with percussion muskets; the Mikado's guards in silken doublets, with breastplates and coats of mail, and numbers of other soldiers of all arms; for in Japan the military profession is as much esteemed as it is despised in China. Besides there were mendicant friars, pilgrims in long robes, civilians with their smooth, black hair, large heads, long necks and chests, thin legs, rather short, and complexions varying from deep copper to dull white. Then came carriages, palanquins, horses, bearers, barrows with rails, and litters of bamboo. Then he caught sight of a few women, not particularly good-looking, muffled up to the eyes, with their teeth blackened according to the taste of the day, flitting about on their little feet, and wearing either canvas slippers, or straw sandals, or clogs of carved wood; but wearing the elegant national costume, called the "kerimon," a sort of dressing-gown, crossed by a silk scarf, the broad band of which spread out behind into an extravagantly large bow, which the modern Russians seem to have borrowed from the Japanese ladies.

Passepartout spent some hours perambulating among this parti-coloured crowd, looking at the rich and curious shops, the bazaars glittering with Japanese jewellery, the restaurants adorned with banners and streamers, where entrance was to him forbidden, and the tea houses where they drink cup after cup of that fragrant hot water, with saki, a spirit distilled from fermented rice, and those comfortable smoking-houses where they smoke a very fine tobacco, and not opium, the use of which is almost unknown in Japan.

At last poor Passepartout found himself in the fields, surrounded by vast rice grounds. There he saw brilliant camellias growing, not on shrubs, but trees; and within bamboo fences were cherry trees, plum, and apple trees, which the natives cultivate more for the sake of their flowers than their fruit, and which grinning and screaming scare-crows protected from sparrows, pigeons, crows, and other destructive birds.

There was not a majestic cedar which did not offer a resting-place to some large eagle; not a weeping willow the foliage of which did not shelter a heron, standing in melancholy attitude on one leg; while everywhere, jackdaws, ducks, kites, wild geese, and numbers of cranes—which the Japanese consider sacred, and which are to them the symbols of long life and happiness—were flying about in all directions.

Wandering about thus, Passepartout spied some violets in the grass.

"Good," thought he, "here is my supper."

But on smelling them, he found them scentless.

"No chance for me," he murmured.

It is true the poor fellow had with great forethought made a good breakfast before leaving the *Carnatic*, but after walking about the whole day, he felt his stomach very empty. He had noticed that neither sheep, nor goats, nor pigs were to be seen in the native butchers' shops, and as he knew it was a sacrilege to kill a cow or an ox, which are kept only for agricultural purposes, he came to the conclusion that meat was a scarce article in Japan. Nor was he far wrong; but in default of butchers' meat, he could have gratified his stomach with either wild boar or venison, partridges or quails, poultry or fish, on which, with rice, the Japanese live almost exclusively. But he was obliged to keep up his spirits, and put off till tomorrow the care of providing himself with food.

Night came, and Passepartout returned to the native town, and wandered about the streets, amongst variegated lanterns, looking at groups of street acrobats, and open-air fortune tellers, and astrologers, with a crowd round their telescopes. Then he revisited the port, studded with the lights on board the fishing boats, attracting the fish by means of resinous torches.

At last the streets grew empty. The sounds of the police officers succeeded. These officers, in their magnificent costumes, surrounded by their escort, resembled ambassadors, and Passepartout laughed to himself, and said every time he met one of these glittering patrols—

"Here comes another Japanese Embassy going to Europe!"

CHAPTER XXIII
IN WHICH PASSEPARTOUT'S NOSE BECOMES
DISPROPORTIONATELY LONG

The next day, Passepartout, exhausted and nearly starved, said to himself he must get something to eat, cost what it might, and the sooner the better. He could have sold his watch, as a last resource, but he would rather have died of hunger.

Now or never was the time for the good fellow to turn the powerful if not melodious voice with which nature had favoured him to account.

He knew a few French and English songs, and he resolved to try them. The Japanese ought to be judges of music, for they every day listened to the sound of cymbals and drums, and they must appreciate European talent.

But perhaps he was too early in the morning to get up a concert, and amateurs, aroused too soon, would not probably remunerate the singer with money bearing the mikado's effigy. He therefore made up his mind to wait a few hours; but as he went along, he reflected he was too well dressed for a wandering minstrel; and the idea came into his head to change his clothes for others more corresponding with his situation, and in so doing he might also get a few coins to boot, which he could immediately apply to satisfy the cravings of hunger.

The next thing to be done was to carry out this resolution. It took him some time to find a native dealer in old clothes, to whom he applied. The European costume pleased the old clothes man, and Passepartout soon left his shop wrapped up in an old Japanese robe, and a one-sided-looking turban on his head, which had lost their colour from use. Moreover he had a few small silver coins to jingle in his pocket.

"Good," thought he, "I can fancy this is carnival time."

His first care, after being thus metamorphosed, was to find his way to a tea house as unpretending-looking as possible, and there he made his breakfast on the remains of a fowl and a little rice, where to find his dinner being as yet a problem.

"Now," thought he, after he had finished, "I must mind what I am about. I have not the resource left me now to sell these rags for others still more Japanese-looking. I must consider how I can leave this country of the sun with as little delay as possible, of which I shall always have a most painful recollection."

Passepartout then thought of visiting the steamers about to leave for America. He thought he would offer his services in the capacity of cook or steward, in return for his passage and food. Once at San Francisco he would soon get over his difficulties. The most important affair was how to get across the four thousand seven hundred miles of the Pacific Ocean lying between Japan and the New World. Passepartout was not the man to be long thinking what to do, and he walked off at once to the port. But the nearer he came to the docks the more difficult it began to appear to put his idea into execution. Why should an American steamer be in want of either cook or steward, and what confidence could one have in him dressed up as he was? and more than all, to whom could he refer to give him a character?

Cogitating thus as he walked along, his eyes fell on a large bill which a sort of clown was carrying through the streets. It was in English, and drawn up as follows: —

THE FULL ACCOUNT

JAPANESE ACROBATIC TROUPE.

The Honourable William Batulcar, Proprietor.

THE LAST REPRESENTATIONS

Previous to their departure for the United States
of America, of the
LONG NOSES! LONG NOSES!

Under the especial patronage of the god Tingou.

GREAT ATTRACTION!

"United States of America!" cried Passepartout, "the very thing I want."

He followed the perambulating clown, and found himself again in the Japanese quarter. A quarter of an hour later he stopped in front of a large booth, decorated with streamers, the walls of which represented, without any regard to perspective, but in most glaring colours, a company of jugglers.

This was the Honourable William Batulcar's establishment, a second edition of Barnum, manager of a troupe of mountebanks, conjurors, clowns, and acrobats, which, according to the posters outside, were giving their last performances before leaving the Empire of the Sun for the States of the Union.

Passepartout walked in, and asked to see Mr. Batulcar. Mr. Batulcar answered in person.

"What do you want?" said he, taking Passepartout at first for a native.

"Do you want a servant?" inquired Passepartout.

"A servant!" cried the Barnum of Japan, caressing the thick, grey beard which grew beneath his chin, "I have here two obedient, faithful servants, which have never failed me, and which serve me gratis provided I feed them well. Here they are," added he, showing his two robust arms.

"So I can be of no use to you?"

"None."

"I am sorry for it. I should like to have left here with you."

"Ah," said the Honourable Mr. Batulcar, "you are as much a Japanese as I am a monkey. What have you dressed yourself up like that for?"

"A man dresses according to his means."

"True. You are a Frenchman, are you not?"

"Yes, a Parisian, from Paris."

"Then you know how to make faces and grin?"

"Upon my word," replied Passepartout, vexed to see that his nationality had prompted the question; "we Frenchmen, we can make faces, it is true, but not better than Americans."

"True again. Well, if I cannot engage you as a servant, I will as a clown. You understand me, my good fellow? In France they exhibit foreign clowns, and abroad French clowns."

"Ah!"

"Yes, particularly after dinner. Can you sing?"

"Yes," replied Passepartout, who used to sing in street concerts.

"But do you think you could sing standing on your head, with a top spinning on the sole of your left foot, and balancing a sword on your right?"

"I should think so," replied Passepartout, recollecting his juvenile performances.

"Because, you see, that is everything," observed the Honourable Mr. Batulcar.

The engagement was made there and then. At last Passepartout had found a situation, he was engaged as odd man in the celebrated Japanese troupe. It was not flattering, but in a week he would be on his road to San Francisco.

The performance, announced with so much flourish of trumpets, was to begin at three, and the noisy instruments of a Japanese band soon began to play in front of the booth. Of course Passepartout had no time to study his part, but he was to give the support of his strong back and shoulders to the great exhibition of the human pyramid, performed by the Long Noses of the god Tingou. This great attraction was to conclude the series of performances.

Before three o'clock the whole of the great booth was filled with spectators — Europeans and natives, Chinese and Japanese, men, women, and children, crowded the narrow benches and the boxes opposite the stage. The band had left the exterior of the booth, and were now hard at work playing their gongs, drums, tambourines, flutes, cymbals, and what not, in front of the stage.

This performance was like every other. But it must be said the Japanese are the first equilibrists in the world. One with a fan and a bit of paper performed the graceful trick of the flowers and the butterflies; another traced a series of words in the air with the blue smoke from a fragrant pipe, and so described a compliment to the audience; another performed some tricks with lighted candles, which he extinguished by passing them before his lips, and then lighted them again one after the other, without ceasing the conjuring tricks he was performing for a moment; another executed a series of combinations with humming-tops; in his hands they hummed, and seemed animated with a life of their own; they spun along pipe stems and edges of sword blades, on wires no thicker than a hair stretched from one side of the stage to the other, round the rims of glass bowls, dispersed into corners, and produced strange musical effects, by combining their various tones. The jugglers flung them into the air, and they were spinning all the time; they put them in their pockets, and still they were spinning when they took them out, till the moment, when, on touching a spring, they burst into showers of fire.

But the principal attraction was the performances of these Long Noses, extraordinary equilibrists hitherto unknown to Europe. These Long Noses form a corporation under the peculiar protection of the god Tingou. Dressed like heroes of the middle ages, they wore a splendid pair of wings on their shoulders; but what distinguished them particularly was a long nose with which their faces were ornamented, and also the use they made of it. These noses were nothing more nor less than bamboos, five, six, and even ten feet long, some straight, some crooked, some smooth, and others covered with tubercles. Now it was on these appendages, which were fastened to their wearers as strongly as possible, that their balancing tricks were performed. A dozen of these followers of Tingou lay on their backs, and their comrades, dressed like lightning conductors, lit on their noses, flitting about from one to the other, and performing the most extraordinary antics.

In conclusion the "Human Pyramid" had been especially announced, in which fifty of the Long Noses were to represent "the Car of Juggernaut"; but, instead of making this pyramid with their shoulders as a base, Mr. Batulcar's artists were to make use of their noses for that purpose. Now one of those who had figured in the base of the car had left the troupe, and as it only required strength and smartness, Passepartout had been chosen to take his place.

The poor fellow felt very miserable when—sad recollection of his youth—he had to put on his middle-age costume, ornamented with parti-coloured wings, and a nose six feet long was fastened on his face. But that nose was his bread-winner, and he resigned himself to his fate.

Passepartout came on the stage, and placed himself by those of his colleagues who were to form the base of the Car of Juggernaut. They all extended themselves on the floor with their noses pointing upwards. A second detachment came and balanced themselves on these appendages, a third above, then a fourth, and on these noses a human monument was constructed reaching up to the cornice of the theatre.

The applause was loud, and the band in the orchestra began to strike up, when the pyramid shook, the balance was lost, one of the noses of the foundation had disappeared, and the monument fell to pieces like a house of cards.

It was Passepartout's fault. Abandoning his place, clearing the front of the stage, without having recourse to his wings, and scrambling up into the boxes, he fell at the feet of one of the spectators, crying, "Ah, my master! my master!"

"You here?"

"Yes, I."

"Well, go to the steamer at once, my man."

Mr. Fogg, Aouda, who was with him, and Passepartout, passed through the lobby to the outside of the booth. There they met the Honourable Mr. Batulcar in a furious passion, insisting on compensation for the "break down." Phileas Fogg appeased him by thrusting some bank notes into his hand, and at half-past six, just as she was about to start, Mr. Fogg and Aouda stepped on board the American steamer, followed by Passepartout, with his wings still on his back, and a nose six feet long, which he had not time to remove.

THE OTHER LOG OF PHILEAS FOGG

There is no need to recount the adventures of the Frenchman after he awoke. After some tense, but comical, episodes in Yokohama, he was reunited with Fogg. They caught the ship to America just before the gangplank was raised.

Passepartout did fail to notify Fogg of the early departure of the liner. The ever-resourceful Englishman chartered a pilot boat. This sailed to Shanghai, where he caught the *Carnatic* and proceeded to Yokohama. Fix was deeply chagrined by this course of events. At least, he told himself that he was. The few impulses of gladness he put down to flaws in his character, flaws that could become fatal for him if he did not master them.

Adding to his chagrin, was his indebtedness to Fogg. That gentleman not only permitted Fix to go with him on the pilot boat but insisted on paying his passage.

Fogg was motivated by a desire to keep Fix handy. He might have to seize a Capellean and extract data from him. Moreover, he suspected that others of his kind—if Fix were a Capellean—were on the ship. If these made contact with Fix, Fogg might spot them.

Fix knew this. He also knew that if they were all just what they pretended to be, Fogg would have treated him as generously. He did not like knowing this. It made Fogg too likable.

Verne says that Passepartout, on meeting his master in Japan, did not inform him that Fix was a detective who intended to arrest Fogg. This was not true. Even if Verne's surface tale was valid, it would be difficult to account for Passepartout's silence. Verne had him say nothing because it was necessary for his plot. Fogg must be kept in ignorance of Fix's mission. Otherwise, Fogg would have rid himself of Fix and so not have been arrested when he landed in England.

CHAPTER XXIV
THE PASSAGE ACROSS THE PACIFIC OCEAN

What happened off Shanghai is easily comprehended. The steamer saw the signals made by the *Tankadere*. The captain, seeing the signal distress flying, bore down to the little schooner. Phileas Fogg paid for his passage the price agreed upon, and John Bunsby, the master, pocketed five hundred and fifty pounds. Then that gentleman, Aouda, and Mr. Fix were transferred to the steamer, which immediately resumed her course for Nagasaki and Yokohama.

Arriving on the morning of the 14th of November, the time the vessel was due, Phileas Fogg, leaving Fix to attend to his own affairs, went on board the *Carnatic* and there he heard, to the great joy of Aouda, and perhaps his own, but at all events he did not show it, that the Frenchman, Passepartout, had really arrived at Yokohama the evening before. Phileas Fogg, who was to leave for San Francisco the same evening, immediately set about finding Passepartout. It was in vain that he applied to the French and English consuls, and after having wandered through the streets to no purpose, he almost despaired of finding Passepartout at all, when chance, or a presentiment, induced him to enter Batulcar's booth. He never could have recognized his servant in his present grotesque accoutrement, but the latter, while lying on his back, saw his master up in the gallery. He could not help moving to attract his notice, and hence the balance was lost, and consequent breakdown of the whole.

All this was told Passepartout by Aouda, who related to him how they had sailed all the way from Hong-kong to Shanghai in company with Fix in the little schooner, the *Tankadere*. Passepartout did not move a muscle of his face at the mention of Fix. He thought the time was not yet come to acquaint his master with all that had passed between the detective and himself. Therefore, in the account Passepartout gave of his adventures, he threw the entire blame on himself, and his only excuse was that he had been overtaken by intoxication caused by smoking opium at Hong-kong.

Mr. Fogg listened to this tale very coldly; then he supplied his servant with money enough to provide himself with proper clothes. In less than an hour Passepartout had got rid of his nose and his wings, and there was nothing about him which recalled the votary of the god Tingou.

The steamer carrying the mails between Yokohama and San Francisco belonged to the Pacific Mail Company, and was called the *General Grant*. It was a large paddle steamer of two thousand five hundred tons, well found, and very fast. The enormous beam of her engine went up and down through the hatchway of the engine-room, a piston was attached to one end and a connecting rod to the other, which changing the rectilinear motion to circular was in direct connection with the shaft of the paddles. The *General Grant* was rigged like a three-masted schooner, and could set a considerable quantity of canvas, which greatly assisted her steam power. By making twelve miles an hour she would cross the ocean in twenty-one days. Phileas Fogg was therefore justified in calculating if he reached San Francisco the 2nd of December he would be at New York on the 11th, and the 20th he would arrive in London, thus having gained some hours on that fatal date of the 21st of December. There were numerous passengers on board the steamer, English, several Americans, a large number of labourers for America, and certain English officers belonging to the Indian Army, who were profiting by their leave of absence to travel about the world.

No nautical incident occurred on the passage. In consequence of its great paddle-boxes and its sails the vessel rolled very little. The Pacific Ocean quite justified its name. Mr. Fogg was as calm and uncommunicative as ever, his young companion more than ever attached to him by other ties than those of gratitude. His silent but generous nature had more effect on her heart than she thought, and it was almost in ignorance that she gave way to sentiments which Fogg did not in the least appear to share.

And Aouda took the liveliest interest in his plans. She became uneasy when any incident occurred likely to compromise the success of their voyage. She often talked with Passepartout, who was not long in finding out the state of Aouda's heart. This good fellow had now the blindest confidence in his master; he was never tired of singing his praises; then he cheered Aouda by prognosticating a successful termination of the voyage, telling her the worst part was already accomplished, since they had quitted the fantastic countries of China and Japan, and were now on their return to civilization, and that, lastly, there was only a run on a railway from San Francisco to New York, and a passage in a transatlantic steamer to conclude this supposed impossible journey round the world within the stipulated time. Nine days after leaving Yokohama, Phileas Fogg had performed exactly half the tour of the terrestrial globe.

In fact, the *General Grant* passed the one hundred and eighth meridian on November the 23rd, and was at the exact antipodes of London—out of his eighty days, it is true, he had employed fifty-two, and he had only twenty-eight left to expend. But it must be noticed that if he was only half-way on his tour according to the difference in the meridians, he had really accomplished more than two-thirds of the whole route. What circuits he had been obliged to make between London and Aden, and between Aden and Bombay, from Calcutta to Singapore, and from Singapore to Yokohama! If he had followed the fiftieth parallel, which is that of London, without deviation, the distance would not have been more than twelve thousand miles or so, while Phileas Fogg had been obliged, in consequence of the irregular means of locomotion at his disposal, to traverse twenty-six thousand miles, of which by the 23rd of November he would have already accomplished seventeen thousand five hundred. But henceforward it was a straight course for them, and there was no Fix at hand to throw obstacles in their way.

It happened, too, that on the 23rd of November Passepartout was greatly delighted. It will be recollected how obstinate he was in keeping London time by his famous family watch, thus finding the time wrong in all the countries he passed through. Now, on that day it was neither too fast nor too slow, but agreed with the ship's chronometer exactly.

Passepartout would have liked to know what Fix would have to say if he had been there.

"That rascal told me a lot of stories about meridians and the sun and the moon," repeated Passepartout. "I was quite sure one day or another the sun would regulate itself by my watch."

Passepartout did not know that if the dial of his watch had been divided, as some Italian clocks are, into twenty-four hours he would have had no reason to triumph, for the hands would have shown nine in the evening, when on board it was nine in the morning—that is to say, the twenty-first hour after midnight—exactly the difference which exists between London and the hundred and eightieth meridian.

But if Fix had been able to explain this purely physical effect, Passepartout would certainly have refused to admit it, had he been able to understand it; and it is not impossible that if the police agent had shown himself unexpectedly on board at that moment, Passepartout would have come to an understanding with him on a different subject, and in a very different manner.

Now, where was Fix at this moment? Fix was actually on board the *General Grant*. On arriving at Yokohama, the agent, leaving Mr. Fogg, whom he expected to meet again in the course of the day, went immediately to the English Consul's office. There he at last found the warrant which, having followed him from Bombay, was already forty days old—a warrant which had been forwarded to him from Hong-kong by the same *Carnatic*, on board which he was supposed to be. Judge the detective's disappointment! the warrant was inoperative. Fogg had left the English territory, and it was now necessary to get a warrant of extradition before he could take him.

"So be it," said Fix to himself, cooling his anger, "my warrant is useless now, but it will do in England. This rascal, I think, intends to return to England, believing he has thrown the police off the scent. Well, I shall stick to him still. As for the money, I hope there may be a little left. But what with voyages, bribes, trials, fines, elephants and all sorts of expenses, my man has already spent more than five thousand pounds. After all the Bank can afford it!"

So having made up his mind he went on board the *General Grant*. He was there when Mr. Fogg and Aouda arrived—to his great surprise he recognized Passepartout also in his acrobat's costume. He hid himself immediately in his cabin in order to avoid an explanation which might compromise everything, and thanks to the number of passengers he calculated in not being seen by his enemy, when on that day precisely he came face to face with him in the forepart of the vessel.

Passepartout took Fix by the throat, with no further explanation, and, to the great satisfaction of certain Americans who immediately offered to back him, he gave the unfortunate detective a fearful thrashing, which proved the superiority of French over English boxing. When Passepartout had finished he felt calm and relieved. Fix got up in a pitiable state, and looking at his adversary, he said very coolly to him—

"Have you done?"

"For the moment I have."

"Then let me speak a word to you."

"If I do—"

"In your master's interest."

This coolness got the better of Passepartout, and he followed the police agent. They both sat down.

"You have given me a thrashing," said Fix. "I expected you would. Now listen to what I have to say—till now I have been against Mr. Fogg, but now I am on his side."

"At last?" cried the Frenchman; "so now you believe he is an honest man?"

"No," coolly replied Fix, "I still think him a thief—stop, let me say what I have to say. As long as Mr. Fogg was on English territory it was my interest to detain him, as I was in daily expectation of a warrant for his arrest. I have done everything I could with that view. I sent the Bombay priests after him, I made you drunk at Hong-kong, I separated you from your master, I made him miss the Yokohama boat."

Passepartout listened and clenched his fists.

"Now," continued Fix, "Mr. Fogg seems determined to return to England. Well, I shall follow him. But in future I will take as much trouble to remove whatever obstacles may come in his way as I have hitherto taken to accumulate them. You see my game is now changed, and it is changed because my interest demands it. I say your interest is the same as mine, because it is only in England that you will find out whether you have been in the service of an honest man or a rogue."

Passepartout had listened to Fix very attentively, and he was convinced that Fix was really sincere in what he said.

"Are we friends?" asked Fix.

"Friends, no," replied Passepartout. "Allies, yes, under certain conditions, but, at the least appearance of treachery I shall wring your neck."

"Agreed," quietly replied the detective.

Eleven days afterwards, the 3rd of December, the *General Grant* entered the bay of the Golden Gate and arrived at San Francisco.

Up to this time Mr. Fogg had neither gained nor lost a single day.

THE FULL ACCOUNT

THE OTHER LOG OF PHILEAS FOGG

The ship which Fogg took for San Francisco was the *General Grant*. This belonged to the Pacific Mail Steamship Company and was a paddle wheel steamer also fitted with three masts bearing large sails. At an expected speed of twelve miles an hour, it would cross the Pacific in twenty-one days. Fogg calculated that he would disembark at San Francisco on the second of December. From there he would travel by train to New York City, arriving on the eleventh of December. From New York he would take a ship to England. The twentieth of December would see him in London, ahead of the required arrival date of the twenty-first.

Verne says that, nine days after leaving Yokohama, on the twenty-third of November, the ship crossed the 180th meridian. Fogg had gone exactly halfway around the Earth since this imaginary line was at the antipodes of London. Though Fogg had only twenty-eight days to traverse the second half of his journey, he had actually completed two-thirds of his circuit. To get to the 180th meridian, he had been forced to make long detours. But the course from then on would he comparatively straight.

On this twenty-third of November, according to Verne, Passepartout made a happy discovery. His watch, which he had not adjusted to the various time zones, now agreed with the sun.

Passepartout, Verne says, did not know that if the face of his watch had been divided into twenty-four hours (like Italian watches), the hands of his watch would have indicated the true chronometry. They would have shown him that it was not nine in the morning but nine in the evening. That is, they would indicate the twenty-first hour after midnight, exactly the difference between London time and that of the 180th meridian.

As we know, Fogg had no watches, having expended them in Bundelcund. Verne did not know of the incident at the rajah's palace, but he also says nothing at this time of Fogg having a watch. Why this gentleman, who conducted himself strictly by the chronometer, lacked a timepiece, Verne does not say.

Fix had stayed in his cabin until the twenty-third, when he felt that he must leave it or go mad. While walking on the forward deck, he ran into Passepartout. He also ran into blows of the fist from the seemingly enraged valet. Passepartout was genuinely angry at the trick that Fix had played on him. But even if he had not been, he would have pretended to be. The role he was playing demanded it. Besides, if Fix were a Capellean, it was fun to pummel him.

Fix tried to defend himself but soon found that the Frenchman was the superior boxer. Lying on the deck, he said, "Are you finished?"

"Yes—for this time," Passepartout said.

"Then let me have a word with you."

"But I . . ."

"In your master's interest."

They sat down in an area distant from the other passengers, who had regarded the encounter with enthusiasm, some even making bets.

"You've thrashed me," Fix said. "Good. I expected it. Now listen. Until now I've been Mr. Fogg's adversary. But I'm now in this with him."

"Aha! You're convinced he's an honest man!"

What the devil is this one up to now? he was thinking.

"No," Fix said coldly. "I think he's a rascal."

He proceeded to tell Passepartout his plan, which was to help Fogg win his bet. He would, however, only be doing this so he could get him back on English soil. There it would be determined whether or not Fogg was innocent.

"Are we friends now?" Fix said.

"No," Passepartout said. "Allies—perhaps. At the least sign of treachery, I'll twist your neck."

Passepartout had a double meaning in his threat, of course.

Verne then says that, eleven days later, on the third of December, the ship entered the bay of the Golden Gate. Mr. Fogg had not gained or lost a day.

This is true, but Verne did not know what happened the next few days after Fix was knocked to the deck.

While we do not know exactly what Fix and the gray-eyed man were up to during the time they were out of Passepartout's and Fogg's sight, we can reconstruct their activities from Fogg's other log.

At one in the morning, Passepartout was wakened from a fretful somnolence by the ringing sounds from the watch at his ear. He listened for a moment, ascertaining that the series of sounds formed no code he recognized. He hastily put on some clothes and left the cabin. He did not observe the figure standing in the shadow of one of the large lifeboats on davits some fifty feet away.

He was standing watch because Fix was in bed with diarrhea and a high fever. Nemo was not pleased with this course of events, both because it was inconvenient and because it showed him that Nature was even stronger than he. And since he did not care to be seen by any of Fogg's party, he could not leave the cabin when the sun was up. He did have a disguise available. The beard was actually a false one, which he could discard in favor of a false moustache. A wig would give him the appearance of a man approaching old age, and putty would make his nose bulbous. To remove the noticeable wide spacing between the eyes, he had a set of glass eyes to which he attached false eyelids and flesh-colored false skin. The glass eyes were thin shells with blue irises, one-way glass which both the Capelleans and Eridaneans had inherited from the Old Ones along with a few other devices far in advance of Earthling science. These could be set within the hollows of his eyes so that his eyes seemed to be closer together.

Unfortunately, half of the vision of each eye was obstructed. Nemo did not like to use them unless the situation absolutely demanded that he do so. He had elected to stay in his quarters, coming out only at night. Now he was just about to light a cheroot when he saw the Frenchman's cabin door. If it had opened a few seconds later, Passepartout would have seen the light of his match. Cursing (his way of delivering thanks for having been saved from observation), he replaced the cheroot in its case. From his belt he drew a Colt revolver.

He had hoped he would not have to use it, since the noise might alarm the occupants of cabins near Fogg's. He waited hidden in the shadow of the lifeboat until Passepartout had knocked on Fogg's door and been admitted. He started toward Fogg's cabin but had to dodge back under the lifeboat. The door had swung open again. Passepartout emerged and went to Aouda's cabin, next to Fogg's, and knocked. There was an exchange of words, which Nemo could not hear, through the crack by the slightly opened door. Nemo supposed that Aouda was requiring Passepartout to give a password, even though she must recognize his voice. In less than two minutes, Aouda came out dressed in a robe, her black hair hanging to her waistline. Both disappeared into Fogg's cabin.

Nemo walked softly to the door and applied to it a stethoscopic device, another inheritance from the Old Ones. The moonlight falling on his features, showed his alarm, followed by a look of determination. Though he hated to make the noise, there was only one way to enter the cabin. He lifted his right boot and gave the lock a mighty kick. Few locks could have stood up under a kick from Nemo, who was extremely powerful. The lock tore out, and the door banged into the wall with Nemo swiftly leaping through the doorway.

A glance showed him that the three were unarmed. They were sitting at a table. Passepartout's watch, illumined by the swinging petroleum lamp attached to the ceiling, lay on the table. That it was there confirmed Nemo's suspicions that it contained a distorter. In the silence that followed his crashing entrance, he could hear, faintly, the ringings from the watch. And he recognized the Capellean code.

Nemo, pointing the revolver at them, shut the door behind him. Passepartout started to rise. Nemo shook his head. The Frenchman sat down. His eyes and Aouda's were wide, and their skins were pale. Fogg sat as still as if he were in a tintype. His was the only calm face at the table.

"You will slowly rise and move over against the bulkhead," Nemo said. "You will then slowly turn around until you face it. You will then place your palms flatly against the bulkhead."

Though he voiced no curses, he must have been thinking them. The pulses indicated an immediate and emergency action for any Capellean possessing a distorter. Nemo would not have ignored any such call, even from the lowliest. This message was sent by the highest chief of them all. It was directed at the Capellean who was bringing the recently found distorter from China. But it also pleaded that anyone else who might possess a distorter should use it if the Chinese agent failed to reply.

Whoever answered was to set his device on *transmit*, though he must, of course, make sure that no one would come across it while it was left unguarded. That the chief would allow a distorter to be left behind showed how desperate the occasion was. Moreover, that the chief thought that the rajah of Bundelcund was still alive but was willing to take a chance on being transmitted by him indicated the desperation of his situation.

Also, the chief said, if at all possible, bring two men. Three would be preferable, but he could manage with two. He did not say why he wanted the two men.

He would prefer that all be Capellean, but if that was not possible, the man in China—or whoever else might be listening in—must pick up two Earthlings at gun's point and bring them along.

Nemo, having been out of touch with other Capelleans so long, did not know what was behind the message. But it changed his plans for the three Eridaneans. Why did Fix have to be sick at this time? Someone had to be at this end to insure that Nemo and the chief would be transmitted back if need be. If they were not, then Fix would have to take care of the distorter. They were too valuable to lose.

And why did not the Chinese agent answer? Was he sleeping? Was he drunk? Was he in the hands of bandits? Or, horrible thought, had he been taken by Eridaneans? If so, they would have the distorter, and even if they did not know the Capellean code, they could set the distorter on *receive* on the chance of scooping up whoever was at the other end. Or, even more unthinkable, they might transmit a group of heavily armed men.

Still, the intelligence report was that the Eridaneans only had one distorter left. And that was on the table before him. But intelligence reports were not always reliable.

Nemo wanted to go to the chief's aid at once, but he had to make certain preparations which would take at least ten minutes. Perhaps fifteen.

At his orders, Passepartout tore the bed sheets into strips. While he was doing this, Nemo, using one hand, pressed the watch stem to send a message to the chief. Then he held the gun on Passepartout while the Frenchman bound his master's hands behind him and his ankles together. Aouda then tied up Passepartout in similar fashion. Nemo struck her over the head and bound her. With the three strips left over, he gagged the three. For a moment he contemplated using his knife to finish them but decided against it. The chief wanted three bodies, but he needed them alive and able. Very well, he would get them.

First, he must make sure that they could not roll over and so get out of the door, which could not now be locked. He tore off other strips and bound the legs of the three together. Then he soaked the clothes of the three with petroleum from one swinging lamp. He set three other lamps near them so that if they moved in any direction, the vapors from the oil would be ignited by the flames of the three burning lamps.

He pocketed the watch and, closing the door behind him, went after Fix.

Fix was in a half-delirium. When he finally understood what Nemo wanted of him, he protested. He could not possibly walk to Fogg's cabin and then carry the watch back to his own cabin.

"Then you will crawl," Nemo said. "But you had better run, since the noise is going to wake up the entire ship. If you fail to get away with the watch, you will die. I'll make sure of that."

"I just can't do it," Fix muttered.

"Then you will die now," Nemo said.

Fix tried to get out of his bed but fell on the floor.

Nemo swore at him. Nature was proving once more that she was stronger than he.

Or had she?

He picked up Fix and hoisted him over his shoulders and carried him out onto the deck. He hoped that he would encounter no insomniacs strolling the deck, or any of the crew. If he did, he could explain that his friend was drunk and that he was making sure he got to his bed. But he did not want any strange events to be observed by anyone who might remember after the uproar had died down.

If Nature was against him that night, so was that other lady, Chance.

An officer did see him with his burden when he was halfway to Fogg's cabin.

Nemo explained that Fix had been sleeping on the deck and was either drunk or sick. He was returning him to his cabin.

"You are going the wrong way," the officer said. "Mr. Fix has his quarters back there."

"Ah, yes," Nemo said. "I must have gotten turned around."

"I doubt that Mr. Fix is inebriated," the officer said. "He has been very sick, as you must know if you are a friend of his. No doubt, he wandered out onto the deck in a delirium. I will call the doctor and make sure that he is restrained. And I'll see he has a nurse."

"You are very kind," Nemo said, wondering if he could kill the officer and drop him over the railing.

That was taken care of a moment later when they encountered a sailor. The officer insisted that the sailor help Nemo carry Fix back to the cabin. The sailor stood by while the officer went off to rouse the doctor and a nurse. Nemo wished to leave at once but knew that the crewmen would think it strange if he did not show concern for his "friend."

He was not, however, restrained from signaling to his chief the changed situation. He went into the water closet, took out the watch, and sent the coded message. The chief replied that he was not in that much of a hurry now that he knew help was on its way. Nemo wished to ask where the chief was and why he needed so many people, but he heard the doctor enter and thought it better not to stay in the closet too long. He had to get back to Fogg's cabin.

Even so, six more minutes passed before he was able to leave. The captain himself appeared and demanded an account. Nemo gave it. The captain seemed to be satisfied. Nemo said that he would look in on Fix in the morning, and he said good night. He hurried back hoping that Fix would be well enough in the morning to go to Fogg's cabin and pick up the watch. After all, it would be taped to the underside of the table. Even if the crew investigated the cabin, which they might well do once they observed the broken lock, they might not see the watch. Fix could gain entrance later and remove it.

He also hoped that the three Eridaneans would not decide to sacrifice themselves. If they set themselves afire, they would defeat his intention of taking them along. And the fire would bring the attention of the ship to that cabin.

If that happened, then he would go to his own cabin and transport himself to the chief. If need be, they could come back to the *General Grant.* It would mean a change in plans, which the chief evidently did not wish. But that could not be helped.

Nemo also wondered where the chief had gotten his distorter. As far as he knew, the one found in China was the only one the Capelleans possessed. But he did not know everything. That cursed secrecy was an evil not always necessary.

With such thoughts, he entered Fogg's cabin.

The next few empty moments, he had no thoughts at all.

The empty lamp swung against his head as he entered.

When he awoke, he was lying tied up in a fetal position on the table. He knew then that they had taken the distorter from him and secured it to the underside of the table on which he lay.

Passepartout, at Fogg's bidding, looked outside. On returning he said, "No Fix in sight, sir. Could Fix be what he claims to be? Surely, if he were a Capellean, Nemo would have called him to his assistance? He would need him to guard the distorter."

"That could well be," Fogg said. "You will inquire after him sometime this morning. After we return."

Passepartout said, "You are determined to carry out this, if I may say so, mad project?"

"I am."

"Will I be accompanying you and this man, sir?"

"Assuredly."

"We were lucky last time, sir. But now . . ."

"We must find out what is behind this."

Passepartout sighed but said no more.

On a chair lay the weapons which had been taken from various hiding places in Nemo's clothing. There was a knife which had been strapped to his left leg, another in a scabbard on his right leg, one in a sheath suspended from his belt in the rear, and a small cylindrical object the function of which Nemo declined to explain. Passepartout, however, found out how to operate the thing. A small slide on its side, if pressed, would obviously discharge the cylinder's contents from a hole at the other end. Pointing the end close to Nemo's face, he said, "Now, sir, please illuminate me. Or I will activate this and so possibly extinguish you."

Passepartout had no intention of doing so, since Nemo might

wish to die to escape questioning. Nemo suspected this, but he could not be sure. And he did not intend to commit suicide unless he were in a far more hopeless situation.

"It will expel a stream of cyanide," he said.

"Very clever," Passepartout said. He gave it to Aouda to use in case Fix should appear.

Fogg said, "Miss Jejeebhoy, you will reset the distorter for *receive* a minute after we are gone. But I do not believe that you should stay in this cabin. The door cannot be locked, and we can't be sure that Fix won't be coming along. As soon as we've made the transit, you will take the distorter to your cabin and tape it to the underside of your table."

"Why not leave this man . . ."

"Nemo," Fogg said.

"This Nemo here?"

"I do not trust him, however capable Miss Jejeebhoy is," Fogg said. "He has enormous strength and great intelligence and resourcefulness. If we could get loose from our bonds while unobserved, he might be able to do so, observed or not."

Nemo had been hoping that they would reveal just how they had gotten loose, but they were keeping this a secret. He would find out someday; he swore to that.

"Besides," Fogg said, "seeing him bound and gagged may disconcert whoever is at the other end. You may gag him now, Passepartout."

"The clanging will undoubtedly awaken everyone on the ship," Fogg said. "And Fix, if he is a Capellean, will know what is transpiring. If anyone knocks, tell them you are frightened and won't come out. Open the door for no one."

"I understand," Aouda said. Her voice was so soft, so lovely that Passepartout's heart bounced as if on a trampoline. How could Fogg resist such a woman, who so openly adored him?

Aouda said, "The bell-like sounds will have to remain another of those mysteries of the sea."

How prophetic her words were, though even she could not have foreseen that from that night there would be, not one, but two marine mysteries.

Passepartout crawled under the table and set the watch to activate within four minutes. He and Fogg climbed onto the table and stuck their fingers in their ears.

The three men found themselves aboard another ship.

This, however, was a small sailing ship, and the sun stood at an altitude indicating some time around nine in the morning. Fogg knew that this would place them somewhere in the Atlantic, probably between the 15th and the 30th meridians. After this hasty calculation, he had no time for scientific matters.

They had dropped a few inches from the air onto a small deckhouse near the forepart of the ship. They were so close to a mast projecting from the roof of the deckhouse that they could reach out and touch it. Near them, piled on the roof, was an untidy mass of canvas.

The only other human being in sight was on the deck about twenty feet away where he would be sure to be out of range of the distorter field. Pieces of white cotton stuck out of his ears, and he held a revolver.

The sailor did not shoot at once because he must have thought that the two armed men were Capelleans and the bound man was the "slave" he had requested. It was true that he had expected only one Capellean and two bound men and a bound woman, but this may have further contributed to his astonishment. He could not grasp the idea that the situation had been changed.

Nemo, though painfully deafened by the nine clangors, nevertheless acted quickly. He straightened out and pivoted on his side, his long powerful legs coming around to strike both his captors across their ankles.

Passepartout, with the acrobat's quickness of reaction, leaped into the air. Fogg, who should have foreseen this move, since he claimed that the unforeseen did not exist, was knocked off his feet. His shot went wide of the sailor and, of course, informed him that all was not as it was supposed to be. The sailor fired at Fogg, missed, perhaps because of the roll and pitch of the ship, and then ran along the deck toward the stern. Passepartout bounded down in pursuit, even though armed with only one of Nemo's knives. He slipped, fell, rolled, and was back up on his feet at once.

Fogg had sprawled forward, and so was unable to keep Nemo from rolling off the roof of the deckhouse. He fell heavily on his side, and Fogg was after him a few seconds later. However, Fogg did not think there was much Nemo could do from then on. To make sure, he struck Nemo over the head with the butt of his revolver. Blood welled out from the wound, and a second later he suffered from another wound. The sailor, having turned once to fire at Passepartout, had missed. The bullet went downward and hit Nemo in his right arm.

Fogg left the limp and bleeding body and hastened after Passepartout. The sailor had taken refuge behind the rear of the aft cabin, just forward of the wheel. Passepartout waited for Fogg at the companionway to the fore cabin. This could be entered by a sliding door which was already shoved to one side.

Since they had not been in a confined space, and the distorter had been, the clangings had not affected their eardrums as much as the previous time. Their hearing was restored enough so that they could hear each other if they put their heads closely together and shouted. Fogg told his comrade to wait there while he inspected the interior of the aft cabins. Perhaps there was another entrance at the other end of his deckhouse. He had to make sure that the sailor did not try a surprise attack by using this. Before reemerging from the doorway, he would give the password. Thus, if the sailor had entered the other end, and overcame or killed Fogg, he would not be able to take Passepartout unawares.

"I saw the upper part of the wheel over the top of this house," the Frenchman said. "There was no one at it."

"The ship seems to be deserted except for this Capellean," Fogg said. "Very strange. But doubtless it can be explained. This seems to be a brigantine. And it's going on the starboard tack."

"Pardon, sir?"

"With the wind from the right. The jib and foremast staysails are set on the starboard tack. The ship is headed westward."

"Jib? Foremast staysail, sir?"

"The headsails. At the front of the ship. The two middle sails, those triangular-shaped ones, attached to the long boom projecting from the nose of the ship. The lower fore-topsail, the fourth from the bottom of the main mast, seems to have been set, but its head has been torn, probably by the wind.

"The foresail and upper fore-topsail are missing. I would judge that they have been blown from the yards. The main staysail, the lowest of the three triangular sails attached between the two masts, is down. It's that heap on the forward house. The aftersails have been removed. All other sails are furled, even the fore-and-aft sails. The main peak halyards, ropes for lowering and raising the sails, have been broken. Most of them are gone. Before the mainsail can be set, the halyards will have to be repaired. The seas are somewhat heavy, but the ship is not yawing much, that is, changing direction. But we can inspect the ship at a later time. I'm telling you this now so you'll have some idea of what to do if I don't return."

That was not nearly enough for him to know what to do, Passepartout thought.

Fogg, holding the revolver ready, entered the cabin. The open door gave some light. There was a window on the bow end, but it had been covered with a piece of canvas secured by strips of plank nailed into the side of the cabin. The floor was wet, though there was no standing water. This could be accounted for by a heavy sea or rain having come in from somewhere. There was a clock without hands secured upside-down by the two nails to a partition. A table held a slate log and a rack—called by the sailors a fiddle—which kept dishes from sliding off. The rack held dishes but no food or drink was visible nor were there any knives and forks. A piece of canvas evidently used as a towel was on the rack.

Fogg also saw a stove and a swinging lamp.

He looked at the slate log, which would have been used by the chief to make notations while on deck.

"H" stood for the hour; "K," for knots. Though the log said it was for Monday the twenty-fifth, the date was nautical, not civil. The day would have started on noon of the twenty-fifth, not midnight. The twenty-fifth, for the ship, would end at noon of the twenty-sixth, after which it would be November twenty-sixth.

Today was November twenty-seventh. Something had happened at eight in the morning on the twenty-fifth, or a few hours later, to prevent the mate from continuing the log. When the record ended, the island of St. Mary's was about six miles to the southwest.

272

H	K	COURSE	WIND	MONDAY 25th
1.	8			Comes in fresh
2.	8			
3.	8			
4.	8			
5.	8			
6.	8			
7.	9			
8.	9			At 8 P.M. fresh
9.	8			Got in royals & topg. sail
10.	8			
11.	8			
12.	8	E. by S.	West	M.P., rainy
1.	8			
2.	8			
3.	8			
4.	8			
5.	8			At 5 made the island of S. Mary's bearingn E.S.E
6.	8			
7.	8			
8.	8			At 8 eastern point bore S.S.W. 6 miles distant
9.				
10.				
11.				
12.				

On the port, or left, side of the cabin was the pantry. Fogg, entering it cautiously, found an open box holding moist sugar, a bag with several pounds of tea, an open barrel of flour, an open box of dried herrings, some rice and kidney beans in containers, some pots of preserved fruit, cans of food, and a nutmeg. These were all dry.

Fogg went back into the mate's cabin and looked around again. On the starboard side was a small bracket holding a tiny vial of oil for, he guessed, a sewing machine. This was still upright. If very heavy seas had been recently met, it would have been thrown to the deck. The bed was dry and showed no damage from water.

He looked under the bed and drew out the ship's ensign and its private signal: WT. The letter "W" had been sewn on. Also under the bed was a pair of stout sailor's boots, designed for bad weather but apparently unused. There were also two drawers. One held some pieces of iron and two unbroken panes of glass. The lower drawer held a pair of log sunglasses and a new log reel but no log line.

The next cabin, the last, was the captain's. He doubted that the sailor was in it. If he had entered it, he surely would have made his presence known by now. However, Fogg entered it slowly, and he kept to the sides of the cabin after he got in. There was a skylight through which the sailor might shoot if he crawled onto the top of the deckhouse.

A harmonium, a reed organ, was by the partition in the center of the cabin. Near it was a number of books, mostly religious, by their titles.

A child's high chair was on the floor along with a chest containing bottles of medicinals. A compass minus its card was on a table. A portable sewing machine was in a case attached to the bulkhead.

Under a bed, Fogg found a scabbarded sword. He removed it, thinking that he could use it. It seemed to be of Italian make and had probably been an officer's.

By the port side of the cabin was a water closet. Still cautious, because the sailor might be hiding there in ambush, Fogg looked within. Near the door was a damp bag. It looked as if it might have been wet by rain or spray entering through the half-covered port-hole on the opposite side.

Curious, Fogg entered the closet. He opened the bag and found ladies' garments, all wet, inside. So the captain had been accompanied by his wife and small child.

The starboard side held two windows, also covered by canvas cut from a sail.

There were no signs of violence anywhere, and the cabin had no aft exit.

Fogg returned to the deck, though not without giving the pass-word first. Passepartout said that the sailor had shown his head around the corner several times but had ducked back each time. Fogg told Passepartout what he had observed. He gave him the pistol, saying, "You hold that man with this. I'll go back to check on Nemo and inspect the fore deckhouse."

With the sword in hand, he walked slowly down the starboard side. Though his gait made him a better target for the sailor, he did not believe that it made him a good enough one. What with the wind and the motion of the ship, accuracy was not to be expected from a revolver at this range, Evidently the sailor, if he saw Fogg, had the same thoughts. No shots were fired.

Just before arriving at the fore deckhouse, Fogg went over to the port side. He looked around its corner. Nemo was gone.

Torn strips of sheet were evidence of Nemo's great strength. He had burst them apart with sheer muscularity. His boots lay by the strips.

Before he had returned on the starboard side, Fogg had looked down the port side. Nemo's still figure had been on the deck. So, the wily fellow had waited until Fogg was out of sight, because he knew that Passepartout, watching for the sailor, would have his back to him.

Fogg spun around, hoping that Nemo had not passed him going aftward while he was going forward. But he had. He was running barefoot, as swiftly and as silently as a tiger. He was only about ten feet from the Frenchman's back.

Fogg gave his first yell in years and ran toward the two. Passepartout, half-deafened, did not hear him. Nemo struck him on the back of his neck with his left fist. The Frenchman was hurled face forward into the deckhouse wall. He crumpled, and Nemo picked up the revolver. Grinning, he turned toward Fogg. Triumphant he might look, but he was pale, and blood ran down his right arm and dripped from his hand. His right arm seemed to be useless, since it hung down at his side and, though right-handed, he held the revolver in his left.

Fogg half-spun to port and raced toward the deckhouse. If Nemo was firing at him he could not hear the reports, but the knowledge that he probably was made him increase his speed. He went around the side of the deckhouse and then to its forepart. Hidden momentarily from the two enemies, he stood there, breathing hard. So now events were suddenly in Nemo's favor. Passepartout was out of the action, perhaps forever, and Nemo and the sailor each had a revolver.

After making sure that Passepartout could not imitate Nemo's feat, the two would proceed toward the bow. One would come along the port rail; one, by the starboard rail. Their paths would converge at the place where Fogg now stood. He could attack one with his sword, but the other would quickly join the man he attacked. At point-blank range, they would not miss.

The fore deckhouse was about thirteen feet square and six feet above the deck. It would contain the fo'c'sle or crew's quarters, the galley, and, perhaps, a cabin for the second mate. It would not afford a good hiding place or even a mediocre one.

Fogg looked upward. He could still run to one of the rope ladders formed of transverse ropes called ratlines and attached to the shrouds, pairs of ropes from the mastheads which gave lateral support to the masts. If he went up a ladder, he could at least get away from them for a while. If he then went out onto the yards, he would force them to use both hands while getting close enough to him so they would not waste their bullets. Perhaps he could attack them then with his sword. If he were an acrobat such as Passepartout, he might go up the main mast to one of the middle triangular sails and ascend by its ropes to the aft mast. If he could get down quickly enough, while the two were still aloft, he could seize the wheel and change the direction of the ship. If it swung around violently enough, it might dislodge the two.

Fogg did not, however, follow his desperate plan.

Instead, he slid open the wooden door on the forward cabin and darted inside. This was on the port side of the deckhouse and seemed to be the second mate's. It held a sea chest the examination of which Fogg deferred. He went through another sliding door into the crew's quarters, placed closest to the bow. His log does not mention his feelings at this point, but we may suppose that even the face of the imperturbable Fogg lit up with delight.

There, as he had hoped, was the watch, taped to the ceiling of the fo'c'sle. He tore it loose and, holding it to his ear, ran out of the entrance onto the deck of the bow.

The watch was emitting, in Eridanean code, a stream of ringing sounds. Aouda had set her distorter on *receive*.

If he set the Capellean distorter for *transmit* he could escape. That meant leaving the enemy distorter, Passepartout, and the explanation of the mystery of the ship behind him. As for the first, he must submit to it if he were transmitted. As for the third, it was better to survive at the price of ignorance. As for the second, it was probable that Passepartout was dead. He was doomed even if Fogg stayed here and tried to fight with only the sword.

He stood for about five seconds, five seconds during which his enemies would be approaching.

Six seconds after this, the two Capelleans were dismayed—and deafened again—when nine clanging sounds seemed to tear the air around them and buffet their eardrums. Both, we may presume, swore at the same time they turned pale. Both, we know, started to run into the cabin under the assumption that they would find only the device. The foxy Eridanean had undoubtedly taken the only way out. He must have removed the distorter from the ceiling and taped it to the underside of a table and been transmitted back to the *General Grant.*

Nemo must have been blaming himself for not having first retrieved the device. But he could console himself with the thought that if he had done so, he, instead of Fogg, might have been trapped in the deckhouse.

The Capelleans met at the forward entrance of the deckhouse. The sailor arrived first and so was ahead of Nemo in entering the fo'c'sle. He halted because, to his astonishment, the watch was still taped to the ceiling. That was all he saw. The edge of Fogg's sword struck the top of his head. He dropped; the revolver fell from his hand. And Fogg picked up the revolver.

And Nemo? After the first moment of chagrin, not unmixed with panic, he backed out of the companionway.

The affair had not suddenly become reversed. It had just evened out. Neither side held a particular advantage at this moment. Both were armed. Fogg was shut up in the deckhouse, but Nemo was losing blood and strength.

The gray-eyed man got onto the top of the deckhouse and proceeded to remove his coat and his shirt. He tore his shirt into strips and bound them around the arm. The wound, fortunately, was only a flesh wound, and blood seemed to stop flowing after a few moments. Nevertheless, he might as well have had only one arm, and the gorilla-like power of his muscles had drained out of him.

He decided that he could afford to desert his post for a few minutes. Fogg would not dare to make a dash for the outside. At least, not for a while. Nemo would finish off the other fellow and then return to the deckhouse. Fogg would still be crouching near a bulkhead or under some furniture. He would know that Nemo could break the deckhouse windows and fire from there. If he had not been so overwhelmed by the thought of Fogg escaping, he would have done that at once. Of course, if he did use the windows, he stood a good chance of receiving Fogg's bullets in his face. It would be discreet to remain away from them.

Eventually, Fogg would be driven out of the deckhouse by thirst and hunger. He would not have access to the galley. Nemo had ascertained from his chief that the galley was partitioned off from the fo'c'sle and second mate's cabin. Even if Fogg knocked a hole through the partition, he would not find much food. Most of the supplies were kept in the pantry, which was in the deckhouse aft.

Nemo moved softly away from the roof of the deckhouse only because it was his nature to do so. He did not have to fear that Fogg would hear him. Fogg would still be deafened by the clangings.

Nemo had proceeded about thirty feet toward the stern when the nine clangings struck again. He whirled. What the devil was Fogg doing now?

Had he indeed departed this time? Or was he setting the same trap? And, if he had gone, would he not be quickly back with help? There was nothing to prevent Fogg from setting the distorter to revert automatically to *receive* within a certain time.

But Fogg might be hoping that he would think just this and so rush in to turn the distorter off before Fogg & Company would return.

Nemo was in a highly indecisive state, a foreign one to this man of great intelligence and speedy action. If he entered either entrance to the fore deckhouse, he would be exposed to fire from a man whose coolness and accuracy with arms had been proven in Bundelcund.

Moreover, Fogg would be in semidarkness. The windows were covered by shutters, and while he could destroy these to let some light in, he would be exposed. Fogg would expect him to try that and so would be ready for him. The deckhouse was built of thin planking through which Fogg's bullets could find him even if Nemo stood to one side while tearing off the canvas coverings.

He stood on the deck for a minute, and then he turned away. If only Fogg did not find the papers on the chief. The distorter itself would have to be abandoned. That could not be helped.

And if only Passepartout were not dead.

Nemo did not expect Fogg to surrender to save Passepartout. That happened only in novels. Fogg would know that he would be killed if he did surrender. Nemo would no longer consider keeping him as a prisoner. The two of them might possibly be able to sail the ship to some port, but Nemo could not stay awake long enough for this. And he could not take any more chances on a live Fogg. The Englishman was too wily.

Passepartout was sitting with his back against the bulkhead of the main cabin. His forehead and nose were bloody, and his eyes were dull.

Nevertheless, he spat at Nemo.

"Good! You are still alive!" Nemo said.

Passepartout did not reply.

Nemo searched him but found no weapons. He picked up Passepartout with his left hand, his revolver stuck in his belt, and propelled him forward. The Frenchman sprawled out onto the deck, but, after being raised again, he managed to stay on his feet.

"If your master is willing to make a bargain by which we will all gain, though some loss by all is inevitable, then you will stay alive," Nemo said.

He pushed Passepartout ahead of him with the end of his revolver until they had reached the fore deckhouse. Standing by the entrance to the second mate's cabin, Nemo shouted out the terms. His own voice sounded distant, and he was not sure that Fogg was yet able to hear him. Or, for that matter, that he was even in the cabin. Fogg could have slipped out while he was busy with the Frenchman, but he did not think so.

After a short silence, Fogg's voice came faintly.

"Very well! Provided that you tell me what happened to the people on this ship. I don't expect you to tell me anything about your own people which might reveal your secrets."

"I can't tell you much because our man didn't have much time to impart anything but a bare outline."

To hear him, Fogg had to be close to the door. Perhaps if he were to make two quick shots, one on either side of the door? The bullets would go through the thin planking. But no, it was too risky.

"It all seems mysterious," Nemo said. "But similar things have happened before and doubtless will happen again. As you may have observed, there are signs of a hasty departure but none of violence.

The vessel has a cargo of seventeen hundred barrels of alcohol contained in spruce and red oak barrels. This is highly volatile, and any rupture of barrels could be a source of explosion or fire. But such was not the case. This ship was not abandoned because of that.

"The sailors left their clothing, sea boots, oilskins, and their tobacco pipes. So the situation was of such a nature that it let no time for taking articles which a sailor would normally not leave behind. Especially the pipes. It is obvious that the misfortune did not occur during meal time, since there are no places set for meals.

"According to . . . to our man . . ."

"His name was Edward W. Head, and he was the cook and steward," Fogg said. "He had his papers on him. That his name was Head is significant, I believe. He must be your chief."

"Only a coincidence," Nemo said. "We have abandoned that ancient, but useless, custom of using names which indicate a person's function."

"Perhaps," Fogg said.

Nemo wondered what else he had found on Head.

"Is he dead?" Nemo said.

"Yes."

"You may have noticed that the navigation book, sextant, and chronometer are missing," Nemo said. "Evidently the captain—his name was Briggs, by the way—had time to grab these. Other articles, such as clothes, were left behind. Nor were provisions from the pantry stored on the yawl."

"The yawl? What about the main lifeboat, the longboat?"

"That was left behind at New York. It was damaged during the loading of the barrels. Several fell out of the sling on it, and Captain Briggs did not want to delay the ship while it was being repaired. The yawl could hold ten people, but it was smaller and not as seaworthy as the longboat."

"The last hour marked on the deck log was eight A.M., November twenty-fifth," Fogg said. "And after that?"

"Between nine and ten o'clock, the *Mary Celeste* was within several miles of the Dollabarat shoals," Nemo said. "Those are dangerous shoals about three and a quarter miles southeast of the Formigas rocks. The Formigas are, it is thought, the peaks of submerged mountains. The *Mary Celeste* was not close enough to be in any peril and would have passed on safely, but . . ."

Nemo wondered why Fogg was having him give this lengthy explanation. Was he hoping to drag out the time before their departure because he had planned some trick which required time to prepare?

Well, there was nothing he could do about it. But if things suddenly went wrong for him, he would kill Passepartout at once. And perhaps this prolonged talk might turn to his advantage, if he could think of something.

"One of those inexplicable but frequently occurring calms befell the ship. At any other place, the *Mary Celeste* could have ridden it out. But now, her sails sagging, the ship was borne by the currents toward the Dollabarat shoals. These have taken many a victim. And it looked as if they would soon fasten their teeth into the hull of another. Captain Briggs had the light sails furled and the mainsail lowered and the ship hove to on the starboard tack. This was to ensure that, if the wind should rise in time, it would blow against the sails and stop its headway. Then the yawl might catch up with the ship, and the crew could board it.

"After this, the captain ordered that the ship be abandoned."

"The yawl lay across the main hatch. This was unsecured while a section of the port rail, which you no doubt saw is missing, was removed. There was no time for a leisurely departure; everything was done in a few minutes. The yawl was lowered without tackle, and the main peak-halyard was unroven. It was used as a towline for the yawl with an end still attached to the gaff."

(The gaff was the spar upon which the head of a fore-and-aft sail was extended. The halyard was about four hundred feet long, and where it was fastened to the gaff it would be about eight feet above the deck.)

"The captain took the ship's papers, chronometer, and sextant. A sailor tried to get a compass; that is why the binnacle is displaced and the compass was broken in the haste to extract it. There was no time to get the other compass. The ship had drifted too close to the rocks.

"At this point, Head refused to get into the yawl with the others. He believed that his only chance of survival lay in using the distorter.

If he were in the yawl, he would have to leave behind both the distorter and witnesses. He could, of course, shoot the nine people in the boat, but his revolver held only six cartridges at a time, and he might be overpowered before he could reload or perhaps even before he had finished firing. He decided to take his chances on the ship itself. If he could get the attention of . . . of one of us who had a distorter, he could be transmitted. Still better, if he could get enough men transmitted to the *Mary Celeste* and the calm did not last, then he could sail it to Europe."

Why, Fogg wondered, had Head taken passage on a brigantine as a cook and steward and not proceeded to Europe by a steam liner? Was it because he thought that the Eridaneans would be looking for him on the passenger ships? Had he hoped to slip across on this sailing ship, quit or desert at Gibraltar, and from thence go in disguise to England? What was he carrying that was so valuable? The distorter? That was certainly valuable enough, but why had he not waited in America until the Chinese agent got to England so he could transmit himself to there? Another Capellean could have brought the distorter at a later time. If it were the distorter itself that was responsible for all this secrecy and haste, he could understand Head's actions. But he felt that there was some other reason.

Stuart, if he were aware of Head's existence and his mission, would have set his people to look for Head. Because of the overstrict security system, he had not informed Fogg of this. Or, perhaps, all this had started after Fogg left England and Stuart had not been able to get news of this through to him.

Fogg determined to make another search of Head's body before he left the cabin.

Nemo said, "Captain Briggs raved when Head refused to get into the yawl. He called him a coward and a mutineer and threatened him with all the consequences of mutiny. But there was little he could do and no time to do it in if he could do it. The yawl departed and presently was at the end of the towline. Briggs was waiting to see what would happen. If a breeze arose in time, the ship would sail away from the shoals. The yawl would be rowed up to it while the line was taken in, and the *Mary Celeste* could be boarded. He must also have thought that Head, to regain favor and get any charges dropped, would steer the ship and give any other assistance he could.

"But a wind did arise, filling the square sails, and the ship moved away from the shoals. It was however, going westward in a direction opposite to its original course. The towline became taut and was pulled at an angle away from the ship. It broke. The yawl, though rowed desperately toward the ship, could not catch up."

"And why didn't Head bring the ship about?" Fogg said.

"Because he was afraid that he could not depend on Briggs' gratitude. Briggs was a stern New England skipper who would probably arrest him and charge him with mutiny even if Head had saved the whole company."

Was Nemo telling the whole truth? Had the sudden strain really snapped the towline? Or had Head severed it to make sure that Briggs would not get back aboard? By the time the yawl made land or its passengers were picked up by another ship—if they did not perish before this at sea—Head would be long gone.

As for the story of the panicky and premature abandonment; that could be true enough. About two hundred and thirty-two derelicts were found every year. Sometimes, the crews were picked up by other ships. Sometimes, they were never seen again. Sometimes, the reasons for the hasty desertions were unknown. A fire, an explosion, too much water in the hold. Sometimes, no reasons could be found by the investigators.

The case of the *Mary Celeste* was only one of many—if it were ever found. Many ships were just swallowed up by the ocean.

"The ship went through several squalls, hence the damage to the sails and the wetness of the floors and garments in some of the cabins," Nemo said. "There was little that Head could do about them, and they were not serious. He was mainly concerned with making contact with our people who had distorters. He did not even bother shutting the doors or the fore and lazaret hatches though he did wash the dishes.

"He was beginning to despair, because if a violent storm did hit the ship, it would surely go down with him aboard."

"He will despair no more," Fogg said.

Fogg told Nemo to wait a few minutes before the truce arrangements were put into effect. This delay would upset Nemo, who would wonder what Fogg was up to. Fogg did not worry about this. He only wanted time for another inspection of the corpse.

Being a very tidy man, he cleaned up the blood on the floor with a piece of canvas. Later, he would use sea water to remove all traces of blood from the floor and water and lemon juice to cleanse the sword. The latter he would put back in its scabbard under the captain's bed. Fogg wished to leave the ship much as he had found it.

He stripped the body, felt the clothes, and then ripped them open with his jackknife. He found nothing in them. The boots were taken apart, but these revealed nothing. Head seemed to have all his original teeth; there were no caps concealing hollows in which objects could be kept. With some repugnance, he probed the anal cavity but found it to be only as nature intended it.

Possibly, the skin bore schematics or writing in some type of invisible ink. He had no means to bring these out. Should he drop the body into the sea or take it back to the *General Grant* for more tests? There was bound to be a hullabaloo because of the three series of clangings, and when these sounded for the fourth time, announcing his arrival, more uproar would ensue. Every cabin might be searched, and it would be more than embarrassing to try to explain Head's corpse.

Before finishing his examination, he pulled on the corpse's hair again to make sure that a shaved head with a code on it was not below a wig. Head's hair seemed to be his own.

Fogg arose and went to the doorway. He declared that he was ready to start disarmament proceedings. Passepartout thoroughly frisked Nemo while Nemo held his revolver at Passepartout's head. The Frenchman announced that Nemo seemed not to have concealed any weapons since the inspection on the *General Grant*.

Nemo frisked Passepartout with the same results.

Passepartout then moved away, stopping when he came to the railing.

Nemo grasped the barrel of his Colt in his right hand, which retained enough strength for this task. He prepared to eject the cartridges from the magazine. Fogg threw the sword and jackknife and Head's knife outside. He stood in the doorway, holding his revolver by the barrel. Together, as Passepartout slowly counted, the two got rid of their cartridges.

Fogg stepped outside onto the deck, his cartridges in one hand. Nemo backed away until he was by the starboard railing. Fogg backed away to the port railing. At a signal from Passepartout, both men, one by one, in unison, tossed their cartridges into the sea. Fogg had removed his coat and shirt before coming out of the deckhouse to ensure that he would not be able to palm any cartridges. This was unnecessary, since the cartridges could be seen sailing away over and into the sea.

Passepartout threw the knives into the ocean. Nemo had permitted the Frenchman to do this because he did not think he was in a condition to hurt him even if Passepartout did come at him with a knife.

Nemo had wanted the sword to go overboard, too, but Fogg had insisted that all articles aboard were to be restored to their original positions, except for Head, of course.

This was a ticklish moment. Nemo could make a dash for the sword. If Passepartout picked it up first, Nemo thought he could dodge the first feeble slash and close in with Passepartout. Even if Passepartout threw it overboard, Nemo would have the others at a disadvantage. Wounded though he was, and still suffering a strong headache from the two blows on his head, he felt that he was physically superior to the combination of the others.

It was then that Fogg reminded him that Aouda was waiting at the other end with the cyanide expeller. She had orders to use it if Nemo appeared alone.

Despite all this, Nemo suddenly decided that he would attempt to overpower them. If he could get Fogg over the railing and into the sea, he could deal easily enough with the Frenchman. He would not kill him, because he might need him to transmit the proper code to Aouda. But there were many ways to make him yield that information. And if Passepartout should somehow refuse, or die, then he would send a message to the man from China. The fellow surely must be listening by now. Or, if that failed, he would turn the ship around toward the east again and hope that another ship would sight the *Mary Celeste*.

It was at this moment that Nemo was stricken with a fit of shaking. Whether it was the first time or not, we do not know. Fogg was startled, because he had not observed anything like this while serving under Nemo. From later accounts by another Briton, the fits became more numerous and one phase of them became permanent. What the nature of the disease was, no one knows. Perhaps his neural charges, restrained too long, damped a part of his brain.

In any event, on this occasion Nemo began shaking violently all over. This lasted for about a minute, after which he seemed to regain a partial control. Now only his head, with the face thrust forward, oscillated in a curiously snake-like fashion. This, with his high domed forehead and the large widely spaced eyes, made him look like a king cobra.

After perhaps sixty seconds, the nervous motion ceased. He had become even paler, and he looked very weary. He passed his hands over his eyes and groaned loudly enough for Passepartout to hear him.

"Great God! Enough! Enough!"

Then he said, "I can't do it!"

Neither of the Eridaneans knew what he meant by this, but we may deduce that he had planned a final attack on them but now realized that he could not carry it out.

Passepartout took the sword to the captain's cabin, cleaned it as required by Fogg, and put it back in its scabbard under the bed. When he returned, he found that neither Fogg nor Nemo had moved.

The next step was to dispose of Head's corpse and clothing. Nemo had recovered enough to assist with this. While Fogg held the feet of the body, Nemo supported the other end with one arm. He failed to let loose of the corpse at the same time as Fogg, and, for a second or so, his hand passed over Head's face. Fogg thought nothing of this incident except that it indicated Nemo's sickness and consequent lack of coordination.

The fo'c'sle was cleaned up so that no traces of blood remained. Fogg brought an open box from the lazaret. He placed it upside-down on the deck. This was near the opening in the port rail left by its removal for access of the yawl. Its underside held the distorter, set for *transmit* in three minutes.

The three crowded upon the box and linked arms. Fogg was counting on either the roll of the ship sending it into the water after the weight on it was relieved or heavy seas carrying it off. He hoped that the transmission would take place before the three men were precipitated off the box by the ship's rolling. He had given Aouda more instructions, and she, using the watch which Fogg had purchased for her in Hong Kong, timed the action exactly right. She turned her distorter on about six seconds before Fogg's began operation. The three, accompanied by the ear-paining clangings, appeared on top of the table in Aouda's cabin.

Aouda had thrust the end of the expeller up toward Nemo's face. He made no motion until told by Fogg that he could leave. He looked slightly surprised, as if he had expected that, now he was outnumbered, he would be taken prisoner again. Certainly, if the situation had been reversed, he would have taken advantage of it. He bowed and walked out of the cabin into a crowd of near-hysterical passengers.

Since they could not hear yet, Fogg and Aouda communicated with pencil and paper.

Yes, Aouda wrote, there had been much running about and screaming. After a while, most of the passengers, chattering loudly but over their panic, had returned to their cabins. Some had stayed on deck; some had repaired to the bar, which was opened at their insistence.

The two series of clangings which had followed Fogg's activation of the distorter to fool the Capelleans had brought everybody boiling onto the decks again. Some passengers had insisted that the center of the noise was in the cabins near Aouda's. Yes, a passenger check had been made, and an officer had talked with her through the door. Yes, she had overheard the discovery of the shattered lock on Fogg's door, and crewmen had been searching for him. But in this turmoil, who could find whom? The broken lock could be attributed to the efforts of a thief to get into Fogg's cabin while the panic was on.

Fogg thought that it was unfortunate that this could not be kept out of the newspapers. Both Capelleans and Eridaneans, reading of the mysterious bell-like noises on the *General Grant* would know that the distorters had been used. They would be watching the ship when it discharged its passengers.

The reader is doubtless wondering why Verne did not describe the mysterious noises. The answer is that he would have if Fogg had been in any way connected with them by the authorities. Or, if there had been a logical explanation for the noises, Verne might have included them. But since the bell-like sounds were only one more of the many mysteries of the sea, Verne, as a disciplined novelist, did not see why he should include the incident. If he had included every interesting, but irrelevant, event, *Around the World in Eighty Days* would have been twice as long.

It is also possible that Verne never even heard about the clangings.

Late the next day, Passepartout met Mr. Fix on the promenade of the forward deck. Though somewhat pale and shaky, Fix had regained most of his strength. Nemo had told him all that had happened. Fix, Nemo said, was to continue to play innocent. He must say nothing of his sickness to Passepartout, who would guess that was why Fix had not accompanied Nemo.

Fix told Passepartout that he had been sleeping peacefully until the first of those terrible belling noises awakened him. What did Mr. Passepartout know about these?

The Frenchman said he knew no more than anybody else. After some small talk and some large drinks, he returned to Fogg. Perhaps, he said, Fix was only a detective.

Fogg replied that could well be. And now, would he sit down with Miss Jejeebhoy and hear what Fogg knew about Nemo? There was no sense in keeping it secret any longer, if, indeed, there had ever been any sense in it. They should understand what sort of man they were up against.

In 1865, Fogg had been summoned by the chief to a secret meeting. He, Fogg, had been on a long mission in the eastern Mediterranean. But he had been replaced by another and told to hurry to London. That he was to have a *tête-à-tête* with the chief and not get his orders via cards or other means indicated the seriousness of the situation. On a train to Paris, Fogg was surprised to see the chief enter his compartment. The chief said he had reason to believe that the proposed meeting place was under Capellean surveillance. So he had intercepted Fogg in France.

The chief had learned that the man called Nemo (no one knew his true name) was about to launch a very disturbing project. The word "launch" was used in a double sense, since this project involved a submersible vessel. After the vessel had been built, it would venture onto the seas on a pirating expedition.

"Ah, the *Nautilus!*" Passepartout said. He, like most of the world, had read in 1869 Professor Pierre Arronax's narrative, edited and agented by the everbusy Jules Verne.

Fogg continued. "This Nemo has an inventive genius which is, alas, not dedicated to the world's good. It has been devoted to the good of the Capelleans, of course, who rationalized that the goal justifies the means.

"Nemo had almost completed the submersible vessel, which was far beyond anything else in its scientific advances. Part of the ingenious devices which enabled it to operate derived from knowledge handed down by the Old Ones. The rest was due to Nemo's almost superhuman intelligence. The submersible would bring in an enormous amount of wealth, both from looting ships and recovering sunken treasure. With this at their disposal, the Capelleans could make much more effective war on us. For one thing, they could hire great numbers of criminals to use against us. These, of course, would not know the ultimate identity of their employers, but they would not need to do so."

"I never suspected that the *Nautilus* was of Capellean origin!" Passepartout cried. "But Arronax's account makes him out to be a hero!"

"Yes, for those who have not read the account carefully," Fogg said. "A close reading soon evaporates the clouds of the Byronic hero which Nemo managed to gather about himself. He was, to put it simply, a pirate. A bloodthirsty money-hungry pirate who sent hundreds of the innocent to a watery grave. It is evident that he kept Professor Arronax, his valet, Conseil, and the harpooner, Ned Land, alive only because of his need for intellectual companionship and to feed his ego. Conseil and Land were not his mental equals, but if Nemo had killed them, Arronax would have refused to talk to him.

"Nemo, as I said, is a mathematical and engineering genius. But even he, if he were only an Earthling, could not have designed and built the motors to drive the *Nautilus* at fifty miles per hour or have created the metal alloys to withstand the pressure of the ocean at forty-eight-thousand feet. He told Arronax that it was electricity

which propelled the submersible. Was it this or the power of the atom itself that he used? In either case, he must have had access to some information handed down by the Capellean Old Ones. From this he deduced the rest, though it took a great genius to do that.

"One of our spies learned of the orders Nemo had placed with various industries all over the civilized world, including the States. After all, the Americans, whatever their other deficiencies, are splendid engineers. Nemo was bringing these specially made parts to a remote island and putting them together there. Our chief told me to get admitted into Nemo's confidence and to sabotage the vessel. I obeyed the first and expected to be able to do the second. Through certain channels, I learned that Nemo was recruiting a crew from different countries. Most of these, poor deluded fellows, were patriots. They came from countries which lay under the heels of oppressors. Nemo told them that he would be waging a deadly war against the oppressors. He hinted that he himself came from a land which was suffering under British rule. To make it appear that he was an Asiatic Indian, he wore glass lenses which gave his eyes a black color, and he often talked as if he had been exiled from his native country after an unsuccessful revolt against the British.

"He even had a common ship's language which he taught the crew to master enough to obey commands in this tongue. This, I believe, was the dialect of Bundelcund. Nemo had spent much time in Bundelcund, a good part of it as the aide to the rajah before the rajah became a traitor to the Capelleans. In fact, I would not be surprised to learn that Nemo had talked the rajah into becoming a renegade. Nemo's motto should be, not *Mobilis in mobili*, the swift among the swift, but *Aut Nemo aut nemo*. Either Nemo or nobody.

"Be that as it may, I was enlisted as Patrick M'Guire, an Irishman who hated the English. I was part of the crew that terrorized the seas from 1866 through 1868. I was equally guilty of sinking all those ships, since I had to play out my role. I told myself that these would have been sunk anyway. I had to cooperate in this so that I could sooner or later stop Nemo's nefariousness. In fact, without me aboard, the *Nautilus* might operate for decades. Nevertheless, I felt guilty.

"And imagine my state when I learned, after the affair was over, that I had participated in sinking a vessel on which my own father was a passenger. I was guilty of patricide."

At this point, Aouda, tears coursing down her cheeks, put her hand on Fogg's. He did not seem to notice it. At least, he did not withdraw his hand.

"That it was not intentional did not ease my conscience one bit.

"From the time that the *Nautilus* plunged into the sea on her maiden cruise, I looked for an opportunity to sink her and with her its commander. But in those crowded quarters, where a dozen eyes are always on you, I had no chance. After we rammed the USS *Abraham Lincoln*, we picked up Arronax and his companions. Events went much as the professor described them, though much happened of which he was ignorant.

"And then we were pulled into the maelstrom off the Lofoten Islands. Even that mighty whirlpool might not have defeated us if I had not had my first chance to act. While the others were occupied at their posts, and frozen with the terror of the maelstrom, I destroyed the circuits which controlled the steering."

"Ah, then it was you who was responsible for sinking that accursed submersible!" Passepartout said.

He had completely abandoned his original concept of Nemo as a battler against evil, a tortured and lonely genius whose only mission in life was revenge against the oppressor.

"Yes. But I should have blown it up long before that, even though it meant that I, too, should die. Arronax, Conseil, and Land, as you know, escaped. So did I. So did Nemo. Perhaps others did. I do not know. I thought at the time that I was the only survivor. Several months later, I was back in London. The chief and I assumed that Nemo had died. Then I saw him on the second of October in the shade of that doorway near the Reform Club."

"But," Passepartout said, "is this man all bad? What about the portrait of the woman and two children which Arronax said hung on the wall of Nemo's cabin? Did not the good professor see Nemo stretch out his arms to the portrait, kneel before it, and sob deeply? Does a man with no heart behave so?"

"He undoubtedly does not lack all sentiment," Fogg said. "It has been established that even the most hardened criminal may love his mother, his wife, his children, or his dog. I do not know the history of his familial connections. To tell the truth, I was surprised to learn that he had a wife and children. But I do not think that his marriage could have lasted long. His intellect is so lofty that he regards all others, man or woman, as mental pygmies. And he is an excessively imperious and moody man. Perhaps his wife left him, taking the children with her. That may be why he wept. His self-image was bruised; if anyone were to leave, it should be he.

"At any event, he did not always have the portrait on the wall. You may have noticed, in Arronax's account, that he himself observed the portrait only after being on the *Nautilus* almost a year and a half. Surely, if he had seen it before, he would have commented on it? Now I, who was aboard from the beginning, only saw it put up twice. Both times were on July second; it was a second of July when Arronax witnessed the sad scene. This date must have some significance to Nemo, but of what only he knows."

"Then, sir, if I understand you aright," Passepartout said, "Nemo was not an Indian patriot who gathered a crew from all over the world to fight oppressors. He was a pirate."

"Most of his crew were patriots, yes. But Nemo was using them. They believed that he was turning his treasures over to underground organizations to finance their revolutions. No such thing. Most of the wealth went either to the Capellean exchequer or into his own bank accounts.

"As for the portrait, the woman and children looked very European; they looked far more English than Hindu."

"But Aouda looks European."

"She could pass for a Provençal or an Italian, true."

"Pardon me, if I persist, sir," Passepartout said. "What about the professor's final scene with Captain Nemo? Did he not hear Nemo sobbing, were not his last words, 'God Omnipotent! Enough! Enough!' Did not Arronax wonder if this was an outburst of sorrow or a confession of remorse?"

"You observed the fit suffered by Nemo while we were disarming on the *Mary Celeste*? Nemo looks, and is, a giant in stature and strength. And he has, like all Capelleans, the elixir which should enable him to live to a thousand years. This, as you know, increases resistance to disease. But it does not make us invulnerable to disease. I am certain from my observations that Nemo is doomed to last no longer than most men. He is inflicted with some sort of nervous malady. Its effects have been few so far. But they will increase. And part of this affliction is an infrequent but blinding and sickening headache. Perhaps this is caused by a tumor, though I suspect that damage caused by undischarged traumas is responsible. But when he was crying out 'Enough! Enough!' he was, I believe, calling for a cessation of his pain. That he, a zealous atheist, called on God indicates the extent of his torture. And that he spoke English in this painful moment, when a man is likely to revert to his native language, is significant."

"He did not speak in French? But Arronax . . ."

"Failed to mention that it was in English. No, Nemo is a native of some English-speaking land, most probably of Ireland. He could speak Gaelic fluently when talking to one of his Irish crewmen, though it was evident that it was not the speech he learned from his parents. I, though, posing as an Irishman, claimed to be from Dublin and ignorant of all but a few phrases of the Celtic."

"Poor man!" Aouda said. "To be suffering so and thus doomed to die early when he could live to a thousand years! Indeed, the elixir will only prolong his agonies. Without it, he would die in a few years, his sufferings mercifully ended."

"Do not waste sympathy on him," Fogg said. "Nor allow his sickness to cause you to underestimate him. We must be on guard the rest of our voyage on this ship. I do not trust him not to break his oath to us to keep the peace until we land at San Francisco."

Nemo

CHAPTER XXV

WHICH GIVES A SLIGHT GLIMPSE OF SAN FRANCISCO.
A PUBLIC MEETING

It was seven in the morning when Mr. Fogg, Aouda, and Passepartout, set foot on the American continent, if the floating quay on which they disembarked could be so called; these landing places, rising and falling with the tide, rendered the loading and discharging of vessels more easy. Clippers of all sizes lay along them, steamers from all countries, and those saloon boats with several decks, which ply up and down the Sacramento and its tributaries. There are collected the productions of a commerce which extends to Mexico, Chile, Peru, Brazil, Europe, Asia, and all the islands in the Pacific.

Passepartout, in his joy on touching American soil, at last thought he would show his agility by springing out of the boat, but when his foot touched the landing stage it went through a rotten plank. He was rather mortified at the manner in which he set foot on the new continent, and gave such a shout that it frightened away the flock of pelicans and cormorants which usually occupied those places.

Mr. Fogg, as soon as he landed, inquired at what hour the first train started for New York. It was at six in the evening. Thus Mr. Fogg had a whole day to spend in visiting San Francisco. He sent for a carriage for Aouda and himself. Passepartout mounted the box, and the vehicle drove off to the International Hotel. From his seat Passepartout looked with great curiosity at this vast American city; wide streets, the low, but regularly-built houses, churches, and other places of worship in the Anglo-Saxon style of architecture; immense docks, warehouses like palaces, some in wood, others in brick; innumerable vehicles in the streets, omnibuses, tramway cars, and not only Americans and Europeans on the pavement, but Chinese and Indians, altogether composing a population of more than two hundred thousand inhabitants. Passepartout was surprised at what he saw. The legendary city of 1849 was no more, the city of bandits, incendiaries, and assassins, crowded thither in quest of plunder, a vast rendezvous of all the outlaws of the world, where they gambled for gold dust, with a revolver in one hand and a bowie knife in the other. But those "fine old times" were gone. San Francisco now presented the appearance of a great commercial city; the lofty tower of the City Hall, whence the night watchmen can overlook the whole town, commanded a view of all the streets and avenues, cutting one another at right angles; among which appeared squares, green with trees and shrubs, and then a Chinese town, which seemed to have been imported from the celestial empire like a box of toys; no more sombreros, no more miners in scarlet shirts in quest of "placers," no more natives with feathers in their hair, were now visible; but in their place silk hats and black coats, worn by gentlemen, active and busy. Certain streets, among others Montgomery Street—what Regent Street is to London, the Boulevard des Italiens to Paris, and Broadway to New York—were lined with splendid shops, displaying in their windows the products of the whole world.

When Passepartout reached the International Hotel it seemed as if he had never left London. The ground floor was occupied by an immense bar, a sort of buffet, which offered, gratis, to all comers, dried beef, oyster soup, cheese and biscuits, &c., payment was only made for what was drank, ale, port, or sherry. That seemed very American to Passepartout.

The hotel restaurant was very comfortable. Mr. Fogg and Aouda sat down at a table and were served abundantly with Lilliputian dishes by the hotel's waiters.

After dinner Phileas Fogg, accompanied by Aouda, left the hotel, in order to go to the consul's office and have the official *visa* inscribed on his passport. On the pavement he found his servant, who asked him if it would not be prudent to buy a few Enfield rifles and Colt's revolvers before starting. Passepartout had heard talk of Sioux and Pawnee, who are in the habit of stopping trains like the Spanish brigands. Mr. Fogg replied it was a useless precaution, but left him to do as he thought proper. He then went off to the consul's office.

Phileas Fogg had not proceeded two hundred yards when, "by the greatest possible chance," he met Fix. The police agent testified his extreme astonishment. What! Mr. Fogg and he had crossed the Pacific together and they had not met! Under any circumstances it was an honour for Fix to meet a gentleman to whom he was so much indebted, and as his affairs required his presence in Europe he should be enchanted to continue his journey with so pleasant a companion.

Mr. Fogg replied the honour would be his, and Fix—who was anxious not to lose sight of him—asked permission to accompany them in their visit to the place, which was of course granted.

So Aouda, Fogg, and Fix took a walk through the streets; they soon found themselves in Montgomery Street, where the traffic was enormous—on the pavement, in the middle of the road, on the tramways, in spite of the perpetual circulation of carriages and omnibuses, at the shop doors, at the windows of all the houses, and even on the roofs, were numbers of people. Men were walking about carrying large placards among the different groups. Banners and streamers were fluttering in the wind. Every one was shouting out—

"Hurrah for Camerfield!"

"Hurrah for Mandiboy!"

It was a public meeting, such, at least, was the idea of Fix, and he communicated his idea to Mr. Fogg, adding—

"Perhaps we shall do well, sir, to keep out of this crowd—there is nothing to be met with there but blows."

"True," said Phileas Fogg, "and though they may be political they are nevertheless blows."

Fix smiled at this observation, and in order to look on without being incommoded, Aouda, Fogg, and he took their stations on the top of a flight of steps leading from a terrace at the upper end of Montgomery Street. Opposite them on the other side of the street was a large open air office, between a coal wharf and a petroleum store, towards which the different streams of people seemed to set. And what was the object of the meeting? What was its purpose? Phileas Fogg was absolutely ignorant. Was it a question of appointing some great civil or military functionary, a governor, or a member of congress? One would be justified in thinking so on seeing the extraordinary agitation in which the crowd was.

At this moment there was a great stir in the crowd, every hand seemed in the air; some, tightly shut, seemed to rise and disappear again in the midst of shouts—a very energetic method of voting.

"This is evidently some public meeting," said Fix, "and the question at issue must be of some importance. I should not be surprised if it had something to do with the Alabama question, though that has been settled."

"Perhaps so," replied Mr. Fogg.

"At all events there are two champions in the field, the Honourable Mr. Camerfield and the Honourable Mr. Mandiboy."

Aouda, hanging on the arm of Phileas Fogg, surveyed this tumultuous scene with the greatest surprise, and Fix went and inquired of some one standing by what was the cause of it, when a more decided movement took place. Hurrahs, abuse, frantic shouts, and blows began to be exchanged. Banner staves became offensive weapons, shoes and boots were flying in the air, and a revolver or two added their reports to the vociferations of the crowd.

The mob was approaching the steps and had reached the lower ones. One of the parties was evidently repulsed, but the lookers-on could not tell whether the advantage remained with Mandiboy or Camerfield.

"I think we had better get away," said Fix, who was anxious Mr. Fogg should not be hurt or got into trouble. "If there is any question about England connected with this row, we might be seriously compromised."

"No English citizen—" began Mr, Fogg. But he had no time to finish his sentence. Behind him a fearful struggle now began, and there were frantic shouts of—

"Hurrah, hip—hip—hip! hurrah! for Mandiboy!"

It was a band of voters coming to the rescue, and taking the Camerfield party in flank. Mr. Fogg, Aouda, and Fix found themselves between two fires. It was too late to retreat. Such a torrent of men, armed with loaded canes and life-preservers, was irresistible. Phileas Fogg and Fix, in trying to protect the young lady, were roughly hustled. Mr. Fogg, phlegmatic as ever, tried to defend himself with the weapons with which nature has armed every Englishman, but with no effect. An immense fellow, with a red beard and red face, who seemed the leader of the band, raised his fist to strike Mr. Fogg, and would have seriously injured him if Fix, in his anxiety to save him, had not received the blow in his place. An enormous bump immediately appeared under the detective's hat, which was completely crushed.

"Yankee!" cried Fogg, giving his adversary a look of supreme contempt.

"Englishman!" returned the other.

"We shall meet again."

"When you please. Your name?"

"Phileas Fogg. Yours?"

"Colonel Stamp Proctor."

The tide swept on. Fix was knocked down, but got on his legs again; his clothes were torn, but he had received no serious injury. His paletot had been torn up the middle of his back, and his trousers resembled those worn by certain Indians who begin by cutting the bottoms off. Fortunately, Aouda had received no injury, and Fix alone was any the worse.

"Thanks," said Mr. Fogg, to the detective, as soon as they became clear of the crowd.

"Do not mention it," replied Fix, "let us go this way."

"Where?" asked Mr. Fogg.

"To a tailor."

A very necessary visit. The clothes of both were in rags, as if they had been fighting on account of the two honourables, Mandiboy and Camerfield.

An hour afterwards they returned to their hotel with new hats and coats.

There Passepartout was waiting for his master with half-a-dozen central fire spring bayonet revolvers. When he saw Fix with Mr. Fogg he frowned, but Aouda having told him in a few words what had happened, Passepartout's brow grew smooth again. Fix, it was clear, was no longer an enemy. He kept his word.

After dinner a coach was sent for to convey the party and their baggage to the station. Just as they got into the vehicle, Mr. Fogg said to Fix—

"Have you seen anything of Colonel Stamp Proctor?"

"Nothing," replied Fix.

"I shall return to America and look for him," said Phileas Fogg, very coolly. "It is not proper that an English citizen should be treated in that manner."

The police agent smiled, but made no reply. But one might see Mr. Fogg was one of those Englishmen who, if they will not tolerate duelling at home, will fight abroad when their honour is concerned.

At a quarter to six the travellers were at the station, and found the train ready to start. Just as Mr. Fogg was about to step into the carriage he noticed one of the railway officials close by, so he said to him—

The Full Account

"My friend, was there not a disturbance at San Francisco today?"

"There was a public meeting," replied the official.

"But I fancied I noticed a certain degree of excitement in the streets."

"It was only a meeting held on account of an election."

"The election of a commander-in-chief, at least," said Mr. Fogg,

"No, sir, of a police magistrate."

At this Phileas Fogg got into the carriage, and the train started.

The Other Log of Phileas Fogg

Mr. Fogg, as soon as he landed in San Francisco, learned that the next train for New York City left at six in the evening that day. He took rooms for the three in a hotel and then started out for the British consulate with Aouda. He had gone only a few steps from the hotel when he ran into Passepartout. The Frenchman was waiting for him so he could get permission to buy some Enfield rifles and Colt revolvers. Verne says the Frenchman wanted them in case they were attacked by Indians en route to the American Midwest. Both he and Fogg, of course, were thinking more of the defense against the Capelleans than against the Sioux or Pawnee.

A few paces further on, Fogg met, "by the greatest chance in the world," Mr. Fix. The detective pretended great surprise. Could it be true that he and Mr. Fogg had crossed the Pacific Ocean together and not once encountered each other? Since Fix owed Mr. Fogg so much, he would like to accompany him. Could he go with him on his tour of this pleasant American city, so agreeably Old-Worldish in many aspects?

Mr. Fogg said that he would be honored, and Fix went with the two. On Montgomery Street, the three ran into a great crowd. Every place was jammed with people yelling and screaming slogans and carrying big posters and flags.

"Hooray for Camerfield!"

"Hooray for Mandiboy!"

Fix said that it was a political meeting and hence to be avoided. Americans got violent when they encountered opposition to their political beliefs, and the two parties were out in force today. Mr. Fogg may have thought that the same could be said for Englishmen—and it was true in those days—but he did not say so. Instead, he made another of his classical remarks.

"Yes, and blows, even if they are political, are still blows."

Shortly thereafter, a fight did break out. The three British subjects found themselves caught between the Camerfieldians and the Mandiboyans. Most of these were armed with canes loaded with lead or billies, and a few had revolvers. Fists, canes, billies, cudgels, and booted feet were used vigorously and, often, indiscriminately. The trio was standing on top of a flight of steps at the street's upper end but found this position no guarantee of safety. The tide of ruffians swept them off the steps.

Fogg used his fists to protect Aouda. A large muscular chap with a red face and an even redder beard aimed a blow at Fogg. Fix stepped in and took the fist. His knees gave way, along with his silk hat. He staggered back up onto his feet but with glazed eyes. He was destined to carry a large lump on top of his head for the next few days.

"Yankee!" Fogg said, looking contemptuously at the red-bearded rogue.

"Englishman! We'll meet again!"

"When you please," Fogg said.

"What is your name, sirrah?" the American said.

"Phileas Fogg. And yours?"

"Colonel Stamp Proctor."

The avalanche of bodies stormed by. Fogg thanked the detective for his noble interpositioning. Neither was badly hurt, though the clothes of both looked as if they had jumped off a train going at sixty miles per hour. Aouda was, if not untouched, unbruised.

The three repaired to a tailor shop. One hour later, they were back at the hotel in new clothes. On the way, Fogg considered the incident with the colonel. Perhaps he was only a Frisco bully. But that name, Stamp Proctor! Could he be the Capellean proctor, the supervisor, the monitor, of the U.S.A. for the enemy? Did the Stamp indicate that another of his functions was the assassination, the stamping out, of Eridaneans? Or was his name only a coincidence? Nemo had said that the Capelleans were abandoning the old custom of using functional names. Nemo, however, was a liar. And even if he were telling the truth, the reform might not yet have been put into effect.

He told himself that he should not have taken a tour but should have remained, as was his habit, in his room. And why had he broken this habit? He had wanted to show Aouda the city.

Fogg also thought about Fix. He had rushed in to take the blow meant for him. Why would he do this if he were a Capellean? Was it to convince Fogg that he was only an Englishman who would defend another Englishman in Yankeeland? This did not seem likely. If Proctor were a Capellean, he would not want his efforts frustrated. Fix, in fact, should have helped Proctor.

But he had not. On the contrary.

After dinner, Fogg said to Fix, "Have you seen this Proctor again?"

"No."

"I will return to America to find him," Fogg said calmly. "It would not be right for an Englishman to permit himself to be treated in that manner without retaliation."

Fix smiled but did not reply. Fogg wondered what he was thinking. As for his speech, it was true enough. After this was over, he would be back looking for the colonel. As an Englishman, he would have done it for the sake of honor. As an Eridanean, he would be doing it to eliminate a Capellean—if Proctor were such.

CHAPTER XXVI

IN WHICH THEY TRAVEL BY AN EXPRESS TRAIN
ON THE PACIFIC RAILWAY

O cean to Ocean"—as the Americans express it, and these three words ought to be the general designation of the Grand Trunk line, which traverses the United States of America at their greatest width. But in reality the Pacific railway is divided into two distinct parts, the Central Pacific, between San Francisco and Ogden, and the Union Pacific, between Ogden and Omaha—there are five distinct lines which put Omaha in frequent communication with New York.

In former days, under the most favourable circumstances, a traveller would be six months going from New York to San Francisco. Now it takes seven days.

New York and San Francisco are thus united by an uninterrupted metal ribbon, which is not less than three thousand seven hundred and eighty-six miles long. Between Omaha and the Pacific the line runs through a district still full of Indians and wild beasts—a vast extent of territory which the Mormons began to colonize in 1845, after they had been driven from Illinois. It was in 1862 that, in spite of the opposition of the Southern members, who wanted a more southerly route, that it was decided the line should run between the forty-first and forty-second parallel.

President Lincoln, of lamented memory, himself fixed

the end of the new series of lines at the town of Omaha, in the State of Nebraska. The works were begun and carried on with that activity so peculiarly American when free from the trammels of law courts and offices. The rapidity of the work did not affect its being well executed. On the prairies they advanced at the rate of a mile and a half per day. A locomotive, running on rails laid the evening before, brought up the rails for the next day, and worked along them as fast as they were laid. The Pacific Railroad throws out several branch lines in its course in Iowa, Kansas, Colorado, and Oregon. When it leaves Omaha, it runs along the left bank of the Platte river to the junction of its northern branch, follows the southern branch, crosses the Laramie territory and the Wahsatch mountains, turns Salt Lake, arrives at Salt Lake City, the Mormon capital, plunges into the Tuilla Valley, skirts the American desert, Cedar and Humboldt mountains, the Sierra Nevada, and descends by Sacramento to the Pacific without a gradient on the whole line exceeding one hundred and twelve feet per mile, even in crossing the Rocky Mountains.

Such was the long artery which the trains ran over in the space of one week, and which would enable Phileas Fogg — he hoped so, at least — to take the Atlantic steamer at New York on the 11th of December for Liverpool.

The carriage in which Phileas Fogg found himself was a sort of long omnibus on eight wheels, and so arranged as to be able to run on sharp curves. There were no compartments in the interior, two rows of seats with a passage between them leading to dressing rooms, with which every carriage is provided. The carriages communicated with each other the whole length of the train, and the travellers could move to and fro, and visit the saloon, balcony, restaurant, and cafe cars. There were no theatre cars as yet, but their time will come some day.

Boys selling books and newspapers, and sellers of liquors, eatables, and cigars were in no want of customers.

The train had left Oakland Station at six in the

evening. It was now night—a cold, gloomy night, with a sky threatening snow. The train was not going very fast, including stoppages not more than twenty miles an hour, at which rate, however, it might reach Omaha within its time. There was not much conversation in the car, and soon the travellers fell asleep. Passepartout was close to the police agent, but he did not speak to him. Since their quarrel their relations with one another had cooled considerably; sympathy and intimacy had vanished. Fix was just the same as he always had been, but Passepartout kept a reserved attitude, ready to strangle his former friend on the least suspicion of treachery. About an hour after the train left the station it began to snow; the snow, however, was so fine it could not obstruct the train. They could only distinguish through the windows an immense white sheet, against which the curls of steam seemed grey. At eight a steward entered the car and informed the travellers it was time to turn in—the carriage was a sleeping car, which in a few minutes was transformed into a dormitory. The backs of the seats were folded back, mattresses ingeniously stowed away were unrolled, berths were improvised in a few moments, and every traveller soon had a comfortable bed, protected from the eye of curiosity by thick curtains, at his service. The sheets were white and the pillows soft. All they had to do was to lie down and go to sleep, which they all did, just as if they were in a steamer's cabin, while the train sped along across the State of California.

There is little irregularity in that part of the territory which lies between San Francisco and Sacramento. This part of the line, under the name of the "Central Pacific" road, first started from Sacramento and advanced eastward to meet that coming from Omaha. From San Francisco to the capital of California, the line ran directly north-east along the American river which empties itself into San Pablo Bay. The hundred and twenty miles between these important rivers were accomplished in six hours, and towards midnight while in their first sleep the travellers passed through Sacramento—consequently they saw nothing of this important city, the seat of the legislature of the State of California, nor its fine quays, nor its broad streets, nor its splendid hotels, its squares, and its churches.

The train in quitting Sacramento, after passing the junction, Rochin, Auburn, and Colfax stations, entered the defiles of the Sierra Nevada. It was seven in the morning when they passed through Cisco station. An hour later and the dormitory was an ordinary car once more, and the travellers could catch glimpses through the windows of the picturesque points of this mountainous region. The railway track followed the windings of the Sierra, here, clinging to the mountains' sides, there impending over precipices, avoiding abrupt angles by the boldness of its curves, and plunging into narrow gorges which seemed to have no issues. The locomotive lighted up like a shrine, with its great lantern, its shrill bell and its cow-catcher, mingled its shrieks and bellowings with the noises of cascades and torrents, and entwined its smoke with the black branches of the firs.

There were few or no tunnels or bridges along the line—it wound along the sides of the mountains, not doing violence to nature by trying to discover the shortest road by the straightest line.

About nine the train penetrated the State of Nevada by the Carson Valley, always keeping in a north-easterly direction. At twelve it left Reno, where the travellers had been allowed twenty minutes for lunch.

From that point the railroad running along Humboldt River rose towards the north for several miles as it follows its course, then it bends eastward and did not leave the river again till it reached the Humboldt ranges, where it has its source, almost at the eastern extremity of Nevada State.

After lunching, Aouda, Mr. Fogg and his companions took their places again in the car, and watched at their ease the varied landscape passing before their eyes—extensive prairies—mountains showing their profiles against the horizon—creeks with their foaming eddies. Sometimes a herd of bisons seemed at a distance like a moving dam. These numerous armies of ruminating beasts often offer an insurmountable obstacle to the advance of a train—thousands of these animals have been seen to spend several hours in crossing the line in compact ranks; the locomotive is then obliged to wait until the line is free.

This was just what happened now, around noon a herd of ten or twelve thousand buffaloes blocked the line. The engine after decreasing its speed tried to make use of its cow-catcher, but the crowd of cattle was so dense it was obliged to stop.

They could see these buffaloes, as the Americans incorrectly call them, marching along with a slow step, sometimes bellowing alarmingly. They stand higher than the bulls of Europe, with short legs and tails, a very high shoulder, wide horns, and the head, neck, and shoulders covered with a long mane. It is useless to try and stop or divert their course, when they have once taken a particular direction. They form a torrent of living flesh which no dam could restrain. The travellers standing on the platforms gazed at this strange spectacle. But the man of them all who had the least time to lose, Phileas Fogg, kept his seat, and philosophically waited until it would please the buffaloes to allow him to pass. Passepartout of course was furious at the delay caused by these animals—he wanted to discharge his arsenal of revolvers at them.

"What a country!" cried he; "trains actually stopped by nothing but cattle, and there they go in procession without hurrying themselves in the least. I should like to know if Mr. Fogg had allowed for this in his programme! and the engine driver who is afraid to send his locomotive into this herd of cattle."

The engine driver was too wise to try to overcome such an obstacle—he might have crushed the first buffalo in two with his cow-catcher, but, however powerful the engine might be, it must have been thrown off the line, and the train would have been in distress.

The best they could do was to wait patiently, and make up for lost time by increased speed. The passage of the buffaloes lasted three long hours, and the line was only free by nightfall—the last ranks of the buffaloes were crossing the line as the leaders were disappearing on the southern horizon.

It was eight when the train cleared the Humboldt ranges, and half-past nine when it entered Utah territory, the region of the great Salt Lake, the strange country of the Mormons.

CHAPTER XXVII

IN WHICH PASSEPARTOUT LISTENS TO A
SERMON ON MORMONISM, PREACHED AT THE
RATE OF TWENTY MILES AN HOUR

During the night of the 5th of December, the train continued in a south-easterly direction for about fifty miles; then for about the same distance it bore to the north-east, as it approached the great Salt Lake.

About nine in the morning Passepartout went out to take the air on the platform. The weather was cold, the sky grey, but the snow had ceased. The disc of the sun, looking larger in the mist, seemed an enormous piece of gold, and Passepartout was trying to calculate its value in pounds sterling, when he was diverted from that useful occupation by the appearance of a very strange person. This personage, who had taken the train at Elko station, was a tall dark man, with black moustaches, black stockings, black silk hat, and black trousers, white cravat, and dog-skin gloves—he might have been a clergyman. He went from one end of the train to the other, and over the door of every car he wafered a written notice.

Passepartout went and read one of these notices, which informed the public that the Elder William Hitch, Mormon missionary on train No. 48, would hold a conference on Mormonism from eleven to noon in car No. 117; inviting all those gentlemen to attend who desired to be instructed in the mysteries of the Latter-day Saints.

"I shall certainly go," thought Passepartout, who knew nothing about Mormonism but its practice of polygamy, the basis of Mormon society.

The news soon spread in the train, which contained about a hundred passengers. Of this number, thirty, at most, attracted by the advertisement, took their seats at eleven o'clock on the benches of car No. 117.

Passepartout figured in the front row of the faithful. Neither his master nor Fix thought it worth the trouble.

At the hour appointed William Hitch rose, and in an irritated tone, as if he had been contradicted already, exclaimed—

"I tell you Joe Smith is a martyr, his brother Hiram is a martyr, and the persecutions of the prophet by the government of the Union, will make a martyr of Brigham Young also! Who dares to contradict me?"

No one dared to contradict the missionary, whose excitement was a strong contrast with his naturally calm expression. But his anger was doubtless explained by the fact that Mormonism was then subjected to some severe trials. For the United States government had just reduced these independent fanatics, but not without some trouble. It had made itself master of Utah, and had forced it to submit to the laws of the Union, after having imprisoned Brigham Young on a charge of rebellion and polygamy.

Since then the prophet's disciples redoubled their efforts, and, until the time came for action, resisted by words the authority of Congress.

Thus Elder Hitch practised proselytism even on the railway.

Then he related the history of Mormonism from Biblical times, giving force to his words by the tones of his voice and extravagance of his gestures. How, in Israel, a Mormon prophet of the tribe of Joseph published the annals of the new religion, and left them by will to his son Mormon; how, many ages later, a translation of this precious book, written in the Egyptian character, was made by Joseph

Smith, junior, a Vermont farmer, who revealed himself as the mystical prophet, in 1825; how, in fact, a heavenly messenger appeared to him in a forest blazing with celestial light, and committed to his hands the annals of the Lord.

At this moment some of the audience, who did not much care about the missionary's retrospective account, left the car; but William Hitch continued, informing them how Smith, junior, with his father, his two brothers, and a few disciples, founded the religion of the Latter-day Saints; a religion which not only in America, but in England, Scandinavia, and Germany, could count among the faithful, artisans, and a number of persons belonging to the liberal professions; how a colony had been founded in Ohio; how a temple had been built at an expense of two hundred thousand dollars, and a town also at Kirkland; how Smith became a banker, and received a papyrus containing an account written by the hand of Abraham, and other celebrated Egyptians, from an itinerant exhibitor of mummies.

This tale was getting rather tedious, and the audience became somewhat thinner; the public now did not consist of more than twenty persons.

But the elder did not trouble himself about this, and he went on to tell them how Joe Smith became a bankrupt in 1837; how his ruined creditors tarred and feathered him; how, some years after, he was living more honourable, and more honoured than ever, at Independence, in Missouri, the head of a flourishing community, which reckoned no less than three thousand disciples, and then, pursued by the hatred of the Gentiles, he had fled into the Far West.

There were still ten of his hearers left, among them honest Passepartout, who was listening with both ears open. They then were told how Smith, after a long persecution, reappeared in Illinois, and founded, in 1839, Nauvoo-la-Belle, on the borders of the Mississippi, the population of which consisted of twenty-five thousand souls; how Smith made himself mayor, supreme judge, and commander-in-chief; how, in 1843, he declared himself a candidate for the presidency of the United States, and how, at last, being drawn into an ambuscade at Carthage, he was thrown into prison, and assassinated by a band of men in masks.

By this time Passepartout was absolutely the only hearer left; the elder, looking him in the face, and fascinating him by his words, reminded him that, two years after Smith's murder, his successor, the inspired prophet, Brigham Young, abandoning Nauvoo, came and established himself on the shores of the Salt Lake, and there, on that wonderful territory, in the middle of that fertile district, on the road followed by the emigrants, who crossed Utah, on their way to California, the new colony, thanks to the polygamous principles of Mormonism, increased enormously.

"And that is the reason," added William Hitch, "why the jealousy of Congress is aroused against us—why the soldiers of the Union have invaded the soil of Utah—why our prophet and chief, Brigham Young, has been thrown into prison in scorn of all justice! Shall we yield to force? Never! Driven from Vermont, Illinois, Ohio, Missouri, and Utah, we shall still find some independent territory where we can fix our tents—and you, my faithful hearer," added the elder, looking sternly at his only auditor, "will you set up your own there under the shadow of our flag?"

"No," bravely answered Passepartout, retreating in his turn, and leaving the enthusiast preaching to himself.

During the discourse the train had made rapid way, and about half-past twelve it reached the north-west point of the great Salt Lake. There one could embrace, at one glance, the aspect of this inland sea, which is also called the Dead Sea, and into which an American Jordan empties itself. A beautiful lake, a wild, rocky frame, encrusted with white salt; a splendid sheet of water, which once covered a much more considerable space, but with time its shores, encroaching by degrees on its extent, have increased its depth.

Salt Lake is about seventy miles long and thirty-five wide, and lies three thousand eight hundred feet above the level of the sea, very different from Lake Asphaltite, whose depression is twelve hundred feet below the sea level; it contains much salt, and its waters hold a fourth of their weight of solid matter in solution; their specific weight being one thousand one hundred and seventy, and after distillation one thousand. Fish cannot live in it, and those brought down by the Jordan, Weber, and other streams, soon die; but it is not true that its waters are so dense that a man could not sink. Around the lake the country was admirably cultivated, for the Mormons are good agriculturists; ranchos and corrals for domestic animals, fields of corn, maize, Indian millet, luxuriant meadows, everywhere hedges of wild roses, clumps of acacias, and euphorbium; such would have been the appearance of the country six months later; at present the earth was covered with a thick layer of snow.

At two o'clock the travellers descended at Ogden Station. As the train would not start till six Mr. Fogg, Aouda, and their two companions had time to visit the City of the Saints, by the branch line from Ogden. Two hours sufficed to visit this entirely American city, and as such, built on the model of all the towns in the Union; like chess boards, with "the solemn sadness of right angles," as Victor Hugo expresses it.

The founder of the City of the Saints could not shake off that feeling for symmetry which distinguishes the Anglo-Saxons. In this singular country, where the men are certainly not up to the level of their institutions, everything is done on the square, towns, homes, and follies.

At three then the travellers were walking about the streets of the city, which is built between the banks of the Jordan and the foot of the Wahsatch Mountains. They noticed there were few or no churches, but as public buildings, the prophet's residence, the court-house, and the arsenal; and houses of bluish bricks, with verandahs and galleries, and surrounded by gardens, bordered by acacias, palms, and locust trees. A wall, constructed of clay and pebbles, surrounded the town. In the principal street, where the market was held, were a few hotels, with flags flying from them, and among others, Salt Lake House.

Mr. Fogg did not find the city very populous. The streets were nearly empty, except near the temple, which they only reached after traversing several quarters surrounded by palisades. Women were tolerably numerous, which is explained by the singular domestic arrangement of the Mormons. But it must not be supposed that all Mormons practice polygamy. They are free to do so or not, but it must be observed that female Mormons are most anxious to marry, as according to their religion the Mormon Heaven admits no unmarried females. These poor creatures seemed neither at their ease nor happy; some of the wealthier wore a black silk open jacket, under a cloak or shawl of unpretending appearance; the others were only dressed in calico.

Passepartout could not help looking at these female Mormons, several of whom were charged with the felicity of one Mormon husband, without a certain degree of fright. According to his idea the husband was the most to be pitied. It seemed terrible to have to guide so many of these ladies through the breakers of life, and to lead them in a body to the Mormon paradise, with the prospect of meeting them there again in company with the glorious Smith, who ought to be the chief ornament of that delightful spot. He certainly felt no vocation for it, and he fancied, perhaps wrongly, that the female citizens of great Salt Lake City cast rather alarming glances at him.

Fortunately, they could not stay much longer in the City of the Saints. At four o'clock the party found themselves again at the station, and took their seats in the car. The whistle was sounded for starting, but just as the driving wheels of the engine began to turn, they heard cries of, "Stop, stop!" Trains stop for no one. The gentleman calling was evidently a Mormon behind his time. He ran till he lost his breath. Fortunately for him there were no gates or barricades to the station. He rushed on to the rails, jumped on the steps of the last car and rolled exhausted on to one of the benches. Passepartout, who had been watching this performance with great interest, came and looked at him, when he learned that he had taken flight in consequence of a domestic scene.

When the Mormon had recovered his power of speech, Passepartout took the liberty of inquiring very politely how many wives he had; for from the manner in which he had decamped he gave him credit for having at least twenty.

"One, sir," replied the Mormon, raising his hand to heaven, "one, and that was enough."

CHAPTER XXVIII

IN WHICH PASSEPARTOUT CANNOT SUCCEED IN
MAKING PEOPLE LISTEN TO REASON

On leaving Salt Lake at Ogden Station, the train tore for an hour as far north as Weber River, having run over nine hundred miles since it left San Francisco. From this point it took an easterly direction through the irregular wooded depths of the Wahsatch Mountains. It was in this part of the territory, lying between these and the Rocky Mountains properly so called, that the American engineers had to encounter their most serious difficulties; consequently, on this part of the line the Government subsidy rose to forty-eight thousand dollars a mile, while it was no more than sixteen thousand on the plains; but the engineers, as has been before observed, temporised with nature instead of affronting her, turning difficulties instead of overcoming them, and thus, to reach the great basin, only one tunnel, fourteen thousand feet long, has been driven in the whole length of the time.

Up to that time the track had reached its highest point of elevation at Salt Lake. Thence it described a lengthened curve, dropping down to Bitter Creek Valley, and rising again to the point which divides the waters of the Pacific from the waters of the Atlantic. There were numerous creeks in this mountainous region. It was necessary to cross Muddy Creek, Green Creek, and others often in boats. Passepartout was becoming more impatient the nearer they reached their goal, but Fix wished they were already out of this difficult district. He dreaded every delay, and was in a greater hurry than even Phileas Fogg to set foot on English soil.

At ten in the evening the train stopped at Fort Bridger station, and twenty miles farther on it entered Wyoming State—the ancient Dacotah— following the whole length of Bitter Creek Valley, whence part of its waters escape, forming the hydrographic system of the Colorado.

The next day, the 7th of December, they stopped for a quarter of an hour at Green River station. Plenty of snow had fallen during the night, but as it mixed with the rain, it could not impede the progress of the train. Nevertheless the unfavourable weather rendered Passepartout uneasy, for the accumulated snow, by blocking the wheels of the cars, would certainly have once more endangered Mr. Fogg's success.

"What an idea!" thought he, "to travel in winter! Why could he not have waited for the fine season, to increase his chance?"

But while the good fellow was only thinking of the state of the weather, and the fall in the temperature, Aouda was much more frightened, and from a very different cause.

Now several passengers had got down from the cars at Green River and were walking about the platform, waiting for the train to start, and through the window the young lady had recognised Colonel Stamp Proctor, the American who had so grossly insulted Phileas Fogg at the San Francisco election.

As Aouda did not wish to be seen, she drew back from the window. This circumstance had a great effect on the young woman. She had attached herself to the man who, cold as he might be, gave her every day unmistakable signs of devotion. She hardly knew herself, perhaps, the depth of the sentiment with which her protector had inspired her, and this sentiment, which she fancied was only gratitude, was far more than that. Her heart, therefore, sank within her when she recognised the coarse personage whom sooner or later Mr. Fogg intended to call to account for his conduct. It was evidently only chance which had thrown Colonel Proctor in their way again, but there he was, and it was necessary, at all events, to prevent Phileas Fogg catching a glimpse of his antagonist.

When the train went on, Aouda, taking advantage of a moment when Mr. Fogg was asleep, put Passepartout and Fix in possession of the state of things.

"Is that fellow Proctor in the train?" cried Fix. "Well, madam, before he has anything to say to that—to Mr. Fogg, he must settle with me. I think I was by far the most insulted of the two."

"And besides," remarked Passepartout, "I will take him off your hands, Colonel though he may be."

"Mr. Fix," replied Aouda, "Mr. Fogg would allow no one to fight his quarrels. He told me he should return to America to find this man again. If he sees Colonel Proctor we cannot prevent a meeting, which might have a deplorable result. He must not see him!"

"You are quite right, madam," replied Fix. "A meeting would ruin all. Victorious or not, Mr. Fogg would be delayed, and—"

"And," added Passepartout, "that would be to play the Reform Club's game. In four days we shall be in New York! Well, if for four days my master does not leave the car, we may trust that chance will not bring him face to face with that cursed American. Now we must contrive to prevent—"

The conversation ceased, for Mr. Fogg woke up, and was looking out of the window, flecked with snow, at the landscape.

But soon after, and without being overheard either by Aouda or his master, Passepartout said to the detective—

"Would you really fight on his account?"

"I would do everything to bring him back to Europe alive," quietly replied Fix, in a tone which showed his resolution to do what he said.

Passepartout felt a shiver run through him, but his trust in his master never wavered.

And now how was Mr. Fogg to be kept in the compartment, to prevent a meeting between the colonel and himself? It was not very difficult, as he was naturally not much inclined to stir, and very little curious. The detective, however, thought he had hit on a plan, for some moments after he said to Phileas Fogg—

"Time passes slowly, sir, in the train."

"Just so," replied Mr. Fogg, "but it does pass."

"On board the steamers," resumed the police agent, "you used to play at whist."

"Yes," replied Fogg, "but it would be difficult to do so here, for we have neither cards nor players."

"As for cards we can buy them easily—they sell them in all the trains in America. As for partners, if that lady—"

"Certainly, sir," replied Aouda quickly; "I can play at whist. It forms part of a young Englishwoman's education."

"And I," returned Fix, "have the reputation of being a tolerable player. Now, we three and a dummy—"

"As you please, sir," replied Phileas Fogg, delighted to resume his favourite game, even in the train.

Passepartout was dispatched to find the cards, and soon returned with two packs, counters, and a table covered with cloth. The game began; Aouda knew enough of the game to play tolerably, and she even was complimented by Mr. Fogg. The police agent was a very good player and quite a match for Mr. Fogg.

"Now," said Passepartout to himself, "we have him—he will stay where he is."

At eleven in the morning the train had reached the point which separates the waters of the two oceans, at Bridger Pass, a height of seven thousand five hundred and twenty-four feet above the level of the sea, one of the highest points attained by the line in crossing the Rocky Mountains. After going about two hundred miles further, travellers would find themselves at last on those widely extended plains which reach to the Atlantic, and which nature has made so favourable to the construction of a railroad.

On the declivity of the Atlantic basin the first rivers, branches, or affluents, of the North Platte River showed themselves. The whole northern and eastern horizon was bounded by this immense semi-circular curtain which forms the northern part of the Rocky Mountains, overlooked by Laramie Peak. Between this bend and the railway lie wide, well-watered plains. On the right rose the first slopes of a mountainous mass which stretches about southward to the sources of the Arkansas River, one of the great tributaries of the Missouri.

At half-past twelve the travellers caught a glimpse of Fort Halleck which commands this region. A few hours more and the Rocky Mountains would be crossed. It might be hoped now that no accident would attend the passage of the train through this difficult country. It had ceased to snow. It was a dry frost. Large birds, frightened by the engine, flew off into space; no wolves, no bears were to be seen on the plains. It was a vast and naked desert.

After a comfortable lunch served in their own car, Mr. Fogg and his partners had just recommenced their game, when several shrill whistles were heard and the train stopped.

Passepartout put his head out of the door, and could see nothing to cause a stoppage—there was no station in sight.

Aouda and Fix were afraid for a moment that Mr. Fogg would get out of the car, but contented himself with saying to his servant—"Go and see what is the matter."

Passepartout jumped out of the car. About forty passengers had already left their seats, and among them was Colonel Stamp Proctor.

The train had stopped at red signal, which blocked the line. The driver and the guard were talking rather excitedly with the signalman who had been sent on to meet them, by the station master at Medicine Bow, the next stopping-place; some of the passengers came up and took part in the discussion. Among others the said Colonel Proctor, with his loud voice and insolent manner.

Passepartout, who had joined the group, heard the signalman say—

"No, you cannot go on—the bridge at Medicine Bow is shaken and could not support the weight of the train."

The bridge in question was a suspension bridge across a rapid about a mile from the place where the train had stopped. From what the signalman said it was in a ruinous state, several of the rods being broken, and it was impossible to risk crossing it. He did not at all exaggerate when he said they dared not attempt it. Besides, careless as Americans usually are, when they take it into their heads to be prudent, it would be madness not to be so.

"I say," cried Colonel Proctor, "I suppose we are not going to stay here and take root in the snow?"

"Colonel," replied the guard, they have telegraphed to Omaha station to send us a train, but it is not likely to be here in less than six hours."

"Six hours!" ejaculated Passepartout.

"Yes, about six hours," returned the guard; "besides it will take us all that time to walk to the station."

"But it is only a mile off," said one of the passengers.

"Yes, about a mile, but on the other side of the river."

"And cannot we cross it in a boat?" asked the colonel.

"Impossible! the creek is swollen by the rains. It is a rapid, and we shall have to go ten miles round to the north to find a ford."

The colonel let fly a volley of execrations, now at the company, then at the guard, and Passepartout was in such a rage he could not help chiming in with him.

This was a material obstacle, which set all his master's bank notes at defiance. Disappointment was general among the passengers, who, without taking delay into account, saw themselves obliged to walk fifteen miles across a plain, covered with snow. There was great noise and grumbling, which would certainly have attracted Phileas Fogg's attention had he not been absorbed in his game.

Passepartout found himself under the necessity of informing his master, and, with his head down, he was turning back to the car, when the engine-driver, a true Yankee, named Forster, called out—

"Gentlemen, perhaps there's a way of getting over it."

"Over the bridge?" asked a passenger.

"Over the bridge."

"With the train?" asked the colonel.

"With the train."

Passepartout had stopped, and was listening to the engine-driver.

"But they say the bridge is dangerous," put in the guard.

"Never mind," replied Forster, "I think by sending the train at it at top speed we might have a chance of getting across."

The devil! thought Passepartout.

A certain number of passengers were immediately attracted by this suggestion. Colonel Proctor was particularly pleased at it; he thought it very practicable. He called to mind that engineers had once proposed to cross rivers without bridges, merely by sending trains at full speed, &c., and at last many of those interested in question took the engine-driver's side of the question.

"We have fifty chances out of a hundred of crossing," cried one.

"Sixty," said another.

"Eighty, ninety, to a hundred."

Passepartout was astounded; though he was ready to do anything to effect the passage of Medicine Creek, he thought this suggestion a little too American. "Besides," thought he, "there is something still more simple which might be done, and these people have never even thought of it."

"Sir," said he, to one of the passengers, "the engine-driver's proposal seems rather hazardous, but—"

"Eighty chances to a hundred," replied the passenger, turning his back on him.

"I am well aware of it," said Passepartout, turning to another, "but a simple idea—"

"Ideas are useless," replied the American addressed, shrugging his shoulders. "Since the engine-driver says we can cross, we shall cross."

"No doubt," replied Passepartout, "we shall cross, but perhaps it would be prudent—"

"What! prudent!" cried Colonel Proctor, roused by the word used. "At full speed, don't you hear, at full speed!"

"I know—I understand," repeated Passepartout, who never had a chance of finishing his sentence, "but it would be more prudent, or, if the word shocks you, more natural—"

"Who? what? how? what is that fellow talking about?" they cried out all around him.

The poor fellow did not know whom he could get to listen to him.

"Are you afraid?" asked the Colonel.

"I afraid!" cried Passepartout. "Well, let us go. I will show these fellows a Frenchman can be as American as they are."

"Take your seats!" cried the guard.

"Oh, yes; take your seats directly! But nothing shall prevent my thinking it would have been more natural if we had first crossed the bridge on foot, and the train had followed us."

But nobody heard this sensible observation, and nobody would have acknowledged it was a reasonable one if they had. The travellers had taken their seats. Passepartout sat without mentioning what had happened. The whist players were still intent on their game. The locomotive gave a shrill whistle. The engine-driver backed his engine for more than a mile—like a man taking a run before he jumps. Then a second whistle; he began to move forward; went faster; the speed became something frightful; nothing was audible but the panting of the engine; the pistons worked twenty strokes to the second; the axles smoked in their boxes. One could feel the train was flying along at the rate of a hundred miles an hour, and hardly touched the rails at all. Speed had the best of weight, and they got over! It was like a flash of lightning—they saw nothing of the bridge. The train jumped, one might say, from one bank to the other, and the driver could only stop his engine five miles beyond the station.

The train had hardly cleared the river before the bridge, completely ruined, fell with a crash into the rapids of Medicine Creek.

CHAPTER XXIX

IN WHICH DIVERS INCIDENTS ARE RELATED WHICH ARE
ONLY MET WITH ON THE UNITED STATES RAILROADS

That same evening the train continued its route unimpeded, passed Fort Landers, and through the Cheyenne Pass and reached Evans Pass. This was the highest point on the line, eight thousand and ninety-one feet above the ocean level. The travellers had now only to descend to the Atlantic, across these boundless plains levelled by nature.

A branch from the grand trunk line led to Denver, the capital of Colorado. This territory is rich in gold and silver mines, and has already more than fifty thousand inhabitants.

They had now accomplished thirteen hundred and eighty-two miles from San Francisco in three days and three nights. In all probability four days and four nights would give them time to arrive in New York. Thus, Phileas Fogg was not behind time. In the night Walbach Camp was passed on the left. Lodge Pole Creek ran parallel with the line following the straight boundary line between the states of Wyoming and Colorado. At eleven they entered the Nebraska territory, passed near Sedgwick, and touched at Julesburg on the southern branch of the Platte River.

It was at this point that the Union Pacific Railroad was inaugurated on the 23rd of October, 1867, of which General

J. M. Dodge was engineer-in-chief. Here two powerful locomotives stopped, drawing nine carriages of guests, among whom were Mr. Thomas C. Durant, the vice-president. Cheers were given, and the Siouxes and Pawnees gave a scene of Indian warfare; there was a discharge of fireworks; and the first number of a journal called the *Railway Pioneer* was printed at a portable press. Thus was celebrated the inauguration of this grand line, an instrument of progress and civilisation flung across the desert, destined to form a link between cities and towns which as yet had no existence. The whistle of the locomotive, more mighty than the lyre of Amphion, would soon cause them to rise from the soil of America.

At eight in the morning Fort MacPherson was left behind. Three hundred and fifty-seven miles lay between this point and Omaha. The railway followed the windings of the southern branch of the Platte River. At nine they came to the important town of North Platte, built between those two arms of that great stream, which meet round here and thence form one single artery, a considerable tributary to the Missouri, whose waters it runs into a little above Omaha.

The one hundred and first meridian was passed. Mr. Fogg and his partner had recommenced their game. No one complained of the length of the journey, not even the dummy. Fix had begun by winning several guineas, which he was on the point of losing again, but he was not less absorbed in his game than Mr. Fogg. That morning the latter had been singularly fortunate. He held trumps and honours repeatedly. At a certain moment, after having determined to play a bold game, he was just about to play a spade, when from behind his seat he heard a voice say—

"I should play diamonds."

Mr. Fogg, Aouda, and Fix looked up. Colonel Proctor was standing close to them. Stamp Proctor and Phileas Fogg recognised one another immediately.

"Ah, it is you, Englishman, is it, who was going to play a spade?" cried the Colonel.

"And who does play a spade!" coolly replied Phileas Fogg, throwing down the ten.

"Well, I chose it should be diamonds," returned Colonel Proctor, in a tone of impertinence.

And he made an effort to take up the card played, adding—

"You know nothing about the game."

"Perhaps I may be a better hand at another," said Phileas Fogg, rising.

"You can try if you like, son of John Bull," replied the Colonel, in a bullying tone.

Aouda turned pale. She seized Phileas Fogg by the arm, who gently shook her off. Passepartout was ready to spring on the American, who was staring at his antagonist most insolently. But Fix had risen, and going up to Colonel Proctor, said:

"You forget you have to deal with me first. You not only insulted, but struck me."

"I beg your pardon, Mr. Fix," said Fogg, "this quarrel is mine only. By asserting that I was wrong to play a spade the Colonel has insulted me afresh, and he must give me satisfaction for it."

"When you like—when you like—and with what arms you like."

Aouda tried in vain to restrain Mr. Fogg, and the police agent was equally unsuccessful in transferring the quarrel to himself. Passepartout would have thrown the American out of the carriage, but a sign from his master quieted him. Phileas Fogg left the car, and the American followed him on to the balcony.

"Sir," cried Mr. Fogg, to his adversary, "I am in a great hurry to return to Europe, and any delay would be very prejudicial to my interests."

"Well! what is that to me?" replied Colonel Proctor.

"Sir," continued Mr. Fogg with great politeness, "after our meeting at San Francisco, it was my intention to have returned to America and sought you out, as soon as I had finished the business which now requires my presence on the Old Continent."

"Indeed!"

"Will you give me a meeting in six months?"

"Why don't you say in six years?"

"I said six months, and I shall be punctual at the place of meeting."

"You want to shuffle out of it," said Stamp Proctor; "at once or not at all."

"Very well," returned Mr. Fogg; "are you going to New York?"

"No."

"To Chicago?"

"No."

"To Omaha?"

"That is no business of yours; do you know Plum Creek?"

"No," replied Mr. Fogg.

"It is the next station we come to. The train will be there in an hour. It stops there for ten minutes. In that time we can exchange a few shots."

"Very well," said Mr. Fogg, "I will get out at Plum Creek."

"And I think you may chance to stop there," added the American, brutally.

"Who knows!" returned Mr. Fogg, and he turned to the car, as cool as before.

There he began to reassure Aouda, telling her such braggarts were never dangerous.

Then he begged Fix to be his second in the meeting about to take place. Fix could not refuse, and Phileas Fogg went on with the interrupted game, and played a spade with the greatest calmness and self-possession.

At eleven the whistle of the engine announced their approach to Plum Creek station. Mr. Fogg rose, followed by Fix, and went out on the balcony, followed by Passepartout carrying a pair of revolvers. Aouda remained in the carriage as pale as death. At that moment the door of another car opened and Colonel Proctor showed himself, followed by his second, a Yankee of the same stamp as himself. But just as they were about to step down on the line the guard ran up and called out—

"No one gets down here!"

"Why not?" asked the Colonel.

"We are twenty minutes behind time, and the train doesn't stop."

"But I am going to fight with this gentleman."

"Sorry for it," returned the guard, "but we start again immediately: there is the bell ringing now."

The bell was ringing, and the train started.

"I am really very sorry, gentlemen," said the guard, "and under any other circumstances I should have been glad to have obliged you. But, as you have not had time to fight here, why not fight as we go?"

"That might not suit this gentleman," observed the Colonel with a sneer.

"Perfectly," returned Mr. Fogg, "perfectly."

"We are all of us in America after all," thought Passepartout; "and the guard of the train is a perfect gentleman."

And he followed his master.

The two principals and their seconds, preceded by the guard, passed through the cars to the last on the line, in which there were not more than ten or a dozen travellers. The guard asked them to have the goodness to leave the car free for a few minutes to two gentlemen, who had an affair of honour to settle.

Of course the travellers were too happy to be agreeable to the two gentlemen, and they retired into the balconies.

The car being about fifty feet long was very well suited to their purpose. The two antagonists could walk up the middle between the seats and fire at one another as they chose. There never was a duel more easily arranged. Mr. Fogg and Colonel Proctor, each armed with a six-shooter revolver, entered the car; their seconds, who remained outside, closed the door. At the first whistle of the engine they were at liberty to fire. Then after a space of two minutes what remained of these two gentlemen would be removed from the car. Nothing could be more simple; so very simple that Fix and Passepartout could hear their own hearts beat.

They were waiting for the signal agreed upon, when suddenly savage yells were heard followed by pistol shots, but which did not proceed from the duellists' car. On the contrary, the reports were repeated from the front part of the train all along its line — while cries of terror proceeded from the interior of the cars.

Colonel Proctor and Mr. Fogg, revolver in hand, immediately hurried from the car, and rushed to the front, where the struggle and noise was greatest.

They were not long in perceiving the train was attacked by a band of Sioux.

This was not the first attempt of those bold marauders. They had stopped the trains more than once before. According to their usual plan about a hundred had jumped on the steps without waiting for the train to stop, and clambered into the cars like a clown at a circus springing on to a horse at full gallop.

These Sioux were armed with guns from which the reports came, and to which the travellers, who were nearly all armed, replied with pistol shots. The Indians had first got upon the engine; they had half killed the engine driver and stoker with blows from their clubs. A Sioux chief tried to stop the train, but, being ignorant how the regulator ought to be handled, had let on the steam instead of shutting it off, and the engine was flying along at increased speed.

At the same time the Sioux had invaded the cars; they climbed along the roofs, broke open the doors, and fought hand to hand with the travellers. They flung the trunks and baggage of the passengers on the line, broke them open and plundered them. The yells and shots never ceased.

But the passengers defended themselves bravely. Some

of the cars were barricaded, and were besieged like moving fortresses, carried along all the time a hundred miles an hour.

From the beginning of the attack Aouda had shown great courage. With a revolver in her hand she defended herself boldly, firing through the broken windows at every attacker who showed himself. About twenty Sioux, mortally wounded or killed, had fallen on the line, the wheels of the cars crushing those who fell out of the balconies on the rails. Several passengers were lying on the benches severely wounded, either by gun-shots or by blows from the Sioux clubs.

An end, however, must be put to the struggle, which had lasted ten minutes, and could not fail to end in favour of the Indians if the train was not stopped. Fort Kearney station was not more than two miles distant, where there was an American detachment, but if they passed it, before they could reach the next the Sioux would have possession of the train.

The guard was fighting by Mr. Fogg's side when he was brought down by a ball. As he fell he called out—

"We are all lost if the train is not stopped within five minutes."

"It shall be stopped," said Phileas Fogg, preparing to quit the car in which he was.

"Stay where you are, sir!" cried Passepartout, "this is my business."

Phileas Fogg had no time to stop him. He opened one of the doors, and succeeded, unseen by the Indians, in crawling under a car; then, while the balls were flying about above his head, he crept from one car to the next, hanging on by the chains, helping himself along by the brakes, and thus reached the first car of the train.

Then, hanging on by one hand, between the luggage van and the tender, he unhooked the coupling chains, but could not succeed in unscrewing the bar which joined the carriages to one another, if a sudden jump of the engine had not broken it, and the train, detached from the flying engine, remained by degrees behind.

The train still moved on for several moments from its own impetus, but the brakes were applied from the interior of the cars, and at last it stopped within a hundred yards of Kearney station.

The soldiers hurried up, attracted by the firing. But the Sioux did not wait for them, and before the train had stopped the whole band had decamped.

But when the passengers were counted on the station platform several were found to be missing, among them the courageous Frenchman, whose devotion had just saved their lives.

The Other Log of Phileas Fogg

There were 3,786 miles of railway to be traversed from San Francisco to New York City. Between the ocean and Omaha, Nebraska, the railroad passed through a rugged land dangerous with beasts and wilder Indians. Part of the territory was occupied by the Mormons, a comparatively peaceful people, though regarded by most Gentiles of that time as uncivilized. The train, averaging only twenty miles per hour because of the many stops, would take seven days for the journey. That is, it would if buffalo, natives, storms, floods, washouts, breakdowns, and avalanches did not interfere. If the schedule were met, however, Fogg would arrive on the eleventh of December to catch the steamer from New York for Liverpool, England.

At eight o'clock, in the midst of falling snow, the car in which Fogg and party rode was converted into a dormitory. At noon of the next day, the train stopped for a lunch break of twenty minutes at Reno, Nevada. At twelve o'clock, the train was forced to stop until nightfall to let a vast procession of buffalo cross the tracks. At thirty minutes after nine in the evening, the train crossed into Utah.

On the night of the fifth of December, the train was about a hundred miles from the Great Salt Lake. Though Fogg was not aware of it, this was the day that the brigantine *Dei Gratia* discovered the

Mary Celeste sailing along without a soul aboard. If Head had trusted to his luck, he would have been put aboard the *Dei Gratia* and would, on the twelfth of December, have disembarked at Gibraltar. It is true that he would have been held up by a court of inquiry, but he could have escaped. Thus it would have added one more element of mystery to a case that has puzzled savants and the public and originated many false stories for a hundred years. Even the name of the ship is known to most people as the *Marie Celeste*. This error is no mystery, however. This derives from an incorrect notation in the New York City pilotage record of the seventh of November, 1872. The error was even perpetuated in the archives of the U.S. State Department, and the American newspapers continued to use the false name.

Perhaps the most influential in spreading this error was A. Conan Doyle, who refers to the ship as the *Marie Celeste* throughout his well-known story, "J. Habakuk Jephson's Statement."

On the seventh of December, the train halted for fifteen minutes at the Green River Station in the Wyoming Territory. Several passengers got off to unlimber their legs. Aouda, looking through the window, became alarmed. She had seen Colonel Stamp Proctor on the platform.

Verne says that it was only chance which brought Proctor on the train, but we know better. Verne also says that Fix, Aouda, and Passepartout conspired to keep Fogg from learning that the colonel was a passenger on another car. This was one of Verne's novelistic insertions. Aouda, in fact, woke Fogg up to tell him about Proctor.

Fogg merely asked if Aouda and Fix could play whist, and they were soon playing.

Aouda, using the cards as code transmitters, asked Fogg what he intended to do about Proctor. Fogg replied, "Nothing—for the moment."

"Why not, if I may ask?"

"The time and place are not appropriate."

The train soon bore them over the Rockies through snow. Some distance past Fort Halleck, the train unexpectedly stopped. The alarmed passengers, with the exception of Fogg, poured out. They discovered the engineer and conductor talking to a signalman. He had been sent from Medicine Bow, the next stopping place, to halt the train. A suspension bridge over some rapids was in too ruinous a condition for the train to chance crossing it.

An American, Forster, proposed that the train back up so it could get a running start. If it gained enough speed, it would practically jump over the bridge.

After some hesitation, the passengers, with one exception, agreed. Passepartout, using the logic that distinguishes the true Gaul, asked why the passengers did not walk over the bridge? Why ride on the train, which might be precipitated into the abyss?

He was overruled by all and so rode trembling while the train, going a hundred miles an hour, shot across the perilous stretch. No sooner had the rear wheels of the rear car passed onto land than the bridge, with a great noise, fell into the chasm.

Passepartout, wiping his brow, thought that there must be something in the air of this continent that made all its inhabitants mad.

The whist game was resumed. When the train was in Nebraska, a voice familiar to three of the players spoke behind them.

"I should play a diamond!"

It was Proctor, who pretended that he had not recognized the Englishman until that moment.

"Ah, it's you, the limey? It's you who're going to play a spade?"

"And who does play it," Fogg said, throwing down the ten of spades.

"Well, it pleases me to have it be diamonds," Proctor said. He reached out as if to grab the card, saying, "You don't know anything about whist."

"Perhaps I do, as well as another," Fogg said as he got to his feet.

Fix also rose. He said, "You forget that it is I whom you have to deal with, sir. It is I whom you not only insulted but struck."

Fogg understood what Stamp was doing. He would try to kill Fogg openly in a duel of honor. These were not uncommon in the territories, but Nebraska had been admitted as a state on the first of March, 1867. Did the state forbid duels and enforce the law with harsh penalties? It did not matter. Proctor did not seem to think that legal retribution would follow. Indeed, he was doing exactly what Fogg had expected. That was why Fogg had endured Proctor's insults and had forced him to come to him. If Fogg won and was then arrested, he could plead that he was not the aggressor.

"Pardon me, Mr. Fix," Fogg said. "This is my affair alone."

The colonel said, indifferently, that the time, place, and weapons were up to Fogg.

Out on the platform, however, Fogg did try to talk Proctor into a delay. Proctor sneeringly refused and intimated that Fogg was a coward who, once safe in England, would never dare return. Seeing that the colonel was set on having the duel now, and that he had plenty of witnesses to prove that he had tried to put off the affair, Fogg agreed to exchange shots at the next stop. Unflustered, he returned to his car. Aouda tried to talk him out of it but without success. Fogg asked Fix if he would be his second. Fix replied that he would be honored. Passepartout understood that this request was one more test of the detective.

A little past eleven in the morning, the train stopped at Plum Creek. Fogg got off, only to be told that the train could not delay more than a minute. It was twenty minutes behind schedule, and the time must be made up. Fogg got back on. The conductor then approached the two participants with the suggestion that they fight in transit.

Fogg and the colonel agreed. The duelists, their seconds, and the conductor walked to the rear car. There the conductor asked the dozen or so passengers if they would leave until the two gentlemen concluded their argument. They left, happy at some excitement relieving the tedium.

The car was fifty feet long. Fogg stood at one end; Proctor, at the other. Each held two six-shooter revolvers. The conductor left, and the two seconds closed the doors of the car. After the engineer blew the whistle of the locomotive, the two would advance toward each other, firing as they wished.

Before Fogg and Proctor could start shooting, the train was attacked by about a hundred mounted Sioux. The two duelists were the first to fire against the Indians; they agreed without a word spoken to each other to put off the duel until this peril was over. If they survived this attack, they could resume their quarrel.

As many may remember from Verne's account, some Sioux

boarded the engine and stunned the engineer and fireman. The chief of the Indians, trying to stop the train, opened instead of closed the steam valve. The train was soon roaring along at one hundred miles per hour. This made it vital that the passengers somehow stop the train at Fort Kearney. If the train went on past it for any distance, the Sioux would have time to overwhelm the passengers. Many of the Indians were aboard it now, shooting and battling hand to hand with their enemies, who were indeed palefaces at this time.

Passepartout had been frightened at the illogic of the others when they rode the train across the ruined bridge. But when logic demanded action, he cast aside his fears. Logic now required that the train be stopped in time. Bravely and expertly, since he was an acrobat, he crawled under the cars on their chains and axles. He loosened the safety chains between the baggage car and the tender, and a violent jolt drew the yoking bar out. The locomotive and coal tender soon passed out of sight while the cars rolled to a stop. The troops from Fort Kearney attacked, and the Indians fled. Unfortunately, Passepartout was carried away on the tender.

CHAPTER XXX

IN WHICH PHILEAS FOGG SIMPLY DOES HIS DUTY

Three travellers, including Passepartout, were missing. Had they been killed in the fight, or were they taken prisoners by the Sioux? No one could tell.

The wounded were numerous, but it was ascertained that none were mortally. One of the most severely wounded was Colonel Proctor, who had received a ball in the groin. He was conveyed to the station with the other travellers, whose injuries required immediate attention.

Aouda was quite unhurt. Phileas Fogg, who had exposed himself bravely, had not received a scratch. Fix was wounded in the arm, but only slightly. But Passepartout was missing, and tears filled the young widow's eyes.

All the passengers had left the train. The wheels of the carriages were blood-stained; there were fragments of flesh adhering to the spokes. The last Indians were then disappearing in a southerly direction, towards Republican River.

Mr. Fogg stood motionless, with his arms folded; he had to come to a very serious decision. Aouda, close by him, looked up in his face, without saying a word. He understood the meaning of her look.

If his servant was a prisoner, was it not his duty to risk everything to rescue him from the Indians?

"I will recover him, dead or alive," said he to Aouda.

"Ah, Mr. Fogg!" cried the young woman, taking him by the hand, which was wet with tears.

"Living," added Mr. Fogg, "if we lose not a moment."

In acting thus Phileas Fogg sacrificed himself completely. He had just pronounced sentence of ruin on himself. One day's delay must make him miss the steamer from New York to London. His bet was irrecoverably lost. But he did not hesitate to do what his heart told him was his duty.

The captain in command at Fort Kearney was there. His men—about a hundred in number—were standing to their arms in case the Sioux should make an open attack on the fort.

"Sir," said Phileas Fogg, "there are three passengers missing."

"Dead?" asked the captain.

"Dead or prisoners. It is this doubt I have to dispel. Is it your intention to pursue the Sioux?"

"This is a serious matter, sir," replied the captain. "These Indians may continue their retreat beyond the Arkansas. I dare not abandon this fort of which I am in charge!"

"Sir," insisted Fogg, "the lives of three men are in peril."

"No doubt. But can I risk the lives of fifty for the sake of three?"

"I cannot say whether you can do so, I only say you ought!"

"Sir," returned the captain, "no one here can teach me my duty."

"Be it so," said Phileas Fogg, coolly, "I shall go alone."

"You, sir," cried Fix, who had just come up, "you go alone in pursuit of the Indians?"

"Would you have me leave that poor fellow to perish, to whom all of us now living are indebted for our lives? I shall go."

"Well, you shall not go alone," cried the captain, affected, in spite of himself. "No, you are a brave man! Thirty volunteers!" he called out, turning to his men.

The whole company stepped forward. The captain chose thirty, and an old sergeant put himself at their head.

"I thank you, captain," said Mr. Fogg.

"Will you allow me to accompany you?" asked Fix.

"You must do as you think proper, sir," replied Phileas Fogg. "But if you wish to do me a service you will stay with Aouda. If anything should happen to me—"

The detective grew suddenly pale. Separate himself from the man he had followed so pertinaciously, step by step? Let him risk himself in this manner?

Fix looked at him attentively, and in spite of his precon-ceived opinion, in spite of the struggle within him between feelings and duty, his eye fell before that honest and calm look.

"I will stay with her," said he.

Mr. Fogg shook hands with Aouda, and gave her his precious bag, and then started with the sergeant and his small detachment.

Before marching he said to the men—

"My friends, there are a thousand pounds for you if you rescue the prisoners!"

It was then a few minutes past midnight.

Aouda retired to a room in the station, and there she waited, thinking of Phileas Fogg, his simple generosity and quick courage.

He had sacrificed his fortune, and now he was about to risk his life, and all that without saying a word, from a sense of duty.

In her eyes Phileas Fogg was a hero!

But Detective Fix's thoughts did not run at all in the same direction, and he could not control his agitation, as he walked feverishly up and down the platform. His feelings had momentarily got the better of him, but now he was Fix the detective again. Fogg was gone, and he saw the folly of which he had been guilty. How could he have consented to separate himself from a man he had just followed all round the world? His professional feelings came into play. He accused himself, and treated himself as if he was a superintendent of police, lecturing himself on his simplicity.

"I have been a flat," thought he. "The other fellow has told him what I was—he is off, and I shan't see him again! Where can I fall in with him? But how could I let him throw dust in my eyes in such a way? I, Fix, with an order for his arrest in my pocket! I certainly am little better than an idiot!"

So argued the police agent, while the hours crept on so slowly. He did not know what to do. Sometimes he thought he should like to tell Aouda everything. But he could see how she would receive him if he did. What course could he take? He felt tempted to set off across those white plains in pursuit of Fogg. He fancied it would not be impossible to find him again. The footsteps of the detachment were still visible in the snow. But under a fresh layer of snow all trace would soon disappear.

Then Fix became discouraged. He felt an unconquerable desire to give up the game. Now just then an opportunity of leaving the station at Kearney and of continuing his journey presented itself.

About two in the morning, while snow was falling heavily, they heard a continuous whistle coming from the east.

A great shadow, preceded by a yellow light, advanced slowly, and looming very large in the mist, which gave it a fantastic appearance.

But no train was then expected from the west. The assistance telegraphed for could not be there yet, and the train from Omaha to San Francisco could only pass the following day. It was soon explained. This engine, which came so slowly on, and whistled so continuously, was the one which after it had been released from the train had continued its rapid course, carrying with it the unconscious engine driver and stoker. After running for several miles, the fire got low, for want of fuel, the steam perforce diminished, and at last it had come to a standstill, about twenty miles beyond Fort Kearney station.

Neither driver nor stoker were killed, and after remaining for some time insensible, they recovered their senses.

The engine was standing still. When the driver found himself on the plains, and the engine all alone, without cars attached to it, he understood what had happened. How the engine had become detached from the train he could not conceive, but there was no doubt that it had remained behind, and was in distress.

The driver did not hesitate for a moment what he should do. The easier plan was to continue his course to Omaha; to return to the train which the Indians were probably still engaged in plundering, the more dangerous.

Never mind! Some wood and a few shovels full of coals were thrust into the furnace. Steam was got up, and at about two in the morning the engine made its way back to Kearney station.

It was very satisfactory for the passengers, when they saw the engine once more attached to the train. They could continue their journey, so miserably interrupted.

When the engine arrived, Aouda left the station, and addressing herself to the guard, she said—

"Are you going to start soon?"

"At once, madam."

"But the prisoners, our unfortunate companions? What is to become of them?"

"I dare not stop the train, madam," replied the guard. "We are now three hours behind time."

"And when will the next train from San Francisco be here?"

"Tomorrow evening, madam."

"Tomorrow evening! but it will be too late, then! We must wait!"

"Impossible!" returned the guard. "If you intend to go, you must get into the carriage at once."

"I shall remain here."

Fix had overheard this conversation. A few minutes before, when all chance of getting on seemed removed, he had decided on leaving Kearney station, and now that the train was ready to start, and he had only to take his seat, some irresistible influence kept him back. The platform seemed to burn his feet, and yet he could not tear himself away from it. His doubts and hesitations began over again, and his rage at having failed was choking him. He decided on carrying the contest to the end.

However, the passengers and some of the wounded, among others Colonel Proctor, who was in a critical state, had taken their seats in the cars. They could hear the humming of the heated boiler and the steam issuing from the valves. The driver blew his whistle, the train began to move on, and soon disappeared, mingling its clouds of steam with the falling snow.

Detective Fix had remained behind. Some hours passed. The weather was very bad and it was bitterly cold. Fix sat motionless on a bench in the station. Perhaps he was asleep. Aouda, in spite of the snow and wind, left the room which had been given up to her at every moment. She would go to the end of the platform and try to see through the drifting snow, and penetrate the mist which circumscribed the horizon around her, and to hear a sound. But there was nothing to be seen or heard. She would then return to the room, and brave it again a few moments later on the same fruitless errand.

Evening drew on, and the little detachment had not returned. Where could it be at that moment? Had it overtaken the Indians? Had it been in a fight or were they wandering about lost in the mist? The commandant of the fort was very anxious, though he did his best to dissimulate it.

When night came the snow ceased in some degree, but the cold became more intense. The gloomy immensity before them was sufficient to awe the most courageous. Absolute silence reigned over the plain—neither bird nor beast broke the infinite stillness.

All night Aouda, full of gloomy presentiments, wandered about the edge of the prairie. Her imagination carried her on with the band, and showed her a thousand dangers. It would not be easy to describe what she suffered during those long hours.

Fix remained motionless in the same place, but he could sleep no more. Once a man went up to him and spoke to him, but he motioned him to leave him, and only shook his head in reply.

So passed the night. At dawn the half visible disk of the sun struggled through the mist above the horizon. One could now see objects about two miles distant. Phileas Fogg and his companions had gone southward. Nothing whatever was visible in that direction. It was then about seven. The captain was extremely anxious, and did not know what course to pursue, whether to send a second detachment to the assistance of the first, and so sacrifice, perhaps, more men, with a very slender chance of seeing those who had been already sacrificed. But he was not long in hesitating. He called up his lieutenant, and was giving him the order to make a reconnaissance to the southward, when shouts were heard. Was it a signal? The soldiers hurried out of the fort and at a distance of half a mile they saw the detachment returning in good order.

Mr. Fogg was marching in front, and by him Passepartout and the two other travellers who had been rescued from the Sioux. They had fought the Indians about ten miles south of Fort Kearney. A few moments before the arrival of the soldiers Passepartout and his companions had begun to struggle with their captors, and the Frenchman had knocked down three with his fists when his master and the detachment hurried forward to his assistance.

All, rescuers and rescued, were received with cries of joy, and Phileas Fogg distributed to the soldiers the reward he had promised them, while Passepartout with some show of reason observed to himself—

"I must confess I have cost my master dear."

Fix without speaking looked at Mr. Fogg, and it would have been difficult for him to analyse the feelings which struggled within him. As for Aouda, she had taken Mr. Fogg's hand in hers and pressed it, without being able to say a word.

Meantime, Passepartout was looking about for the train at the station. He expected to find it there, ready to start for Omaha, and he hoped they might be able to recover the time they had lost.

"The train! where's the train!" cried he.

"Gone," replied Fix.

"And the next one, when?" asked Phileas Fogg.

"Not till this evening."

"Ah!" was all that impassive gentleman said.

THE OTHER LOG OF PHILEAS FOGG

Aouda, who had coolly shot a number of Sioux, was untouched. Fogg was also unwounded. Fix had a slight wound in his arm. Colonel Proctor had not been so lucky. He had received a ball in his groin which had not only incapacitated him but might result in his death. Through his pain, he glared at Fogg, who coolly stared and then turned away.

Verne assumed that it was a Sioux bullet which had struck Proctor. Fogg records that it was he who put the colonel out of action. As soon as he saw that they would be safe, he had shot the colonel. He would have put the bullet in the man's head if he had been absolutely certain that he was a Capellean. In any event, he wanted to make sure that he would not be delayed.

As it turned out, he was held up anyway. On being informed that Passepartout and several other passengers had been carried off, he determined to go after them. This meant that the train would leave without him and that he would probably not catch his steamer at New York. He did not hesitate. He could not desert the brave Frenchman, knowing that he would be horribly tortured by the warriors. He shamed the captain of the troopers into getting thirty volunteers to accompany him on a rescue expedition. That Fogg offered five thousand dollars to be split among the troopers may have had something to do with their willingness to face the Sioux. And that Passepartout was carrying the distorter may have had something to do with Fogg's insistence on going after him. However, in view of his character, it would be well to dismiss this unworthy thought.

Fix, be it noted, stayed behind. He did not believe that any of the party would return. He would have liked to volunteer, because this would have removed the last of Fogg's suspicions about him. But at the thought of what the Indians did to their captives, he quailed.

Afterward, he cursed himself for a coward. But what a brave fellow that Fogg was! Eridanean or not, he . . . But no! Such thoughts were treasonable. He paced back and forth before the station house. Should he enter and make himself known to Proctor? Or was the colonel even aware that he, Fix, was a Capellean? If so, he had made no recognition signal. And if Proctor did not know, then Fix would have a perfect excuse for his inaction. Nemo, who had stayed behind in San Francisco, had only instructed him to stick close to Fogg. He was to report on Fogg's activities when an agent made contact with him.

The train pulled out, leaving Fix and Aouda behind. Watching it dwindle on the vast prairie, Fix suddenly lost his sense of security at having at least followed Nemo's orders. He was not supposed to leave Fogg for any reason. And he had refused to go with him! What would Nemo say? He knew well what he would say. Unless Fogg did come back, Fix was lost. Nemo would say that Passepartout and Fogg might have used the distorter to get away from both Sioux and Capelleans. Fix would argue that this was not likely. To use the distorter, Fogg would have to rescue Passepartout first, and how could he do that? Besides, it was thought that the Eridaneans had only one distorter left. Where was the other one needed for their transmission?

Nemo would reply that it was uncertain that the enemy had only one device. Moreover, what was to prevent the wily Fogg from repeating the *Mary Celeste* incident with the distorter now carried by the Chinese agent? Indeed, the Chinese agent may have been killed by the Eridaneans, who would then be in possession of a second distorter.

And this had happened because Fix had not been able to help Nemo on the *General Grant*. And had Fix been as sick as he said he was? Perhaps he had been malingering. And so on. A fatal so on.

Fix went into the station house. If he had no internal fire to warm him, he could at least get an external fire from the stove. But he went out again almost at once. He felt a need to be punished. He would sit out here and freeze until Fogg came back. At least, until the sun arose. The sun. It was said to be ninety-three million miles away. He had heard Earthlings exclaim with wonder at this inconceivable distance. He had always snickered inwardly when this happened. What did they know of the mindreeling stretch of interstellar space? His own homeland was forty-five light-years away. A man walking twenty miles a day would take four million and six hundred and fifty thousand days to travel to the sun. Almost thirteen thousand years. Yet that was a mere stroll to the corner greengrocer's for one who walked to Capella.

His homeland? Why did he call it that? In reality, he had never seen it nor had any of his ancestors. He and they were homebodies, Earthlings, in fact. They had always been restricted to this tiny far-off planet. Only the Old Ones could call Capella home, and even those who had come from it were probably all dead.

The original settlers had stopped here because they had thought that it might make a site for another fort. Also, because they had to make scientific survey of this unknown planet. They had to ascertain, among other things, if it held sentients. And, if it did, if the sentients were dangerous to Capella. That had happened over two hundred years ago. The sentients then, and now, were a long way from interstellar, or even interplanetary, flight.

By the time they attained the latter, they would probably kill themselves, the whole planet, too, with nuclear wars or, even more probably, global pollution. It was doubtful that their technology, and its intelligent use, would ever match their ability to create social stupidities. If it did, it would be too late. Or so said the original Old Ones. The mystics among them claimed that man was descended from some type of now-extinct ape. The simian strain would never die out, no matter how far the physical appearance of the human species got from the simian. They were inherently committed to dirt and dissension.

But if they had proper guidance?

If the Old Ones had been able to land in force, instead of in a single scoutship, they could have conquered the sentients. These, guided by the Old Ones' superior wisdom and knowledge, could have been set on the right path. But the Old Ones had to hide while they observed. Otherwise, they would have been killed, no matter how many thousands they might have slaughtered.

The Old Ones were just completing their report on Earth when the Eridaneans landed. There had been war, and both spaceships had been damaged beyond repair. And so both forces had gone underground. With surgery, they had remodified their bodies to pass for humans. After a while, because of their small numbers, they had enlisted a few Earthlings as allies. Through infant adoption, secret education, the bloodsharing ceremony, and, strongest of all, the millennium medicine, they had secured the loyalty of their allies. There was also the Great Plan which would make mankind long-lived and happy.

But first, the Eridaneans must be exterminated.

Fix shook with the cold. He was freezing to the core of his brain. The fires were going out. Still, there were enough to cast some shadows. Now he could see, suddenly, without the obstacle of the shadows. He must be frozen through and through. Emotions were dead; only logic could live in this extreme cold. If the Capelleans and Eridaneans were so highly advanced, why had they ever thought it necessary to make war on each other? War was all right for the Earthlings, since they were so retarded. They did not know any better. They were still like baboons. But why the two peoples from the stars?

The Old Ones had said—or so he had been told—that the Eridaneans had started it all. They were not quite as advanced as the Capelleans, not at least in social wisdom. They had attacked the Capelleans somewhere on some outpost planet many millennia ago. And the Capelleans had been forced to fight or become extinct.

The sun rose. Fix became a little warmer though no less confused.

Shortly after seven, he heard a shot. He rushed out toward the sound with the soldiers and found Fogg, Passepartout, and two other passengers marching with the volunteer troopers. Aouda, too choked up to talk, could only hold Fogg's hand. Fix was happy yet ashamed. Passepartout was lamenting how much he had cost Fogg in money and time so far. Then he looked around for the train and became even more desolate on finding that it had gone on.

Phileas Fogg was twenty-four hours behind schedule.

CHAPTER XXXI

IN WHICH DETECTIVE FIX TAKES PHILEAS FOGG'S
INTERESTS SERIOUSLY TO HEART

Phileas Fogg was twenty hours behind time. Passepartout, the involuntary cause of it, was in despair; he had been the ruin of his master.

At that moment the detective came up to Mr. Fogg and said —

"Is it really true, sir, that you are very much pressed for time?"

"Very much so, indeed," replied Fogg.

"I have a reason for pressing the question," continued Fix. "Your object is to be in New York on the 11th, before nine in the evening, when the steamer leaves for Liverpool."

"A most important object."

"And if your journey had not been interrupted by the Indians, you would have arrived in New York the morning of the 11th."

"Yes, about twelve hours before the steamer left."

"Well, now you are twenty hours behind; between twelve and twenty the difference is eight; you have to recover eight hours, will you try to do so."

"On foot?" asked Mr. Fogg.

"No, in a sleigh," replied Fix, "a sledge with sails. A man has proposed this mode of conveyance."

That was the man who had spoken to Fix during the

night, and whose offer Fix had declined. Phileas Fogg made no answer to Fix, but the latter having pointed out the man in question, who was walking up and down before the station, that gentleman went up to him. A few moments afterwards, Mr. Fogg and the individual, an American, named Mudge, went into an outhouse below the fort.

There he was shown a strange-looking vehicle, a frame on two long beams, rather raised in front, like the runners of a sleigh, with sufficient room to hold five or six persons. About a third of the length from the front of the frame was a mast on which was set an immense long sail, the mast was supported by wire shrouds, and a forestay on which a jib was set—behind a sort of rudder served to steer the vehicle.

It was in fact a sloop-rigged sleigh. During winter, over the frozen plains, when the trains are delayed by snow, these vehicles make rapid passages from one station to another; they carry enormous canvas, more than a racing cutter could, without risking going down, and with the wind aft, they glide along as fast, if not faster, than an express train over the frozen prairies.

In a very short time a bargain was struck between Mr. Fogg and the owner of this land craft—the wind was in their favour. There was a strong breeze from the west. The snow was hard, and Mudge engaged to convey Mr. Fogg to Omaha station in a certain number of hours. There they would find plenty of trains, and several lines of rails to Chicago and to New York. It was not impossible they might recover the time lost, so there would be no excuse for hesitating to make the attempt. Mr. Fogg did not wish to expose Aouda to the risk of such a journey in the open air, with the cold rendered excessive by the speed at which they would travel, he therefore proposed to leave her under the care of Passepartout at Kearney station, with instructions for him to bring her to Europe, by a better route, and under more favourable circumstances.

But Aouda refused to leave Mr. Fogg, and Passepartout was delighted at her determination. In fact he would not have left his master on any account as Fix was to accompany him.

What the police agent's thoughts were would be difficult to say. Had his previous conviction been shaken by Fogg's return, or did he think him still a very clever rascal, who, after having made the tour of the world, believed he would be safe in England? Perhaps Fix's opinion about Phileas Fogg was somewhat modified. But he was not the less decided to do his duty, and more impatient than any of them to hasten his return to England.

At eight o'clock the sleigh was ready to start. The travellers took their places, and wrapped themselves up close in their travelling rugs and blankets. The two sails were set, and the vehicle started at a rate of forty miles an hour, over the frozen snow.

The distance from Kearney to Omaha is in a straight line—a bee line, as the Americans call it—at most, two hundred miles, if the wind held the distance could be done in five hours. If no accident happened to prevent it, the sleigh ought to arrive at Omaha at one in the afternoon.

What a journey it was! The travellers, squeezed close together, could not speak for cold, which increased by the speed at which they were going; the sleigh glided as lightly over the surface of the plain as a boat on the water, without the accompanying swell. When the breeze came along the surface of the earth, it seemed as if the sleigh was raised from the ground by its canvas. Mudge at the helm kept it straight, and by his skilful management of the tiller avoided the lurches she had a tendency to make. All the sails were full. The jib drew clear of the lug sail; he set a topsail which added to the speed they were going, which could not be very mathematically determined, but which certainly was not less than forty miles an hour.

"If nothing breaks," cried Mudge, "we shall get there all right."

And it was to Mudge's interest to arrive within the time agreed upon, for Mr. Fogg, true to his system, had offered him an extra reward if he did.

The prairie across which the sleigh was gliding in a

straight line was as level as the sea. It was like a vast frozen lake. The line which ran through this part of the territory ascended from north-west to south-west by Grand Island; Columbus, a town of some importance in Nebraska; Schuyler; Fremont; then Omaha. It followed the right bank of the Platte River throughout its course. The sleigh shortened this route by taking the chord of the area described by the railroad. Mudge was in no fear of being stopped by the Platte River at the small bend which it made just before they reached Fremont, as it was frozen over. Thus their road was quite free from obstacles, and Phileas Fogg had but two causes of apprehension—an accident to their rigging, and a change or a fall in the wind.

But the breeze did not go down; on the contrary, it blew till it bent the mast, which was, however, well secured by its wire rigging, which whistled in the wind like the strings of a violin. The sleigh glided along to a plaintive accompaniment.

"The chords give the fifth and the octave," said Mr. Fogg.

They were the only words he spoke during the journey. Aouda, closely wrapped up in furs and blankets, was as far as it was possible sheltered from the cold.

As for Passepartout, whose face was as red as the sun's disk when he sets in a fog, he enjoyed breathing the biting air. With his natural confidence he had begun to hope once more. Instead of arriving in the morning at New York, they would be there in the evening, and there was still a chance it would be before the steamer left for Liverpool.

He almost felt inclined to shake Fix by the hand, his old ally. He could not forget they owed the idea of the sleigh to the inspector, and consequently their sole chance of reaching Omaha in time. But owing to some presentiment, he kept up his usual reserve.

But under no circumstances could Passepartout ever forget the sacrifice Mr. Fogg had made without hesitation in order to rescue him from the Sioux. In doing so Mr. Fogg had risked life as well as fortune. No, he never could forget that!

While each of the travellers was lost in reflections so different, the sleigh was flying along over a carpet of snow. If it crossed a few creeks, affluent as tributaries of Little Blue River, they never noticed it. Fields and water-courses disappeared alike under a uniform covering of white. The plain was absolutely a desert. Not a village, nor a station, nor even a fort. From time to time they passed like a flash some skeleton tree, twisting its branches in the wind. Sometimes flights of birds of prey rose all together in the air. Occasionally, too, packs of half-starved prairie wolves pursued the sleigh with their horrid howls. Passepartout held his revolver ready to fire at those which might come too near. Had any accident then stopped the sleigh, these savage brutes would have attacked the travellers, who would have been in most imminent danger; but the sleigh held on its way, and soon left the yelling pack far behind.

At twelve Mudge found by certain marks that he was crossing the Platte River. He said nothing, but he was already certain that the station at Omaha was only twenty miles distant.

And in fact in less than an hour their pilot left the rudder, brailed up his mainsail, and lowered his jib, while the sleigh still ran for half a mile under bare poles. At last it stopped, and Mudge pointing to some snow-covered roofs, said—

"Here we are!"

They arrived at last at the station, which is in daily communication by numerous trains with the eastern part of the United States.

Passepartout and Fix jumped out, and shook their benumbed limbs. They then assisted Mr. Fogg and Aouda to leave the sleigh. Phileas Fogg paid Mudge liberally. Passepartout shook hands with him, and they all hurried into Omaha station. The Pacific Railroad, properly so called, stops at this important Nebraska city, which keeps the basin of the Mississippi in communication with the ocean.

To go from Omaha to Chicago the line, under the name of "Chicago Rock Island Line," runs directly eastward, and stops at fifty stations.

A direct train was just going to start. Fogg and his friends had only time enough to get into a car. They had seen nothing of Omaha, but Passepartout confessed he did not regret it, for now it was not a question of sight-seeing.

The train passed quickly into the State of Iowa, by Council Bluffs, Des Moines, and Iowa City; during the night it crossed the Mississippi at Davenport, and at Rock Island entered Illinois. The next day, the 10th, it arrived at Chicago, already risen from its ruins, and seated more proudly than ever on the shores of the beautiful Lake Michigan.

Nine hundred miles separated Chicago from New York. There was no want of trains at Chicago. Mr. Fogg passed immediately from one to the other. The engine of the Pittsburg-Chicago Line started immediately at full speed, as if it was aware that gentleman had no time to spare. It traversed Indiana, Ohio, Pennsylvania, and New Jersey with the rapidity of lightning, passing through towns with names belonging to antiquity, in some of which the streets were marked out, and lines of railways indicated, but not a house yet built. At last the Hudson came in sight, and the 11th of December, at a quarter-past eleven in the evening, the train stopped at the station, on the right bank of the river, before the very pier belonging to the Cunard Line, otherwise called the "British and North American Royal Mail Steam Packet Company." The *China*, bound to Liverpool, had left three-quarters of an hour before!

THE OTHER LOG OF PHILEAS FOGG

Fix knew that Fogg had to be in New York City on the eleventh before nine o'clock in the evening. At that hour the steamer left for Liverpool and another would not be available until the next day. It seemed inevitable that Fogg would miss the steamer. But Fix came to the rescue this time. The evening before, he had been approached by a Mr. Mudge, who had offered to take Fix at once to Omaha, though by a rather unconventional conveyance. Fix had turned him down because he had to wait for Fogg. Now he informed Fogg that all was not yet lost. He could be transported on an ice-sled. This vehicle held five or six persons and was equipped with a mast which held a brig sail and afforded attachment for a jib sail. It was steered by a rudder which dug into the snow.

Would Fogg care to use this craft?

Mr. Fogg certainly would. Presently, the party was being driven by a west wind over the ice and snow of the prairie. The two hundred miles between Fort Kearney and Omaha were covered in five hours. Fix said nothing during the journey, but he was happy. His service in obtaining the ice-sled would be one more item in his favor to reduce Fogg's suspicions of him.

The sled arrived just before the Chicago and Rock Island train was to leave. Fogg and party boarded it and so arrived in Chicago at four in the afternoon of the next day. This city, partially destroyed in the Great Fire of the eighth and ninth of October, 1871, had been rebuilt with some attention to beauty. The party had no time to inspect the new constructions or to take a drive along the superb Lake Michigan. They had nine hundred miles to go and so departed at once on the Pittsburgh, Fort Wayne, and Chicago Railway. On the evening of the eleventh of December, at eleven o'clock, the train pulled into the New York station. This was near the pier of the Cunard line but, unfortunately, the *China* had left for Liverpool forty-five minutes ago.

CHAPTER XXXII
IN WHICH PHILEAS FOGG FIGHTS A BATTLE
WITH HIS ILL LUCK

The *China* seemed to have carried Phileas Fogg's last chance away with her. For no other steamers which ply between America and Europe, neither the French Transatlantic, nor the White Star line, nor the steamers belonging to the Inman Company, nor the Hamburgh line, nor any others, were of any service to him.

The *Pereire*, belonging to the French Transatlantic Company—whose splendid vessels equal in speed, and surpass in convenience, all those belonging to other lines, without exception—did not leave until the 14th; moreover, like the Hamburgh vessels, it did not go direct to Liverpool or London, but to Le Havre, and this additional passage from Le Havre to Southampton in delaying Phileas Fogg would have rendered his last efforts useless.

It was idle to think of a passage by the Inman steamers, one of which, the *City of Paris*, would sail the following day. These vessels are particularly employed in conveying emigrants; their engines are weak, they depend as much on their sails as on steam, and their speed is but moderate. They would take more time to go from New York to England than Mr. Fogg had at his disposal to win his bet.

Mr. Fogg was *au fait* to all this by consulting his *Bradshaw's*, which gave him the daily arrangements of every steamer.

Passepartout was quite beside himself. To have missed the steamer by five-and-forty minutes was his death blow. It was his fault, he who, instead of being of any assistance to his master, had contrived to throw continual difficulties in his way—and when he looked back on all that had happened on their tour, when he added up the sums spent for nothing and solely on his account, when he thought how the enormous sum at stake, and enormous expenditure on this now useless journey had completely ruined Mr. Fogg, he bitterly reproached himself.

But Mr. Fogg never reproached him, and as they left the quay of the transatlantic steamers he only cried—

"We must consult about what is best to be done tomorrow. Come—"

Mr. Fogg, Aouda, Fix, and Passepartout crossed the Hudson in the Jersey City ferry boat, and drove to St. Nicholas Hotel, Broadway. Rooms were taken and the night passed quickly to Phileas Fogg, who slept soundly, but tediously to Aouda and her companions, whose agitation would not allow them to rest.

The next day it was the 12th of December. From seven in the morning of the 12th, to a quarter-past nine in the evening of the 21st, there was at his disposal nine days, thirteen hours and forty-five minutes. Therefore if Phileas Fogg had left the evening before by the *China*, one of Cunard's fastest vessels, he would have reached Liverpool and then London within the time! Mr. Fogg left the hotel alone after having desired his servant to wait and tell Aouda to be ready to start at any moment. He then proceeded to the banks of the Hudson, and looked carefully at all the vessels moored to the quay or at anchor in the river which were about to sail. Many of them had their Blue Peter flying, and were preparing to go to sea with the morning's tide, for in that immense port of New York there is not a day that a hundred vessels do not leave for all parts of the world; but most of them were sailing ships which were useless to Phileas Fogg.

It seemed after all he was destined to fail in his last

attempt, when he noticed a screw steamer at anchor off the Battery, about a cable's length from the shore, and as smoke was issuing from her funnel he concluded she was about to get under way.

Phileas Fogg hailed a boat and went on board the *Henrietta*, an iron steamer with wooden upperworks. The *Henrietta*'s captain was on board; Phileas went aft and asked to see him; he came forward immediately.

He was a man about fifty, a sort of sea dog, who did not look very obliging, with great eyes, a complexion of oxidized copper, red hair and a bull neck—nothing pleasant-looking about him.

"The captain?" said Fogg.

"Here I am."

"I am Phileas Fogg, of London."

"And I Andrew Speedy, of Cardiff."

"Are you about to leave?"

"In one hour."

"You are bound for?"

"Bordeaux."

"And your cargo?"

"Stones in the hold. No freight; I sail in ballast."

"Have you any passengers?"

"None. I never take any—they are always in one's way, and talk too much."

"Is your vessel fast?"

"Between eleven and twelve knots—the *Henrietta* is well known."

"Will you convey me and three other persons to Liverpool?"

"To Liverpool? why not to China?"

"I say Liverpool?"

"No."

"No?"

"No. I am bound for Bordeaux, and I am going to Bordeaux."

"On no terms."

"On no terms whatever."

The captain spoke in a tone which admitted of no reply.

"But the *Henrietta*'s owners?" resumed Phileas Fogg.

"The owners are myself. The vessel belongs to me."

"I will charter her."

"No."

"I will buy her."

"No."

Phileas Fogg kept his countenance. But his situation was critical. It was not the same at New York as at Hong-kong, and the captain of the *Henrietta* was a very different man to the owner of the *Tankadere*. Till now money had always overcome his difficulties, but now money seemed to have lost its power.

But some means must be found of crossing the Atlantic, unless he would do it in a balloon, which would have been very adventurous, and which besides was not practicable.

It seems an idea occurred to Phileas Fogg, for he said to the captain.

"Well, will you take me to Bordeaux?"

"No, not if you were to give me two hundred dollars."

"I will give you two thousand."

"For each person?"

"Yes, for each person."

"There are four of you?"

"Four."

Captain Speedy began scratching his forehead, as if he intended to rub the skin off. Eight thousand dollars to be earned without change of destination. It was well worth his while to lay aside his antipathy to passengers for once. Besides, at that price they are no longer passengers, they are valuable goods.

"I am off at nine," said Captain Speedy, coolly, "if you and your people are here."

"We shall be on board at nine," replied Mr. Fogg, no less coolly.

It was then half-past eight. He landed from the *Henrietta*, got into a coach, drove to St. Nicholas, fetched away Aouda, Passepartout, and even the inseparable Fix, to whom he very civilly offered a passage, and all this with the same calm demeanour, which never abandoned him under any circumstances.

At the moment the *Henrietta* got under way they were all on board.

When Passepartout heard what their last passage cost, he uttered a vocal gamut of "Oh's!"

As for Detective Fix, he said to himself that decidedly the Bank of England would not get out of that affair without loss. In fact, when they arrived in England, admitting that Mr. Fogg did not throw a few bundle of notes into the sea on purpose, more than seven thousand pounds would have already come out of the famous bag of bank notes.

THE OTHER LOG OF PHILEAS FOGG

Fogg seemed to be beaten. The Inman liner would not leave until the following day and was not fast enough to make up the lost time. The Hamburg ships went directly to Le Havre, France, which meant that the trip from Le Havre to Southhampton and thence to London would make him too late. A French liner did not depart until the fourteenth.

Mr. Fogg only said, "Tomorrow, we will consult about what is best. Come."

They took the Jersey City ferry over the Hudson and a carriage to the St. Nicholas Hotel on Broadway. The next morning, Mr. Fogg went out alone (according to Verne). Actually, Passepartout trailed him by about sixty feet to detect any shadowers or intercept any Capellean assassins. If Proctor had been sent to kill Fogg, it seemed unlikely that another attempt would not be made in New York. Yet, nothing of this nature happened. Perhaps Proctor was after all only a Western ruffian. But why were the Capelleans leaving him alone? What was behind this? If one thing was sure, they had not given up on him.

Mr. Fogg inquired along the banks of the Hudson for any vessels that seemed about to depart. There were many of this kind, recalling Whitman's phrase of "many-masted Manhattan," but sailing ships would be too slow. At the end of his quest, Fogg saw, anchored at the Battery, a steam-driven freighter with the usual auxiliary sails. The puffs of smoke from its stack indicated that it would soon be leaving. Fogg hired a boat and was rowed to the *Henrietta*. It was bound for Bordeaux and was carrying only ballast for this trip. Its captain, Andrew Speedy (neither Capellean nor Eridanean despite his functional name), loathed passengers. He refused to take Fogg and party at any price nor would he think of going anywhere but to Bordeaux. However, at the offer of two thousand dollars for each passenger, Speedy relented. As Verne says, passengers at this price are no longer passengers but valuable merchandise.

Speedy gave Fogg an unalterable half hour to get all aboard. Fogg hurried in a cab to the hotel and returned with the others just in time. (New York was having traffic problems even in 1872, but the fact that Fogg was able to make such speed shows that the problem was not as bad as now. Or perhaps Fogg ignored all traffic laws.) An hour later, the *Henrietta* passed the lighthouse marking the entrance to the Hudson, turned past Sandy Hook, and was in the sea.

CHAPTER XXXIII

IN WHICH PHILEAS FOGG SHOWS HIMSELF
EQUAL TO ANY EMERGENCY

An hour afterwards the *Henrietta* passed the lighthouse at the entrance to the Hudson, turned the point at Sandy Hook and found herself in the open sea. In the course of the day she ran down Long Island, passed Fire Island light, and took an easterly course.

At noon the following day, the 13th of December, a man mounted the bridge to ascertain where they were. This man ought certainly to have been Captain Speedy; not at all—it was Phileas Fogg.

Captain Speedy was, on the contrary, under lock and key in his cabin, and was yelling and shouting in a manner which betrayed a very excusable though violent state of rage.

What had happened was very simple. Phileas Fogg wished to go to Liverpool, the captain would not take him there. So Phileas had agreed to take his passage for Bordeaux, and during the thirty hours he had been on board had managed matters so well, that by dint of bribery he had brought over the whole crew, which was on very bad terms with the obstinate and uncivil captain, to his side—the crew was rather a mixed one—and that is why the *Henrietta* was making her course for Liverpool. Only it was very clear, from the manner in which Mr. Fogg managed the vessel, that he had been to sea.

Now, how the adventure ended will be seen in the sequel. Aouda, however, was very uneasy, but said nothing. Fix had at first been in despair. Passepartout was delighted.

The captain had said the *Henrietta* would do between eleven and twelve knots, and this proved to be correct, for she kept up that rate of going.

If then—how many ifs there were still—if the sea was not too heavy, and the wind did not veer round to the east, and if no accident happened to the ship or machinery, the *Henrietta* in nine days, reckoned from the 12th to the 21st, might accomplish the three thousand miles which separate New York from Liverpool. It is true that, on his arrival, the affair of the *Henrietta*, added to the Bank of England business, might take the gentleman farther than he calculated upon.

For the first days of their voyage they had very favourable weather. There was not too much sea, the wind seemed steady in the north-east; they were able to use their sails, and under her canvas the *Henrietta* went like a mail steamer, and everything seemed to favour their progress.

Passepartout was in a state of great delight, his master's last exploit, the consequences of which he would not anticipate, excited his enthusiasm. The crew had never had so gay and active a fellow on board. He struck up a friendship with all the crew, and astonished them with his acrobatic tricks. He gave them glasses of grog innumerable. For him they worked their hardest, and the stokers fired up like heroes. His good humour infected them all. He had forgotten the past with its troubles and its dangers, and he only thought of one object so nearly attained, and sometimes he boiled over with impatience, as if he had been heated like one of the *Henrietta* boilers. He often took a look at Fix, and considered him with an eye that said a good deal, but he did not speak to him, for there was no longer an intimacy between these former friends.

Besides, to tell the truth, Fix was utterly at a loss. He was quite bewildered by the taking possession of the *Henrietta*, the buying over of the crew, Fogg's management of the vessel like an experienced sailor; all these circumstances, taken together, were too much for him; he did not know what to think. But, after all, a gentleman who began by stealing fifty-five thousand pounds could very well end by stealing a ship, and Fix naturally came to the conclusion that the *Henrietta* in Fogg's hands was not going to Liverpool at all, but to some part of the world where the thief, now become a pirate, would quietly put himself in safety. This conclusion was very plausible, and the detective began to regret he had ever been concerned in the business.

Captain Speedy, meantime, continued shouting in his cabin, and Passepartout, who was charged with conveying food to him, did so with great precaution, strong as he was. Mr. Fogg never seemed to think there was such a person as the captain on board.

On the 13th they passed the edge of the banks of Newfoundland, a very dangerous place. In winter the fogs last a long time, and there is a great deal of wind. The evening before the barometer fell suddenly and foretold a change of weather; in fact, during the night the temperature fell, the cold became excessive, and the wind veered round to the south-west. This was unfortunate. Mr. Fogg, in order to keep his course, was obliged to furl his sails and trust to steam.

Still the vessel's progress diminished in consequence of the state of the sea, the long waves of which broke over her stern. She also pitched violently, which also stopped her somewhat. The breeze became a squall, and it seemed already very likely the *Henrietta* could not be kept head to wind. Now, if they were obliged to run before it, they could not tell where they might be driven.

Passepartout's countenance was an index of the sky, and for two days he was in a state of mortal anxiety. But Phileas Fogg was a bold sailor, who knew how to face the sea, and he kept on his course without decreasing steam-power. When the *Henrietta* did not rise over a sea she plunged through it, and her bridge was sometimes swept by the waves, but she battled on. Sometimes the screw was out of the water, when a mountainous wave lifted her stern; but still she kept on.

All this time the wind was not as high as they feared it might be. It was but a squall travelling ninety miles an hour. It still blew fresh, and, unfortunately, always from the south-east, and they could set no sail; and, as we shall see, it would have been very serviceable to help the steam-power had they been able to do so.

The 16th of December was the seventy-fifth day since they left London, and as yet the *Henrietta* was not very much behind time. Half the passage was accomplished, and the dangerous part was passed. One might almost anticipate success.

Passepartout did not like to give an opinion. He still hoped, and if the wind was against them they would still depend on their steam.

That day the engineer went and had a long conversation on the bridge with Mr. Fogg.

Passepartout, from a presentiment, felt uneasy, without knowing why; he would have given one of his ears to hear with the other what the engineer was saying. He caught a few words, and among others, he heard his master say—

"You are sure of what you say?"

"Certain, sir; you must not forget that since we left we have had all our fires going and though we had fuel enough to take us with half-steam power to Bordeaux, we have not sufficient to carry us with full power from New York to Liverpool."

"I must think it over," said Mr. Fogg.

Passepartout understood now. Their coals had evidently run short.

"Well," thought he, "if my master gets over that he will be a clever fellow;" and having met Fix he could not help telling him what he had heard.

"Then," replied the police agent, grinding his teeth, "you still believe we are going to Liverpool?"

"Of course I do."

"Idiot!" replied the detective, walking off, and shrugging his shoulders.

Passepartout was on the point of resenting the appellation, the true meaning of which he well understood; but he said to himself, poor Fix must be very much disappointed, and his vanity wounded, in having been all round the world on the wrong scent, and he passed it over.

And now what could Phileas Fogg do? It is rather difficult to guess, but it seemed that phlegmatic gentleman had made up his mind, for the same evening he sent for the engineer, and said to him—

"Keep your fires up, and go on as long as the fuel lasts."

A few moments afterwards the *Henrietta*'s funnel vomited more smoke than ever.

The vessel continued going ahead at full speed; but two days later, the 18th, the engineer, as he had said, was obliged to tell Mr. Fogg, they had not a day's coal left.

"Don't let the fires down on any account," said Mr. Fogg.

That day, after taking an observation, Phileas Fogg told Passepartout to let Captain Speedy out. It was about the same as if he had ordered him to go and unchain a tiger, and he went below, saying to himself—

"He will certainly go mad."

A few minutes afterwards a bomb appeared on the poop, to an accompaniment of oaths and execrations; that bomb was Captain Speedy. It was clear he was going to burst.

"Where are we?" were the first words he uttered, nearly suffocated with rage, and surely if he had a tendency to apoplexy he must have died.

"Seven hundred and seventy miles from Liverpool," replied Mr. Fogg, with great calmness.

"Pirate!" roared Andrew Speedy.

"I sent for you, sir."

"Sea robber!"

"Sir," continued Phileas Fogg, "to beg you to sell me your ship."

"No! by all the devils in hell, no!"

"Because I shall be obliged to burn her."

"Burn my ship?"

"Yes; at least, her upperworks, for we are short of fuel."

"Burn my ship! A vessel worth fifty thousand dollars!" cried Speedy, who could hardly articulate.

"Here are sixty thousand," replied Phileas Fogg, offering the captain a roll of notes.

This had a wonderful effect on Speedy. No American could stand the sight of sixty thousand dollars without experiencing a peculiar sensation. In a moment the captain had forgotten his anger, his imprisonment, and all his wrongs. His vessel was twenty years old. It was a very good bargain. The bomb would not burst now, for Mr. Fogg had taken out the tube.

"Shall I have the hull as well?" said the captain, in a singularly soft tone.

"The iron hull and the engine, too. Is it a bargain?"

"A bargain," and Andrew Speedy took the notes, counted them, and thrust them into his pocket.

During this scene Passepartout turned gradually white, and Fix nearly had a fit.

About twenty thousand pounds already spent, and Fogg must give away the hull and the engine, nearly the entire value of the vessel! It is true the sum stolen from the bank was fifty-five thousand pounds.

When Andrew Speedy had pocketed the money—

"Sir," said Mr. Fogg, "do not be surprised at what I have just done. You must know I lose twenty thousand pounds if I am not in London the 21st of December, at a quarter to nine in the evening. Now I missed the steamer at New York, and you refused to take me to Liverpool."

"And right I was in so doing," cried Andrew Speedy, "for I have made at least forty thousand dollars by it!"

Then he added—

"Do you know something, Captain—"

"Fogg."

"Captain Fogg. Well, there is something of the Yankee in you."

And having as he thought paid his passenger a great compliment, he was going below, when Phileas Fogg said to him—

"Now the ship is mine?"

"Certainly, from the keel to the truck; as far as the woodwork is concerned, you understand."

"All right. Now, my men, clear away all her cabin fittings, and fire up with them."

That day the poop deck, cabins, bunks, and forecastle were broken up and burnt.

The next day, the 19th, the masts and spars followed. The masts were cut off at the deck, and then sawn into blocks. The crew worked with a will, and Passepartout did the work of ten men.

The next day, the 20th, the sails, bulwarks, and a greater part of the deck was burnt. The *Henrietta* was little better than a hulk. But that day they sighted the coast of Ireland and Fastnet light.

But at ten the *Henrietta* was only abreast of Queenstown, and Phileas Fogg had only twenty-four hours to get to London! Now the *Henrietta* would require all that time to reach Liverpool, even with full steam power, which was just beginning to fail the bold gentleman.

"Sir," said Captain Speedy, who had at last taken an interest in Fogg, "I am truly sorry for you. Everything goes against you. We are only off Queenstown now."

"Ah," said Mr. Fogg, "is that Queenstown whose lights we now see?"

"Yes."

"Can we enter the harbour?"

"Not for three hours; only at high water."

"We must wait then," replied Mr. Fogg, quietly, without

showing the least sign on his face of any intention to make a final attempt to overcome his ill luck.

Queenstown is a port on the Irish coast, where the transatlantic steamers stop to leave their mails, which are conveyed to Dublin by an express train in waiting for them. From Dublin they are carried on by very fast steamers to Liverpool— thus gaining twelve hours on the fastest vessels.

Phileas Fogg expected to gain twelve hours too. Instead of arriving on board the *Henrietta* the next evening at Liverpool, he would be there at noon, and consequently would have time to reach London before a quarter to nine in the evening.

About one in the morning, at high water, the *Henrietta* entered Queenstown harbour, and after a hearty shake of the hand from Captain Speedy, left him on board the cut-down hulk of his late vessel, which was still worth half the price he had been paid for her.

The passengers disembarked immediately.

Fix at that moment felt a savage temptation to arrest Mr. Fogg. But he did not. He was in a fearful state of mind about him. Whether he had his doubts—whether he believed he was after all mistaken, we cannot say. Under any circumstances, however, he never lost sight of him. They all got into the train together, at Queenstown at half-past one in the morning, arrived at Dublin by daybreak, and embarked at once on one of those steel cylinders called steamers, which always go through the water instead of over it.

At twenty minutes to twelve, the morning of the 21st of December, Phileas Fogg landed at Liverpool. He was only six hours distant from London!

But at that moment Fix came up, put his hand on his shoulder, and showing his warrant, said—

"Are you Mr. Phileas Fogg?"

"Yes, sir."

"Then I arrest you in the Queen's name!"

THE FULL ACCOUNT

THE OTHER LOG OF PHILEAS FOGG

Passepartout, it can be presumed, regretted not having been able to tour Manhattan. Due largely to immigration from Europe, New York City held a million people. It was, generally, a dirty, drab, drunken, corruptly governed city with many slums. Muggings, killings, brawls, and mob violence were common. The guidebooks warned newcomers not to walk out at night except in better areas well lit by gas. Despite this, the visitor with means might enjoy it. Passepartout would have liked to drive through the recently constructed Central Park, even if slums did ring it. Trinity Church was the tallest structure in town and, though it would be nothing unusual in London, it was notable in contrast with its surroundings. Passepartout might also have wanted to view the new residential areas with their brownstone fronts and the business sections with their cast-iron façades. He could have compared the mass-transportation problems vexing New York City with those vexing London. If he had talked to the Gothamites, he would have heard rumors of gunrunning to Cuban revolutionaries and the seriousness of the epizootic disease which was killing horses. He would have noted that it was only because of this "horse influenza" that Manhattan's streets in summer were not as foul with manure and the air as thick with huge horseflies and a compound of dust, coal smoke, and manure particles as were London's.

All this was not to be. Passepartout also had more to think about than the rather sleazy exotica of Baghdad-on-the-Hudson. Mr. Fogg had locked Captain Speedy up in the master's own quarters.

Mr. Fogg, seeing that Speedy was adamant about not changing his course to Liverpool, had bribed the crew to cooperate with him. This was, as Speedy screamed behind his door, mutiny on the high seas and piracy, the penalty of which was hanging by the neck until dead. Fogg heard him with his customary serenity and continued to give orders from the bridge. It is here that Verne says (truly) that Fogg's management of the craft showed that he had once been a sailor.

As for Fix, he was fighting a tendency to admire Fogg more and more. He was also wondering why he had received no orders in New

York concerning Fogg. Doubtless, Nemo had changed his plans, but it would be nice to know what was going on. Perhaps one of the crew was a fellow Capellean charged with killing the Eridaneans even if he had to blow up the vessel to do it. Fix did not like to contemplate this plan, since it would mean his own demise. And, to tell the truth, he admitted, he was getting more and more excited about the wager. Several times, he had to remind himself that he had no business rooting for the chap.

On the sixteenth of December, half the trip across the Atlantic was behind the *Henrietta*. She had passed safely through the Newfoundland Fogs and a storm. But now the chief engineer informed Fogg that the fuel supply was running out. The ship did have enough coal to go on "short steam" at a reduced speed to Liverpool. The furnaces were still on "full steam."

Fogg, after some deliberation, told the engineer to keep the fires at maximum until the coal was all gone. On the eighteenth, Fogg was told that the fuel would be exhausted sometime that day.

Near noon, Fogg sent for the captain. His face purple, Speedy bounded onto the bridge. "Where are we?" he cried.

"Seven hundred and seventy miles from Liverpool," Fogg said calmly.

"Pirate!"

"Sir, I have sent for you . . ."

"Pickaroon!"

". . . to ask you to sell me the ship."

"By all the devils, no!"

"Then I shall be forced to burn her."

"What, burn the *Henrietta*!"

"The upper part at least. The coal has run out."

"Burn my ship? A ship worth fifty thousand dollars!"

"Here are sixty thousand," Fogg said. He handed him the money.

Here Verne makes his classical remark: "An American can hardly remain unmoved at the sight of sixty thousand dollars."

True, but Verne's ethnicism is evident in this statement. Few of any nationality, then or today, would not be emotionally affected on being presented with this sum.

Speedy forgot his hate. Money, more than music, soothes the savage beast. He was getting by far the best of the bargain.

"I will still have the iron hull?" he said.

"The iron hull and the engine. I am only buying the wood and all other combustible substances. Is it agreed?"

Fogg then gave the order to strip off all the interior seats, bunks, frames and other furniture and to put them into the furnaces.

The next day, the nineteenth, the fires received the masts, spars, and rafts. On the twentieth, the railings, fittings, and most of the deck and upper sides followed. On this day, the hulk was within sight of the Irish coast and the Fastnet lighthouse. At ten that evening, Queenstown appeared. This was the Irish port where trans-Atlantic steamers put in to deliver the mail. From there express trains sped to Dublin, from which the mail was carried by fast boat to Liverpool. This route got the mail into London twelve hours ahead of the ships.

The *Henrietta* waited three hours for high tide, after which it steamed into the harbor and discharged the Fogg party. A little after one o'clock, the travelers stepped onto dry land. Since this was British soil, Fix was in a position to arrest Fogg and clap him into jail. Verne says that Fix was much tempted to do so. But Verne could only speculate on why he refrained.

"What struggle was going on inside him? Had he changed his mind about *his man*?"

No, Fix had not changed his mind. He just could not make it up. The long intimacy with his three enemies had forced him to acknowledge that Eridaneans could be, and were in this case, as human as he. They were, even if the deadly antagonists of his own people, not evil incarnate. He admired Fogg for his undeviating courage, quick-wittedness, resourcefulness, loyalty, and generosity. He liked him. He liked the other two for similar reasons. He liked Fogg far more than he did Nemo, who, he admitted to himself, he hated, feared, and loathed. And he had not liked Stamp Proctor; he had been glad when the colonel's plan to kill Fogg had been spoiled by the Sioux.

Time and again, he told himself that he was thinking wrongly. No matter. He continued to think along the same lines. He could not sleep at night because of his conflicts, and his days were tearing-aparts. What was he to do?

At twenty minutes to high noon, the Fogg party got off the boat at Liverpool. Fogg had only a six-hour train ride to Charing Cross Station, London, and a brief carriage ride to the Reform Club.

Fix could no longer refuse to act. Both the English law and Capellean orders required him to proceed. He put his hand on Fogg's shoulder, a familiarity he would not have dared except in an official capacity. Verne says that he showed the warrant in the other hand, but Verne forgot that Fix had had no opportunity to get a warrant.

"You are really Phileas Fogg?" he said.

No doubt, a variation of Pilate's classical remark flashed through Fogg's mind. What is truth? What is reality? What, or who is the real Fogg?

But he replied, "I am."

"I arrest you in the Queen's name!"

CHAPTER XXXIV

PHILEAS FOGG ARRIVES IN LONDON AT LAST.
IS HE IN TIME?

Phileas Fogg was in prison. He had been confined in the Custom House, and he would be obliged to stay there, until he should be transferred to London.

At the moment of his arrest, Passepartout was about to rush at the detective, but he was held back by two policemen.

Aouda was frightened at the brutality of the proceeding, which she could not understand. Passepartout explained it to her. Mr. Fogg, that honourable and courageous gentleman, to whom she owed her life, had been arrested like a common thief!

The young woman protested against such a charge, her heart revolted against it, and tears began to flow when she found she could do nothing to serve her protector.

Fix felt he had arrested Mr. Fogg because it was his duty to do so, guilty or innocent. That was a question for the law to decide.

The thought then occurred to Passepartout that he was the cause of this fresh misfortune! Why had he concealed what he knew from Mr. Fogg? When Fix confided to him that he was a police agent, why had he taken upon himself not to inform his master? Had the latter been warned he could no doubt have given Mr. Fix proofs of his innocence, and so proved his mistake; and under no circumstances would he have carried this unlucky police agent about with him at his own expense, whose first care was to arrest him the moment he set foot in the United Kingdom. When he thought of his blunders and his imprudence, the poor fellow experienced all the pangs of remorse. He cried, it was painful to see him. He would have liked to have blown his brains out.

Aouda and he remained under the portico of the Custom House, in spite of the cold. Neither of them would leave the place—they wanted to see Mr. Fogg again.

That gentleman was well and completely ruined, and that at the very moment he had nearly won. This arrest was a final blow. On his arrival at Liverpool he had just nine hours and fifteen minutes to present himself at the Reform Club, and he only wanted six to go to London.

Just then if any one could have got into the guard-room at the Custom House, they would have found Mr. Fogg, calm and quiet, seated on a bench. It could not be said he was resigned, but to all appearance this last blow had not any effect on his placid demeanour. There he sat calm and expectant—of what? Had he any hope still? Or did he still believe in succeeding with the prison door closed upon him?

Whatever it might have been, Mr. Fogg had laid his watch carefully down on the table, and was watching the hands as they moved around. Not a word escaped his lips, but his eyes were singularly set.

Under any circumstances his situation was terrible, and for those who could not read his conscience it might be summed up thus:

If an honest man Phileas Fogg was ruined.

If a rogue he was taken.

Had he any thought of escape? Did it occur to him to see if he could find means to leave the guardroom? One might almost think so, for at a certain moment he got up and walked round the room. But the door was fast, and the window barred, so he sat down again and took out the journal of his tour—to the line on which these words were written—

"21st of December, Saturday, Liverpool."

He added—

"80th day, 11 h. 40 A.M."

Then he waited.

One o'clock struck at the Custom House. Mr. Fogg noticed his watch was two minutes too fast by that clock.

Two o'clock. Supposing he started at that moment by an express train, he might still get to London and reach the Reform Club before a quarter to nine. His brow contracted a little.

At thirty-three minutes past two he heard a voice outside; the sound of doors opening and shutting. He could hear Passepartout's voice, and that of Fix.

Phileas Fogg's eyes grew brighter.

The guard-room door opened, and he saw Aouda, Passepartout, and Fix rush up to him.

Fix was out of breath. He could not speak.

"Sir," he stammered, "sir—forgive—most unfortunate likeness—thief arrested three days since—you—free."

Phileas Fogg was free! He walked straight up to the detective—he looked him full in the face; he, with the only rapid movement he ever made in his life, or ever would make, drew his right arm back, and with the precision of an automaton, he knocked the unfortunate detective down.

"Well hit," cried Passepartout; "that is a good blow straight from the shoulder."

Fix fell; he did not speak. He only had what he deserved. Fogg, Aouda, and Passepartout left the Custom House directly. They jumped into a cab and were soon at the railway station, and Phileas Fogg inquired if there was an express about to start for London.

It was forty minutes past two, the express had been gone thirty-five minutes. Phileas Fogg ordered a special train.

There were several fast engines with steam up, but in consequence of other arrangements the special could not leave before three.

At which time Phileas Fogg having said a word about

something extra to the engine driver, started for London, accompanied by the young widow and his faithful servant.

He had five hours and a half to do the distance between Liverpool and London—easy enough when the line is clear—but they were obliged to stop more than once, and when he reached the station it was ten minutes to nine by all the clocks in London.

Phileas Fogg, after accomplishing his tour round the world, arrived five minutes too late.

He had lost his bet.

The Other Log of Phileas Fogg

Fogg went quietly into custody in the Custom House. He would, he was informed, be transferred the next day to London.

Passepartout tried to attack Fix but was restrained by several policemen. Fix did not prefer charges against him, as he could have done for this attempted assault. One, he felt that the Frenchman was justified. Two, Passepartout was still carrying the distorter. If the Capellean chiefs still wished to get hold of it, which they surely must, they could do so much more easily if Passepartout were at large.

Aouda was paralyzed with astonishment. Contrary to what Verne said, Aouda understood what was happening. But, since Fix had not tried to arrest Fogg in Ireland, the three Eridaneans had assumed that he meant to wait until they reached London. Just as they had had plans to tie him up and leave him behind in Ireland, so they had intended to take care of him at London. They even thought that he might mean to wait until after Fogg had won the bet.

Evidently, Fogg had overlooked this particular section of the foreseen.

That gentleman, calm as ever, sat in a locked room in the Custom House and read the London *Times*. Among other items attracting his interest was a story about the *Mary Celeste*. This had first been noted by the *Times* of the sixteenth of December in its *Latest Shipping Intelligence* section. The derelict had been brought into Gibraltar by a prize crew of three from the British brigantine *Dei Gratia*. Not many details were as yet available, but the ship had a cargo of seventeen hundred barrels of alcohol and was seaworthy.

Verne says that, while in this room, Mr. Fogg carefully put his watch on the table and looked at its advancing hands. Verne wonders what Fogg was thinking at this time.

This incident is a curious one. Except for one previous occasion in Verne's book, Fogg had no watch to consult. He had relied on Passepartout's watch. Furthermore, if he had had a watch, why would he have fallen into the same error that Passepartout made about the time zones? Fogg, according to Verne, thought that that day was the twenty-first of December. It was, in reality, the twentieth. Would Fogg, who was a veteran sailor by Verne's own admission, one who had been everywhere and seen everything, who was highly educated, have not known what happened when the ship crossed the 180th meridian? By no means. Verne must have known this. But he was eager to provide drama and suspense. He cannot be blamed for using this little piece of trickery in his narrative. After all, he got it from the public report issued by Fogg himself. The Englishman had to create some excuse for the events that were to follow his incarceration in Liverpool. His fertile imagination supplied one which Verne was eager to accept.

So, when Verne says that Fogg wrote in his journal that day, "21st December, Saturday, Liverpool, 80th day, 11:40 A.M.," he is inserting his own fiction. Indeed, Verne adds more imaginative detail by writing that Fogg noticed that his watch was two minutes fast. If he took the express train at that very moment, he would just make the quarter to nine deadline.

It was at this time that Fix was told that the real thief, a James Strand, had been arrested three days ago. Fogg was in the clear. Stammering, Fix related the news to Fogg.

Phileas Fogg walked up to Fix, gave him a steady and cold look, and knocked him down with one blow of his fist.

Fix, lying on the floor, felt that he still had not been properly punished. But he at least could salvage something from the incident. Fogg evidently believed him to be nothing more than a meddling detective.

This incident shows that Fix was as ignorant of the real date as Passepartout. Otherwise, he would not have believed that Fogg had lost his bet because he had arrested him.

But if Fogg knew that he still had plenty of time, why did he hit Fix?

The answer is obvious. As Phileas Fogg, English gentleman, he could be expected to resent being arrested by a man whom he had so generously treated. He had to play out his role.

The party, minus Fix, took a cab and arrived at the station at twenty minutes before three. They were thirty-five minutes too late to catch the express.

Fogg ordered a special train but could not get one until three o'clock. He wondered if Nemo's hand was in this delay, if Nemo was planning to have unauthorized passengers on board. Before the train left at three, Fogg thoroughly searched the locomotive, tender, and his car. Satisfied that these hid no one, he signaled the train to depart. It soon roared along at a speed that should have brought them to London in five and a half hours. There were, however, unexpected delays.

When Fogg stepped from the car at Charing Cross, he was five minutes late. (Or would have been if this had been the twenty-first.)

All the clocks of London were striking ten minutes to nine.

As noted, this remarkable phenomenon has been commented on by various critics and translators. The original French version contains no footnotes about this, so it may be presumed that Verne thought this singularity was unique to the clocks of the English, an eccentric people all told.

Fogg made no such mistake. He knew that, somewhere in London, a distorter was being used. As far as he knew, the Eridaneans had only one, so it must be a Capellean's. Probably, the man from China was using his to transmit himself to London, which meant that they had at least two now. Had the box with the distorter taped on its underside failed to be washed off the *Mary Celeste*? Had it been stolen by a Capellean sent to Gibraltar for that very purpose? Surely, that must be the explanation.

CHAPTER XXXV

IN WHICH PASSEPARTOUT DID NOT LET HIS MASTER
REPEAT THE SAME ORDER TWICE

The next day the inhabitants of Savile Row would have been surprised if they had been told Mr. Fogg had returned home. Both doors and windows were still closed — outside no change whatever was apparent.

After leaving the station, Mr. Fogg had ordered Passepartout to buy some provisions and then he went home.

He had received the blow which ruined him with his habitual composure. Ruined! and by a clumsy police agent! after having safely travelled so far. After overcoming so many obstacles, braved so many dangers, and having found time to do some good actions on his road, to fail on entering port from a piece of brutality which he could not have foreseen; it was terrible indeed. A very insignificant sum remained of the large amount of money he had taken away with him. The twenty thousand pounds at Baring's were all he possessed, and these he owed to his friends of the Reform Club. After the money he had spent, had he won his bet he would have been no richer, and he probably had not sought to enrich himself, being a man who betted for honour's sake. But this bet was his complete ruin. However, he knew what he had to do.

A room in the house had been arranged for Aouda. The

young woman was in despair. From certain expressions Mr. Fogg let fall she believed he was meditating something dreadful.

Passepartout, without betraying himself, kept a strict watch over his master, as he was aware to what deplorable extremes the English are sometimes carried when labouring under the pressure of some fixed idea.

But first of all the faithful fellow had gone into his own room and turned off the gas, which had been burning for eighty days—he had found a bill from the gas company in the letter box, and he thought it was about time to put a stop to an expense for which he was responsible.

Mr. Fogg went to bed, but did he sleep? Aouda could not rest, and Passepartout watched all night at his master's door like a faithful dog.

The next day Mr. Fogg desired him very briefly to attend to Aouda's breakfast. He only wanted a cup of tea and bit of toast himself. He hoped Aouda would excuse his presence at breakfast and dinner as his time was so occupied in putting his affairs in order. In the evening he would ask her permission to have a short conversation with her.

Having received his instructions for the day, Passepartout had only to attend to them. He looked at his master and could not make up his mind to leave the room— his heart was full, his conscience filled him with remorse, for he accused himself more than ever of having been the cause of this irreparable disaster. Yes! if he had only warned Mr. Fogg, if he had told him of the detective's plans, Mr. Fogg would certainly not have brought the police agent with him to Liverpool, and then—

Passepartout could hold out no longer.

"Master, sir, Mr. Fogg," he cried, "curse me, for I am to blame, that—"

"I blame no one," replied Phileas Fogg, calmly, "go."

Passepartout left the room and went in search of Aouda, to whom he communicated his master's intentions.

"Madam," he added, "I can do nothing; I have no influence over my master, but you—"

"What influence can I have?" replied Aouda. "Mr. Fogg is not to be influenced by any one. Has he ever understood the feeling of gratitude I entertain for him? Has he ever read my heart? My friend, you must not leave him for a moment. You say he is going to speak to me this evening?"

"Yes, madam; it is probably to arrange about your situation in England."

"We must wait, then," replied Aouda, pensively.

Through the whole of this day, which was Sunday, the house in Savile Row seemed still unoccupied, and for the first time since he lived there Phileas Fogg did not go to his club when it struck half-past eleven by the clock at the Houses of Parliament; and why should he go to his club? His friends could not expect him there; for, as the evening before, at a quarter to nine, on Saturday, the 21st of December, Phileas Fogg had not appeared in the saloon at the Reform Club, his bet was lost. He had not even any occasion to go to his banker for the money, his adversaries had in their hands his cheque for the amount, and all Baring Brothers had to do was to pass the twenty thousand pounds to their credit.

So Mr. Fogg had no occasion to go out and he did not go out—he remained in his room, and put his affairs in order.

When at last Passepartout became so miserable he could not remain alone, he knocked at Aouda's door, went into her room, sat down in a corner, without speaking, and looked at her.

About half-past seven in the evening, Mr. Fogg asked if Aouda would receive him, and in a few moments the young woman and himself were alone in the room.

Mr. Fogg took a chair and sat down by the fire opposite Aouda. His face did not betray the least emotion. Mr. Fogg, on his return, was the same as Mr. Fogg on the eve of his departure.

He sat for five minutes without speaking, then, looking at Aouda, he said—

"Madam, can you forgive me for bringing you to England?"

"I, Mr. Fogg," replied Aouda, trying to still the beating of her heart.

"Allow me to finish what I have to say. When I decided on bringing you away from that distant country, become so dangerous for you to remain, I was a rich man, and it was my intention to have put a part of my fortune at your disposal. Your life would have been a free and happy one. Now, I am a ruined man."

"I know it, Mr. Fogg, and I will in my turn ask you if you will forgive me for having followed you? — and — who knows! perhaps in delaying you I have contributed to your ruin."

"Madam, you could not have remained in India, and your safety was not assured until you were sufficiently far removed, that those zealots could not have obtained possession of you again."

"Then, Mr. Fogg, not content with having saved me from a horrible death, you thought yourself obliged to secure my position in a foreign country."

"Yes, madam," replied Fogg, "but circumstances have gone against me. Still the little I have left I wish to dispose of in your favour."

"But you, Mr. Fogg, what is to become of you?" asked Aouda.

"I, madam," he coldly replied; "I need nothing."

"But how do you look on your future prospects?"

"As I ought," replied Fogg.

"But under no circumstances could want overtake such a man as you? Your friends —"

"I have no friends."

"Your relations, then."

"I have no longer any."

"I pity you, then, Mr. Fogg, for solitude is a sad thing — no one to whom you can confide your griefs? They say that misery shared by another is always to be supported."

"They do say so, madam."

"Mr. Fogg, then," said Aouda, who rose and held out

her hand to that gentleman, "will have a friend and relation in me. Will you take me for your wife?"

As she spoke Mr. Fogg rose; there was an unusual light in his eyes, and a quivering on his lips. Aouda looked up in his face. The sincerity, honesty, grimness, and yet softness in the glance of a noble woman, who dares everything to save him to whom she owes everything, first astonished and then penetrated him. He closed his eyes for a moment, as if to avoid her look. When he opened them—

"I do love you," said he, simply. "Yes, by all that is most sacred, I love you, and I am all yours, and yours only."

"Ah!" cried Aouda, pressing her hand to her heart.

They rang for Passepartout. He came at once.

Mr. Fogg was still holding Aouda by the hand. Passepartout understood it all, and his big, round face became as radiant as a tropical sun.

Mr. Fogg asked if it was not too late to warn the Reverend Samuel Wilson, the rector of the parish of Marylebone. Passepartout smiled his happiest smile, and said—

"It is never too late."

It was then five minutes after eight.

"For tomorrow, Monday?" said he.

"For tomorrow, Monday?" asked Mr. Fogg, looking at Aouda.

"For tomorrow, Monday," replied Aouda.

Passepartout ran off at once.

CHAPTER XXXVI
IN WHICH PHILEAS FOGG'S NAME IS AGAIN
AT A PREMIUM

We ought now to inform our readers that a change had taken place in public opinion when it was known that the actual Bank robber—a certain James Strand—had been taken at Edinburgh, the 17th of December. Three days previously Phileas Fogg was a criminal, actively pursued by the police, and now he was a gentleman of the highest respectability, who was strictly carrying out his eccentric tour round the world.

What an effect this announcement created in the papers! People began betting again, and Phileas Fogg's name was quoted on 'Change at a premium.

That gentleman's five colleagues at the Reform Club passed those three days rather uneasily. Phileas Fogg, whom they had thought no more of, was brought forward once more. Where was he now? on the 17th of December, the day Strand was arrested. No news had been received of Phileas Fogg since he left, seventy-six days before. Had he broken down in his attempt? had he given it up, or was he still following out the route agreed upon before starting? or would he the Saturday following, the 21st of December, make his appearance at a quarter to nine in the evening in the saloon at the Reform Club? During these three days the anxiety which existed in London society is not to be described. They sent telegrams to America and Asia for news of Phileas Fogg. The house in Savile Row was watched morning and evening—no news. Nor had the police any information regarding Fix, the detective, who had so pertinaciously followed the wrong scent. But this did not put a stop to the betting, which became very heavy. Phileas Fogg, like a race-horse, had got to the last turn. They no longer laid odds against him; the paralytic old Lord Albemarle backed him at evens.

Therefore there was a great crowd in Pall Mall that Saturday evening; betting men were numerous in front of the Reform Club. The circulation was impeded, they argued and wrangled, and the police had some trouble in keeping the mob in order, which became greater the nearer the time drew on for Phileas Fogg to arrive.

That evening the two bankers, John Sullivan and Samuel Fallentin, Andrew Stuart the engineer, Gauthier Ralph, the bank director, and Thomas Flanagan, the brewer, were waiting anxiously in the large saloon.

At the moment the clock indicated twenty-five minutes past eight Andrew Stuart rose, and said—

"Gentlemen, in twenty minutes the time agreed upon between us and Mr. Phileas Fogg will have expired."

"At what o'clock was the last train due from Liverpool?" Flanagan asked.

"At twenty-three minutes past seven, and the next is not due till ten minutes after twelve."

"Well, then, if Phileas Fogg had come by the twenty-three minutes past seven train he would be here now. We may consider we have won the bet."

"We must wait awhile before we give an opinion," observed Fallentin; "you know Fogg is a most eccentric person, and his punctuality is well known. He is never too late nor too early, and I should not be the least surprised to see him walk in here to the minute."

"And if I was to see him I should not believe it," rejoined Stuart, who, as usual, was very nervous.

"The truth is," said Flanagan, "Phileas Fogg's undertaking was an absurdity. Let him be as punctual as he may, he could not control the unavoidable delays which were sure to arise, and the loss of two days would be sufficient to compromise his journey."

"You must recollect, sir," added Sullivan, "we have never had a single telegram from him, and yet there was no want of telegraphic communication along his road."

"He has lost, gentlemen," resumed Stuart, "lost a hundred times over. You know the *China*, the only steamer from New York, by which he could have arrived from Liverpool in time, came in yesterday. Here is a list of the passengers from the *Shipping Gazette*, in which his name does not appear. Under the most favourable circumstances he can hardly be at this moment even in New York. I consider he will be twenty days over his time, at least, and old Lord Albemarle will lose his five thousand also."

"That is pretty clear," said Gauthier Ralph, "and all we have to do will be to send his cheque to Barings' tomorrow to be cashed."

It was now just forty minutes past eight.

"Five minutes more," said Stuart.

The five gentlemen looked at one another. Their hearts beat a little faster, for it was very exciting even for men who played high. But they would not let their anxiety appear, and Andrew Fallentin accordingly proposed a rubber.

The minute hand of the clock now pointed to eighteen minutes to nine.

"I would not sell the four thousand pounds which I have in the bet for three thousand nine hundred and ninety-nine pounds," said Andrew Stuart, as he sat down to play.

The players had taken up their cards, but they could not keep their eyes from the clock. Certainly they felt the minutes never seemed so long.

"Forty-three minutes past eight," said Thomas Flanagan, cutting the cards for Gauthier Ralph.

There was a dead silence. The large room was perfectly

still, but outside they could hear the clamours of the crowd, and now and then a shrill cry. The pendulum continued to beat the seconds, and the players could hear every one of them.

"Forty-four minutes past eight," said Sullivan, in a voice which betrayed involuntary emotion.

Only one more minute and the bet was won.

Andrew Stuart and his companions could not go on playing. They threw down their cards.

They began counting the seconds.

At the forty-second, no one, nor at the fiftieth!

But at the fifty-fifth they could hear outside thunders of applause, hurrahs, and even oaths.

The players left their chairs.

By the fifty-seventh second the door of the saloon was thrown open, and before the pendulum had made its sixtieth stroke Phileas Fogg appeared, followed by the crowd, which had forced its way into the club, and quietly said—

"Here I am, gentlemen."

CHAPTER XXXVII

IN WHICH IT IS SHOWN THAT PHILEAS FOGG
WON NOTHING BY HIS TOUR ROUND THE WORLD
EXCEPT HAPPINESS

Yes, Phileas Fogg himself.

It will be remembered that at five minutes past eight in the evening—about twenty-five hours after their arrival in London—Passepartout had been desired by his master to see the Reverend Samuel Wilson, respecting a certain marriage which was to take place the following day.

Passepartout set out on his errand with pleasure. He hurried off to Mr. Wilson's house, who was not yet come home. Of course he was obliged to wait, and he did wait at least twenty minutes.

It was thirty-five minutes past eight when he left the Rector's house—but in what a state! Without his hat, running as he had never run in his life, upsetting people as he flew along the pavement.

In three minutes he was back in Savile Row, and fell down out of breath in Mr. Fogg's room.

He could not speak.

"What's the matter?" said Mr. Fogg.

"Sir," he stammered, "marriage—impossible!"

"Impossible?"

"Impossible for tomorrow."

"Why?"

"Tomorrow is Sunday."

"Monday," replied Mr. Fogg.

"No, today—Saturday."

"Saturday? Impossible!"

"Yes, yes!" cried Passepartout. "You have made a mistake of a day—we arrived twenty-three hours in advance—but there are only ten minutes!"

Phileas Fogg rushed out of the house, jumped into a cab, promised the cabman a hundred pounds, and after running over two dogs, and against five carriages, reached the Reform Club.

The clock showed forty-five minutes past eight when he appeared in the saloon.

Phileas Fogg had accomplished the tour round the world in eighty days!

Phileas Fogg had won his bet of twenty thousand pounds!

And now, how could so exact and particular a man have made this mistake of a day? How was it he believed it was Saturday evening when he arrived in London, when it was only Friday, the 20th December, only seventy-nine days after his departure?

This is the reason he was mistaken, and it is a very plain one.

As he advanced eastward, Phileas Fogg was going towards the sun, and consequently for him the days diminished four minutes for every degree he crossed in this direction.

Now, there are three hundred and sixty degrees on the earth's circumference, and these degrees multiplied by four give exactly twenty-four hours, that is to say, the day he had gained without knowing it. In other words, while Phileas Fogg moving eastward saw the sun pass the meridian eighty times, his friends in London only saw it seventy-nine times. That is why on that very day, which was Saturday and not Sunday as Mr. Fogg fancied, his friends were waiting his appearance in the Reform Club saloon.

And Passepartout's celebrated family watch, which had always kept London time, would have shown this also as well as it did the hours and minutes if it could have shown the days too.

So Phileas Fogg had won twenty thousand pounds. But as he had spent about nineteen thousand on his journey, the pecuniary result was but small. However, that eccentric personage's object was not money, but victory. Even the thousand pounds remaining he divided between honest Passepartout and that wretched Fix, to whom he bore no ill-will. But for correctness' sake he deducted the cost of nineteen hundred and twenty hour's gas from the former's wages.

That same evening Mr. Fogg, as cool as ever, said to Aouda—

"Is this marriage still agreeable to you?"

"Mr. Fogg," replied Aouda, "it is I who ought to ask you that question. You were a ruined man, you are now a rich one."

"Excuse me, madam, this fortune is yours. If you had not thought of it my servant would not have gone to the Reverend Mr. Wilson, and I should not have known I was mistaken in my calculation, and—"

"Dear Mr. Fogg," said the young widow.

"Dear Aouda," responded Phileas Fogg.

The marriage took place forty-eight hours afterwards, and Passepartout, splendidly attired, gave the bride away. Had he not rescued her, and did he not deserve that honour?

The next morning, as soon as it was light, Passepartout began knocking at his master's door.

The door opened, and Mr. Fogg appeared.

"What is it, Passepartout?"

"Why, sir, I have just discovered—"

"What?"

"That we might have done it in seventy-eight days only."

"Certainly we could," replied Mr. Fogg, "but by not

crossing India. But if I had not crossed India I should not have found Aouda, she would not have become my wife, and—"

And Mr. Fogg quietly shut the door again, and this is how Fogg won his wager. He had gone round the world in eighty days. He had employed every means of conveyance in doing so, steamers, railways, carriages, yachts, elephants, and sleighs. He had displayed in this undertaking his wonderful qualities of coolness and exactness. But, after all, what had he gained by all his labour—what had he profited by this journey?

Nothing, do you say? Nothing, indeed, except a charming wife who—improbable as it may seem—made him a very happy man. And, in truth, who would not go round the world for as much?

THE OTHER LOG OF PHILEAS FOGG

After leaving Charing Cross Station, Fogg ordered Passepartout to buy some food for their stay at No. 7, Savile Row, that night. Fogg and Aouda would proceed straight to his house for a night's rest. There was plenty of time to win the bet. In fact, Fogg planned to make his entrance into the Reform Club only a few minutes before his time was up. Stuart might be angry at this delay because he had important information or orders for him. But Fogg desperately needed that night. The anxieties and terrors had been accumulating in him to the bursting point. He had to discharge at least some to keep his psychic boiler from exploding. About six hours of therapeutic emission of neural current would restore him.

On the way, however, he changed his mind about Stuart. He would have to tell him that he was at No. 7. The Capelleans were up to something; the clangings showed that. By indulging himself, he might be ruining his own people, not to mention himself.

As they passed a telegraph office, he ordered the cab to stop. He took only a little time to write the telegram since it consisted of one codeword with his name in code. Directing the clerk to send a messenger at once if a reply came, he left the office. The cab soon drew up before his house. Fogg did not enter it for a few minutes. The front of the house looked as he had left it. The light from Passepartout's gas jet was shining through a narrow opening between the blind and the windowsill. Fogg led Aouda quietly into the house. Both held revolvers. Fogg had smuggled these into England, adding this crime to piracy on the high seas. A thorough search of each room revealed nothing untoward.

Presently Passepartout entered with the provisions. He deposited the bags in the pantry and hurried upstairs to his own room. The jet had not been turned off by Fogg, who thought, correctly, that this was his valet's duty. Passepartout reached out to extinguish the flame, then held his hand. Why turn it off now when he would be needing it?

He went downstairs and removed the mail from the letter box. On seeing the bill from the gas company, his eyes bugged. He would never be able to pay off his debt, not unless he worked for nothing for eighty days and then some. Fogg, being a stickler, even if a hero, would not bear the expense himself.

The night lurched, bumped, and groaned by. Aouda reached vainly for sleep in her room. Fogg sat in his chair in his room and delved into his own mind. He had to be as careful in his probing as an electrician without a schematic trying to find the cause of a malfunction in a tangled mass of high-voltage equipment. One mistake, and he could be severely injured or even killed. From time to time, a shudder passed through him. His pupils dilated or contracted. His nostrils flared. His ears and scalp twitched. His fingers fastened upon the arms of his chair as if he would tear the leather off. Sweat poured out all over him.

Now and then, he groaned. Pain, hate, loathing, contempt, and horror twisted his face in succession. He soundlessly mouthed words he should long ago have verbalized. Sometimes, his body became rigid and shook as if he were in a grand mal seizure. Sometimes, he was as limp as if he were newly dead.

Dawn came while Passepartout watched outside Fogg's door. If he heard sounds that seemed as if Fogg were hurting himself or even killing himself, he was to hasten in. But this had not occurred, though there were moments when he was about to interfere.

Shortly after dawn, Passepartout, looking through the keyhole, saw Fogg sleeping in bed. The crises were over, for that night at least. Fogg had told him that it would take at least three sessions to discharge most of the heavy stuff.

The Frenchman went to his own room then to perform some therapy on himself. Since he was much less self-controlled than Fogg (as who wasn't?), and had a temperament which naturally discharged anxieties more easily than Fogg's, his therapy was shorter and less dangerous. After an hour, he went to sleep.

Fogg, looking haggard and pale, rose late that morning. By noon he had regained his customary healthy appearance, though he acted as if he still had much energy bound up in him. Aouda came down for breakfast about twelve. She, too, was pale and had bags under her eyes.

At half-past seven that evening, the occupants of No. 7 heard the clanging of fire-wagon bells. Looking out the windows, past the curtains, they saw by the gaslights many people, including their neighbors, hurrying up Savile Row. The bells became louder, and two fire-wagons, each drawn by a team of horses, sped by. The bells had no sooner died out than the boom of an explosion rattled the windows. Passepartout, quivering with curiosity, asked if he could not leave the house to find out the source of all this excitement.

"No," Fogg said. "Someone might see you and thus know that I am back. I prefer to keep it secret until the last moment."

Passepartout thought that that was not likely, since everybody, servants and masters, seemed to have rushed off to the fire or whatever it was. They did not know what he looked like, and he would take care to be back before they returned to Savile Row. But he did not argue. He could not, however, refrain from looking between the curtains several times. Just as he was about to turn away from his latest peek, he saw a hansom cab stop two houses from No. 7. The horse drawing it stood for several seconds while the driver, perched high on a seat at the rear of the two-wheeled carriage, shouted at it. The passenger turned around and in turn shouted at the driver through the opening in the roof. The horse, quivering, took several more steps forward. The driver stood up to lash his whip at it. A moment later, the horse suddenly collapsed, causing the cab to tilt even more forward and precipitating the driver off to one side and onto the street.

The occupant of the hansom must have been startled, since he did not open the door for at least a minute. Then he got out slowly on the other side, where he examined the driver, who had not moved after striking the street. Presently, he rose from the driver, looked around at the deserted street, and then headed for the nearest house across the street. He leaned on a heavy walking cane, dragging his right leg somewhat. He wore a long heavy cloak against the late December cold. On his head was a military cap, probably an officer's. He knocked on the door so hard that Passepartout could hear the banging. Receiving no answer, he turned and walked with awkward and slow three-legged gait to the next house. He must be some officer who had returned wounded from India or some far-off place, Passepartout thought. His bronzed skin indicated a long residence in the tropics.

Meanwhile, the driver had sat up and then fallen back again. The horse had not moved.

Passepartout did not go out to help the man, since he had been forbidden to leave. The officer, however, would soon work his way to No. 7. What should he do? Passepartout thought. The poor fellow on the street evidently needed help. Well, he would go ask Fogg for his orders.

The officer had just turned toward Fogg's house when Passepartout saw a man in the uniform of a telegraph officer runner on the opposite side of the street. Could he be bringing a message to No. 7? Fogg had said that he might be getting one. Yes, he was crossing the street at an angle toward No. 7. This relieved Passepartout's predicament. He had orders to open the door only for a telegram. He could not help it that the officer would arrive at the same time as the messenger. Fogg could not reasonably refuse help to the injured man; besides, it would look suspicious if he did.

Though he kept on the latch chain, he opened the door. Now he saw, coming up the street, a chimney sweep. And, down the street, on the other side, the door of a house opening. A young man, bare-headed and in a dressing gown, stepped out. Evidently, he had been sleeping and had just awakened. Looking out, perhaps wondering why the servants were gone, he had seen the fallen man. This was good. Passepartout could direct the officer to him, telling the officer at the same time that he was unauthorized to leave the house.

The officer reached the door first and addressed him through the opening in a rich baritone.

"There's been an accident, as you can see. My driver seems to have broken his arm and also suffered head injuries. I'm afraid that he has been drinking. Could you run for the nearest doctor?"

Now that the officer was closer, Passepartout could see the cold blue eyes under heavy lids. These, combined with the bushy eyebrows, the thin, projecting nose, heavy black moustache, heavy lips, and strong jaw, combined to form a ruthless yet sensual face. Passepartout did not care for him, but, after all, it was the driver who needed medical attention.

"There is a Doctor Caber several blocks from here, sir," the Frenchman said, remembering that Fogg had told him so before retiring. "I cannot leave the house, but you might send that sweep after him. Or perhaps the messenger would oblige you?"

The runner had drawn to within a few feet of them. He was an exceptionally broad-shouldered fellow with a bushy moustache and long hair, both streaked with gray. His bulbous red nose indicated his chief occupation when not on duty.

"Ah, perhaps I could, my good fellow!" the officer said. He pointed the cane through the opening at Passepartout. The Frenchman saw the round hole in its end.

"But I do not care to," the officer said. "And don't think about trying to leap away. This is an air gun disguised as a walking stick. It can, and will, drive a rifle bullet through you at this range. So open up for us or suffer the consequences."

The messenger must have had concealed a pair of bolt cutters under his cloak. Their ends appeared and closed on the latch chain, which fell apart. The door was pushed violently inward against Passepartout, and he staggered backward. Despite the officer's demand for silence, Passepartout gave one loud cry. The officer, no longer crippled, lifted the air gun and brought it down over Passepartout's head. Passepartout ducked so that he did not receive the full impact. Stunned, he still had sense enough to throw himself to one side. He had intended to bounce up onto his feet but found that his legs failed him. The officer ran at Passepartout with the messenger close behind him. In a flash, Passepartout recognized him, under the dyed hair and the false nose, as Nemo. He tried to get up again, but this time the stick came down fully on his head.

A few minutes later, according to the clock on the mantel of the fireplace, he awoke on the floor. His head hurt. His hands were bound behind him, and he was gagged. The only other occupant of the room was the hansom driver, recovered from his "broken arm." He was a tall, very stooped man in his early forties. He bore a resemblance to Nemo but lacked the widely spaced eyes and was much darker in eyes and skin. He held a peculiar weapon in one hand. Passepartout thought it must be an air gun. It was small enough to be concealed under a cloak.

The minutes throbbed by, along with his head, as the clock hands progressed. About ten minutes later, Passepartout heard footsteps on the staircase. He twisted his neck, not without pain to his head, to see who was coming. He was shocked. This was a stranger. How many others had invaded while he lay unconscious?

The newcomer also carried an air pistol. He was tall and looked as if he were in his late forties. He had bold aquiline features on which was an arrogant and predatory expression. His peculiar yellow-green eyes and sharp profile made him look like a hungry fish-eagle.

"They're still locked in his room," he said. "Nemo says there's no hurry to take them. We want as little noise as possible. The people are starting to come back from the fire. Moran is stationed in the back with his air rifle. If they try to get out of the third story window, he'll drop them. He won't miss, that one."

The other frowned and said, "Why don't we just break down the door and storm them? If they get off a few more shots, they're not likely to draw much attention. The sounds will be confined in their room. But if Fogg shoots out the window, the sound will carry a long distance."

"Your brother says no. Too many people returning. Evidently we didn't provide them with a large enough spectacle."

He laughed harshly and said, "We should have set the whole block ablaze."

"Nemo knows what he's doing," the tall dark man said. He looked at Passepartout. "While they're holed up, we can work on this frog. You should enjoy that. You've had so much practice."

"Excellent!" the man with yellow-green eyes said. "But what is to keep the other two from killing themselves?"

"Nothing. But that's the way Nemo wants it. You ask too many questions."

The other looked as if he did not like that. Though he did not carry himself as if he were or had been a soldier, he radiated the air of one who had been in command of many and would like once more to be.

"Also," he added, "how do we know that Fogg doesn't have secret escape routes?"

"I presume that the house was examined while Fogg was gone," the tall dark man said. "Why don't you ask Nemo?"

"We're always left in the dark," the predatory-looking man said.

The tall dark man shrugged and then walked over to Passepartout. He looked at him.

"I wonder if he knows anything we don't."

"The code?"

"It's been changed since he started on his trip, and we know the old one now. But he'll have some items of interest for us, I'm sure."

"We'll have to keep the gag on, since we wouldn't want the neighbors to hear his screams. So we'll leave the right hand untouched. He has to be able to write out the information."

"What if he uses his left hand to write with?"

"We'll find out."

The tall dark man said, "Before the entertainment begins, I have to revive the horse and get the cab out of the way. It's a wonder that someone hasn't noticed the beast. Where's the kitchen? A pailful should do it."

He left the room, and the yellow-green-eyed man sat down. He seemed disgruntled.

Jealousy, Passepartout thought. He was jealous of Nemo's authority. If only he could work on that. But that was a forlorn hope even if Passepartout could talk. And he couldn't talk.

A familiar voice came from the head of the stairs. Yellow-green eyes rose and walked to its foot.

"Yes?"

"Yes what, Vandeleur?"

"Yes, sir."

"Hold the colonel for a minute. I have another idea."

"Yes, sir."

Vandeleur? Passepartout thought. Where had he heard that name before?

The colonel's footsteps sounded, and he entered holding a large pail from which water sloshed.

"This should be enough to get the beast back onto its legs," he said, chuckling, "We must thank Moran sometime for discovering this rare Oriental drug. One pill, and the beast drops seemingly dead at a precisely calculated moment. One pailful of water, and it is resuscitated in a minute."

"I know that," Vandeleur said.

Now Passepartout remembered where he had heard Vandeleur's name before. He must be the notorious Englishman whose duel with the Duc de Val d'Orge, one of the best swordsmen of the world, had been in all the French newspapers. The Duc had lost a hand during the encounter and his wife afterward, since she had run off with Vandeleur. A few years later, Vandeleur had become, for a brief time, the dictator of Paraguay. He had eventually been forced to flee because of a rebellion caused by his atrocities. The Duchess had died during his flight, some said under circumstances which did not reflect credit upon Vandeleur. He had also, it was said, been of service to the British government during the Indian mutiny, but his exploits were such that the government did not dare acknowledge them. There was also a story afloat that he had never backed away from a duel with any man, except one, the equally notorious Captain Richard Francis Burton. Vandeleur's admirers, however, claimed that the government had interfered because Vandeleur was then engaged in the delicate and extremely important task of recovering the jewels of the baronet, Sir Samuel Levy. The duel would be resumed whenever Vandeleur and Burton happened to meet again, which was not likely, since both were seldom in England.

Passepartout shivered. With such men holding them prisoner, what chance had they?

Vandeleur said, "Your brother wants you, Colonel."

The tall dark man set the pail down and called up the stairs, "Shall I come up?"

"No," Nemo said. "Don't forget to stay out of the way of the horse when he first revives. The drug sometimes causes the beast to go into a frenzy. Hang onto his head for a minute, keeping out of the way of his hooves, and he'll soon be quiet."

"I haven't forgotten," the colonel said. "I'm no green recruit."

"Also," Nemo said, "I want you to take a message to Nesse I. Tell him to listen for our signals. We may use the distorter after all. There's too much chance of the police or the neighbors getting curious. Those Reform Club swine may send somebody over to ascertain if Fogg has at least gotten home even if he hasn't shown up there. And Fogg's colleagues may try a rescue attempt. He surely must have notified them that he was back."

"Why didn't you think of that before we came here?" the colonel said somewhat sulkily.

"Because, my dear brother, I had expected to overpower these Eridaneans at once. I didn't know how inept my help was."

"You were with us," the colonel said.

"Yes, and I should have handled the Frenchman myself. He would never have been able to get that shout out, and we would not now have Fogg and the woman giving us a problem. And pray shut up, brother, while I tell you what else you must do."

"All right," the colonel muttered.

"After you've delivered my message, stay at Nesse I. We don't want too many coming and going here. Remember, Fogg's a celebrated man, and if we hadn't lured his neighbors away, they'd be down around our ears by now."

"I'll miss all the fun. Can't Vandeleur go instead?"

"Do I have to repeat everything?" Nemo said in an exasperated tone. "You are dressed like a cabbie. What if someone should see a gentleman drive off a hansom?"

"Very well," the colonel said reluctantly. He turned and went to the pail.

Nemo's voice came sharply. "Can't you wait until I'm through? You will take one of the distorters with you. Nesse doesn't have any, and I think it'd be better that we be transmitted there than to the other place, which is too close to the heart of London."

"Which one?" the colonel said. "Passepartout's or the one you made?"

The one you made! Passepartout thought. Then that was why Nemo stayed behind in San Francisco! And it was his arrival via the distorter that caused the clangings. That was sorry news indeed! Nemo could *manufacture* distorters! But how had he been able to accomplish something that both Eridaneans and Capelleans had been trying to do without success for two hundred years? The original Old Ones had brought some distorters with them, those still in use, but they had lacked the knowledge to make new ones. And their desire to take some apart for analysis had been unfulfilled because opening them would cause them to blow up.

The distorter which Head had carried! Was that one which had been recently manufactured? Had he taken passage as a mere cook-steward on a small merchant sailing vessel to avoid the Eridaneans covering the liners? Had he done this because the chief of the Eridaneans knew that he was coming to Europe with the distorter?

Where then had Nemo gotten the knowledge to make a new distorter? Surely, from schematics. Where had he gotten them? From Head? But Fogg had examined Head's clothing and body, and Nemo had been examined by both Passepartout and Fogg. Still, Nemo had not been frisked again after returning to the *General Grant*.

Could Nemo have removed the schematics from Head's body during the disarming and the cleaning up of the *Mary Celeste*? The only time he had been close to Head after he had been searched was when he had helped Fogg throw the corpse overboard.

Somehow, he had gotten hold of the schematics. And he had made two new ones in San Francisco while Fogg's party was traveling east. One of the new distorters would have to be left behind. He had brought with him the other distorter when he was transmitted, undoubtedly by the device brought to London by the man from China.

And he had carried the new distorter with him to Fogg's house just in case he would not be able to get hold of Passepartout's.

The colonel went up the steps and returned a minute later. He left the house with a hard slam of the door. Nemo called out, "The fool! Will he never go quietly?"

Valdeleur got up to look through the window. He gave a cry and clutched the curtains. Then he said, "The idiot!"

He whirled and ran to the foot of the staircase and called up, "Your brother's in trouble!"

Passepartout could hear the heavy footsteps of Nemo as he ran to the room overlooking the street. A moment later, his boots sounded on the floor as he returned and on the steps as he descended. He strode to the curtains, pulled Valdeleur roughly aside, and looked out.

He swore and said, "I told him! He was to keep his body away!"

He swore again, ran to the door, opened it, and then closed it again.

Passepartout heard a shrill whinnying, the clatter of hooves, and a scream. Shouts from down the street came faintly.

Valdeleur swore also.

"The beast knocked him down and the hansom rode over him!"

He turned to Nemo.

"What do we do now?"

Nemo said, "Oh, the fool! He'll pay for this!"

"In more ways than one," Valdeleur said. "He's unconscious, the bloody blighter!"

"How he ever got to be a colonel is understandable only if you know the general level of intelligence of Her Majesty's officers," Nemo said. "But how I could be brother to him and that other idiot is explainable only by the fact that we had different mothers!"

"I didn't know that," Valdeleur muttered. "That explains why your brother's named James, too."

"And a fine lot of confusion that resulted in, too!" Nemo said. "She would insist on naming him after her father, even if my father objected!"

His expression became even harder. He said, "That's neither here nor there."

He went back up the stairs. Presumably, he was notifying whoever was stationed at the door of Fogg's bedroom of the situation.

Passepartout groaned behind the gag. If only Mr. Fogg and

Aouda had known about this, they could have made a break. With only one man at their door, they might have gotten loose.

Aouda was in her room and wondering if Phileas Fogg would ever ask her to marry him.

If she were called away on another mission, she might never see him again. If he did not ask her soon, he might not get a chance even if he wished to do so. Perhaps he was hesitating now only because she was a Parsi. Still, she could pass for a European, and their children would be even more European-looking than she.

But she doubted that her Parsi origin had anything to do with his failure to speak up. What did Fogg care about the opinions of others? No, his difficulty was his inability to express his deepest feelings. He had too much self-control, which meant, in effect, that in many things he could not control his true self.

Fogg, in his room, was thinking about asking Aouda to marry him. But what kind of life could he offer her? It was true that, once she started having children, she would be exempt from missions. Yet, she would know no ease of mind. He would be gone for long periods, in peril most of the time, and could be expected to be killed at any time. Moreover, if the Capelleans found out where she lived, they would kill her and perhaps the children, too.

At that moment, both Fogg and Aouda heard Passepartout's cry.

Fogg ran out into the hall with a revolver in his hand. A few seconds later, Aouda came out of her room. She was holding a Colt six-shooter.

Fogg gestured for her to go to the other end of the hall so she could command the approach up the servants' staircase. He hurried to the landing off the big central staircase. As he did so, he heard bootsteps clattering on the stairs. He got to the landing just in time. Three men were running up the second-story stairs, and all were armed with weapons which he instantly recognized as air pistols. He also recognized two of the men. One was a neighbor, the dissolute wenching young baronet, Sir Hector Osbaldistone. The other was Nemo. He had torn off the eye-mask which half-blinded him and the putty nose and false moustache.

Fogg's shot and Nemo's went off almost at the same time and both missed. The three men retreated down the stairs.

A shot sounded behind him. He whirled and saw smoke curling from Aouda's pistol, and then he saw Aouda stagger back until she hit the wall. She slid down, dropping the pistol and clutching her right shoulder. Blood welled out from between the fingers of her left hand.

Fogg, crying, "Aouda, Aouda," ran down the hall to her. She was pale, and her eyes looked strange, but she was able to murmur, "The bullet only creased me."

He removed her hand and saw that it had done more than just burn the skin or break it. It had skimmed the upper part of her right breast but had gone into her flesh just below the collarbone. It seemed to have emerged without striking the shoulder bone, though he could not be sure. She was bleeding from both wounds profusely and would soon be in deeper shock, or even dead, if the bleeding were not stopped.

But if he attended to her, the staircase would be left open to the enemy.

She could not continue to man her post here, and he could not defend both positions. There was only one thing to do.

He lifted her and carried her down the hall and into his bedroom. Blood dripped from her and left a trail. Again, that could not be helped.

In the bedroom, he placed her on his bed and then locked the door. From the medicine chest in the bathroom he got dressings and bandages, which he applied in a feverish haste. For once, he was not serene.

Aouda stared at him and muttered something. He said, "Shh, dear!" and put a finger lightly over her lips. A few minutes later, he completed the bandaging. Some of her color seemed to be returning, though he was not sure that his hopes were not supplying it for his eyes. He started to move a heavy bureau toward the door when he heard a door slam down the hall. They were now on this floor and, though they had the trail of blood to follow, were searching the other rooms anyway.

Presently, the knob turned on his door. He fired his revolver at a point just above the knob. If he hit anybody he could not hear anything to indicate so.

A moment later Nemo's voice came to him. "We have you, Fogg.

There's a man out in the garden with an air rifle. He'll drop you without fail if you so much as even show yourself at the windows. He's the best shot in the East and perhaps in the West, too. We have the Frenchman and his distorter, and we can shoot our way in at any time."

"Not without loss," Fogg said calmly.

Nemo said something Fogg could not hear distinctly. Footsteps sounded as a man walked heavily away. Fogg shoved the bureau toward the door but decided not to bring it against the door. He would leave it several feet away and would place burning oil lamps on its top and at its bottom. If they did try to storm him, he would shoot both lamps. The paraffin oil (called kerosene by the Americans) would form an impenetrable barrier, and some of it might even splash on the invaders and set them afire. The dangerous disadvantage of this was that he and Aouda would have to get out of the room to escape being burned alive. Aouda might be incapable of getting out by herself, in which case he would have to lower her on a rope made out of bedsheets. This would make both of them somewhat easy targets for the rifleman in the garden.

That would have to be taken care of when it occurred. Fogg would throw out his last lamp and hope that its burning would illuminate the garden enough for him to see the rifleman. Also, the fire might be seen by the neighbors behind him, and an alarm would, he hoped, force the Capelleans to run. He could, of course, shoot out the window now and try to attract the attention of the neighborhood. But he had heard the fire wagons and the explosion and had comprehended that the explosion was a trick to draw his neighbors away for the time being.

He set the third lamp, as yet unlit, by the window, peered between the curtains, and then turned away. The sky was overcast; the garden was in an impenetrable darkness. If only there were snow there, he might be able to see better what the garden held.

After turning off the jet light, he got some brandy for Aouda and lifted her head so she could drink. Some blood had spread beyond her bandages, but the flow seemed to have stopped.

"Did you hear all that?" he whispered.

"Yes," she said.

"He hasn't much time to do whatever he is going to do," he said. "And the neighbors will surely be back soon. At least, some of the servants will have to return; they won't want to take the chance of displeasing their masters by staying away too long. And our chief is sure to reply to my telegram. Perhaps even now the house is under surveillance by our people."

"I trust you to see us all through," Aouda said weakly.

"One way or the other," Mr. Fogg said.

"Did I hear you call me *Aouda dear*?"

"You were not mistaken," he said.

"Would that mean . . . ?"

"It would."

She smiled slightly, and her eyes looked brighter.

"I have been waiting to hear you say that," she said. "And then . . ."

"And then . . . ?"

"And then kiss me."

Fogg stooped over and kissed her lightly. Straightening, he said, "I dare not press my ardor, Aouda, since you are in no condition to receive anything but a tender nursing. But would you marry me?"

"If we had a minister, immediately," she said.

Passepartout, meanwhile, watched Nemo and Vandeleur as they watched the scene on the street. According to their comments, which were frequently asterisked by oaths, the plight of the colonel had attracted a number of people returning from the excitement. From Vandeleur's exclamations, the first to reach the colonel was a street boy, a ragged and dirty urchin. "He's not helping him!" Vandeleur said. "He's robbing him!"

"What?" Nemo said, and he opened the curtains a trifle more.

"He's taking the distorter!" he said. "He's running away with his wallet and the watch!"

Vandeleur turned to his chief for orders and saw then that he was in no condition to give them. He had been seized with a fit of shaking.

Vandeleur said, "By God, you aren't fit to command us!" He started to open the door, but Nemo, by a great effort of will, overcame the shaking. He bounded forward and struck Vandeleur on the back of his neck with the barrel of the air pistol. Vandeleur crumpled. Nemo shut the door.

Though his body had quit shuddering, Nemo's head still oscillated. And when he spat out his recriminations at Vandeleur, he seemed to Passepartout to resemble a giant snake even more.

"Did you think you could really catch that guttersnipe? What did you think would happen when you dashed out of a house supposedly uninhabited? And so you think that I am not fit to command?"

Vandeleur did not answer. Nemo kicked him heavily in the ribs and snarled, "Get up!"

Vandeleur groaned but made no effort to rise.

Nemo placed the flats of his palms against the door and leaned against it for a moment. When he pushed himself away a moment later, the oscillations had ceased. He started to turn away, and his composure, only just regained, was immediately lost.

Passepartout, with his acrobat's skill and agility, had gotten to his feet though his ankles were bound together. He had advanced across the room in a series of very small hops. Any small noise he might have made was drowned out by the exclamations of the two Capelleans. When he had seen Nemo starting to run toward him, he had crouched low, leaped high into the air, and kicked out in a double-sabot.

The heels of his boots caught Nemo on the side of his jaw. Nemo crashed sideways into the door and slumped to the floor. Passepartout fell heavily on his back, hurting the arms tied behind his back and knocking the wind out of him. For a moment he writhed in agony. Vandeleur groaned again and rolled over onto his side. Nemo, sitting with one side against the door, his head on his chest, seemed completely unconscious.

Passepartout, his breath regained, got to his knees with a jerk of his body. With another violent contortion, he got to his feet.

Vandeleur managed to struggle to all fours. He shook his head, an action which must have pained his injured neck, because he groaned.

There was a slight cracking sound as the Frenchman disjointed his arms. He brought them up and over his head and now had his arms in front of him. If Nemo had been able to see him, he would have understood how the three Eridaneans had managed to get free of their bonds in the cabin of the *General Grant*.

It was at this moment that someone banged on the front door and that he heard a voice raised in some room in the back of the house.

Passepartout fumbled desperately in Nemo's clothes for a knife. The banging on the door continued, and now he recognized Moran's voice as the captain approached. He was asking why in blue blazes someone had not brought the promised hot coffee and brandy? Post or no post, he was coming in for a moment. His hands were so cold that he couldn't even handle the air gun properly.

Passepartout brought a knife out of one of Nemo's boots and slashed at the ropes binding his ankles. Moran's footsteps became louder; he was just about to enter the room.

Vandeleur got onto his feet and lurched toward the Frenchman. Passepartout turned and slashed at him, gashing him on the left side of his face. Vandeleur screamed and stumbled back with one hand held over the wound. Blood spread out between his fingers and ran down his neck.

Still holding the knife, Passepartout ran across the room and raced up the steps. Just as he was about six steps from the first landing, he heard a shout behind and below him. He cleared the six steps and dived forward. He slid forward, stopped, rolled over, and saw a hole in the ceiling just above the landing where the missile from the captain's air rifle had struck. He got onto his feet and sped down the hallway. At its far end was the staircase used by the servants. If he could get to that and then back down, he might escape from the house. But it was a long way to go, and Moran was not far behind him, and if he caught him while he was still in the hall, he would probably not miss.

He dared a glance behind him. The captain had halted a few steps past the end of the hall and was bringing up his weapon to his shoulder.

Passepartout threw himself to one side so hard that he rebounded from a door. The door opposite was part way open, offering an opportunity which he could not afford to dismiss. He staggered sidewise into it and fell through. He was up quickly and locked the door. He stuck the hilt of the knife between his teeth and sawed at the rope around his wrists. The knob rattled; the door crashed as Moran vainly hurled his body against it. Passepartout cut the last fibers and stood up, his hands free.

Moran's voice shouted down the hall; somebody shouted back. Evidently Moran would be telling them to guard the door while he returned to the garden. Passepartout quickly pulled back the curtains and opened the window. He could drop one story to the walk below and dash across the garden. But Moran would be out almost as quickly, and he would have too much time to aim while Passepartout tried to scramble up over the eight-foot-high wall. No, that was out.

He swore a few Gallic oaths. He had hoped to go through the door from which he had rebounded and so have access to a street window. There he could have shouted to the people in the street or even have dived through a window. But now he was in the same situation as Fogg and Aouda.

Nemo, on coming to his senses, may or may not have had another seizure. It is safe to assume that his jaw, head, and side hurt and that he raved at his aides and threatened horrible punishments. Then he turned his attention to the banging on the door. He opened it a crack. By the illumination of the nearby gaslight, he saw Fix. Fix was dressed in a messenger's uniform.

Beyond, two men were carrying off the still form of the colonel on a stretcher. Leading them was a man carrying a leather bag. Doubtless, this was the Doctor Caber who lived near Fogg. He was bringing the colonel to his house to wait for the ambulance.

"Go away!" Nemo said through the crack. "Go away, you fool! The situation has changed!"

"What?" Fix said, and then, hesitatingly, "But you must read this telegram!"

Nemo could see that everybody in the crowd was turned to watch the colonel being carried off. He opened the door, reached out, grabbed Fix by his coatfront, and yanked him inside. He shut the door and said, "I must, must I?"

"Yes," Fix said. He looked curiously around in the light afforded by the single gas jet. "What's happened?"

"Never mind that," Nemo said. He tore the envelope from Fix's grasp. It had been opened, so obviously Fix had read it.

"Just as you told me, sir," Fix said. "I stopped the real messenger, and I showed him that I was a detective. I told him that I had to have the telegram because it was evidence in a criminal case. I gave him two shillings to assure his cooperation, then read the message and hurried here as swiftly as I could."

"Shut up!" Nemo said. He walked over to the gas jet and read the telegram silently the first time and loudly the second time. It was evident that he did not like what he read either time.

RELEASE THE THREE UNDAMAGED BY 8:30, AND YOU MAY GO UNTOUCHED. WE HAVE NESSE I. THE OLD ONE IS NO MORE. CONGRATULATIONS. YOU ARE NOW THE CHIEF. CONSIDER THE CONSEQUENCES.

CHIEF OF ERID

Fix put his hands in his pockets to conceal their trembling. He said, "What does all that mean?"

"It's obvious," Nemo said scornfully. "They managed to locate Nesse I when I arrived because of the noise made by the distorter. It took them some time, which is why I got away before they found it. They've killed our chief, the last . . ."

He paused, thinking of the effect on their morale if they knew that the last of the Old Capelleans was dead. He was too late. The others understood what he meant.

"The Old One is dead!" Fix said, almost wailing.

"Perhaps," Nemo said. "The Eridanean may be lying, you know, and probably is. But he's not lying about his knowledge of the situation here. So he's giving us until eight-thirty to produce Fogg, the Frenchman, and Jejeebhoy unharmed. If we don't, we'll probably be invaded, no matter how many Earthlings are attracted by the battle."

Fix started to the curtain as if he meant to look outside.

Nemo said, "Belay that! They're out there somewhere."

He stood for a moment in thought, softly rubbing his jaw, on which a swelling had appeared.

"Get Osbaldistone and Vandeleur back down here."

"And what about . . . ?"

"The others? They won't know they've been left unguarded. They won't open the door for fear they'll get a ball in the head. I want everybody to be acquainted with this new situation. Moran can be told later; if they saw him coming back into the house, they might try to leave by the windows. Hurry!"

Fix went upstairs and quietly got Vandeleur and Osbaldistone away from their posts. On the way down from the second floor, he whispered the news to them. Vandeleur said nothing. The baronet went gray. "The last of the Old Ones is dead," he murmured. "What do we do now?"

"Nemo says that the Eridaneans may be lying about that," Fix said. "But I doubt it. They must have taken Nesse I; otherwise, how would they have even known that that is what we call the prime headquarters? But Nemo is the first chief now."

Nemo affirmed everything that Fix had said. "But don't feel that the Eridaneans have any advantage over us because they might still have an Old One to lead them. For all we know, they don't have any either. Even if they do, what about it? The Old Ones were no more intelligent than we. In fact, their very alienness has handicapped us, in my opinion. It takes a genuine human being to know how to fight human beings, and now we Capelleans have one—myself—to lead them! Now we can conduct our war as we please and with a more realistic goal."

Fix wondered what Nemo meant by *more realistic*. Was he intending to abandon the Grand Plan, to use the Race for private gain only, mainly his own private gain?

Osbaldistone said, "But what about the sharing of the Blood? There is no more Blood from the Stars to mingle in our veins at the puberty ceremonies."

"So what?" Nemo said, glaring. "The Blood itself has no intrinsic value. Its only value is symbolic. From now on the blood of the human chief will be used in the ceremonies. Capelleanism is an ideal; its goal is the conquest of Earth for the good of the Earthlings. The Earthlings must be saved from themselves."

"But the way things are going, the Eridaneans might win!"

"That's close to treason," Nemo said. "It is true that the end is near, since neither we nor the enemy probably number more than a hundred each, if that. But I have a plan. We'll conduct a campaign such as the Old Ones were too inflexible, too unintelligent to conceive. We'll concentrate, bring in our people, who are scattered all over the globe, reorganize, and launch a hunt which will not stop until we have run every Eridanean to the ground and killed him. And . . ."

"Only a hundred each!" Fix said.

Nemo looked as if he wished he had not said so much. Then he said, "Enough of the future. The present is what counts, and, for the present, we must retreat. The enemy has won this round, but it'll be the last he'll win."

He took Passepartout's watch from his coat pocket and snapped the lid on its back open.

"We'll retreat, but only after Fogg and company have been eliminated," he said. "Then we use the distorter to get to Nesse II. Vandeleur, you're carrying the tape for . . ."

He stopped, his mouth hanging open. First, he paled. Then he became red.

"This isn't the Frenchman's watch!" he cried. "This doesn't have any controls! It's just a watch, that's all, just a watch!"

Fix became numb.

Vandeleur said, "What do you mean?"

"I mean those swine have tricked us!" Nemo said. "That Fogg! He must have taken the distorter and given the Frenchman a watch to carry so we'd think . . . he . . . he . . . Fogg . . . has the watch with the distorter!"

Fix said, "Then we're trapped! We can't get out!"

"No, by all the furies!" Nemo said. "We'll get it from Fogg!"

"Sir," Fix said, "why don't we just accept their terms and leave quietly?"

Fix, half-stunned, lay on the floor. He tried to rise, but, seeing that Nemo was about to hit him again, decided to stay where he was.

"Do you think for a moment they'd keep their word any more than we would ours?"

He turned away, and Fix thought it safe to get up. He was scared to speak up, but he felt that he must. Their salvation depended upon it.

"Sir," he said, "if Fogg gave his word, we'd be safe. He wouldn't go back on his word."

Nemo swung back to face him. "What, an Eridanean's word is good?"

"Eridanean or not, Fogg would not betray us because then he'd be betraying himself," Fix said. "I know the man well."

"Perhaps you know him too well!" Nemo said. "Perhaps he has seduced you into turning traitor?"

"Exactly my thinking," Vandeleur said.

Fix trembled, but he said, "Not at all. But I do know that Fogg, whatever else he may be, is a true man. He would not break his oath, not even to us."

"Not *even* to *us*!" Nemo said. "Just what do you mean by that?"

He threw the watch against the fireplace so hard that the works burst out.

"Fix, I've had my doubts about you for a long time. There is only one way you can convince me you're not a traitor; only one way you can keep from dying as a traitor."

"Yes, sir," Fix said. He tried to keep his face from twitching.

"We must have that distorter and have it quickly. There is no time for subtlety now; we must storm Fogg's room. You will lead us into it."

And so he would die, Fix thought. Fogg wouldn't miss the first man who entered. Fix would be the sacrifice, and Nemo would, in effect, have executed him. And why? Because Nemo thought Fix to be a traitor.

"Well, Fix?" Nemo said.

"If that's the way it has to be," Fix said.

"That is the way it has to be."

"Will you see that my family is taken care of?" Fix said.

"Take care of a traitor's. . . ?" Vandeleur said, but Nemo interrupted him with a, "Quiet!"

Fix said, "I am no traitor."

Nemo's voice became softer. "Vandeleur is too hotheaded. We're all disturbed by this, but now is no time to get panicky. Yes, Fix, I promise you that if something should happen to you, your family will not have to suffer."

And what did that mean? Fix thought. That they would be killed quickly?

"We'll get the Frenchie first," Nemo said. "Sir Hector, you'll resume your post at Fogg's door. It's not likely that he'll hear us attacking the Frenchie, but if he did he might deduce that there couldn't be many of us at his door, and he might try to break out. Station yourself to one side, along the wall, so that if he does run out, you'll get the first shot."

Osbaldistone left. Nemo said, "Vandeleur, you'll have a chance to avenge the wound the Frenchie gave you. You will lead the attack."

"Excellent!" Vandeleur said. "But I'd like to carve his face before he dies."

"We don't have time for that," Nemo said. "He must be killed immediately and as silently as possible.

"Now, whatever our losses, we must get into Fogg's room and get it over with at once. That trail of blood indicates that the woman was badly wounded. She is either dead or too hurt to help Fogg, and a good thing, too, since she is an excellent shot. Fogg must be killed at once, otherwise he may open the distorter and so blow himself, and possibly all of us, to kingdom come. I don't think he will do that except as a last resort, so it is up to us to see that he has no time for a last resort.

"I imagine that he has placed some furniture before the door as a barricade. We will remove the hinges of the door. At my signal, Vandeleur will shoot the door lock off. The door will be pulled away by Osbaldistone and myself. You, Fix, will take a running jump across the hall and dive over the barricade. Fogg will have his room dark, but we'll turn off the lights in the hall beforehand so our eyes can be adjusted to a lack of light. This will also make it difficult for Fogg to see clearly. As you go over the barricade, Fix, fire once to draw his fire. Then worry about how you are going to land. We'll see the flame from his revolver and know where to shoot then."

Fix knew he couldn't clear that furniture in one dive. And if Fogg had the furniture piled all the way up to the ceiling, he'd be hanging there a helpless target. No doubt, Nemo and Vandeleur would be able to shoot Fogg once they had seen his fire. But Fix wouldn't be able to see that. He'd be dead. And for what? For a man who had used him, not to advance the interests of all Capelleans but only to advance his own.

Nevertheless, he said nothing. Words would be useless. He took his Webley from his pocket and followed Nemo to the door behind which Passepartout waited. Nemo used his air pistol to shoot out the lock mechanism. Fix opened the door, and Vandeleur rushed in with an air pistol in one hand and a knife in the other. The room was dark, but Fix carried an oil lamp which lit up enough for them to see that the Frenchman was not in the room. Nor was he hiding in the bathroom or the wardrobe or beneath the bed or behind the curtains. The windows were still locked.

"You said he wouldn't dare open his door and look out!" Vandeleur said.

"He's even more foolish than I thought," Nemo said. "I gave him too much credit for intelligence. Fix, run down and see if he's outside! He may have used the servants' staircase while we were coming up the main one!"

"Yes, sir," Fix said, "but I don't think so."

He started to run off, but Nemo called him back.

"What did you mean by that?"

"He wouldn't desert Fogg and the woman," Fix said.

"You do know these Eridaneans well, don't you?" Nemo said slowly. "Well, run on down and make sure. Then report to me on the third floor."

Fix was back a few minutes later. He found the others trying to revive a stunned Osbaldistone. The door to Fogg's room was open.

"You were right, Fix," Nemo said. "He came up here, hit Osbaldistone on the back of the head, and the three went . . . someplace. They could not have come downstairs, however. I went up the main staircase and Vandeleur went up the other. Osbaldistone just went up, so they have not had time to get far. I doubt they'd stay on this floor; they probably went on up. However, Fogg is so tricky, he may be in a room on this floor."

What a mess! Fix thought. Nemo might be a great brain, a genius at mathematics and engineering, but when it came to affairs in which lightning thought was needed, not a gigantic ratiocination, he did not do so well. He was also too arrogant, too egotistical. He underestimated everybody else. Perhaps he would learn a lesson from this and use his genius in a more appropriate manner. But what did Fix care about him? Nemo thought Fix was a traitor, and he'd see Fix die.

Well, he was a traitor, if thoughts made a man a traitor.

Nemo lifted Osbaldistone with one arm and carried the dangling body to the landing off the main staircase. He dropped the baronet, who groaned once but did not recover consciousness.

Nemo said, "Fix, you will pile furniture, curtains, anything flammable, on the landing and the steps of the servants' staircase. Vandeleur, you'll do the same for the main staircase. After the piles are completed, soak them with paraffin oil. We're going to burn down the house and with it Fogg, the Frenchman, the woman, and the distorter. The fire will bring a large crowd, into which we'll disappear. We'll meet at Nesse III."

He looked at his watch. "A quarter after eight. Fogg has thirty minutes to get to the Reform Club. He is going to lose that bet, since he will be in Hell before then."

Fix shuddered at the image of Fogg and Passepartout and the beautiful and gentle Aouda screaming in the flames.

It took about ten minutes for the two to carry out wooden tables and chairs, curtains, bedsheets, and feather pillows and stack them on the stairs and the landings. Vandeleur and Nemo then began bringing out lamps, but not enough of these were filled with oil to satisfy Nemo.

"We'll turn on the gas jets, too," he said, "but I want to get a fire going that will absolutely prevent those three from getting over the piles. Fix, you go into the cellar and see if there are extra cans of oil. On the way back, notify the captain of what we are doing. Tell him to return to his post then and to wait until we leave before he goes over the wall. Determine that he has ladders or some means of getting over the back wall, since it will be dangerous to go through the house once the fires have thoroughly started. The jets won't be turned on until just as we leave, but the chances of an explosion will be high. Have you got that straight?"

Fix said, "Yes, sir," and he hurried off. He went into the deep and gloomy cellar, which was not as deep or as gloomy as his thoughts. A few minutes later, he emerged with two large cans of oil. There were several step ladders against the cellar wall which Moran could use. In the front room, he put the cans down and went to a sideboard from which he decanted a half-tumbler of brandy. He poured this down, stopping only when he coughed. Tears running down his cheeks, he put the tumbler down. Then, not so pale and shaky, he walked toward the rear of the house. On reaching the main rear door, he looked out into the darkness. Moran was a darker shape among the shadows, crouched by the side of a huge stone urn. Fix opened the door and said, "Captain, come here quickly! I have a message for you."

Nemo looked at his watch again. Soon, the gentlemen in the Reform Club and the great crowd outside would see the flames rising and would wonder whose house was burning.

Hearing footsteps coming up the staircase, he turned. Fix, a few seconds later, climbed up over the pile with a big can in each hand.

"Put one down there and take the other to Vandeleur's pile," Nemo said. "We'll set his afire first."

Fix set one of the containers on the floor and walked toward Nemo. Nemo turned away to watch Vandeleur, who was bringing a bundle of curtains to add to the large pile. Fix reached into his coat and brought out his revolver. He held it by the barrel.

Fogg, Aouda, and Passepartout were at a window in a front room on the fourth story. The gaslights below showed an almost deserted street. Four gentlemen were standing talking across the street near the corner light.

"They must be the men Nemo's stationed to intercept us if we should escape," Fogg said. "There's no way of getting away from them. As soon as they see us coming down on this bedsheet rope, they'll come running. We must drop fast and start shooting as soon as we reach the ground."

Aouda, sitting in a chair, said, "I still think I should stay here. I can use only one hand, and I'm not strong enough to hang on with it."

"Nonsense, my dear," Fogg said. "I told you that we will go down together and that I will have one arm around you. Our gloves will keep us from burning our hands."

"But . . ."

Aouda stopped. Fix's voice was coming from the end of the hall.

"Mr. Fogg! Believe me, this is no trap! I have knocked out Nemo and the others! I could not let them burn you alive. Please believe me, Mr. Fogg, and come quickly!"

"It might well be a trick to locate us," Fogg said.

"Mr. Fogg! Nemo said I might be a traitor, and I'm sure he was going to see that I was killed. And God knows what he meant to do to my family. Please believe me. I have a pistol, but it is in my coat, and my hands are in the air. See for yourself. But quickly!"

"It could be true. It's not entirely unforeseen," Fogg said. He walked to the door, unlocked it, and opened it a crack. There was Fix, slowly walking down the hall, his hands held high.

Fogg opened the door a little more, stuck the end of his revolver out, and said, "Come on in, Mr. Fix."

Fix entered. Fogg shut the door and said, "Where are your colleagues?"

"All unconscious, perhaps dead," Fix said. "I called Moran in and hit him over the head with the butt of my gun. Then I went upstairs and hit Nemo when his back was turned. Osbaldistone was still senseless, so I only had to make Vandeleur stand with his face to the wall and then hit him, too."

"And you did this for the reasons you stated?"

"Yes, but you'll have to protect me and my family from now on. You will, won't you?"

"Consider it done," Mr. Fogg said.

With Fix ahead of them, for Fogg was not sure that it was not a trap, they went down to the landing. All three of the Capelleans were still unconscious.

"Are you going to kill them?" Fix said.

"Would you want me to do so, Mr. Fix?" Fogg said.

"No. I do not like them, and Nemo would have killed me without mercy," Fix said. "But to slay them in cold blood . . ."

Fogg did not reply. He was searching Nemo's clothing. Within a few seconds, he pulled a small flat leather case from a pocket and took out of it small oblong papers covered with writing and diagrams that could only be seen plainly under a magnifying glass. He said, "I was hoping he'd still be carrying these."

"What are they?" Aouda said.

"The schematics for the distorter. But how did Nemo get them from Head's body?"

"Head had them stored inside his glass eye," Fix said. "Nemo removed it when he helped you throw Head's body overboard."

"I should have raised Head's eyelids and looked at his eyes," Fogg said. "But where did Head get the schematics?"

"It was an American Eridanean who found out how to manufacture distorters," Fix said. "Head discovered that he had done so—how, I don't know—and killed him, burned down his laboratory, and fled with the schematics and the distorter which the American had made. Your chief must have found out about this at once, which is why Head took passage on the *Mary Celeste* to avoid the Eridaneans looking for him on the liners."

Fogg put the schematics in his pocket, looked at Passepartout's watch, and said, "And those men outside?"

"They are either loungers or Eridaneans waiting to see if Nemo will surrender you to them." He told Fogg about the telegram from the Eridanean chief.

Fogg looked at his watch again. "Let's go," he said.

"Where?" Aouda said.

"To the Reform Club. We have exactly ten minutes to get there if I am to win the bet."

Verne says that Passepartout dragged Fogg outside by the collar, hailed a cab, and the two drove off at a reckless speed, running over two dogs and overturning five carriages. This is true, except for the dragging by the collar. But Aouda and Fix followed in another carriage at a somewhat slower pace. Aouda's wound did not permit her to be jostled much, and, moreover, she stopped long enough to inform the gentlemen on the corner, who were indeed Eridaneans, that they were safe and that Fix was now one of them. She also told the gentlemen to pick up the Capelleans in Fogg's house.

These hastened to do so, but, alas, they were too late to catch Vandeleur, Moran, and Nemo. These had recovered and fled, leaving Sir Hector behind. As the Eridaneans entered the front door, the trio went over the back wall of the garden.

Osbaldistone was carried out as if he were drunk and driven off in a cab. What happened to him thereafter, no one knows.

As everybody does know, Phileas appeared three seconds before his time was up. He collected twenty thousand pounds, though he had spent nineteen thousand during the journey, his last expenditure being a hundred pounds to the cabman who drove to the Reform. The remaining thousand pounds, he split between Fix and Passepartout. Within two days, Fogg and Aouda were married, and Verne ends his narrative on a happy note.

But what of the story behind Verne's? The other log of Fogg ends on the day he took Aouda as his bride. No other literature on this subject has ever been turned up, so we must reconstruct the postlude. Fortunately, we have common sense and some narratives of a few other authors about some of the people Fogg met to help us build a reasonable sequel.

The Eridaneans and Capelleans, with Nemo out of the way, and through Fix's offices, must have made a truce or perhaps even an alliance. Many on both sides felt, as Fix did, that there was no sense in continuing this secret and gory war which could end only in extermination for one side and near-extermination for the other. Besides, life as a mere Earthling was hard enough without adding to it the perils of Capelleanism and Eridaneanism.

Moran, we know from the writings of a certain Dr. John Watson, went back to India and stayed there for years. After retiring as a colonel, he rejoined his chief in London.

The chief, whom Watson called Professor James Moriarty, seems to have abstained from a criminal career for some years. Probably, the shock of being outwitted by Fogg and of losing the chieftainship of the Capelleans accelerated his illness. Nemo became a teacher for a while, but, after recovering much of his health, went back into business. He formed a vast criminal ring, though he succeeded in keeping his part in it unknown for a long time. Eventually, he experienced a bad fall—and falls—near the little Swiss village of Meiringen. It was symbolically and esthetically appropriate that a man who started his career in the water should end there.

Nemo's brother, the colonel, had been so injured by the frenzied horse that he retired from the army. However, he did go back to his evil ways when older, though not as his brother's partner. He appears briefly in a semifictional book by Robert Louis Stevenson, *The New Arabian Nights*.

Vandeleur plays a more important role in the same book.

Fogg retired to Fogg Shaw in rural Derbyshire, where he tinkered around in his laboratory and raised a number of children, all as handsome as he or as beautiful as their mother.

Fix continued to be a detective, though he now served only one master, or mistress in this case, Her Majesty.

Passepartout settled down as manager of Fogg's estate and married a local girl.

And what of the Grand Plan?

From the situation of the world today, we may assume that it was abandoned.

What about the distorters?

Did the Eridaneans and Capelleans decide to throw the few remaining devices, along with the schematics, into the ocean? Or did some greedy person steal them? That we hear no more of the nine great clangings means nothing. It may be that someone, perhaps Fogg, invented a means for suppressing or canceling these noises. In which case, some of the many mysterious and seemingly impossible disappearances of things and people in this world may be explained.

Whatever happened to the distorters, the important thing is that Fogg and Aouda and Passepartout and Fix lived happily for many years. They may still be living for all anybody knows.

Fogg may even have thought that, after a hundred years, the public could be informed of the true story.

That Phileas Fogg's initials and your editor's are the same is, I assure you, only a coincidence.

ADDENDUM

The following article appeared in *Leaves from The Copper Beeches*, published for The Sons of the Copper Beeches Scion Society of the Baker Street Irregulars, by the Livingston Publishing Co., Narberth, Pa., 1959.

A SUBMERSIBLE SUBTERFUGE OR PROOF IMPOSITIVE

H. W. STARR

A familiar literary phenomenon is the novel which is actually autobiography, biography, or factual narration disguised as fiction. We see it in the work of Thomas Wolfe, Dickens, Watson, and a score of other writers; and perhaps we may find it also in two novels that we have all read as children: Jules Verne's *Twenty Thousand Leagues under the Sea* and *The Mysterious Island*. The popular impression of the most interesting character of this saga, an individual using the alias Captain Nemo, is that of an Indian prince, a disillusioned and embittered idealist, sickened by civilization, who gathered a little band of kindred spirits, devoted to him and tenderly cared for by him, and vanished forever into the depths of the sea in a marvellous submarine which he had secretly assembled. Yet if we examine these tales we find certain inexplicable and absolutely irreconcilable inconsistencies appearing in them—for example the dates. According to *Twenty Thousand Leagues*, the *Nautilus* is recorded as first being observed by seafarers in 1866 and vanishing

433

in the Maelstrom in 1868,[1] at which time Professor Aronnax and his companions escaped from the vessel. Yet we are surprised at the beginning of *The Mysterious Island*,[2] when Captain Nemo is a silvery-haired old ruin, the last survivor of a company of at least twenty-four sailors and two officers, living in solitude on Lincoln Island, that the date is given as 1865![3]

---

[1] Jules Verne, *Twenty Thousand Leagues under the Sea*, transl. P. S. Allen (Chicago: McNally, 1922), pp. 3, 471.

[2] Jules Verne, *The Mysterious Island* (New York: Scribner's, 1924).

[3] Discrepancies of this sort are innumerable: the captain must have had time to design and build the submarine, collect a large crew, wait for the crew to die off one by one, age from a vigorous man apparently in his thirties or forties (the period of *Twenty Thousand*) to sixty years of age (*Mys. Is.*, p. 458), and retire to Lincoln Island—a sequence of events that would seem to require about twenty years. Yet, according to the data in *Mys. Is.*, all this occurred between 1858, the date of the suppression of the Sepoy Rebellion, and 1865, a bare seven years. The reference to the Sepoy Mutiny in the *Mys. Is.* (p. 456) cannot be an error—it is lengthy and explicit—nor may we simply assume another and much earlier rebellion is meant, for the detailed description of the *Nautilus* shows that much of its construction was based on improvements made on scientific discoveries of the 1850s or later (the work of Ruhmkorff and Bunsen, for example, *Twenty*, pp. 98, 125). Even more significant is the reference by Captain Nemo (*Twenty*, p. 105) to fishing experiments at great depths made in 1864, experiments that he could not possibly have known of after he was cut off from society and which he clearly considered when designing the *Nautilus*. In other words, the vessel was not launched until 1864 or 5—if not later. To add to this total confusion, in the *Mys. Is.* (p. 457) the date of the professor's escape from the *Nautilus* is given as June 22, 1867 (in *Twenty Thousand* it is 1868—see p. 471), but Captain Nemo dies on October 15, 1868, a much older man than a few months or a year could account for (*Mys. Is.*, p. 468). Furthermore, the colonists of Lincoln Island, totally cut off from civilization from 1865 to 1869, have heard, *before* their arrival in 1865, of Aronnax's adventure, which could not, of course, have been made public until 1867 or 8. On p. 454 of *Mys. Is.* (Oct. 15, 1868) Captain Nemo says he has passed "three long years in the depths of the sea" cut off from any communication with civilization—a statement which is in conflict with practically every other date in both books! Some vague notion of a certain inconsistency in dates seems to have worked its way into M. Verne's consciousness, for in two notes (*Mys. Is.*, pp. 306, 455) he remarks that his leaders may observe "some

There are other inconsistencies. According to the *The Mysterious Island,* Nemo is an Indian Prince Dakkar, and presumably at least some of such a man's followers would be Indians. This could hardly have escaped the observation of Professor Aronnax, who for months watched them fishing and working about the *Nautilus.* Yet never does it seem to occur to him that any are from the Indian subcontinent. Instead, he says that all are Europeans.[4] No matter how dubious in the eyes of modern science identification of nationality from appearance may be, it is unlikely that a veteran biologist would mistake, after close and repeated observations, some two dozen Hindus for Europeans— especially Irishmen! Furthermore, in *The Mysterious Island* (p. 460) Captain Nemo defends the sinking of the hostile warship witnessed by Professor Aronnax on the grounds that he "was in a narrow and shallow bay—the frigate barred my way." Yet the Professor's account (*Twenty Thousand,* pp. 473–82) unquestionably proves that for over twenty-four hours Captain Nemo deliberately lured the frigate to follow him until it suited his whim to turn and sink her.

Many more such instances may be piled up, but I think the conclusion is too obvious for us to cite them. *The Mysterious Island* is a work of fiction turned out by a professional novelist who, after some editing of the manuscript of Professor Aronnax to ensure its popular sale, decided to capitalize on its success by writing an entirely imaginary sequel and, in doing so, to rehabilitate a rather brutal man by painting him as a Byronic hero with a heart of gold—a procedure thoroughly compatible with the literary fashion of the day. We must dismiss it, and with this dismissal must also vanish any and all reliance upon this later volume's account of Captain Nemo's character, moral values, and life as "Prince Dakkar."

Having disposed of *The Mysterious Island* as a source of information, let us now turn our attention to *Twenty Thousand Leagues.* Since this volume appears to be a novelist's rewriting or editing of Professor Aronnax's memoirs, we may put some faith in

discrepancy in the dates; but later again, they will understand why the real dates were not given at first." Unfortunately, there is absolutely nothing in the book which would lead the readers to such an understanding.

[4] See p. 148, where the professor is sure some of them are Irish, French, Slavs, Greeks, or Candiotes, but "the European type was discernible in each one of them."

H. W. Starr

matters of fact observed by the professor. However, we should be more cautious in acceptance of matters of interpretation, for here the romantic Byronic aura which Aronnax and Verne saw surrounding the captain may mislead us. Consider the concept of Captain Nemo as the half-noble, half-ruthless, golden-hearted, disillusioned idealist, who loves the oppressed in general, his crew in particular, and who has provided an "Ark of Refuge" for a selected few to whom he is bound by ties of mutual devotion. Just how does the man Nemo really treat this crew of his? First of all, we should estimate how many men are on the *Nautilus*. From various bits of information it is clear that he cannot have had fewer than twenty-four crewmen in the original group and he may have had thirty or more.[5] The living quarters provided for these men are very interesting. The description of the berthroom in which they seem to have spent practically all of their existence when not engaged in their duties indicates that the room could not have measured more than 22 feet by 16 feet.[6] If we

---

[5] When the *Nautilus* is imprisoned by an iceberg in south polar waters it is necessary for the crew, working in two shifts which must have been of approximately equal numbers, to dig it out. In the first shift, "a dozen of the crew . . . and in their midst" Ned Land and the captain get to work (*Twenty*, p. 414). Even if we count Ned and the captain as part of this "dozen," we find ten men in each shift, a total of 20. A more normal reading of the text would give 12 to a shift, totalling 24. To this figure we must add the man previously killed by an accident in the engine room and the tenants of the coral cemetery (pp. 210–30 *passim*). The number of graves is not stated, but the plural is repeatedly used and the specific number *two* is not employed. Hence we may assume a minimum of three men were buried there. Consequently, the original complement of the *Nautilus* must have consisted of Captain Nemo, one officer (or originally more), and at least 24 crewmen—probably 28 sailors or even over 30. One might argue that there cannot have been many more since only about ten (p. 448) accompanied Captain Nemo and his three prisoners in their poulp chopping activities, a situation that certainly seems to require the full strength of the ship's company. On the other hand, the very limited deck space of the *Nautilus* might have made a larger number than 14 axe swinging enthusiasts more of a menace than a help.

[6] The length given by the professor is 16. The maximum exterior width of the Nautilus was 26 feet. If we subtract two feet for the thickness of the remarkably strong hull and two more for the passageway down which the

line this room with tripledecker berths, we can just fit twenty-four men[7] (the smallest possible number) into these quarters, generously leaving clear in the center a floor space of 10 feet by 16 feet, in which they may dress, store their clothes, eat, lounge, and otherwise amuse themselves.[8] These are slum conditions of the foulest sort. But perhaps Captain Nemo, whose bedroom is described as "severe almost . . . monkish,"[9] lived under equally Spartan conditions? Well, his private[10] suite, into which the crew never intruded, consisted of the following apartments in addition to his fifteen foot bedroom; a dining room (15 feet long) equipped, among other articles, with "exquisite paintings" and with oak and ebony sideboards bearing "china, porcelain, and crystal glass of inestimable value" (p. 81); a

professor walked (he went from one end of the ship to the other, passing the closed door of the crewroom [p. 98], the interior of which he never saw; hence we must admit the existence of this passage), we reach the figure 22. Since we have no assurance the room was halfway from the bow of this tapering vessel, the correct figure may be only 18 or 20 feet.

[7] We assume that somewhere in the vessel was a cubbyhole where the lieutenant could swing his hammock in solitary grandeur.

[8] There is no reference to any mess or recreation room for them, nor is it easy to see from the description of the vessel (pp. 81–108 *passim*) where any such cabin could have been located unless the extremely bare room by the stair well (containing one table and five chairs, p. 63) was occasionally used as a mess. However the paucity of its furnishings and the fact that the professor and his friends were incarcerated there whenever the captain wanted them out of the way suggests that this was the brig. Question: If a hoosegow of this size (20' x 10', p. 62)—and space is at a premium on a submarine—was needed on the *Nautilus*, does it not indicate that Captain Nemo expected (and perhaps had) either a good deal of trouble from his devoted crew or a considerable body of other prisoners at one time or another?

[9] Apart from the nautical instruments on the walls, a few toilet articles, and some large paintings (p. 483) on the wall which the professor rather inexplicably failed to see for the first nine or ten months, it contained only "a small iron bedstead, a table," and a chair or two. See pp. 91–92.

[10] And private it was, by gum! With the exception of the steward who served the meals and was so severely disciplined that he didn't dare show even a flicker of resentment after Ned Land had half choked him to death (p. 74) and the mate, who appeared only to mark the submarine's position on the chart, no member of the ship's company is ever recorded as entering the entire forward part of the *Nautilus*.

library (also 15 feet in length and running like the former room, the width of the ship) containing overstuffed divans upholstered in brown Morocco, movable desks, a huge table for periodicals, cigars, a bronze brazier for a cigar lighter, and a private collection of 12,000 books (pp. 85–87); a magnificent museum-drawing room (30 feet by 18 feet) provided with an arabesques ceiling, pictures "of great value" by Raphael, Leonardo, Titian, Rubens, etc. ("the greater part of which" Professor Aronnax "had admired in the galleries of Europe"), statues of bronze and marble, a large piano-organ, an invaluable collection of marine life in "splendid glass cases," and pearls some of which were "larger than a pigeon's egg" and which surpassed the most valuable pearl hitherto known.[11] With this[12] at his disposal, I think that one can see how Captain Nemo managed to survive the hardships of that severe, almost monkish bedroom.

In any event, the account does not fit the concept of a loving master served by an admiring group of acolytes. It does, however, fit the picture of the sybaritic commander of an old-fashioned warship living in luxurious quarters and ruling with an iron hand a crew of tough fighting men whose fear of their captain and expectation of high financial gain may make them willing to put up with physical discomfort.

One or two puzzling events are reported by the professor. The events we can accept, but his interpretation is less reliable. On a very rough day when the captain, the mate, and the professor are on deck, the two officers observe through a telescope an object so distant that the professor (whose vision seems normal) is unable to see even a speck with his naked eye. The officers are greatly excited, the professor and company are heaved into the brig again, doped, and a ship is sunk by the *Nautilus* (pp. 216–220). These are the facts; the interpretations that we are given is this: Captain Nemo on first sighting the ship immediately recognized it—necessarily by its flag—as belonging to that unidentified nation which he so loathed, and consequently rammed it with the ship spur mounted on the bow of his submarine. Yet a little thought shows us that this cannot be entirely correct:

---

[11] That of the Imaum of Muscat (pp. 88–90).

[12] Thus out of a total length of 232 feet (65 feet of which was the engine room) 75 feet of the *Nautilus* had been set aside for the exclusive use of the captain.

if the ship was so far away that Professor Aronnax was unable to distinguish it at all with the naked eye, how could the man Nemo even with a telescope possibly recognize its colors?[13] The conclusion, therefore, is that the one way Nemo could know that here was the ship upon which he had designs was by being given information that at this date and in this location, just one particular vessel could be expected. Yet our saline recluse could possess up-to-date information concerning shipping only from some source external to the *Nautilus*. And of this supposition we have confirmation. He appears to have devoted considerable effort to scooping up the treasure from the sunken ships in the Bay of Vigo. About a million dollars in gold (pp. 300–01) he sent ashore in the pinnace after his intermediary, one Nicholas Pesca (an amphibious individual who appears to have devoted most of his time to swimming from one island of the Cyclades to another), had, during an evening dip, swum out to the *Nautilus* (p. 299). The interpretation which Captain Nemo skillfully plants in the professor's mind (pp. 326–27) is that he, as a friend to all oppressed groups, has devoted his wealth to the Cretans, who at this time were in revolt against Turkish rule. The facts are that he is in the habit of sending part of his takings ashore and that he does have certain connections with civilization which might supply him with data concerning shipping and cargo schedules.

Now, following Watson's method (since we dare not arrogate to ourselves the techniques of the Master), let us see what conclusions we can come to concerning the puzzling character of the man Nemo:

1. He had a wide educational background—especially in biology, music, sculpture, painting, and history.

2. He must have been a genius of breathtaking stature in the fields of mathematics, physics, and theoretical

---

[13] Should it be argued that the telescope was tremendously powerful—let us say 20, 30 power, or more—anyone who has tried to use such an optical instrument will reply that without placing it on a tripod mounted on a firm foundation one will find it almost impossible to see anything whatsoever. I doubt that on a pitching deck any instrument of much more than 10 or 15 power could be used effectively—and that would be utterly inadequate in this situation.

engineering[14] to have designed such a submersible as the *Nautilus.*

3. Yet, strange to say, although Nemo surely had a reasonable acquaintance with the handling of ships by the time Professor Aronnax met him, we cannot be quite so certain that his practical maritime experience is very extensive. There seem to be curious lapses here. As a sailor the worthy captain is constantly—and accidentally—bumping into things: three passenger ships (not to be confused with the deliberate rammings), one iceberg, the Maelstrom, and the island of Gilboa. Furthermore, wonderful though the design of the vessel is, it has features which an experienced marine engineer would hardly incorporate into its design. For example, quite unlike almost all large vessels of the last thousand years or more—submarine or surface—it has no cutwater unless the very slight elevation of the deck provided a most inadequate one, for the bow is completely conical as it tapers to a sharply pointed spur. Since the deck elevation is only about a yard above water level, this means that in anything but a dead calm at any speed above the barest crawl tons of water would be constantly deluging the pilot's cage whenever the *Nautilus* traveled on the surface.[15] Walking on deck when the vessel was under way must have

---

[14] The engines of the *Nautilus* are described as run by electricity alone (a modern submarine usually has two sets, one electrical and one diesel), but their tremendous power and their speed of 50 M.P.H. lead one to the strong suspicion that they were really atomic engines. Furthermore, the incredible strength of the vessel far surpasses that of any submarine of today. The *Nautilus* survived a descent to a depth of 48,000 feet (p. 357)—more than ten times the level reached by a bathyspheric descent of 1949, which in its turn attained a depth far greater than any twentieth-century submarine can reach. The mathematical genius required for this engineering feat is vastly beyond our own day, for it almost seems that such construction could be achieved by only someone capable of putting into practice the principle of molecular adaptation. This, however, must remain speculative.

[15] The fact that the pilot could seldom see where he was going may have had something to do with the perpetual collisions which dot the *Nautilus'* career.

been a singularly damp—not to say hazardous—procedure. Indeed, the design of the *Nautilus* is amazing in its total subordination of the everyday needs of navigation to sheer military utility. It is an armored ram, but such a ram as could never be found in any classical trireme, Venetian war gallery, or nineteenth-century ram. It is a cigar shaped cylinder with pointed ends, one surmounted with a spur, retractable pilot and lantern cages, and collapsible railing—streamlined, in fact, so that the entire submarine may pass completely in needlelike fashion through a hostile vessel. So extreme a design is hardly necessary merely to sink a ship, and it reveals an appalling savagery of purpose in the designer which ill consorts with a bitter and disillusioned yet golden-hearted friend to the oppressed.

4. He is clearly a man of commanding and domineering personality, a man who rigidly draws the caste line.[16] This combination of an arrogant personality and a marked distinction between groups is of course to be observed in many walks of life, but it is particularly noticeable in those who follow two professions: officers in military organizations and teachers. Nemo, however, repeatedly shows an extreme aversion to the human race in general, a quality not exceptionally common in military men, but one which is frequently to be found in members of the pedagogical profession after several years spent in the refreshing experience of purveying sweetness and light to large quantities of Youth.

5. Finally, the captain is definitely a man of somewhat dubious ethics. No matter how romantic a light is cast over his activities, he is guilty of destruction of shipping, murder, and possibly theft. To put it bluntly, he is simply a pirate, a pirate who has turned to financial advantage his extraordinary

---

[16] Note that, as has already been observed, the sailors are not admitted to his quarters nor is even the mate allowed there save in performance of his duties. Furthermore, his treatment of the three prisoners shows that he accepts the professor as more or less his social equal and very decidedly does not accept Ned Land or the well educated servant Conseil.

scientific skill and who maintains on land perhaps a small[17] but necessarily a widely distributed network of secret agents, who at prearranged meetings provide him with essential information concerning the shipment of valuable cargoes.

On the basis of these conclusions I think that we can now advance the hypothesis which has already occurred to the reader: Is it not likely that the portrait of Captain Nemo in *Twenty Thousand Leagues under the Sea* is a portrayal of a sinister figure well known to us—Professor James Moriarty? Let us examine some of the resemblances—or apparent lack of resemblances:

(a) Physical appearance: At first glance Nemo and Moriarty seem to have little in common save their high foreheads and stature, but consideration of their respective ages will modify this assumption. When first encountered in 1867 Captain Nemo is described as between thirty-five and fifty years of age, but when one realizes his strength, endurance, and agility, it is evident that between thirty-five and forty would be a much more accurate estimate.[18] There seem to be no differences[19] that the passage of twenty-five years will not account

[17] No very elaborate organization would be needed, since most of the information could be picked up from the daily newspapers. Incidentally, the reader should note (pp. 299–300, 325) that after the professor has blundered into the saloon and witnessed frogman Nicky Pesca and his cohorts collecting their cut, the captain tells him that the gold ingots came from the sunken galleons in Vigo Bay. He had to make up some story to account for what the professor had witnessed. If this one happened to be the truth, very well—but, as far as we can tell, the gold delivered on Feb. 14 (p. 297) may have been looted from the ship we know the captain sank on Jan. 18 (pp. 214–15).

[18] He takes a tremendous undersea hikes which exhaust the others, attacks a huge shark with a hunting knife, hacks up giant cuttlefish with an axe, and floors the Herculean Ned Land with one punch.

[19] Here one slight hitch regrettably manifests itself: Nemo's eyes are described as black (p. 64); Moriarty's were gray ("Empty House," p. 563). Professor Aronnax makes his observation on the day after the collision of the *Nautilus* and the *Abraham Lincoln*, and it is possible that the phrase "black eyes" may refer to the ocular disfigurement likely to occur under such conditions: Appealing though this explanation may be, there is a more plausible one. We may be sure that M. Verne edited and polished the Aronnax manuscript for publication. Had the professor omitted to mention the color of Nemo's

for. (In passing we may note that the Nemo-Moriarty identification here solves a problem which must have puzzled many Sherlockians: no matter how enraged Moriarty was, how willing to die, and how tricky the footing at Reichenbach may have been, he never would have hoped that a stooped, sedentary, elderly ex-mathematics professor could succeed, without even employing the element of surprise, in a physical assault upon a thirty-eight year old, six-foot athlete well known for his boxing, wrestling, and single-stick ability. Those of us in the teaching profession have often eyed the athletes infesting the rear row with thoughts of homicide drifting through our minds; yet we would only dream of a bare handed assault. If Moriarty were Nemo, though, the picture changes: a former athlete at the age of sixty or so may still possess great physical strength, and the consciousness of his youthful prowess and experience in violent conflict gives him the mental attitude which in a moment of desperation would make such an attack possible.[20])

Captain Nemo could hardly have been born later than 1831; Mr. Edgar Smith[21] has speculated that Moriarty was born about 1846, but so late a date seems improbable. It would make Moriarty about forty-six years old at the time of his death; yet the descriptions of his physical appearance in the "Final Problem" (pp. 544–45) and *The Valley of Fear* (p. 910) are more appropriate to a man in the sixties or even in the seventies than to a man in the forties. If we placed his birth about 1830 he would be around sixty-two at the time of his death, an age which agrees with the physical descriptions and with the approximate birth-date of Nemo.

(b) Educational level: Mr. Smith indicates that Moriarty came from a cultured background, as Nemo did. Both men were fond of

---

penetrating eyes, Verne would have been sure to supply it and, being a confirmed Gallic romanticist, would have made them the black eyes of the Byronic hero-villains of the exotic Gothic novel tradition—not to be confused with the superior Anglo-American literary code which requires all heroes to have steely gray eyes.

[20] Holmes seems to be aware of Moriarty's physical prowess: "There cannot be the least doubt that he would have made a murderous attack on me." ("Final Problem," p. 551).

[21] "The Napoleon of Crime," *Baker Street and Beyond* (Morristown, N.J.: Baker Street Irregulars, 1957).

art. Nemo had thirty old masters[22] and Moriarty kept, at considerable risk, a very expensive Greuze in his study *(Valley of Fear,* pp. 910–11).

(c) Manner: Moriarty was a teacher, a member of a family with some military tradition (his brother, we know, was a colonel), and of so forceful and dominant a personality that the unhappy Porlock wobbled in his dishonest boots at a mere glance from the Napoleon of Crime. He obviously had little devotion to humanity in general. All are traits we have noted in Nemo.

(d) Biographical data: We know surprisingly little about Moriarty's life.[23] Certainly it would have been possible for him to drop out of sight for three or four years[24] during his thirties without Holmes' taking any particular notice of it. So brilliant a criminal could have buried all tracks so effectively that even the master could not uncover the Nemo episode after a quarter of a century.[25]

(e) Mathematical and scientific genius: This has been amply demonstrated for both men.[26]

---

[22] The one picture that seems to have had personal significance for Nemo was a portrait of a young woman and two children hanging on his bedroom wall (p. 483). This is taken by the casual reader to represent Nemo's presumably defunct spouse and offspring; but is it not more probable that on this occasion, having just completed a particularly juicy mass murder, the youthful Moriarty, who so early in his career might well suffer from a pang or two of conscience, was stretching out his arms to the portrait of his mother and her two wee bairns, James Moriarty and James Moriarty?

[23] See Smith, *op. cit.* Moriarty wrote his treatise on the binomial theorem when only twenty-one, got a mathematical chair on the strength of it, acquired a dubious reputation, left the university, set up in London as an army coach (military tradition again), and formed a vast criminal organization. We do not know any of the pertinent dates.

[24] No more time would be needed. The *Nautilus* was first observed in 1866, and M. Aronnax implies that there were no further sightings of it by ships after 1868. Moriarty would have realized that the game was definitely up after Aronnax's escape and that it would be far too risky to continue his venture once the *Nautilus* was generally known to be a piratical submersible. He got out while the getting was good.

[25] Yet it is odd to note in W. Baring-Gould's *Chronological Holmes,* pp. 157–77 *passim,* that out of the ten or so Holmes cases involving maritime matters, eight occurred during Moriarty's lifetime.

[26] It seems clear from the studies of Mr. A. C. Simpson, "The Curious Incident of the Missing Corpse," *BSJ,* n.s. IV (1954), 23–24, and Mr.

(f) Another curious point of resemblance is to be found in Nemo's interest in scientific men. Clearly the only sensible thing for a pirate captain to do when he found Aronnax, Land, and the valet squatting on top of the *Nautilus* was to attach a few heavy weights and drop them overboard. A man who practiced wholesale murder could have had no moral scruples about so trifling a gesture, but Nemo, a proficient amateur biologist, had discovered that one of these men was an internationally famous zoologist whose works were in his own library—and by this time the captain, whose only associates were a crew of hardbitten buccaneers, must have been desperately lonely for intellectual companionship. Consequently he saved Aronnax. (Incidentally, observe the smug satisfaction with which Nemo-Moriarty impresses his superiority upon a professional colleague such as M. Aronnax. There can be no doubt that this man was a college teacher.)

(g) A young mathematical genius of criminal tendencies is very likely to start his illegal career[27] by engaging in some activity in which he can exploit his special talents. Only later, when Moriarty had the time, the capital, and the foundation provided by his information service for the *Nautilus*, would he develop a vast organization of pickpockets, burglars, thugs, and gunmen. Members of these particular criminal strata are not found on the campus in very great numbers.

It is, therefore, difficult indeed for the writer to resist the identification of Professor Moriarty and Captain Nemo and to refrain from suggesting that here we have the first major step up in a spectacular criminal career whose final step down was a long one to the bottom of Reichenbach Falls.

Smith that Moriarty had done very advanced work in atomic theory, and the obviously atomic engines of the *Nautilus* have been noted above (n. 14).
[27] Outfitting the *Nautilus*, Captain Nemo said, cost about $1,737,000 (*Twenty*, p. 108), a sum which it does not seem likely the young Moriarty would have on hand. However, there is such a thing as credit, and since his orders were placed with dozens of different firms, the man whose *Dynamics of an Asteroid* dropped the scientific press cold in its tracks would surely have the timing and mathematical ingenuity for the necessary juggling. One fears that Messrs. Creusot, Penn, Laird, Scott, Cail, Krupp, Hart, *et al.* had a long wait before their bills were paid.

Only a Coincidence: Phileas Fogg, Philip José Farmer, and the Wold Newton Family

Win Scott Eckert

Phileas Fogg lives!
   And so do Sherlock Holmes, and the jungle lord, and Doc Savage, and the insidious Doctor Fu Manchu.

In 1844, Fogg participated in an Eridanean blood-sharing ceremony, which granted him a lifespan of one thousand years.

Philip José Farmer points out that there is no record of Sherlock Holmes' death.[1] One of Holmes' biographers, William S. Baring-Gould, revealed that the Great Detective developed a Royal Jelly bee pollen elixir which extended his life[2]; he probably perfected the Royal Jelly treatment in 1921.

The jungle lord is immortal. As shown in one of the canonical stories recounting his adventures: he was given an immortality elixir by an African witch doctor in 1912. Later on, in 1933, the jungle lord, his wife, and a few others gained access to Kavuru pills which halted the aging process. The jungle lord shared these with his cousin, Doc Savage, "the Man of Bronze," who analyzed and synthesized the pills, resulting in an unlimited supply to be shared with both their families and their closest associates.[3]

---

[1] Foreword to Farmer's *The Adventure of the Peerless Peer*, Aspen Press, 1974; Dell, 1976.

[2] *Sherlock Holmes of Baker Street*, Bramhall House, 1962.

[3] This is recounted in Philip José Farmer's *Tarzan Alive: A Definitive Biography*

Doctor Fu Manchu independently developed his Elixir of Life in 1929.[4]

In addition to the common thread of immortality, or at least very long life, there is another tie which binds together these amazing men: they are all members of the extensive Wold Newton Family.

The Wold Newton Family takes its name from the cosmic event that spawned it. On December 13, 1795, at 3:00 P.M., a meteorite came plunging to the earth, landing near the English village of Wold Newton. The impact site became part of the local folklore in the countryside of the Yorkshire Wolds in the East Riding of Yorkshire. Pieces of the Wold Cottage meteorite[5] are held in the Natural History Museum in London, and in 1799, Edward Topham built a brick monument to commemorate the event:

Here
On this Spot, Dec[r] 13th, 1795
fell from the Atmosphere
AN EXTRAORDINARY STONE
In Breadth 28 inches
In Length 30 inches
and
Whose Weight was 56 Pounds

———

THIS COLUMN
In Memory of it
was erected by
EDWARD TOPHAM
1799

---

of Lord Greystoke, Doubleday & Co., 1972; University of Nebraska Press Bison Books, 2006.

[4] *The Mask of Fu Manchu* by Shan Greville, edited for publication by Sax Rohmer (1930).

[5] The meteorite is named after the Wold Cottage, the house owned by Edward Topham, who was a poet, playwright, landowner, and local magistrate. Apparently Magistrate Topham was instrumental in the Wold Cottage meteorite's role in promoting worldwide acceptance of the fact that some stones are not of this Earth. The Wold Cottage is still privately owned, and is currently the site of an excellent bed and breakfast; nearby is the Wold Top Brewery, where one can procure the local brew, Falling Stone Bitter.

History also records that several people observed the object in the sky. "Topham's shepherd was within 150 yards of the impact and a farmhand named John Shipley was so near that he was forcibly struck by mud and earth as the falling meteorite burrowed into the ground."[6] A contemporaneous account observes that:

In the afternoon of the 13th of December, 1795, near the Wold Cottage, noises were heard in the air, by various persons, like the report of a pistol; or of guns at a distance at sea; though there was neither any thunder or lightning at the time:—two distinct concussions of the earth were said to be perceived:—and an hissing noise, was also affirmed to be heard by other persons, as of something passing through the air;— and a labouring man plainly saw (as we are told) that something was so passing; and beheld a stone, as it seemed, at last, (about ten yards, or thirty feet, distant from the ground) descending, and striking into the ground, which flew up all about him: and in falling, sparks of fire, seemed to fly from it.

Afterwards he went to the place, in company with others; who had witnessed part of the phænomena, and dug the stone up from the place, where it was buried about twenty-one inches deep.

It smelt, (as it is said,) very strongly of sulphur, when it was dug up: and was even warm, and smoked:—it was found to be thirty inches in length, and twenty-eight and a half inches in breadth. And it weighed fifty-six pounds.

(*Remarks Concerning Stones Said To Have Fallen from the Clouds, Both in These Days, and in Antient Times* by Edward King, Esq. F.R.S. and F.A.S, 1796.)

What many historians fail to adequately record is the presence of eighteen other persons in the immediate vicinity at the time of the Wold Newton meteor strike. We know about these eighteen people through the extraordinary and singular work of one historian. This historian, in fact, has engaged in a rather in-depth treatment of the subject in two scholarly biographical tomes. However, despite the fact that this historian's biographies are often appropriately shelved in the Biography section of libraries, his revelations are generally regarded as fictional.

The historian to whom I refer, of course, is Philip José Farmer,

---

[6] See this website, <fernlea.tripod.com/woldcottage.html>.

and the biographies of which I speak are *Tarzan Alive: A Definitive Biography of Lord Greystoke* (1972) and *Doc Savage: His Apocalyptic Life* (1973). In the course of his researches into the life of Lord Greystoke, Farmer extensively traced the jungle lord's ancestry, and came to discover the ape-man was closely related to several other august historical personages. The nexus of this relationship was the Wold Cottage meteor strike in 1795.

As Farmer uncovered, seven couples and their coachmen "were riding in two coaches past Wold Newton, Yorkshire . . . A meteorite struck only twenty yards from the two coaches . . . The bright light and heat and thunderous roar of the meteorite blinded and terrorized the passengers, coachmen, and horses . . . They never guessed, being ignorant of ionization, that the fallen star had affected them and their unborn." (*Tarzan Alive*, Addendum 2, pp. 247–248.)

The eighteen present were:[7]

Coach Passengers (14)
John Clayton, 3rd Duke of Greystoke, and his wife, Alicia Rutherford – *ancestors of the jungle lord*

Sir Percy Blakeney, and his (second) wife, Alice Clarke Raffles – *Blakeney is from Baroness Emmuska Orczy's* The Scarlet Pimpernel *and sequels*

Fitzwilliam Darcy, and his wife, Elizabeth Bennet – *from Jane Austen's* Pride and Prejudice

George Edward Rutherford (the 11th Baron Tennington), and his wife, Elizabeth Cavendish – *ancestors of Professor George Edward Challenger, from* The Lost World *by Edward Malone, edited for publication by Sir Arthur Conan Doyle*

Honoré Delagardie, and his wife, Philippa Drummond – *ancestors of Hugh "Bulldog" Drummond from H.C. "Sapper" McNeile's (and later Gerard Fairlie's) novels*

Dr. Siger Holmes, and his wife, Violet Clarke – *ancestors of Sherlock Holmes, from the stories and novels by John H.*

[7] It has since been revealed, by researchers inspired by Farmer's original discoveries, that there may have been several more persons present that fateful day, not named by Farmer. I restrict myself herein to Farmer's original findings.

ONLY A COINCIDENCE

Watson, M.D., edited for publication by Sir Arthur Conan Doyle

Sir Hugh Drummond and his wife, Lady Georgia Dewhurst – *ancestors of Hugh "Bulldog" Drummond from H.C. "Sapper" McNeile's (and later Gerard Fairlie's) novels*

Coachmen (4)
Louis Lupin – *ancestor of Arsène Lupin, from novels and stories by Maurice Leblanc*
Albert Lecoq – *ancestor of Monsieur Lecoq, from the novels by Émile Gaboriau*
Albert Blake – *ancestor of Sexton Blake, from the stories by Harry Blythe and countless others*
1 unnamed by Farmer

The meteor's ionized radiation caused a genetic mutation in those present, endowing many of their descendants with extremely high intelligence and strength. As Farmer stated, the meteor strike was "the single cause of this nova of genetic splendor, this outburst of great detectives, scientists, and explorers of exotic worlds, this last efflorescence of true heroes in an otherwise degenerate age."[8] (*Tarzan Alive*, Addendum 2, pp.230–231.)

In addition to the jungle lord and the Man of Bronze, Farmer concluded that influential people whose lives were chronicled in popular literature were part of the Wold Newton Family, including Solomon Kane (a pre-meteor strike ancestor); Captain Blood (a pre-meteor strike ancestor); The Scarlet Pimpernel (present at meteor strike); Fitzwilliam Darcy and his wife, Elizabeth Bennet (present at meteor strike); Sherlock Holmes and his nemesis Professor Moriarty (aka Captain Nemo); Phileas Fogg; Monsieur Lecoq; The Time Traveler; Allan Quatermain; A. J. Raffles; Professor Challenger; Arsène Lupin; Bulldog Drummond and his archenemy, Carl Peterson; the evil Fu Manchu and his adversary, Sir Denis Nayland Smith; Sir Richard Hannay; G-8; Lord Peter Wimsey; The Shadow;

---

[8] Of course, not all the Wold Newton Family members were heroes. Some turned the genetic advantages with which they had been blessed toward decidedly nefarious pursuits.

Sam Spade; Doc Savage's friend and associate Monk Mayfair, his cousin Pat Savage, and his daughter Patricia Wildman; The Spider; Nero Wolfe; Mr. Moto; The Avenger; Philip Marlowe; James Bond; Lew Archer; Travis McGee; and many more.

Farmer's researches, uncovering the cosmic explanation for the almost superhuman nature and abilities of these amazing men and women, heroes and villains, are meticulous, well-sourced, and representative of all his historical endeavors. He not only studied the jungle lord's life, but he actually met and interviewed the ape-man himself,[9] after spending uncounted hours poring over Burke's *Peerage* to uncover his real name, titles, arms, and forebears. He applied a similar depth of focus when researching the life of Doc Savage, discovering Doc's real name, ancestors, and current relatives, as well as the family arms.

After writing the two biographies, Farmer continued to chronicle previously unrevealed exploits of Wold Newton Family members in novels and short stories; often these tales have been mistaken for fiction, but they are entirely consistent with the information he had already uncovered, and many are similarly sourced from newly discovered, and unpublished, manuscripts and diaries.[10]

---

[9] On September 1, 1970, Philip José Farmer conducted "An Exclusive Interview with Lord Greystoke." (Originally published as "Tarzan Lives" in *Esquire*, April 1972; reprinted in Farmer's *Tarzan Alive: A Definitive Biography of Lord Greystoke*, University of Nebraska Press Bison Books, 2006, and in *The Man Who Met Tarazan*, Meteor House, 2021.) The interview ostensibly took place in Libreville, Gabon, West Africa, but Farmer later revealed that the interview actually occurred in Chicago. ("I Still Live!" in *Farmerphile: The Magazine of Philip José Farmer* no. 3, January 2006; reprinted in *The Man Who Met Tarazan*, Meteor House, 2021.

[10] Farmer's prior publication of *A Feast Unknown* (1969), *Lord of the Trees* (1970), and *The Mad Goblin* (1970) may have also added to the impression among some readers that the Wold Newton biographies, novels, and stories are works of fiction. These novels are also sourced, from the memoirs of Lord Grandrith, and cover the exploits of Grandrith and Doc Caliban. Grandrith is also a jungle lord, while Caliban is also a Man of Bronze. However, unlike Greystoke and Savage, who are cousins, Grandrith and Caliban are half-brothers. They share a common history which is not based on the Wold Newton meteor strike. Among Farmer's followers there are several explanations for the discrepancies: (1) The novels are highly fictionalized

Among the first of these was *The Adventure of the Peerless Peer*, edited by Farmer in 1974 from Dr. John H. Watson's unpublished manuscript. Another, *The Other Log of Phileas Fogg* was first published in 1973, and derived from Phileas Fogg's secret notes.

Further books in Farmer's Wold Newton series include *Time's Last Gift* (1972; revised 1977) and *Hadon of Ancient Opar* (1974).[11] *Hadon of Ancient Opar* kicks off the Khokarsa trilogy, which is rounded out by *Flight to Opar* (1976) and *The Song of Kwasin* (2012), the latter coauthored with Christopher Paul Carey.

Ironcastle (1976; reprinted by Meteor House in 2022) is Farmer's translation and retelling of J.-H. Rosny Aîné's *L'Étonnant Voyage de Hareton Ironcastle* (1922), which has several prominent Wold Newton references. Farmer's *The Lavalite World* (1977), the fifth entry in the World of Tiers series,[12] solidly connects to the Wold Newton series. This is not an accident; more on this in a moment.

Farmer also wrote several Wold Newton short stories and pieces in the 1970s: "Skinburn," "The Problem of the Sore Bridge—Among Others," "The Freshman," "After King Kong Fell," "A Scarletin Study," "The Doge Whose Barque Was Worse Than His Bight," "The Obscure Life and Hard Times of Kilgore Trout," "Extracts from

adventures of the real Greystoke and Savage, and Farmer published the books before uncovering and revealing the true backgrounds of these men in *Tarzan Alive* and *Doc Savage: His Apocalyptic Life*; (2) Grandrith and Caliban's escapades occurred much as Farmer documented them, based on Grandrith's memoirs; the two heroes coexist alongside their more famous analogues in the Wold Newton Universe; or (3) Lord Grandrith and Doc Caliban exist in a universe which is parallel, but very similar, to the Wold Newton Universe. Perhaps this alternate universe shares a common past with the Wold Newton Universe, but diverged from it at some point in prehistory. The latter alternative begs the question how Farmer came into possession of Grandrith's memoirs, but solving such a mystery is not insurmountable.

[11] Christopher Paul Carey discusses Farmer's research and sources for *Time's Last Gift* and the Khokarsa trilogy in an afterword to *Time's Last Gift*, Titan Books, 2012; reprinted in Carey's The Grandest Adventure, Leaky Boot Press 2018.

[12] *The Maker of Universes* (1965), *The Gates of Creation* (1966), *A Private Cosmos* (1968), *Behind the Walls of Terra* (1970), *The Lavalite World* (1977), *Red Orc's Rage* (1991), and *More Than Fire* (1993).

the Memoirs of 'Lord Greystoke,'" and others more peripherally connected to the series.

He also continued to write short biographical pieces, including "A Reply to 'The Red Herring,'" "The Two Lord Ruftons," "The Great Korak–Time Discrepancy," "The Lord Mountford Mystery," "From ERB to Ygg," "A Language for Opar," and "Jonathan Swift Somers III, Cosmic Traveller in a Wheelchair: A Short Biography by Philip José Farmer (Honorary Chief Kennel Keeper)."[13]

Farmer returned to the Wold Newton series in a big way in the 1990s, starting the decade with the authorized novel *Escape from Loki: Doc Savage's First Adventure* (1991), and rounding it out with the authorized *Tarzan and the Dark Heart of Time:* (1999; Meteor House, 2018). 2009 saw the publication of the Wold Newton series novel *The Evil in Pemberley House*, coauthored with Win Scott Eckert. Farmer passed away on February 25, 2009, after the completion of *The Evil in Pemberley House* but before publication. The following year Wold Newton short fiction was authorized by Farmer's estate, and new stories based on his research appeared.[14]

Returning to *The Other Log of Phileas Fogg*, it's worth noting that not only is Fogg a Wold Newton Family member, but so too is his primary adversary, Nemo (aka Professor James Moriarty). In fact, they are half-brothers. The dalliance that led to Moriarty's birth also caused Phileas' mother, Lorina Dacre, to divorce his biological father, Sir William Clayton. Lorina Dacre was the daughter of Lord Dacre and Jane Carfax, who in turn was the daughter of Lord Rufton.

Nemo also has several Capellean assistants: Colonel James Moriarty (the very tall dark man with a heavy stoop); Colonel Sebastian Moran; a man named Vandeleur; and a henchman who is "the dissolute wenching young baronet, Sir Hector Osbaldistone."

Colonel Moriarty is the Professor's elder brother. That two brothers Moriarty share the first name James is an oddity found in

[13] These have been collected in *Myths for the Modern Age: Philip José Farmer's Wold Newton Universe*, Win Scott Eckert, ed., MonkeyBrain Books, 2005.

[14] "A Kick in the Side" by Christopher Paul Carey and "Is He in Hell?" by Win Scott Eckert, *The Worlds of Philip José Farmer 1: Protean Dimensions*, Michael Croteau, ed., Meteor House, 2010; "Kwasin and the Bear God" by Philip José Farmer and Christopher Paul Carey, *The Worlds of Philip José Farmer 2: Of Dust and Soul*, 2011; *The Song of Kwasin*, 2015 Meteor House.

Dr. Watson's accounts of Sherlock Holmes. In "The Final Problem" Watson refers to Colonel James Moriarty, and in "The Adventure of the Empty House," Holmes mentions Professor James Moriarty.

Colonel Moran was Professor Moriarty's lieutenant and appeared in Watson and Doyle's "The Empty House." Vandeleur appeared in Robert Louis Stevenson's short story "The Rajah's Diamond," which was published in the collection *New Arabian Nights*. Sir Hector Osbaldistone is a descendant of Sir Francis Osbaldistone, who was seen in Sir Walter Scott's *Rob Roy*.

Fogg's secret log also indicates that before joining Fogg, his valet Passepartout was a valet for Lord Windermere. Oscar Wilde wrote a biographical play about Lord Windermere's wife: *Lady Windermere's Fan: A Play About a Good Woman*. The log also refers to Lady Jane Brandon of Brandon Beeches. Brandon Beeches also appeared in George Bernard Shaw's *An Unsocial Socialist*.[15]

Finally, Fogg's notebooks discuss the Rajah Dakkar of Bundelcund, a renegade Capellean who is killed. This cannot be the Prince Dakkar of Jules Verne's *The Mysterious Island*, which H. W. Starr dismisses as wholly fictional in his essay "A Submersible Subterfuge, or, Proof Impositive."[16] However, if there is a kernel of truth in *The Mysterious Island* (or more than a kernel), then maybe Rajah Dakkar is the Prince's father.

Perhaps the greatest mystery to be found in *The Other Log of Phileas Fogg* is not resolved by Fogg's secret diaries, but rather is contained in Farmer's cryptic concluding comment: "That Phileas Fogg's initials and your editor's are the same is, I assure you, only a coincidence."

What precisely is Farmer hinting at here? That *he is* Phileas Fogg?

---

[15] Lady Jane Brandon, the widow of Sir Charles Brandon, became Sir William Clayton's twelfth wife after his eleventh wife perished in 1874. Sir William, a Wold Newton Family member, was the biological father of Phileas Fogg.

[16] There is a split among post-Farmer Wold Newton researchers regarding the veracity of *The Mysterious Island*, and the validity of many points made in Starr's essay. A few even go so far as to challenge the authenticity of Fogg's notebooks, casting them as an elaborate forgery; others take a more moderate view, and have proposed lines of research which reconcile aspects of *The Mysterious Island* with *The Other Log of Phileas Fogg*.

Perhaps, but there are many established facts about Farmer which probably preclude this delightful notion.

But might Farmer be implying something else, something related to the Wold Newton Family? What follows does not purport to be the final answer to the puzzle of Farmer's enigmatic remarks, but is one potential resolution.

There are many science fiction writers in the Wold Newton Family, some accomplished, successful, and well-known like Farmer; others, not so much. Among these are Leo Queequeg Tincrowdor, Kilgore Trout, and Jonathan Swift Somers III, all three of whom are on a branch of the Family descended from the Shawnessys. Of course, there are numerous other writers in the Family, but many of these are adventurers who have recorded their own deeds and published them with the assistance of other editors and writers. Philip Marlowe and Travis McGee come to mind. Tincrowdor, Trout, and Somers, on the other hand, are of the breed who made writing their primary career, rather than a happy side-effect of lives of daring and bold exploits.

Tincrowdor was born in New Goshen, Indiana, when his parents were on the way to a Terre Haute hospital, in 1918.[17] He attended the University of Shomi.

Somers was from Petersburg, Illinois; he was born on January 6, 1910. He shares a birthday with Sherlock Holmes.

Trout was born in 1907 and spent much time in the city of Ilium, a code name for Troy, New York.

Farmer was friendly with all three men, writing of Tincrowdor's experiences in *Stations of the Nightmare* (1982), and penning brief biographical sketches of Somers and Trout.

In any event, there doesn't seem to be a place for Farmer in the Shawnessy line. Doubtless Farmer attended various Family reunions and gatherings, although perhaps Trout didn't make as many of the reunions as Midwesterners Tincrowdor, Somers, and Farmer.

However, there are others to whom Farmer is more closely related. While he shares with Tincrowdor, Somers, and Trout the experience of being a working writer, he has had some parallel experiences with Tim Howller, Tom Wode Bellman, and Paul Janus Finnegan.

---

[17] Interestingly, Farmer was born in Terre Haute in 1918. At age five, the Farmer family moved to Peoria, Illinois, and Farmer spent much of his life there.

Peoria native Tim Howller was also born in 1918. He appeared in Farmer's short stories "After King Kong Fell" and "The Face that Launched a Thousand Eggs." Like Tincrowdor, he attended the University of Shomi ("Shomi" = Missouri) and he experienced similar college hazing incidents as Farmer, who attended the University of Missouri. It appears as though Tim Howller was an autobiographical version of Farmer himself.

Tom Wode Bellman's roots are in Busiris, Illinois. Bellman, also a science fiction writer, appeared in Farmer's short story "The Light-Hog Incident." Busiris is a code-name Farmer used for Peoria.

As for Paul Janus Finnegan, also born in Terre Haute in 1918, let's back up a few steps.

The image to the right is cropped from Farmer's "The Fabulous Family Tree of Doc Savage (An Extension of the Wold Newton Family Chart of *Tarzan Alive*)" in *Doc Savage: His Apocalyptic Life*. The branch in question is one of many begat by the prolific Sir William Clayton (1799–1902). Sir William's father, John William Clayton, the third Duke of Greystoke (1750–1801) was one of those irradiated when the Wold Newton meteor struck.

According to both *Doc Savage: His Apocalyptic Life* and *The Other Log of Phileas Fogg*, Phileas Fogg (b. 1832) was the biological son of Sir William Clayton. Phileas had a sister, Roxana (b. 1833). These birth dates are clearly documented in *Tarzan Alive*. In 1835, when Phileas and Roxana were very young, their mother, Lorina Dacre, divorced Sir William and married Sir Heraclitus Fogg, who adopted both of the children.

In both *Tarzan Alive* and *Doc Savage: His Apocalyptic Life*, Farmer states that the daughter of Phileas Fogg and Aouda Jejeebhoy, Suzanne Fogg, married French Foreign Legion Captain Armand

Jacot. Suzanne and Armand's daughter, Jeanne Jacot (aka "Meriem"), married John Drummond Clayton, the adopted son of the jungle lord.

At the conclusion to *The Other Log of Phileas Fogg*, Farmer writes that, "Fogg retired to Fogg Shaw in rural Derbyshire, where he tinkered around in his laboratory and raised a number of *children*, all as handsome as he or as beautiful as their mother" (emphasis added).

Suzanne Fogg, at least, is mentioned in the text of both *Tarzan Alive* and *Doc Savage*, but neither she, nor the other Fogg children, are reflected on any of the family tree graphics included in those biographies.

Why?

It should also be mentioned that in *Tarzan Alive*, Farmer refers to Suzanne, Phileas, and Aouda as "late," as in deceased. Yet he concludes *The Other Log of Phileas Fogg* with this:

Whatever happened to the distorters, the important thing is that Fogg and Aouda and Passepartout and Fix lived happily for many years. They may still be living for all anybody knows [due to the alien life-extension process which conferred one-thousand-year lifespans].

Fogg may even have thought that, after a hundred years, the public could be informed of the true story.

That Phileas Fogg's initials and your editor's are the same is, I assure you, only a coincidence.

If Farmer is not implying that he is Fogg, then is he insinuating that he's related to Fogg? The illustrations of Fogg in the Tor Books edition of *The Other Log of Phileas Fogg* (1982) show a character that looks exactly like Farmer. In fact, when Christopher Paul Carey had Farmer sign this edition for him a few years ago, he asked, "Could you please sign your picture?" and Farmer promptly placed his autograph directly under the picture of Fogg on the frontispiece.

Fogg is also very closely related to Kickaha (Paul Janus Finnegan) from Farmer's World of Tiers series. Kickaha also shares Farmer's initials, and is also from Terre Haute, Indiana, where Farmer was himself born on January 26, 1918. Kickaha's parents were Philea Jane Fogg-Fog (a daughter of Roxana Fogg and Hardin Blaze Fog), and Park Joseph Finnegan. Park Finnegan deserted Philea Jane upon learning she was pregnant, and she died shortly after Paul's birth, after which Paul was adopted and raised by Ralph Finnegan, a cousin of Park Finnegan.

Perhaps Farmer is connected both to the Wold Newton Family and the family of Lords from the World of Tiers series. Based on the descriptions in the books, Paul Janus Finnegan (Kickaha) is the spitting image of Farmer, and Finnegan also greatly resembles the Lords called Urthona and Red Orc. In fact, Red Orc strongly implies that Kickaha is half-Lord, and that Kickaha may be his own offspring. Wold Newton scholar Dennis E. Power has speculated that Red Orc was Park Finnegan.[18] However, a Wold Newton researcher very close to Power, Coyle T. Ravin, theorized that Park Finnegan was Red Orc's son, and thus Kickaha is his grandson.[19]

If so, this doesn't negate Kickaha's membership in the Wold Newton Family, which he derives from his mother, a Fogg. As Power noted, Kickaha's mysterious acrobatic knife-throwing uncle was likely Jean Passepartout.

Interestingly, there are incidents in the history of Farmer's family which parallel those in Kickaha's.

Farmer's great-grandfather was Dr. Henry Harvey Park, who was married to Dr. Lida Park. Henry's son, William Albert Park, was either abandoned in 1877 at age two by both of his parents and turned over to a distant relative, George Farmer, or was turned over to George Farmer by Henry Park's wife, Dr. Lida Park, upon Henry's death in 1883. Lida Park took off for Texas with two older daughters and became the world's first female osteopath.[20]

The record is unclear regarding whether or not Lida Park was William Albert Park's mother. But if William was Henry Park's son by a prior relationship, that may explain her willingness to leave him behind.

---

[18] "The Conundrums of Kickaha." *Farmerphile: The Magazine of Philip José Farmer* no. 7, Christopher Paul Carey and Paul Spiteri, eds. January 2007.
[19] "The Stars Are but Reflections." *The Wold Newton Universe: A Secret History.* Dennis E. Power, ed. <www.pjfarmer.com/secret/contributors/no-stars.htm>.
[20] Philip José Farmer. "Maps and Spasms." *Fantastic Lives.* Martin H. Greenberg, ed., 1981. *Pearls from Peoria.* Paul Spiteri, ed., Subterranean Press, 2006.

William Albert Park, Farmer's grandfather, later called Bill (Park) Farmer, deserted his wife Josephine Amanda Dooley and their children in 1912. In 1915, Josephine died in an accident eerily similar to that in which Philea Jane Fogg-Fog perished. George Farmer, Philip's father, never forgave his own father.

Parallel historical events don't dictate a genealogical relationship, but there are indications that Paul Janus Finnegan and Philip José Farmer could easily be cousins. Kickaha is described as six feet, one inch tall and weighing 190 pounds, muscular, and broad-shouldered; his face is strong and craggy with a long upper lip. His voice is a rich baritone. Without a doubt, this could be a description of Farmer. (It would be interesting if they had met in 1946 while Kickaha was going to college on the G.I. Bill. Perhaps they did, and that's how Farmer later came to write of Kickaha's adventures.)

Did William Albert Park, later known as Bill Farmer, even later go by the name Park Joseph Finnegan? Both William Park/Bill Farmer and Park Finnegan had a marry-them, love-them, and leave-them-with-children *modus operandi*.

Let's return to the Foggs for a moment. Farmer tells us that Philea Jane was the youngest of the three daughters of Roxana Fogg. Philea Jane was born when her mother was forty-three. In the World of Tiers novel *The Lavalite World*, Farmer tells us that Philea Jane was born in 1880. If so, then her forty-three year-old mother Roxana would have been born in 1837. However, *Tarzan Alive* indicates Roxana was born in 1833, a year after her brother Phileas. If so, then Philea Jane must have been born in 1876. Philea Jane would have just about been of childbearing age, at forty-two years old, when her son Paul Janus "Kickaha" Finnegan was born in 1918.

As we will see, the discrepancy in Philea Jane's birth year is not the first fact regarding the Foggs that Farmer casts in a shroud of—dare I say it?—fog.

Furthering the confusion, as Dennis E. Power and others have noted, Farmer provided two conflicting lineages for Paul Janus Finnegan. First, Paul Janus Finnegan was the great-nephew of Phileas Fogg by his descent through Phileas' sister Roxana (*Doc Savage: His Apocalyptic Life*). Second, Paul Janus Finnegan was the great-grandson of Phileas Fogg through Phileas' daughter Roxana (*The*

Lavalite World). Much later, Farmer told Christopher Paul Carey that the lineage in *Doc Savage* was the correct version. Nonetheless, we do have a clue that Phileas Fogg had a daughter Roxana, named after his sister.

Philea Jane's two older half-sisters, Wanda and Isis,[21] were born sometime between 1854 and 1871—probably much closer to 1854, since Roxana married her first husband in 1853, when she was 20, and he died in 1871. Yet Farmer tells us that Wanda's son Robert Blake was born in 1917. Even applying the most generous interpretation to the numbers, and supposing that Wanda was born in 1871, she'd be forty-six at the time of Robert's birth, which is highly unlikely. And given that a mid-1850s birthdate is much more probable for Wanda, she cannot be Robert Blake's mother. The same argument might apply to Isis Fogg's son, Richard Henry Benson (aka The Avenger), who was born in 1902. If Isis was born in the 1860s, then Richard Benson could be her son. However, if Isis was born any earlier, then it's unlikely that she's Benson's mother.

The evidence is overwhelming that Farmer omitted a generation between Wanda Fogg and Robert Blake, and possibly omitted a generation between Isis Fogg and Richard Benson.

In *Doc Savage*, Farmer also lists Wanda and Isis with their mother's surname rather than their father's, and does not provide their father's name, thus presenting yet another mystery to be solved at a later date. (He did the same with Wanda and Isis' younger half-sister, Philea Jane, only later revealing, in the novel *The Lavalite World*, the details about her father.)

At this point, Farmer's obfuscations regarding the Foggs appear purposeful. He was too detailed and meticulous in his research for it to be otherwise.

Again, why?

Because Farmer himself is a Fogg.

If Park Joseph Finnegan was a half-human, half-Lord, the son of the Lord called Red Orc, then who was his human mother? A

---

[21] Furthering the confusion, *The Lavalite World* indicates that one of Philea Jane's two older half-siblings was a brother, but since the actual names Wanda and Isis are supplied in *Doc Savage*, we'll assume that Philea Jane's two older half-siblings were sisters. The reference to a brother is a tantalizing hint worth further investigation.

Fogg, a child of Phileas, although the chronology prevents Aouda Jejeebhoy from being the mother of this child. Phileas must have had a daughter, probably sometime in the 1850s. Dennis E. Power suggests that Phileas Fogg met her mother in Ireland while creating the identity of the Irish born sailor Patrick M'Guire, an identity he would use again years later as part of the *Nautilus* crew. Miss Finnegan, the mother of Phileas' daughter, then traveled to America and lived with other Finnegan relatives (see the prior reference to Ralph Finnegan).

Phileas Fogg's daughter would also have been quite young when she was seduced by the Lord, Red Orc, who was using the identity "Dr. Henry Harvey Park," resulting in the birth of Park Finnegan/ William Albert Park/Bill Farmer in 1875. Through some as-yet undiscovered machinations, Red Orc saw to it that the child ended up in the care of the real Henry Park.

If Philip José Farmer is the great-great-grandson of Phileas Fogg, it's obvious why he chose not to disclose this when revealing the genealogy of the Wold Newton Family; he certainly would not want Red Orc to know he knew of their relationship. And although the Eridanean-Capellean conflict ostensibly ended in 1872, he wouldn't want any potential Capellean agents to know he was aware he was descended from a key Eridanean agent.

As for Farmer's shared and parallel experiences with his fellow Family members, I refer you to the blurb Tim Howller—or rather Farmer himself?—provided for an advertisement for the Farmer collection *Venus on the Half-Shell and Others*: "Finally confirmation of my long-debunked many-souls theory of quantum mechanics . . ."

In fact, Christopher Paul Carey has speculated that Farmer and Kickaha are soul-twins: "Perhaps they are twins, the same soul living out two different lives on two different worlds. This is also a theme in the World of Tiers books, with the two Earths, both experiments of Red Orc to see how they would diverge. Perhaps Red Orc was experimenting by leaving one twin (Farmer) on our Earth, and creating the circumstances whereby the other twin (Kickaha) traveled through the gate into the World of Tiers."

If this is the case, then Red Orc was probably behind the freakishly similar "accidental" deaths of Josephine Dooley and Philea

Jane Fogg-Fog, as part of a dark design to create similar backgrounds for his soul-twins.

Since Philip José Farmer is a Wold Newton Family member via his descent from Phileas Fogg (and Fogg's father, Sir William Clayton), it's worth noting that his other children and grandchildren, are also Family members. Farmer's time-traveling daughter, Josie Bauer, from Spider Robinson's Callahan's series, may not have been his biological daughter.[22]

Farmer's membership in the Family explains a lot. When Farmer interviewed the jungle lord, the latter claimed not to know about the Wold Newton Family. Is that likely? The jungle lord was intelligent and educated. He was a member of the British peerage. Surely he knew of the events in his family's past and about the Wold Newton meteor. So why did he grant only Farmer an interview?

Of course Farmer had done amazing research to track down the ape-man, and that was to be rewarded.

But the other reason the jungle lord granted the interview was because Farmer was part of the Family.

---

[22] Josie Bauer is seen in Spider Robinson's *Time Travelers Strictly Cash* and others. Paul Spiteri has speculated that the Eridanean-Capellean conflict continued into the twentieth century, and that the Eridaneans recruited Farmer for some missions involving time travel for ten-year periods. Due to the resemblance between Farmer and Phileas Fogg, the Eridaneans once asked Farmer to pose as Fogg. (See "The Time Distorter" by Paul Spiteri, *Farmerphile: The Magazine of Philip José Farmer* no. 15, Paul Spiteri and Win Scott Eckert, eds. January 2009, and "Le Maréchal" by Paul Spiteri, *The Worlds of Philip José Farmer 1: Protean Dimensions*, Michael Croteau, ed., Meteor House, 2010.) Dennis E. Power's research indicates that Josie Bauer was an adopted daughter of Philip José and Bette Farmer, and the biological granddaughter of the time-traveling Doctor Omega. (See Power's "Bronze Lady Down" in *Doctor Omega and the Shadowmen*, Black Coat Press, 2011.) She must have been adopted during one of Farmer's ten-year sojourns back in time, one in which Farmer's wife Bette accompanied him. When Phil and Bette Farmer had to return to their present time, Josie was probably then cared for by, and later inducted into, the Time Police.

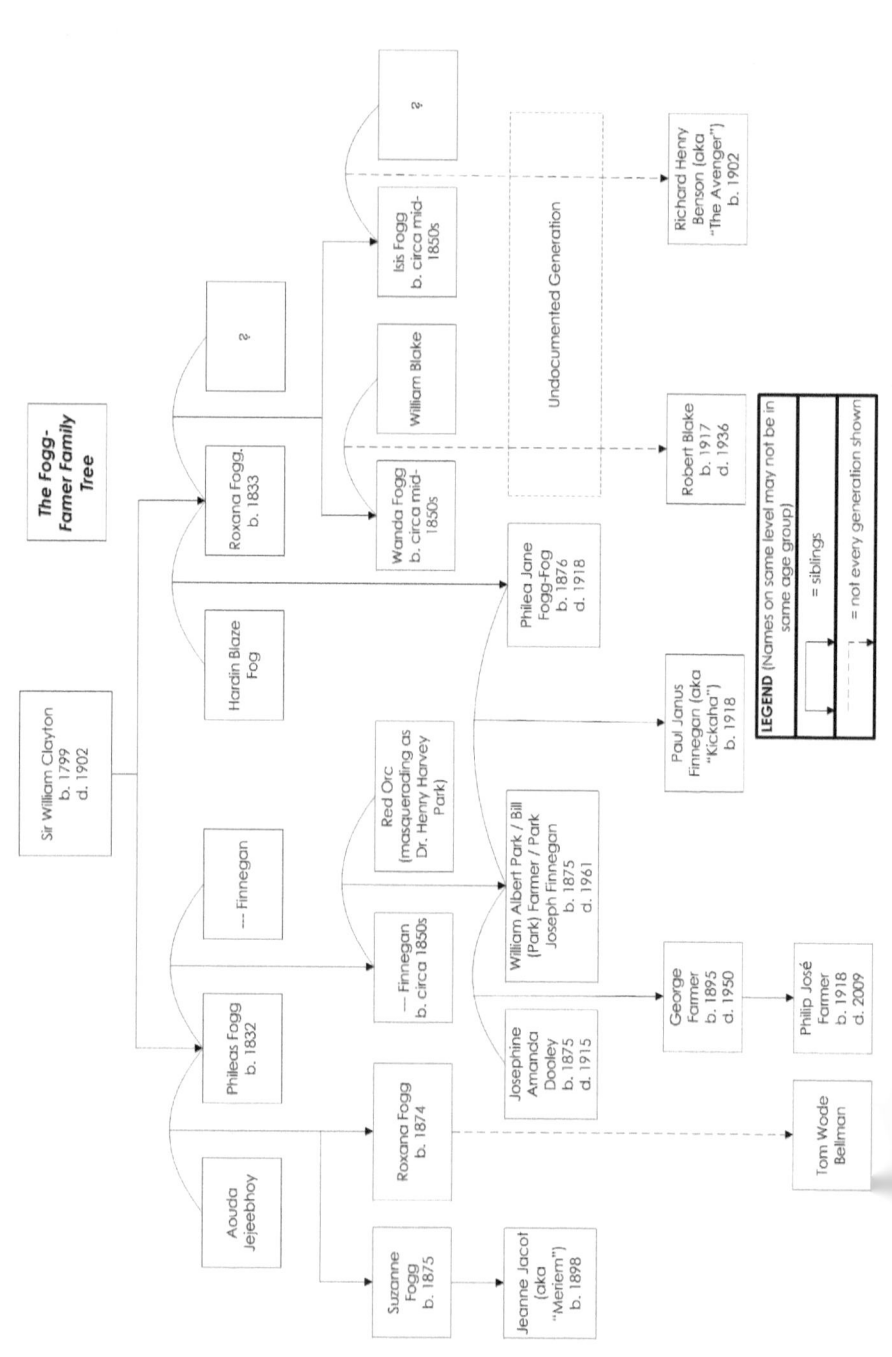

The Fogg-Farmer Family Tree

Sir William Clayton
b. 1799
d. 1902

Phileas Fogg
b. 1832

Aouda
Jejeebhoy

Hardin Blaze
Fog

Roxana Fogg
b. 1833

?

--- Finnegan

Roxana Fogg
b. 1874

--- Finnegan
b. circa 1850s

Red Orc
(masquerading as
Dr. Henry Harvey
Park)

Isis Fogg
b. circa mid-
1850s

William Blake

?

Wanda Fogg
b. circa mid-
1850s

Suzanne
Fogg
b. 1875

Josephine
Amanda
Dooley
b. 1875
d. 1915

William Albert Park / Bill
(Park) Farmer / Park
Joseph Finnegan
b. 1875
d. 1961

Paul Janus
Finnegan (aka
"Kickaha")
b. 1918

Philea Jane
Fogg-Fog
b. 1876
d. 1918

Jeanne Jacot
(aka
"Meriem")
b. 1898

George
Farmer
b. 1895
d. 1950

Undocumented Generation

Robert Blake
b. 1917
d. 1936

Richard Henry
Benson (aka
"The Avenger")
b. 1902

Tom Wode
Bellman

Philip José
Farmer
b. 1918
d. 2009

LEGEND (Names on same level may not be in
same age group)

⌐ = siblings

- - - → = not every generation shown

A Chronology of Major Events Pertinent to
The Other Log of Phileas Fogg

With selected entries from Philip José Farmer's
Tarzan Alive: A Definitive Biography of Lord Greystoke,
Farmer's *Doc Savage: His Apocalyptic Life*,
and other sources

Win Scott Eckert

Mid 1600s
Two rival extraterrestrial races, the Eridaneans and the Capelleans, crash on Earth, stranding the warring aliens. Over the centuries, both races, which are very long-lived, are forced to adopt human guise; they covertly continue their rivalry while living amongst humans. As the aliens die off, many humans are secretly inducted into the ranks of both the Eridaneans and the Capelleans, in furtherance of the conflict. These humans are given an elixir allowing them to live at least one thousand years, barring accidental death. (*The Other Log of Phileas Fogg* [TOLOPF])

November 1795
Sir Percy Blakeney's pocket watch is embossed with the constellation Eridanus, an indication, for those who recognize it, that he is an Eridanean agent. (See the short story "Is He in Hell?" by Win Scott Eckert, *The Worlds of Philip José Farmer 1: Protean Dimensions*, Meteor House, 2010.)

December 13, 1795

Wold Newton meteor strike: Seven couples and their coachmen "were riding in two coaches past Wold Newton, Yorkshire . . . A meteorite struck only twenty yards from the two coaches . . . The bright light and heat and thunderous roar of the meteorite blinded and terrorized the passengers, coachmen, and horses . . . They never guessed, being ignorant of ionization, that the fallen star had affected them and their unborn." *Tarzan Alive*, Addendum 2, pp. 247–248. The meteor strike was "the single cause of this nova of genetic splendor, this outburst of great detectives, scientists, and explorers of exotic worlds, this last efflorescence of true heroes in an otherwise degenerate age." *Id.*, pp.230–231.

John Clayton, third Duke of Greystoke, and his wife, Alicia Rutherford, are both present at the meteor strike, as well as Sir Percy Blakeney (The Scarlet Pimpernel) and Dr. Siger Holmes, among others. (*Tarzan Alive* [TA])

January 1, 1799

Birth of General Sir William Clayton, second son of the third Duke of Greystoke. (TA)

1832

Marriage of Sir William Clayton (his fourth marriage) to Lorina, daughter of Lord Dacre by Jane Carfax, daughter of Lord Rufton. (TA and *Doc Savage: His Apocalyptic Life* [DS:HAL]) Birth of Sir William's son Phileas, a member of the Wold Newton Family. (TA)

1833

Birth of Sir William's daughter Roxana, a member of the Wold Newton Family. (TA)

1835

Birth of Colonel James Clayton Moriarty, son of Sir William Clayton and Morcar Moriarty. (DS:HAL) The illegitimate birth no doubt led to the subsequent (and swift) divorce of Sir William Clayton and Lorina Dacre. (TA and DS:HAL)

A Chronology of Major Events

1836

Lorina Dacre marries Sir Heraclitus Fogg, Bt., of Fogg Shaw, Derbyshire. Fogg, an original Eridanean "Old One," adopts Phileas and Roxana. (TA and DS:HAL)

Birth of Professor James Robert Moriarty. Professor Moriarty is later inducted into the secret ranks of the Capelleans (as is his brother, Colonel Moriarty) and calls himself "Captain Nemo."

See Farmer's *Doc Savage: His Apocalyptic Life* for details on Moriarty's lineage, and proposed modifications to Farmer's genealogy in Rick Lai's "The Secret History of Captain Nemo," *Myths for the Modern Age: Philip José Farmer's Wold Newton Universe*, Win Scott Eckert, ed., MonkeyBrain Books, 2005.

Farmer's genealogical research indicated that Professor Moriarty was a Wold Newton Family member, as he was the son of Sir William Clayton and Morcar Moriarty.

Lai's research led to a different conclusion, that Moriarty was the son of master criminal Dr. James Noel and Morcar Moriarty. Dr. Noel's father, Sebastian Noel and friend of Dr. Siger Holmes, had been present on horseback at the Wold Newton meteor strike.

Whichever genealogy is correct, Professor Moriarty is a member of the Wold Newton Family, although maintaining Farmer's genealogy preserves the half-brother relationship between Moriarty-Nemo and Fogg, and adds a definite mythological weight to their conflict in *The Other Log of Phileas Fogg*.

1842

Sir Heraclitus Fogg battles Capelleans in the Paris sewers. (TOLOPF)

Birth of Jean Passepartout; he is thirty years old in 1872, at the beginning of Verne's *Around the World in Eighty Days*.

1844

Young Phileas Fogg, adopted son of Sir Heraclitus Fogg, undergoes a blood-sharing ceremony that enables him to become a full human-Eridanean and gives him a lifespan of one thousand years. (TOLOPF)

1859

Passepartout is inducted into the Eridaneans. (Date based on unpublished research by Wold Newton scholar Dennis E. Power.)

1866–1868

Fogg, using the alias Patrick M'Guire, is assigned by the Eridaneans to go undercover on the submarine *Nautilus*, commanded by Captain Nemo. Fogg is unfortunately aboard when the *Nautilus* sinks a vessel carrying Fogg's father, Sir Heraclitus Fogg, but is instrumental in sinking the submarine in 1868. (TOLOPF; see also Jules Verne's *Twenty Thousand Leagues under the Sea*.)

1867–1872

Passepartout is ordered by the Eridaneans to change careers, and he becomes a valet in England. He serves first in Lord Windermere's household, and then in a succession of ten more houses over a period of five years. (TOLOPF)

1872

Passepartout's ninth assignment by the Eridaneans is to serve at General Sir William Clayton's manor, Sallust's House, Oxfordshire. The object of the assignment is to determine where Sir William is and the length of his absence. Lady Martha Clayton, Sir William's eleventh wife, assigns Passepartout as butler and household manager, with the plan that he will serve as Sir William's valet when the latter returns. Passepartout never meets Sir William, who, as Passepartout discovers, is off on an African expedition to locate Solomon's lost treasure city of Ophir. Passepartout is then ordered to the household of Lord Phileas Longferry. (TOLOPF)

A Chronology of Major Events

October 2, 1872
Passepartout becomes Phileas Fogg's valet; later that day, Fogg embarks on his whirlwind trip around the world. (Jules Verne's *Around the World in Eighty Days* and Farmer's *The Other Log of Phileas Fogg*.)

November 27, 1872
Fogg and Passepartout battle Nemo and the leader of the Capelleans, appropriately named "Head," on the otherwise abandoned *Mary Celeste*. (TOLOPF) John Gribardsun was also on the *Mary Celeste*, but apparently departed before the arrival of Fogg, Passepartout, and Nemo, unless he somehow managed to remain hidden during their confrontation. (See Farmer's *Time's Last Gift*, Del Rey Books, 1977.)

December 3–4, 1872
On the Oakland Ferry, Fogg and a man named Proctor have a confrontation which leads to a challenge to a duel. Fogg then hires Paladin to escort Fogg, Passepartout, and Aouda from San Francisco to Reno, Nevada, where they are to catch a train to New York.

Proctor follows Fogg and company, continually trying to goad Fogg into a fight. Paladin believes Proctor is motivated more by the money bag that Fogg carries rather than any sense of honor.

During the course of these events, Fogg reveals that his great-grandfather was General Sir Hezekiah Fogg; if Hezekiah had led the British Army, instead of Cornwallis, the United States would now be a province of Canada.

Just outside of Reno, Proctor finally gets Fogg alone and challenges him to a duel once again. In the course of events, Paladin shoots and kills Proctor.

The above information comes from "Fogg Bound," a 1960 episode of the television series *Have Gun, Will Travel*. Evidently neither Verne nor Farmer knew of this particular incident. There are several conflicts with *The Other Log of Phileas Fogg* which are worth discussion.

In *Other Log*, Colonel Proctor was a Capellean agent whom Fogg wounded during a fight with Indians. Fogg had met that Proctor in San Francisco, had a conflict with him over American politics, and then did not see him again until the train was well past Salt Lake City. Interestingly, although Proctor is verbally referred to as "Colonel" in the episode "Fogg Bound," in the credits the character is called "Major Proctor." We may speculate that Major Proctor from "Fogg Bound" was the brother of Colonel Proctor from *Other Log*, and like his brother was also a Capellean agent.

Regarding General Sir Hezekiah Fogg, since Sir Heraclitus Fogg was a long-lived Eridanean Old One, not a human adoptee, Hezekiah was probably one of Sir Heraclitus' previous identities.

December 5, 1872
The brigantine *Dei Gratia* discovers the *Mary Celeste* abandoned in the Atlantic Ocean, with one lifeboat missing.

December 5–7, 1872
Fogg's train is delayed at Green River, Wyoming, where he and a masked lawman, aided by Passepartout and the masked man's Potawatomi companion, attempt to bring a peaceful conclusion to a conflict between Chinese mine workers and the oppressive town leadership. Shan Ming Fu, the leader of the Sublime Order of the White Peacock tong, is, unknown to Fogg, Fogg's half-brother, and in later decades will become an infamous criminal mastermind. (See the short story "Being an Account of the Delay at Green River, Wyoming of Phileas Fogg, World Traveler" by Win Scott Eckert, *The Lone Ranger and Tonto: Frontier Justice*, Moonstone Books, 2018; also included in the volume at hand.)

December 8–9, 1872
As Fogg's train travels through Nebraska, it is attacked by Indians and Passepartout is captured. However, the Indians are not all that they seem. During a several-hour period, Passepartout encounters agents of Dr. Schultz from Jules Verne's *The Begum's Fortune*, as well as Old Shatterhand and Winnetou from Karl May's *Winnetou I*, and Johnny

A Chronology of Major Events

Brainerd from Edward Ellis' *The Huge Hunter; or, The Steam Man of the Prairies*. (See the short story "Passing through the Hands of Steel" by Dennis E. Power, *Tales of the Shadowmen 8: Agents Provocateurs*, Black Coat Press, 2011; also included in the volume at hand.)

December 20, 1872
Phileas Fogg successfully concludes his circuit around the world. (*Around the World in Eighty Days* and *The Other Log of Phileas Fogg*.) With the death of the last Old One (original alien Eridanean or Capellean), the secret conflict between the aliens is apparently ended. After these events, Professor Moriarty abandons his "Captain Nemo" identity and lays low for several years, before resuming his criminal career in the 1880s and '90s under his own name. (See Sir Arthur Conan Doyle's "The Final Problem," "The Empty House," and *The Valley of Fear*.)

1870s
Phileas Fogg and Aouda Jejeebhoy have several children, including Suzanne Fogg. (TA and DS:HAL)

1886
Phileas Fogg is made a baronet. (DS:HAL)

May 26, 1914
John Drummond-Clayton marries (Jeanne "Meriem" Jacot). Meriem's parents are General Armand Jacot and Suzanne Fogg, the daughter of Phileas Fogg. (TA and DS:HAL) John Drummond Clayton is the same Lieutenant John Drummond who was mentioned as the adopted son of the jungle lord in John H. Watson's *The Adventure of the Peerless Peer*, edited by Farmer (Aspen Press, 1974; Dell, 1976; in *Venus on the Half-Shell and Others*, Subterranean Press, 2008). See Farmer's *Time's Last Gift* for much more about the jungle lord.

January 26, 1918
Birth of Philip José Farmer.

1947

Discovery of an extraordinary manuscript (which will later come to be known as Phileas Fogg's other log) at No. 7 Savile Row, Burlington Gardens, London. (TOLOPF)

1962

The other log is identified as being written in a previously unknown language. (TOLOPF)

1971

Sir Beowulf William Clayton, Bt., a noted Oxford linguist and the great-grandson of Sir William Clayton by his tenth wife, discovers Eridanean notebooks in Fogg Hall, Fogg Shaw, Derbyshire. The notebooks assist Sir Beowulf and he translates approximately one third of Fogg's other log. (TOLOPF)

1972

Death of Sir Beowulf Clayton after he shares Fogg's Eridanean manuscript with Philip José Farmer. (See the Wold Newton novel *The Evil in Pemberley House* by Philip José Farmer and Win Scott Eckert, Subterranean Press, 2009; Meteor House, 2014.)

1973

Farmer publishes Fogg's Eridanean manuscript as *The Other Log of Phileas Fogg*.

2140

John Gribardsun—now calling himself "Commander Rhys"—and his wife Jane depart for Capella, in a cryogenic sleeper ship. (See epilogue to *Time's Last Gift* [not included in the original Ballantine 1972 edition].) Perhaps they eventually encountered some of the Capellean "Old Ones."

Being an Account of the Delay at Green River, Wyoming of Phileas Fogg, World Traveler

Win Scott Eckert

December 2, 1872—Oakland, California

B ritt?" the girl asked, slurring a bit. "What an odd name . . ."
    "No ma'am," the man replied. His words came out in a lazy Southern drawl. "It's Bret."

"Britt Re . . ."

He smiled patiently at her and smoothed down the reddish whiskers of his Van Dyke beard. "*Bret*, ma'am. Bret Reagan."

She giggled and put a hand on his knee. She leaned in close and her whiskey-soaked breath came at him in great waves. "That's a funny accent, Bret. Where you from, anyway?"

"Louisiana, ma'am." He set his glass on the bar, untouched, and looked into her bloodshot eyes.

"Well now, Bret, Oakland Long Wharf's a long way from home, ain't it?"

"I hope you can help me, ma'am."

The girl giggled again and waved a strand of stringy blonde hair out of her eyes. "I'm sure I can, Bret. But ya gotta stop callin' me 'ma'am.' I'm Josie." Her hand moved up his thigh.

"Josie, I'm looking for someone."

"Ya done found 'er, Bret." She put her lips near his ear and whispered, "It's jest two bucks—"

"Well, Josie, you see—"

"Now, Mr. Bret, I don't jest do it for dog cheap."

"But that's not really why I came—"

Josie backed away and raised her voice. "Well, why the hell else do ya come down to th' Devil's Addition, 'cept to come? Was th' matter, ya don't like ol' Josie? I ain't even thirty yet!"

Some of the other patrons of the *Casa del Gato* turned from their drinks or card games and stared. The bartender shot a glare their way.

This wasn't exactly going as Bret had planned.

"Now, now, Josie darlin', that's not what I meant, not what I meant at all," he said. "Listen, the fella I'm looking for owes me some dinero. Soon as I find him, well, you and me . . ."

Josie smiled and quieted down. She took another gulp of the whiskey he'd bought her and put a hand back on his knee. "I git ya now, Bret. Waas this feller look like?"

"He got here maybe a couple hours ago," Bret said. "Tall, lanky, dark hair, has a white scar on his cheek that he tries to hide under a scraggly beard."

"Yeah, I seen 'im. Fact, e's upstairs with Lorraine right now."

Bret glanced at the rickety stairway. "You know which room?"

"Well now," she said, "I'll git in trouble if'n I tell ya and ya jest go burstin' in there. Cain't ya wait till e's done?"

He smiled at her. "Josie, if I wait, and he ducks out the back way, I don't get my dinero, and you and me, well . . ."

Josie frowned. "Well, I ain't sure—"

A woman's piercing scream from the upper floor interrupted Josie's protests.

"That's Lorraine," she yelled, but Bret Reagan was already halfway up the stairs, six-gun drawn. He stopped at the top landing and darted a quick look around the corner. The red-carpeted hallway was empty, though a few slightly creaked-open doors showed anxious eyes peering out. Lorraine's screams continued, emanating from the one wide-open doorway, the third down on the right.

Reagan heard the stomp of feet on the hickory wood stairs behind him. He shot once, into the air. "Get back in your rooms, folks, nothing to see here!" As one, the quarter-open doors in the hallway slammed shut.

He pulled the trigger again and yelled back toward the staircase: "Crossfire, stay down!"

The clomping on the stairs halted.

Reagan slipped forward a few feet, six-gun at the ready. Nothing stirred in the hall. Lorraine's cries continued, morphing into sobs.

He dared a quick glance behind him. Nothing. The followers on the staircase continued to lay low, for now.

Bret Reagan tore the false moustache and beard away from his face and stuffed them in his pocket. He shucked his white topcoat, reversed it so that the black lining now faced out, and slipped it back on. He doffed his white hat, tied a black mask tightly around his eyes, and pulled the hat back on his head.

The Lone Ranger shot twice more into the ceiling, and made some noises suggesting the danger still existed, in order to continue to deter any brave souls from downstairs. He kicked in the cheap, flimsy door and dashed into Lorraine's room, both guns drawn, intent on preventing his quarry from striking again.

A quick glance at the girl—Lorraine—revealed her huddled in a corner on the cold wood floor, sobbing in horror, covered only with a shabby blanket. She appeared unharmed, or relatively so.

Not so the Lone Ranger's quarry.

Dave Daffie hung by his wrists from a rafter in the ceiling. A blood-red length of cloth, like a scarf, was knotted tightly around his bruised throat. A dark tongue lolled from a slack mouth.

Daffie's eyes bulged, a look of stark horror forever etched on his features. His feet were bare, boots tossed in the corner. He was shirtless. Small red welts covered his chest and feet. The tips of his fingers and toes were bloody ruins, the nails ripped off.

He had been tortured before being strangled.

The Ranger took all this in within seconds. He closed the door, turned the key, locking it, and shoved a chair under the knob.

He hunched down next to the sobbing girl and examined her. His first impression was correct, she was unharmed. Physically unharmed, anyway.

"Lorraine."

She looked up, as if seeing him for the first time. At the sight of the mask, her mouth opened to give forth another barrage of screams. He clamped a hand over her mouth and then shifted to hold a finger to her lips. "Lorraine, I'm not going to hurt you, I promise. Please, don't scream. Nod if you understand."

The girl nodded and he released her. "It's okay, it's okay," the Ranger said, soothing her. "I need you to answer some questions. Can you do that?"

Lorraine nodded again and wiped the tears from her cheeks. She was pretty, dark haired, and probably only eighteen or nineteen. He felt sorry that her life had come to this, and at such a young age.

"How many were there?" he asked.

"Th-three," she answered quietly.

"What did they look like?"

"They were like those foreigners, those men who built the railroad and work at the docks."

"You mean, Chinese?

"Yeah. Long black hair braided in the back and big flowy shirts and pants."

"Did they all look like that?" the Ranger asked.

"The one in charge, he held a knife to my neck while the others . . ." Lorraine gestured at the hanging body. "He was bald, had a funny little yellow hat. He spoke real quiet, like he was whispering, but he wasn't really."

"What did he say?"

"He was real apologetic. Said he was real sorry and that as long as I was quiet I wouldn't get hurt. Said that the railroad was built on the backs of the Chinese and now they were dyin' in the coal mines and it was gonna end. He and his gang were gonna end it."

"His gang?"

"He had a funny name for it, but it seemed like it was a gang. Called it a 'tongue' or something like that."

"A 'tong?'" he asked.

"Yeah, that's it, tong."

"Think hard, Lorraine," the Ranger said. "Did this tong have a name?"

"I don't have to think too hard, mister," Lorraine said. "He looked at me with those eyes and I almost felt like I was dreamin'. He said to tell whoever came askin' that it was the 'Sublime Order of the White Peacock.' Don't even know what that means, but it don't sound very scary. He made me repeat it to make sure I got it right."

"Okay. How did they get away?"

"The head guy, like I said, he said they wouldn't hurt me, if'n I did what they said. If I didn't, it'd be worse than that guy hanging there."

"Go on," he prodded.

"So, he said I had to wait five minutes after they left before I could start screaming. He said he knew I was gonna scream, but I had to wait five minutes. Or else if I didn't he would come back and find me and string me up like that guy there and slice off my eyelids and shove burning wood slivers up under my fingernails and other stuff I don't wanna talk about."

"So, you stayed quiet."

"Damn right, mister."

"I understand," the Ranger said. "You did the right thing. Is there anything else you can think of?"

Lorraine shook her head no, then grabbed the Ranger's wrist and looked at him hard.

"Just that he said the coal mines were goin' up in flames, startin' with the one that there dead man came from. And mister, that peacock stuff don't sound too scary, like I said. But he scared the dickens outta me, when he said this stuff about the coal mines burnin', his own eyes were afire. They were blazin' *green!*"

December 3, 1872
Sheriff C. Carey
Green River, Wyoming
 DAFFIE DEAD STOP CHINESE TONG PLANS
 GREEN RIVER COALMINE SABOTAGE
 RETALIATION STOP WARN MAYOR
 DECHER STOP ARRIVING TRAIN DEC
 SIXTH INFORM T STOP
Allen King, en route Green River, Care Conductor, Central Pacific, Train 94, Oakland, California.

December 4

Reagan entered the crowded dining car and took a long look. The train, rattling along the steel rails, had just departed Reno, Nevada.

He noted an empty chair at a table for four and made his way down the narrow aisle.

"Please pardon the intrusion," he said, in a slight Southern drawl. He tipped his hat respectfully. "There don't appear to be many empty seats. May I join you?"

The three passengers sat stock still, staring at him, and a palpable air of tension arose.

Then one of the men, whom Reagan estimated to be about forty, stood and bowed slightly. He wore a dark suit of a European cut and a top hat. He nodded without smiling and indicated the vacant seat with a gloved hand. "I am Phileas Fogg of Savile Row, London. Please, do join us."

"Bret Reagan, Baton Rouge, Louisiana, at your service, sir."

The two shook hands and Reagan took the seat next to Fogg. Across from them sat another man and a woman. She was introduced as Aouda, a Parsi who had joined Fogg's party while they had traveled through the Bundelcund region of India. She was darkly beautiful, with coal black hair, wide eyes, and smooth skin with the faintest tint of olive.

Reagan tipped his hat again and gave a friendly smile. "Charmed, ma'am." Aouda nodded gravely at Reagan but said nothing.

"And this," Fogg said, "is my manservant, Passepartout."

Passepartout looked to be about thirty. He wore a brown suit and matching bowler hat, which was affixed firmly atop a round, somewhat cherubic face. He smiled openly at Reagan and the two shook hands across the table. "Pleased to meet you, monsieur! Are you a real American cowboy?"

Bret Reagan chuckled and shook his head. "No, Passepartout, not a cowboy by any stretch." He turned to Fogg. "But tell me, sir. What brings you all the way from London to Nevada, by way of India?"

"My master has made a bet that he can circumnavigate the entire globe in eighty days or less!" Passepartout exclaimed. "He stands to lose an enormous sum if he fails to do so."

"Passepartout, that will be quite enough," Fogg said. The manservant's comically abashed expression made Reagan grin.

"But," Reagan said, "what Passepartout says is accurate? That's absolutely fascinating, sir! And Miss Aouda here joined your expedition as you traveled through India?"

"Mr. Fogg is a wonderful man." Aouda spoke for the first time. "He rescued me from a horrible fate." Reagan could plainly see that the girl felt not only gratitude for the Englishman. She was clearly in love with him.

"Sir, if I may," Reagan said to Fogg. "You and your party looked quite wary, perhaps even tense, when I asked to join you. Nonetheless, you have extended to me the hospitality of your table. For that, I thank you. If you care to share what's troubling you, I'm at your service."

Fogg looked at Reagan for a long while, as if taking the American's measure, and then nodded at Passepartout, who clearly was bursting to tell the tale.

"It was on the Oakland ferry that one of your countrymen made insulting remarks concerning my master's homeland," he began. "Monsieur Fogg, naturally, took exception to this, and the upshot is that this American, a Colonel Proctor, caused us to be late and made several threatening remarks. Facing a wait of several hours, we returned to San Francisco and checked at the British Consulate, where they referred us to a gentlemen gunfighter who resides at the Hotel Carlton.

"Finally, with this escort in place, we made our way to Reno. The Colonel's brother, Major Proctor, and two henchmen dogged our heels almost all the way to Reno. He continually tried to goad Monsieur Fogg into fighting him. Our guide believed Major Proctor was motivated more by the money in Monsieur Fogg's carpetbag than his brother's honor."

Fogg shot a dark look at Passepartout at this comment, and Reagan was sure the Englishman would have stern words with his valet later. The Frenchman, oblivious, glibly continued: "Anyway, just outside of Reno, the Major finally got us alone and challenged Monsieur Fogg to a duel. In the course of which, the man in black—"

"Man in black?" Reagan asked.

"Yes, monsieur, our guide."

"Ah," Reagan said. He had heard of this man. He waved Passepartout to continue.

"Well, monsieur, the man in black was forced to shoot Major Proctor."

"I see," Reagan said. "And you're worried the Colonel may come after you."

"There has been no sign of Colonel Proctor on the trail," Fogg said. "There is really no cause for concern."

"But if Colonel Proctor were to make trouble, Mr. Fogg," Reagan said, "it could cause you further delay."

"Not to mention bodily harm, monsieur!" Passepartout said.

"I thank you for your concern, Mr. Reagan," Fogg said, "but I am confident we will arrive in New York on December 11, with time to spare to catch our steamer."

Passepartout extracted an oversized silver watch with esoteric markings on the cover from a vest pocket. He made a great show of consulting it. "As of this moment, monsieur, we are exactly on schedule—just as my master has foreseen!" he said with pride.

Fogg changed the subject. "My man Passepartout is enamored of American gunfighters." He gestured at Reagan's six-shooters. "Are you one, sir?"

Reagan chuckled. "Me? No sir, Mr. Fogg, not by trade, anyway."

"Then what brings you on this journey, sir?"

Reagan—the Lone Ranger—felt that it was always wisest to stick as closely to the truth as possible when in disguise. "I was deputized by the sheriff of Green River, Wyoming, and sent after a ruthless murderer."

"Then you are a gunfighter!" Passepartout exclaimed.

Reagan smiled and shook his head. "No, no, just a bounty hunter."

"But you return to Wyoming empty-handed," Fogg said.

"Someone else got to him first," Reagan replied.

"Please monsieur, tell us the full story," Passepartout asked.

And so Reagan did.

"The killer was named Dave Daffie. He was the chief of the coal mine in Green River, and by all accounts a brutal ruffian. He beat to death one of the Chinese mine workers, and looked to get away with it. The owner of the coal mine—who also happens to be Green River's mayor—sure didn't have any trouble with it. Said it would teach the 'coolies' a lesson and keep them in line."

"'Coolies,' monsieur?" Passepartout asked.

Being an Account of the Delay at Green River

"Yes, Passepartout," Reagan said. "It's a not-very-nice term for low-wage—almost zero-wage—Chinese laborers. Unfortunately, there's a lot of anti-Chinese sentiment here in America. Many Chinese immigrants worked on the railroad which now connects east and west—the very rails we're traveling over now. After completion of the railway, many of the Chinese transitioned to working in coal mines. In California, Chinese workers are helping to construct an immense system of levees which will aid in agriculture. And yet, many Americans who have no problem with this cheap labor don't want these workers as their neighbors. Just last year, fifteen Chinese were hanged in Los Angeles in a wave of anti-Chinese riots.

"Despite the prevailing sentiments in his town, the sheriff of Green River is a good man and went after Daffie. Unfortunately, Daffie escaped on the Pacific Railroad, headed for California. Word spread quickly that Daffie was a wanted man, and the usual posters were drawn up, with rewards posted, but Sheriff Carey was concerned that no lawmen would 'waste' their time pursuing the killer of a mere Chinese laborer.

"I was passing through Green River," Reagan continued. "The sheriff and I go back pretty far, so he deputized me and I set out after Daffie."

This was a bit of a fib, but he couldn't give away all his secrets. The truth was he and his faithful Potawatomi companion, Tonto, had been in Denver, having just tracked down and brought to justice one of the last stragglers of the notorious Cavendish gang. They had been preparing to head for Texas when they received Carey's message. The sheriff had met the Lone Ranger once before and had sent out a mass telegram to "Allen King," hoping the message would reach the Ranger. The Lone Ranger always checked for telegrams addressed to King wherever he went. It was his way of ensuring he could be reached by key people in his operation, such as Jim Blaine, and his nephew, Dan Reid, Jr.

The Ranger and Tonto had made good time to Green River, and after consulting with Carey, it was decided that the best course of action was for the Ranger to track Daffie, taking the next train, while Tonto camped on the outskirts of Green River to monitor the situation there, in the event of more anti-Chinese violence.

"I finally tracked Daffie to the environs of the Oakland Long Wharf," Reagan told his traveling companions, "which as you know is also the terminus of the Pacific Railroad. Guess he thought he'd made it that far and was safe. The wharf area is a den of iniquity, dirty, fog-shrouded and misty, and littered with saloons and flop houses. I've heard it's much like London's Limehouse district, Mr. Fogg."

"I wouldn't know," Fogg replied.

Reagan nodded and wrapped up the tale with a brief overview of how he had found Daffie dead, omitting the gruesome details out of respect for the lady, Aouda.

"But monsieur," Passepartout said, "why do you return to Green River, if you essentially—*ahem*—failed in your mission?"

"Sheriff Carey is a friend of mine," Reagan said. "I'm worried that once the news that Daffie was killed in California gets back to Green River, folks might make more trouble for the Chinese workers there. One thing I didn't mention . . . it looked like Daffie had been killed by a gang of Chinese. If that gets out . . ."

"I see, monsieur," Passepartout said.

"Besides," Reagan said, smiling, "I left my horse in Green River."

December 5, 1872
Sheriff C. Carey
Green River, Wyoming
BUFFALO CROSSING DELAY SIX HOURS STOP NO SIGN TONG HOPE TO BEAT THEM TO GREEN RIVER STOP ARRIVE APPROX NOON DEC SIXTH STOP
Allen King, en route Green River, Care Conductor, Central Pacific, Train 94, Wells, Nevada.

December 6, 2:00 A.M.—Ogden, Utah

The Lone Ranger, still in his Bret Reagan identity, stepped from the passenger car to the station platform and rubbed his hands to stave off the cold. He could see his breath in the chill of the air. The station was almost pitch black below a blanket of stars which peppered the crisp night sky. Beyond starlight, the sole illumination came from a gaslamp set near the station door.

BEING AN ACCOUNT OF THE DELAY AT GREEN RIVER

Most passengers were asleep or, if wakeful at this late hour, had the good sense to stay on the train where there was at least a modicum of warmth. A few disembarked, as the Salt Lake area was their final destination. Sleepy station workers unloaded large cases and footlockers from the baggage cars at the rear of the train, while the departing passengers filed into the station and out of the cold.

At the same time, the conductor checked the tickets of a few new arrivals who were boarding at Ogden.

Amidst this minor commotion, the Ranger stamped his feet against the chill and paced the platform, waiting for the people to clear out. He had a telegram to send, but he'd decided to wait until the other passengers had sent and received their own messages, or otherwise finished conducting their business in the station house, in order to avoid prying eyes.

As he had already telegraphed Sheriff Carey from the prior stop, he wasn't sure where the men of the White Peacock Tong were. However, the Central Pacific had been the fastest option to get from Oakland to Wyoming, and he had taken the first departing train after the incident at the house of ill repute on the Wharf. He had to be ahead of them, but one couldn't be too careful.

He stepped into the cone of yellow light cast by the gaslamp, turned on his heel, and paced back into the shadows. At the corner of the brick structure, he reversed again.

Something flitted overhead, stirring the air like the passage of a small bird, and in the next second a sharp kick to the back of his knees took his feet out from under him. A loop of cloth cinched around his neck and tightened, cutting mercilessly into his windpipe.

The Ranger tried to pull the cloth loose, but it dug too deeply into his flesh. He began to see stars and knew he was close to blacking out—permanently. He didn't want to attract attention, but breathing trumped everything at this point. He couldn't see his would-be killer behind him, but he didn't need to. His six-gun slipped into his hand and he got a shot off.

The noose immediately loosened and he collapsed to the platform, gasping for precious air. He heard the padding of bare feet on the wooden clapboards as his prospective murderer made his escape.

The Ranger heard the station men and passengers inside coming to investigate, and took off after his assailant, rounding the building's corner. Seeing no sign of the noose-man, he continued all the way around the building, tearing off the murder cloth as he ran and donning his own bandana to conceal the angry red marks that presumably marred the flesh of his neck.

He came back onto the train platform, on the opposite side of the station building from which he had left it. Nonchalantly, he asked the milling folks what the matter was, and looked suitably alarmed when told there had been a gunshot. He made his way through the crowd and inside, where he finally sent his telegram, just as the train whistled.

The conductor yelled for all aboard who were going aboard, and the platform quickly cleared. The Ranger darted over to where he had been attacked and scanned the wooden floorboards.

Drops of blood. Good. He had at least winged his man, though given the man's quick escape, it was not a fatal wound. Also good.

He leapt aboard the train as it began to roll down the tracks and slowly made his way through several carriages back to his own passenger car, keeping a wary eye out.

As he reseated with Fogg's party, Passepartout asked him: "Monsieur Reagan, we heard a shot! It woke us up. Do you know what happened?"

"I'm afraid I don't, Passepartout," Reagan replied. "I was in the station house at the time, sending a telegram."

The Parsi lady, Aouda, seated across from Reagan, shook her head. She reached over and pulled from his inside coat pocket a length of dull yellow cloth, the tip of which he had not noticed sticking out.

"Aouda," Fogg said, embarrassed at her forward behavior, "what in the world—"

"Ask Mr. Reagan," she said, "to loosen his neckerchief."

"Now, Aouda—"

"Mr. Fogg," she said firmly. "Ask him."

Fogg turned to the Ranger. "I'm terribly sorry, Reagan, I don't know what's gotten into her."

Reagan held up a hand. "It's okay, Mr. Fogg. The lady Aouda is mighty perceptive." He loosened his bandana, ever so slightly.

Aouda gasped at the angry red marks about his throat. "Phansigar!"

"Phansigar?" Reagan asked.

"Ruthless robbers and stranglers," Aouda replied. "Your throat bears their marks. They strike quickly and silently using garrotes made of cloth, sometimes using head coverings or kerchiefs known as *Rumāl*. They have terrorized unsuspecting travelers in my homeland for hundreds of years, Mr. Reagan. They are also known as Thuggee!"

"I see," Reagan said. "Thank you, Aouda, that's very helpful. You're right, of course, I was attacked."

"Mr. Reagan, will you be quite all right?" Fogg asked.

"I will, sir. Thank you for asking though, and for your concern," Reagan said. "Let's keep it down, though, I don't want to attract any attention."

"If you'll pardon me," Fogg said, quietly, "it appears you've already attracted some."

The Ranger smiled ruefully.

"Then . . . the gunshot?" Passepartout whispered.

"Yes, that was me," Reagan said. "I clipped him but he got away. I think we should all get whatever sleep we can. I know I'll need it, at least, once I get off the train at Green River."

He tugged his white Stetson down to shade his eyes, put up his feet, and pretended to sleep, one hand on his six-gun.

December 6, 1872
Sheriff C. Carey
Green River, Wyoming
    ATTACKED IN OGDEN STOP TONG MEMBERS SOMEWHERE ON TRAIN STOP ARRIVE GREEN RIVER APPROX EIGHT OR NINE HOURS STOP NOTIFY T TO PREPARE SUITABLE WELCOME STOP
Allen King, en route Green River, Care Conductor, Central Pacific, Train 94, Ogden, Utah.

Bret Reagan stepped out of the carriage and into southwestern Wyoming's early winter noonday sun. He turned back and glanced up at the carriage window, at which sat Fogg and Passepartout. He tipped his hat respectfully, silently wishing them safe travels. This was a short stop and the train would be away in a few minutes.

He scanned up and down the platform, looking for anyone who might resemble his assailant, or other members of the White Peacock Tong. Of course, before last night, he would have assumed that White Peacock members would all be robed, pigtailed Chinese men.

Now he knew better.

He also kept an eye out for Sheriff Carey, assuming that the lawman was aware of the train's arrival and would be at the station shortly.

A tremendous explosion threw Reagan and the other debarking passengers from their feet, and wooden and metal debris rained down over them. He shook his head to clear it and stumbled to his feet. He rushed toward the front of the train and the dying flames, weaving in and around dazed and milling passengers.

Passing the engine, he saw that the blast had occurred some one hundred feet up the tracks. In fact, the tracks had been blown. Only shattered and twisted metal remained of the once-straight and solid steel rails.

Behind Reagan, passengers scurried off the train in alarm. He saw Fogg, Aouda, and Passepartout amidst the others, many of whom were shouting at those remaining to hurry off the train in the event of another explosion. Mixed in with these were cries of speculation that it was an Indian attack.

Reagan raced up and down the length of the train, wondering if this was a distraction. If the White Peacock Tong had been on the train the whole way—however they managed to hide themselves— disembarking at Green River unnoticed would present a problem for them. He ran back to the tail end of the train, toward the baggage cars, in time to see a wagon drawn by four horses racing away. In the wagon were four caskets. Next to the driver was a man in a black hat and black cloak wearing dark smoked-lensed glasses.

The wagon was too far away and was going too fast to give chase. He slapped his open palm on his thigh in frustration.

"You took a terrible chance, *Kemosabe*, getting back on the train in your Bret Reagan identity after being attacked," Tonto said. He handed the Ranger a cup of boiled chicory coffee. "Why not just board the train in a new disguise?"

The Lone Ranger and his friend Tonto, along with Sheriff Carey, sat around a small campfire. Tonto was camped about half a mile outside of town; Carey had taken the Ranger there shortly after the explosion at the Green River train station.

"You raise a good point, Tonto," the Lone Ranger said. He had dispensed with the Reagan disguise and was back in his traditional gray denim, black mask, and white Stetson. "I made some friends on the train. They knew that I—Reagan—was traveling to Green River after running into some trouble in Oakland. They would have raised the alarm if Reagan hadn't gotten back on the train in Ogden. Even so, the members of the White Peacock Tong would probably have kept a special eye on any new passengers boarding at Ogden. It was better to just board as Reagan and stay alert for any additional attacks."

"That makes sense," Tonto said. "Who were these friends?"

"A Mr. Fogg of London and his traveling companion, a lady named Aouda, from India. They're accompanied by Mr. Fogg's valet, a Frenchman named Passepartout. I believe they've taken rooms at the Green River Hotel while the rails are being repaired."

"And you think these, these 'tong' boys blew up the rails?" the sheriff asked. "Why in tarnation would they do that when their real aim is to destroy the coal mine? Why not just get off at Green River to do their business and let the train go on?"

"I think their leader is a real savvy one," the Ranger said. "I'm betting he figured that Reagan telegraphed a warning ahead—which I did—and that it would be easier to get off the train at Green River unnoticed if there was a lot of confusion. So he bombed the tracks, got himself and his men off in the commotion, and disappeared."

"So as soon as the train stopped," Tonto said, "one of them hopped off, ran up the tracks, and set off a stick or two of dynamite. They clearly have the means to destroy the coal mine—or at least put it out of commission for a while."

"But where could they be?" the Ranger asked.

"I've had a few men scout around the town—the saloon, the hotel, pretty much everywhere," Carey said. "There's no sign of anyone unusual. Some passengers, like your friends, have taken rooms at the hotel, but there's only so much room. Most have gotten back on the train to wait for the track repairs. Mayor Decher—he owns the coal mine too—sent for some of the Chinese miners to do the repairs. After all, they originally worked on the tracks before settling here. But the Chinese are nowhere to be found. Boss Decher's in quite a rage, let me tell you."

"'Boss?'" the Ranger asked.

"It's what the townsfolk here call Mayor Decher," Tonto explained. "He's the mayor, and the owner of the coal mine. He controls everything in Green River. Everyone calls him 'boss' and he likes it that way."

"I see," the Ranger said, slowly. Tonto nodded. They both had encountered too many men like Boss Decher in their crusade for justice.

"The train is going to be delayed at least for twelve to eighteen hours," Carey said, "while the rails are being repaired. It would go a lot faster if those skilled Chinese laborers could be found."

"And what of the Chinese," the Ranger asked. "Where could they be?"

Carey had good grace to look embarrassed. "They've gone underground."

"What does that mean?" Tonto asked.

"I've heard stories of other towns that have laws forbidding the Chinese from being out and about on the streets," Carey said. "They use tunnels dug out between the cellars of the buildings to get around. Not quite as bad here—yet. Boss Decher is working on getting a similar law on the books. In the meantime, there are already tunnels . . . most of the Chinese have fled down to 'em—for safety."

"Why is that?" the Ranger asked. "What happened?"

"The townsfolk have learned that Dave Daffie was probably killed by Chinese in Oakland. They're all worked up," Carey said. "I'm guessing Decher has a spy in the telegraph office. He probably received your first telegram to me almost before I did."

The Ranger slapped one gloved hand against the other in frustration. "It's a sure bet where the men of the White Peacock Tong have fled, then. They're being harbored underground by the locals. If we can't rout them out, they'll blow the mine."

"There're veins criss-crossing beneath the whole town," Carey said. "They do that, and the whole place could go up. Lotta people could die."

"Not to mention the danger to all the Chinese locals below ground," Tonto said. "How come Decher and his men don't just go down into the tunnels and bring them out, if they're so concerned about getting them back to work?"

"Decher's worried they could be armed," Carey said. "He's decided to just wait until they start starving and come out of their own accord. When that happens, he plans to hold a necktie social and make an example out of a few of 'em."

"Are there any Chinese still above ground, anywhere?" the Ranger asked.

"Only one I can think of works at the hotel as a jack-of-all-trades," Carey said. "That's where Boss Decher hangs his hat as well. You can usually find him at the bar."

The Lone Ranger rose and headed toward his white stallion, Silver. "Let's ride. It's time for a word with the Mayor."

"And just how do I know you're not another outlaw?" Decher said. He took a large slurp of cheap whiskey. "A man who wears a mask isn't exactly a man I can trust."

Decher, Sheriff Carey, and the Lone Ranger were seated at a rickety wooden table near the bar in the Green River Hotel. The hotel was the nicest place in town. That wasn't saying much—this was a working town and there was little in the way of luxury—but it was enough.

"I'm vouching for him, Mayor," Sheriff Carey said. "I deputized him to go after Daffie, and that's still in effect."

"Well now, Carey, you know I don't exactly agree with you chasing after Daffie in the first place," Decher said. "He was my best man and kept the mine running like clockwork."

"There was a little matter of murder, Mayor."

"No proof poor old Daffie murdered anyone," Decher said. He pursed his fat lips and slurped his drink again.

"That would've been up to a court to decide, Mayor, but Daffie took off before I could arrest him," Carey said. "You know all this, let's stop playing games."

"Games, Sheriff?" Decher's voice lowered. He was a fat man, but there was steel in his voice. "Your little game cost me a good head man, and all over some stupid coolies. They're barely even hum—"

"That's enough." The steel in the Ranger's voice matched Decher's.

"I agree," Carey said. "I've heard enough of this. I have work to do at my office." The sheriff picked up his hat in disgust and left, almost bumping into Phileas Fogg as the latter entered the room.

The Englishman made straight for their table. "Mayor Decher, please pardon the interruption, but is there any update on the rail repairs? I have a schedule to keep . . ." He stopped as he got a good look at the Ranger and then continued, more slowly. "I'm sorry, Mr. Mayor, but what is a masked outlaw doing sitting at your table?"

"I asked myself the same thing, Mr. . . ."

"Fogg."

"Mr. Fogg, the sheriff assures me this masked man's on the side of law and order." Decher slapped his fat stomach in amusement. "I'm not sure I'm supposed to believe that, but he hasn't done anything wrong in my town—yet."

The Lone Ranger stood and shook Fogg's hand. Both men sat down. "The Mayor is right, Mr. Fogg," the Ranger said. "I wear a mask in the service of justice. In fact, I was just trying to convince him of the threat to his town—a threat from the White Peacock Tong."

"There's no such thing," Decher said with derision in his voice. "Do you really think a bunch of coolies could pose a threat to *my* town? And they name themselves after a peacock? What kind of threat is that?"

"A very real threat, I assure you," Fogg replied. "A man I met on the train from Oakland was attacked by one of their members, and almost killed."

At that moment, a young Chinese man approached with a glass of whiskey and set it down hard in front of Decher, splashing the brown liquid on the table and on Decher's suit coat.

"Goddammit, boy, you know how much that coat cost me?" the boss said. "That's coming out of your wages, you—"

"No, it's not," the young man said firmly.

"What did you say to me?" Decher said. He stood up, slowly, his hand sliding toward his gun.

The Ranger also stood and took Decher's forearm in a steel grip. He looked toward the young man. "What's your name, son?"

"I am Wei Ning," he said to the Ranger. "I know you are here to stop them, but it is too late."

"Them?" the Lone Ranger asked.

"Yes, masked man, the Sublime Order of the White Peacock. They have come to protect us." Wei Ning turned back to the Mayor. "Your days of wantonly murdering my people are over. The tong will destroy the coal mine and teach you all a lesson you will not soon forget!"

"Don't be ridiculous," Decher said.

Wei Ning looked at the clock above the bar and said to them, "The whole town will be destroyed. The White Peacock Tong will spread a reign of terror and death upon you. War has been declared. You have one hour. All of you." He turned on his heel, picked up a wooden crate from the end of the bar, and exited by a door to a storeroom.

"I'll send some of my boys to teach him a lesson," Decher said.

"You'll do no such thing," the Ranger said. "You must take this seriously, Mayor. Isn't it the case that the veins of coal are extensive and run all beneath the town? If they really have enough TNT, they could make good on their threat to destroy Green River."

Decher looked dubious, as if rationality and reason were penetrating his narrow-minded thoughts for the very first time.

"Don't you see, Decher? If the tong destroys the mine, any Green River survivors will massacre the rest of the Chinese. We're trying to avoid an all-out race war."

The Ranger turned to the Englishman. "Mr. Fogg, you are traveling with others, if I'm not mistaken? I would get them away from the hotel, and outside the town limits, if I were you."

"I will warn them," Fogg replied, "but then I shall return to assist you." The Englishman departed before the Ranger could protest.

"Decher, get to Sheriff Carey's office," the Ranger said. "My partner, Tonto, is there. Work with them to round up as many men as you can and get the town evacuated, just in case."

"Tonto?" Decher echoed.

"Yes, Tonto," the Ranger said. "He's an Indian. That going to be a problem for you?"

Boss Decher shook his head, as if he still couldn't fathom the possibility of his mine and his town going up in flames. He also was unaccustomed to taking orders from others. Still, he stood. "You said just in case. In case what?"

"In case Mr. Fogg and I are unsuccessful," came the Ranger's grim reply.

The Lone Ranger and Phileas Fogg descended the shaky wooden ladder from the trapdoor in the storeroom behind the hotel bar. The Ranger, mindful of Decher's concern that the Chinese locals were armed, and might shoot first, had one six-gun drawn and held at the ready. Fogg carried a dark lantern in his left hand and a black cane in his right.

"What is your plan, sir?" Fogg asked.

"I want to try to reason with the Chinese, Mr. Fogg," the Ranger answered. "I know they've been mistreated, but a cycle of violence will help no one."

"Strange words from a man who carries two six-shooters."

"Not so strange, Mr. Fogg. I shoot to disarm, not to kill."

They continued to make their way downward through twisting and winding corridors, until finally the air freshened somewhat and they saw hanging lanterns flickering in a widening cavern ahead.

The Ranger stepped into the larger space first. Men, women, and children were camped on thin bedrolls on the earthen floor in a condition of squalor. Many looked cold, and hungry.

On the other side of the grotto, he could see that the tunnel continued downward, presumably connecting to the coal mine proper.

The Ranger and Fogg took two more steps forward and stopped. Some of the refugees—for that's what they were—looked up dully at the two men.

"Please, who's in charge here?" the Ranger asked.

There was a stirring as the rest of the Chinese locals noticed the two intruders, and one man came running toward them.

"You!" It was Wei Ning. "What are you doing here?"

"I came to try and stop this war, Wei Ning," the Ranger said. He holstered his gun and raised his hands as a sign of good faith. "Who's in charge here?"

Wei Ning was angry, but called out. "Grandfather! There are two men here to see you."

An old man shuffled forward.

"This is my grandfather, Ai Wen," Wei Ning said. "He speaks for us."

The Lone Ranger nodded at Ai Wen respectfully. "It is an honor to meet you, sir. I come to ask you to give up the men who belong to the Sublime Order of the White Peacock."

The older Chinese man spoke plainly. "Why should we do that? They come here to help us."

"Sir, I realize that you and your people have been ill treated by the rest of the Green River townsfolk. But the men of the White Peacock Tong cannot help you by destroying the coal mine. Most of you down here will die, and those that don't will be killed by the white survivors out of revenge. Sir, there has to be a better way, a way to peacefully resolve this."

The old man looked skeptical.

Phileas Fogg spoke up: "Sir, while you have no reason to believe us, we are not from Green River. I have met many honorable men, of many different colors and creeds, in my travels around the world—"

Several figures darted out of the shadows and shouldered Ai Wen aside. Two were clearly tong men, not Chinese but rather the Phansigar killers whom Aouda had described. One held a wicked blade, while the other menacingly swung a yellow cloth weighted on either end like a bolo. The three behind the tong men were obviously, from their workman's clothes, local Chinese miners.

The knife man leapt forward. In the next split second, the dagger spun through the air and clattered uselessly against the cave's rock wall. The Thuggee screamed in pain and fell to the ground, cradling his shattered and bloody hand.

Faster than thought, the Lone Ranger had drawn his six-gun and shot the blade out of his attacker's hand!

The other Thuggee feinted at Fogg. Fogg was not fooled and

calmly stood his ground, his response showing a battle hardness that belied his gentlemanlike exterior. The tong man attacked in earnest and Fogg, acting almost as quickly as the Ranger, drew a sword from his black cane. In a whirling frenzy he slashed the strangling garrote to ribbons. He thrust his blade forward and impaled the man's shoulder in a non-lethal strike, putting him out of commission.

The three Chinese miners had stood on the sidelines of the fight, and now two more joined them. Three held heavy metal work tools; the other two wielded knives. They were obviously not warriors, but hardened determination etched their grim visages.

The Ranger and Fogg were surrounded.

"I can't injure or kill these men," the masked man whispered to Fogg.

"Agreed, sir."

The Ranger holstered his gun and Fogg sheathed his sword.

"Ai Wen," the Ranger called out, "please . . ."

The old man stepped forward. He held a flaming torch in each hand. Others stepped forward and the elder Chinese lit their torches.

"I am sorry," Ai Wen said, "but the mines must be destroyed. There is no other way."

Above the drama playing out in the underground mines, on Green River's main street, Tonto, Sheriff Carey, Boss Decher, and Passepartout attempted to coordinate an organized evacuation of the small mining town. The latter two were at one end of the street, near the Green River Hotel and the rail station, while Tonto and Carey were at the far end.

In the confusion, two pigtailed Chinese emerged from the hotel, which Passepartout thought had already been cleared. These men were dressed in flowing green and yellow garments. "Look!" he cried, "tong men!"

Decher spun and drew his gun. "Goddamn Chinese bast—"

A thin throwing dagger sliced into Decher's throat. Blood geysered and the mayor fell face-forward in the dusty street, instantly dead.

The two Peacock Tong men leapt at Passepartout and tackled him to the ground. One pinned his arms against the hard dirt road while the other tried to pummel the Frenchmen into unconsciousness.

Passepartout attempted, mostly in vain, to block the blows. The next instant he realized that the masked man's Indian companion was in the fray.

Tonto and the Chinese man who had pinned the valet's arms were rolling head over heels in the dust. Both men landed on their feet and circled each other warily. A wavy dagger appeared in the tong man's right hand.

In the meantime, his arms freed, Passepartout flipped from his back to his feet in a flash, clearly astounding his opponent, who had not expected such an acrobatic display. The man's astonished pause, however, was short lived and gave way to a flurry of kicks which the Frenchman was hard pressed to block.

Nearby, Tonto caught his man with an uppercut, narrowly avoiding the other's blade. A solid right to the jaw knocked the tong man unconscious. Tonto grabbed the blade from the man's loosening fingers and he tossed it away.

The Indian launched himself toward Passepartout and his adversary, who was getting the better of the Frenchman. Fogg's valet was almost unconscious, bloody and battered. The tong man reached into the Frenchman's vest and withdrew his enormous silver watch.

A single shot rang out and the Chinese fell dead in the road, a bullet from Sheriff Carey's smoking gun lodged in his heart.

Passepartout looked up in gratitude. "Thank you monsieurs, thank you! It's a family heirloom, absolutely irreplaceable." He gingerly tucked the watch back in his vest pocket.

They heard a scuff behind them and whirled as one.

Tonto's man had been faking unconsciousness and was running full-tilt toward the Indian with another wavy-bladed dagger in hand.

Carey shot him dead.

"Ai Wen," the Ranger said, "there *is* another way. The way of peace."

The old man faltered.

"There has been enough death," the masked man continued.

As if to emphasize his point, Wei Ning ran up. "Grandfather, Boss Decher and two of the Chinese men from California are dead!"

"Ai Wen," the Ranger said, "Decher's reign is over. I will work with the mining company's new owners to ensure they honor and value the work your people do."

Ai Wen slowly lowered his torches.

"The law that Decher wanted," the masked man continued, "the law that would have forced your people to live underground as well as work underground . . . that law will never come to be."

Ai Wen dropped the torches and signaled the others to do so. "It is over," he said solemnly.

The Lone Ranger nodded. "It is over."

As the last of the Chinese miners and their families made their way out of the caverns and up into the brisk, but fresh, winter's air, a sibilant, almost hissing voice called out from behind the masked man and the Englishman.

"Mr. Reagan. Mr. Fogg."

Startled, the two men turned.

Two green eyes burned and danced in the inky depths of the cavern, like emerald fireflies, or angry hornets.

Below the eyes, a grate slid open on a dark lantern and a slice of kerosene-fed light illuminated the face in which the jade eyes were set.

The face was that of a Chinese man in his early thirties, handsomely satanic. His head was shaved and he wore a yellow skullcap. His black robes were of silk and prominently embroidered with a stylized white peacock surrounded by smaller dragons and other arcane symbols.

"I am Shan Ming Fu."

The Lone Ranger nodded. "The head of the Sublime Order of the White Peacock."

"The very same," the tong leader replied. "You have thwarted my attempts to bring about change in Green River, and indeed to change the lot of my people in this country."

"I have also done my best to help your people," the Ranger said, "at least on a small scale in this tiny town. And my methods involve less loss of life or limb than yours."

Shan Ming Fu nodded. "You have earned my respect. Grudgingly, but you have earned it. But you have administered a setback to me. You can provide compensation which will make me whole."

"What setback?" the masked man asked.

"The reputation of being the only Mandarin willing to take on oppressors for the sake of ordinary Chinese workers would be a great foundation for the growth and expansion of my Order. I would have gained great prestige among the immigrants and their families."

"And what is it you wish?"

"Nothing of import. It is a matter of honor which can be satisfied with a small token."

"Which is?"

Shan Ming Fu gestured to Phileas Fogg. "This man's servant carries a watch. It is an ornament of great beauty. Give it to me and you shall hear from me no more."

"Absolutely out of the question," Fogg said with his usual calm.

The tong leader turned his blazing green eyes upon the Englishman. "It is only out of regard for our shared paternity that I do not strike you down where you stand."

"I have no idea what you're talking about." For the first time, Fogg's characteristic composure was shaken.

"Sir," the Lone Ranger interrupted, "you have suffered no harm which requires compensation. You showed the immigrant Chinese workers your willingness to help them. Daffie and Decher are dead. Your prestige remains intact, and in fact will only grow due to the events here, which you helped shape."

Shan Ming Fu turned back to the masked man. The unblinking green eyes burned but there was an inhuman coldness behind them. He nodded. "I am outmaneuvered. My respect for you is well placed. I shall follow your progress, and that of your descendants and their descendants. I expect great things."

There was a burst of green flame which temporarily blinded the Ranger and Fogg. When their eyesight cleared, Shan Ming Fu was gone.

Fogg turned to the Ranger. "Mr. Reagan?" he asked quizzically.

The masked man gave a slight smile. "The very same."

December 7

The Lone Ranger and Tonto walked toward the Green River station platform as the train prepared to depart.

"*Kemosabe*," Tonto said, "from what you told me, the tong leader said many strange things in the cavern below. The comment to Mr. Fogg, for instance."

"Yes, Tonto, and Mr. Fogg clearly did not want to discuss it further."

"But even more strange," Tonto continued, "was the remark about your descendants."

"I don't understand that one either, Tonto," the Ranger replied. He gave a dry chuckle. "Perhaps Shin Ming Fu thinks he'll live forever."

The Lone Ranger and his friend arrived at the platform and raised their hands as the train pulled away. From the carriage window above, they saw Fogg, Aouda, and Passepartout waving in farewell.

"*Kemosabe*, one more thing." Tonto said. "While you were speaking with Mr. Fogg, I overheard an interesting conversation between the lady Aouda and Mr. Fogg's valet."

"Oh?"

"Yes, it seems they saw a man they feared, a Colonel Stamp Proctor, on the train platform. They agreed to tell Mr. Fogg as soon as they boarded. Given what you told me about their prior encounter with the Colonel, and with his late brother, Major Proctor, shouldn't we follow and help Mr. Fogg?"

The Lone Ranger smiled. "My friend, after what we've just been through, I have a feeling Mr. Fogg can more than take care of himself."

THE END

Author's Note:

Despite the best efforts of the Lone Ranger and Tonto in Green River, anti-Chinese racism lived on in Wyoming and throughout the Old West. In 1885, disputes over hiring practices at the local coal mine, and ongoing racial tensions, resulted in a terrible anti-Chinese race riot and massacre in Rock Springs, Wyoming (Rock Springs and Green River are both located in the same area, Sweetwater County).

Jules Verne's novel *Around the World in Eighty Days* provides many specific dates, which were quite helpful in establishing the timeline of this adventure.

And yet, there is an oddity in the chronology, as documented by Verne, which impacts the arrival date of Fogg's train in Green River, Wyoming. Here is the timeline of the train's journey, December 3–11, 1872, from San Francisco (technically, Oakland) to New York City, as described in *Eighty Days*:

December 3

6:00 P.M. – Fogg's train departs Oakland.

December 4

12:00 Noon – Train stops at Reno, Nevada (western border of Nevada).

December 5

12:00 noon – Still in Nevada, now near eastern border; stopped for buffalo crossing until nightfall.

6:00 P.M. – Train resumes journey.

9:30 P.M. – Train crosses into Utah; about one hundred miles from the Great Salt Lake.

December 6

2:00 A.M. – Verne's tale indicates Fogg's party reaches Ogden at "two o'clock," but does not specify A.M. or P.M. A 9:30 P.M. crossing into Utah on December 5 leads to a 2:00 A.M. arrival in Ogden on December 6. Verne also recounts that the train stopped in Ogden for six hours and that Fogg and company had time to pay a two-hour visit to Salt Lake City; this implies a 2:00 P.M. arrival in Ogden rather than 2:00 A.M., for who would sightsee in Salt Lake City in the middle of the night? However, a 2:00 P.M. arrival makes no logical sense, based on the prior documented times. In addition, Salt Lake City is almost forty miles from Ogden; it is doubtful that Fogg would risk his schedule with an eighty-mile-round-trip diversion. This alone makes the six-hour stop more questionable, and one suspects that Verne elongated the time Fogg's party spent in Utah, by eighteen hours or more, for his own reasons. We shall make the assumption that there was a slight delay of an hour in Ogden, and that Fogg and his party resumed their journey at 3:00 A.M. on December 6.

12:00 noon – *Eighty Days* indicates the train makes a fifteen-minute stop at Green River, Wyoming on December 7. Yet, Green River is about eight hours away from Ogden at 20 mph. Logically, the date of the stop in Green River is December 6, not December 7.

December 8

Early afternoon – Train is attacked by Sioux in Nebraska; Passepartout is carried away on the tender.

December 9

Morning – Passepartout is rescued, but the train is gone, the entire incident of Passepartout's seizure and rescue occupying approximately eighteen hours. Fogg is in Fort Kearney, Nebraska, and is almost twenty-four hours behind schedule.

December 10

1:00 A.M. – Fogg and Co. arrive in Omaha and almost immediately catch a train bound for Chicago.

4:00 P.M. – Fogg and Co. arrive in Chicago.

December 11

11:00 P.M. – Fogg and Co. arrive in New York City, two hours too late to catch their scheduled steamer.

It is now clear that there is a gap in the records of Fogg's transit between Ogden, Utah and Fort Kearney, Nebraska—a gap now covered by a period of almost twenty-four hours, December 6–7, 1872, in Green River, Wyoming. The delay having been resolved, the train departed Green River on the morning of December 7 and the remainder of Fogg's journey unfolded according to the timetable Verne outlined in *Eighty Days*.

Why did M. Verne alter the details of Fogg's transit through Utah and compress the time spent in Green River—indeed, eliminate the

Green River incident altogether? As Philip José Farmer has said in his *The Other Log of Phileas Fogg*, Verne, whom Farmer calls a good and disciplined novelist, fictionalized his account, made insertions, and eliminated other information as needed.

However, the events at Green River might have seemed to Verne to be worthy of inclusion, if for no other reason than the severe impact to Mr. Fogg's schedule. Why replace them with an unnecessary and frankly humdrum layover at Salt Lake? The truth is, Shan Ming Fu's representatives were everywhere—even France. It is not unlikely that Shan Ming Fu or his agents would have persuaded M. Verne to suppress the Asian mastermind's role in these events, and Verne decided it was wise to eliminate the Green River story in its entirety rather than attempt to tell half of it.

Given the many wonderful stories that Verne lived to tell between the 1873 publication of *Around the World in Eighty Days* and his death in 1905, we cannot disagree with his decision.

Passing through the Hands of Steel
Dennis E. Power

December 8, 1872

H ot moist kisses became freezing wet stings.

As the dream arms of a San Francisco belle faded away, Passepartout passed from darkness to blinding light. His eyes stung from the glare of a winter's storm, flesh chilling as sleet and snow covered his hair, exposed skin, and sodden clothing. A ceaseless drumming accentuated his throbbing pain.

Patches of dark dry earth and winter-browned, frost-tipped grass flitted across his vision at a dizzying speed. Bleary eyes gazed over a horse's curved, muscled flanks. Lying on his right side, he was face down over the back end of a galloping horse. As the pounding in his head subsided, he noticed the pain in his arms, legs, back, hands, and feet. He had been what the Americans so charmingly called hog-tied and thrown over the back of a horse. The tied lump of hands and feet had been looped to the rear of a saddle.

His fingers were cold and stiff from the winter's chill, so he flexed and warmed them. Once they were limber, he gingerly felt the rope binding him. The knot was simple. Untying it would take mere seconds, but if he loosened the rope, he could fall and land beneath the horse. Doing this when the horse was galloping would perhaps not be healthy. He ignored the burning strain on his leg and arm muscles and withstood the jarring and bouncing of the horse, waiting for the right opportunity to make his move.

What fate awaited him, he was not certain. Passepartout had been standing on a train car platform when several war-painted natives in buckskins surrounded him and beat him down. They had attacked and overwhelmed the train that he and his employer, Monsieur Fogg, were using to traverse the wilds of America. During their attack, the natives had injured the engineer and fully opened the steam valve, hurtling the unmanned train down the tracks.

Passepartout had clambered over several cars to reach the engine of the runaway train. He had prevented it from being derailed by disengaging the engine car from the rest of the train. Then, he had fallen prey to the not-so-noble savages and been carried away.

"*Was wir sollte, über den Franzosen tun?*" (What should we do about the Frenchman?) shouted one of the Indians.

Passepartout barely heard him over the pounding din of hooves crunching through the frozen ground. And so, for a moment, he thought he had misheard.

"Keep him alive until Herr Schultze says otherwise. However, guard the hunchback with your life," answered another Indian in the same language.

Passepartout wondered if the blow to his head had scrambled his brains. The natives were speaking German! A Mormon missionary's lecture he had recently heard claimed that Indians were of the Lost Tribes of Israel. As such, they might have spoken Hebrew—but their speaking the tongue of Goethe was inexplicable.

"Once Fogg is either killed or captured, we can kill the Frenchy or take him back to Steel City to become a slave," added another German-speaking Indian.

Passepartout was as fluent in German as he was in English. Once the alleged Indians' conversation sank into his muddled mind, he grew infuriated. Passepartout had no love for Germans, especially since the invasion of France two years past. Since he knew he was dealing with bogus Indians, Passepartout decided to escape sooner than later.

Wiggling his fingers free, he then loosened the loops confining his feet. He scooted up to a higher, more horizontal position on the horse's back by shifting his weight slightly. He grabbed onto the saddle and kicked his feet loose. Passepartout then swung his feet about in an arc that gave the unsuspecting rider a clout to the head. Although the blow was relatively weak, the startled rider dropped his reins.

Passepartout pivoted and let his captor have a *revers* to the throat. This prevented the rider from crying out and sent him flying off of the galloping horse. Rolling forward, Passepartout seated himself in the saddle and gained control of the horse with his legs. After he finished untwining the rope from his hands, he took hold of the horse's neck.

The thick snowstorm helped cover Passepartout galloping his mount directly into the path of the nearest horse. This horse reacted to the sudden proximity of another animal and tried to get out of the way. His rider thought his mount was being troublesome and bore down the reins. Passepartout's horse shied away from colliding, but brought Passepartout close enough for a vault onto the other horse.

His feet landed upon a wrapped tarpaulin behind the saddle. He heard a loud grunt. The Indian who had been struggling to regain control of his suddenly difficult horse turned at the noise, shocked to see Passepartout standing on his horse.

He could not have known that this particular valet had once been a circus rider!

Passepartout batted the head of this second faux-Indian with the rope still looped around one wrist. A knotted end struck an eye and the rider clawed at the stinging orb. A follow up blow to the side of the head unmounted him.

Passepartout slipped into the vacated saddle and grabbed the reins. Whipping his head around, he quickly took in his situation.

About twenty yards away ahead was a single rider. The thick snowfall, the clamor of pounding hooves, and the howling of the winter's wind had hidden his attacks so the man remained unaware that his two companions had fallen. Off to Passepartout's side, a large body of Indians rode towards the east.

The saddle contained a boot with a rifle and also two bags with ammunition, dried food, and water. Passepartout lifted the tarp and looked into the face of a gagged, blindfolded young man. Since he did not have time to free the boy, he covered him back up.

Passepartout turned his horse and galloped off to the west.

Although he knew that it was the opposite direction of Fort Kearney, he hoped to gain some distance before his absence was realized. Once he had lost the war party, he would circle back towards the fort.

Passepartout had gained perhaps a mile before his horse was spotted and given chase. Further off to the west rose a group of hills. Passepartout galloped towards them, wanting to gain the high ground before the natives caught up with him.

However, the gap between him and his pursuers closed far too quickly for his liking. The main body of forty or so riders were shrouded in a white fog created by the churning of snow and frosted earth, but one lone man outdistanced the main group. As the distance between them closed, Passepartout heard the whoops and cries of the warriors intermixed with some Germanic curses.

When he arrived at a small cluster of grass and brush-covered hills, Passepartout urged the tired horse upwards. Near the summit of the largest hill, Passepartout found a hollow with brush cover. He jumped from the horse and, in a short time, untied the captive young man and removed the saddle, rifle and saddlebags. Since there was not enough brush to hide the horse, he reluctantly chased it off. He loved horses too much, to shoot it and use it as a barrier. He propped the saddle up over a slight rise in the hollow, spread out the tarpaulin, and crawled under it.

The snow quickly covered the oiled canvas sheet and, he thought, would provide some warmth and cover.

The lone rider and the group of Indians swung further west, following the freed horse. It would not take long for them to realize that they had been deceived.

Passepartout loaded and readied the gun, being careful that it remained out of sight.

The young man dropped down beside him and crawled underneath the oilcloth. "Did Mr. Henry send you?"

Passepartout shook his head, "No, monsieur, I am a victim of circumstance and was captured by the Sioux as they raided my train. They took me prisoner when I stopped the train from being derailed."

"The Sioux!" snorted the young man. "They aren't Sioux, leastways not entirely. That's an unholy mob of renegades from the Sioux, Apache, Arapaho, and other tribes. They're led by a man named Santer. I'm Johnny Brainerd."

Although Passepartout inwardly winced at the American's brash mannerisms, he smiled and gave Brainerd a slight bow of the head. There seemed very little remarkable about him. He was a handsome youth, despite being small in stature and having a hunched back. Passepartout wondered if the youth had been captured for purposes of ransom.

He barely had time to introduce himself when a rider arrived at the foot of the hill. A cloud of snow and dust indicated that the other riders were not far behind. As the man's horse climbed the slope, Passepartout took aim with the rifle's silver blade sight and fired.

He meant to shoot off the rider's hat, but being unfamiliar with the weapon, he planted a shot right between the horse's eyes. Man and mount tumbled sideways down the slick snowy hill. A pang of regret washed over Passepartout for killing the beautiful animal. The sentiment faded when Gallic practicality made him concede that, without his horse, the man had become less of a threat.

When the rider stood up, apparently unharmed, Passepartout shot again. This time, he hit what he was aiming for: the ground next to the man's feet. The Indian turned and ran down the hill, not stopping until he had met up with the rest of the band.

"Nice shooting, Mr. Passepartout. My old friend Baldy could not have done any better, God rest his soul."

Below them, the single rider was making gestures to the Indians, motioning for them to split into two groups and make their way around the hill.

"Gosh! Santer is going to have them flank us," Brainerd whispered to Passepartout, who had come to the same conclusion on his own. He fired the rifle twice, once at either end of the group of Indians, warning them not to move. One of the Indian braves shouted something, raised a spear defiantly at Passepartout, wheeled his horse, and made a dash away from the rest of the group and towards their position. Passepartout fired once more and the defiant brave flew from his horse. The remaining group turned their mounts and moved further back away from the hill where Passepartout was positioned. The third German-speaking Indian, whom Brainerd had said was named Santer, followed the rest.

Once they were further away from the hill, the Indians spread out once more. Passepartout shot at their feet. In response, a warrior nocked and shot an arrow. The arrow landed quivering in the dirt a few dozen yards away from where Passepartout and Brainerd were hidden. Santer gave the Indian who had shot the arrow a rifle butt stroke to the face. He screamed orders at the rest. Passepartout assumed that they were being told not to shoot at them.

Santer turned to face the hill, peered upwards, and shouted in German accented English, "Give us the boy and we will let you go, Herr Passepartout. We only wished to delay Herr Fogg by taking you. That part of the mission is accomplished, so we do not need you any longer. We want the boy, not you."

The young man regarded him with a trusting face. Passepartout instinctively knew that giving the boy to Santer was the wrong thing to do. "Why do they want you so desperately? Is your family rich?" Passepartout asked in a whisper.

To Passepartout's surprise, the boy laughed. "Not rich yet, but one day . . . Once I get my factory set up. I am an inventor, that's why they want me. Or rather, that is why their boss wants me."

"Boss?" Passepartout asked, not certain of this American term.

"Their leader, Herr Doktor Schultze. He is building a city in Oregon named Steel City based on technology and industrialization. He wants me to work for him. Initially, I agreed, but when I learned that his ultimate goal was to create superior weapons of war so that Germany could conquer Europe, I changed my mind. He wants me to redesign my Steam-Man and mass-produce it. When I refused, Doctor Schultze's hired hand, Santer, and his two owlhoots, kidnapped me from my St. Louis home."

At Passepartout's request, Brainerd described the Steam-Man he had built eight years before. A ten-foot tall steam-vehicle, it was shaped like a man with a top hat. The driver sat in the hat. With spiked feet, it could move as fast as a locomotive. Its arms could lift great weights and were versatile enough to kill a bear or a buffalo. The Steam-Man's main drawback was that, like a train, it needed to haul its own fuel and did so in a cart, which trailed behind it. This hampered its mobility. Brainerd had been redesigning the engine so that it would use a more efficient fuel than wood, such as whale oil or petroleum.

Passepartout had a horrifying vision of battalions of metallic juggernauts barreling through the French countryside, rolling over the French army and crushing the life and spirit of his beloved country. He became determined more than ever to not let Johnny Brainerd fall into this Santer's hands.

Santer gestured for a couple of his henchmen to move towards the hill and asked with some impatience, "So are you going to give us the boy, or not?"

"I think not, monsieur!" Passepartout shot at the feet of the Indian who had moved closest to the hill. His shot clipped him against his shin, scoring a deep wound and possibly breaking the leg. His companion scurried back leaving the wounded man on the ground.

Seeing Passepartout's puzzled look, Brainerd said, "The one you winged is a Pawnee; the other one is a Cheyenne. Normally, they are enemies. They work for Mr. Santer, but not with each other, get it?"

"*Oui*," Passepartout murmured. He had run across the same phenomenon recently in his travels through India and Africa. The various native groups were forced into a peace not of their choosing through the imposition of imperial might, or through a mutual hatred of the colonial powers. He suspected that if the colonial powers were ever to leave Africa or India, the various groups would almost immediately be at one another's throats.

Over the next hour or so Passepartout and Santer played a game whereby Santer would try to catch Passepartout unaware and send one of his hired men to climb or skirt the hill. Passepartout sent them back with well-placed shots near their feet.

"You know, we aren't going to harm the boy," Santer shouted. "He is just going to work for us—and for a very good sum, too."

Brainerd shot Passepartout a sour look at that.

Santer approached once more. "How much do you make working for that Englishman? He seems to have forgotten you. I doubt if he will come after you!" Although Passepartout could not clearly see Santer's face in the waning afternoon light, there was no mistaking the guile in the next words. "Perhaps you are not as valuable to him as we thought. He holds you in such high regard that he abandons you in this land of native warriors . . . We can pay you three times your year's salary if you help us out. Give us the boy and, when you catch up with Fogg, make certain he does not make it back in time to win his bet. Get a little payback for leaving you out in the Great American Desert."

His curiosity piqued, Passepartout could not help but ask, "Why are you so interested in stopping Monsieur Fogg. You cannot be members of the Reform Club?"

"Do you really think the wager is confined to Herr Fogg and that decadent club? *Nein*! The betting has spread over the world. Herr Doktor Schultze has bet against Fogg for quite a sum of money and has taken steps to ensure that the Englishman fails."

Because of the various setbacks that Fogg had encountered upon his voyage, Passepartout had come to believe that a conspiracy created by the Reform Club existed to stop him. For a time, he had believed that their fellow traveler Fix was an agent of the Reform Club, until Fix had revealed that he was a detective for the Peninsular and Oriental Company on Fogg's trail for a bank robbery.

Passepartout realized now that such a conspiracy did exist, although not specifically from the Reform Club. This Herr Doktor Schultz, through his agents, was probably behind both the Indian attack and the damaged bridge that had nearly stopped the train at Medicine Bow, Wyoming. He wondered if the annoying Colonel Stamp Proctor who had challenged Fogg to a duel was also an agent of this Herr Doktor Schultze.

As the afternoon sun waned, Santer grew more crafty; he had his hired renegades crawl up the hill on their bellies, making them harder to see and harder to hit. Passepartout responded to this new challenge by also being bolder. He stood on his knees and blasted at the areas near the Indians until he either scored a hit or drove them back. The ammunition emptied from the bags at a furious rate.

Santer had counted upon this. "Herr Passepartout, you cannot hold out much longer. I know how much ammunition Hans and Fritz had. Soon, you will have none and then, *mein freund*, it will be the curtains for you. Give us the boy now, and we will let you leave with your life."

Passepartout counted the remaining bullets and made his decision.

Passing through the Hands of Steel

"Pardon me for being blunt, Monsieur Brainerd, but can you run with your condition?"

"You mean, do I lurch and limp like Quasimodo?" Johnny Brainerd answered with a wry smile.

"*Oui*," Passepartout answered, coloring with embarrassment.

"My gait is fairly normal, although the weight of my hump throws my balance a little to the left. Why do you ask? Are we going to make a run for it?"

"I suggest that you do so, monsieur. I will use what little ammunition I have to hold them off so you can get away as far as you can under the cover of darkness."

Brainerd shook his head and set his chin firmly. "I will not leave you to be butchered by these warriors."

While Passepartout admired the young man's spirit, he tried to reason with him and get the young man to accept the reality of the situation. However, Brainerd remained adamant in his refusal to leave Passepartout. His nobility left Passepartout with a moral dilemma.

When Santer and his men overwhelmed their position, as they were certain to do, Passepartout had meant to save one bullet to use on himself rather than be subjected to the tender mercies of the renegades. However, he knew he could not allow Brainerd to fall into their hands either. Although the young inventor would not be killed, he would no doubt be severely tortured until he used his creative genius for this Herr Doktor Schultze. France would certainly be the first target of the madman's quest for domination and so, the first nation to be crushed by Brainerd's juggernauts.

Although Passepartout did not much care for the current leaders of his country, despite his exile, he was still a patriot and still considered himself an agent of France, as he had been for years.

While a young itinerant street singer, Passepartout had aided Chief Inspector Gevrol on several occasions. Chevalier Dupin had also called upon Passepartout's aid. When he was still a child, Dupin had put him in the circus to hone his natural acrobatic and acting abilities.

As Dupin's agent, Passepartout had, while posing as a gymnasium teacher, uncovered and thwarted a Prussian plot to assassinate Napoleon III. Later, while working as a fireman, he had, at Dupin's request, investigated and stopped an arson ring. His efforts were brought to the attention of his imperial majesty and Napoleon III had personally requested him to undertake a delicate assignment in 1867, which, through no fault of his own, he had failed. As a consequence, he had been exiled.

Passepartout's exile had meant that he was unable to be present to defend France when Germany had invaded. Although Napoleon III had fallen from power, Dupin had informed him that the new government viewed his former agents with suspicion. If Passepartout returned home, he would have an unpleasant welcome. The Frenchman knew that this suspicion would eventually subside, but, until then, he was still effectively exiled.

Monsieur Dupin had suggested that he seek employment with Monsieur Fogg, having known somehow that Fogg would dismiss his previous valet. Although he did not know how Dupin had foreseen the trip around the world, Passepartout realized that he had been sent to aid and guard Fogg,

Although Passepartout considered his connection to the French government finished, he still wanted to do what was best for his country. Despite not being able to return to his homeland, Passepartout had no desire to see it crushed beneath the iron heels of a voracious Germany.

The sun set and Passepartout realized that, if any rescue were forthcoming, it would have already arrived. He remained convinced that for the sake of France, Jack Brainerd could not fall into Doktor Schultze's steely hands.

So resolved, Passepartout braced himself for the final act. He carefully counted his shots until only two bullets were left. One for Brainerd, and one for himself. Passepartout comforted himself with knowledge that he would not have to live with the consequences of this heinous act; at least, not for very long. Blissfully unaware of what Passepartout planned, Brainerd smiled encouragingly at him, despite knowing that their situation was all but hopeless.

Passepartout closed his eyes and gathered his will to quickly swing the rifle around and shoot Brainerd before his conscience got the better hand, and before Brainerd realized that Passepartout had betrayed him.

A horrendous scream startled Passepartout and his hand twitched, firing the rifle. Passepartout cried "*Mon Dieu!*" as the bullet left the gun.

Tired of the stand off, one of Santer's Indians had decided to make a charge up the hill. He streaked upward screaming a war cry, his spear and tomahawk poised to strike. Fortune's hand guided the unaimed shot, which plowed through the charging brave's chest.

Biting his tongue in self-mortification, Passepartout cursed himself for having wasted one of the two remaining bullets. The deed he knew needed done was going to be even harder to perform now. Passepartout would not only have to live with the guilt of his act, but certainly the enraged Santer would allow his native minions to do what they wished to him. Doubtless, he would suffer for untold hours or days under the cruel ministrations of their barbaric artistry. Yet Passepartout would gladly suffer the tortures of the damned, if it meant that France would live!

Passepartout had once knifed an old man in the back, but never suffered a second's qualm over the act. The old man had been about to torch an orphanage and would have killed dozens of children, not out of malice or hatred, but simply because they were in the way. Yet, killing Brainerd was different. It was an expedient elimination; the sort of killing Passepartout had once vowed never to do. Each time he broke the vow, he died a little himself.

Santer screamed a long string of words that Passepartout could not translate, yet he understood their meaning. Since he knew Passepartout was out of ammunition, Santer told the braves to capture them. As a howl went up from the slopes below, Passepartout bit the inside of his cheeks, he turned, aimed the gun at Johnny Brainerd's head and fired.

The bullet struck the ground about a foot from Brainerd's prone head. Tears stung Passepartout's eyes as he cursed his weakness. He could not bring himself to kill this innocent young man, even though he knew that it could mean the extinction of France.

Brainerd gazed up at Passepartout with a wistful smile on his face; his eyes glimmered with compassion and understanding. Passepartout immediately realized that Brainerd knew that Passepartout had intended to kill him and had understood why. Shame and guilt flared over Passepartout and he turned away from the young man to face the coming onslaught

Suddenly, from out of the night, thunder cracked, and cracked again. At each crack, one of the dim, night-blurred figures in Santer's mob fell. Several voices shouted: "Inya-Nape!" or "Winnetou!"

Passepartout strained to peer through the moonlit darkness until he saw a silvery glint off to the west. His eyes adjusted to the dark and he saw two riders galloping across the plain. One was an Indian dressed in buckskins who rode a horse so black it shone silver in the night. The other rider was a white man, also dressed in buckskins, but wearing some sort of mask across his eyes. Both fired rifles at the Indians who had been charging up the hill. Their rifles seemed to have an endless supply of ammunition. The rapid and continuous gouted flames reflected on the glossy coats of the horses, briefly making them steeds of fire.

A cloud of dust and snow rising behind them, the horses galloped across the plain with such a speed his vision in the dim light had trouble keeping up with them. The Indian raised his rifle and shouted, "*A he ya eh Silberbüchse!*"

As his friend reloaded, the Indian charged forward and fired his rifle with deadly accuracy from a full gallop. Santer's men either scattered or gathered their nerve to attack the new arrivals.

Passepartout was surprised when the masked white man jumped off of his horse without his rifle and fought the Indians with just his bare hands. Yet, at every swing of his fists, an Indian brave sank to the ground unconscious or dead.

Brainerd danced with excitement. "Mr. Henry started using my designs after all!" Brainerd stiffened after a second and peered intently down the hill, moving his head back and forth, "Santer. Where is Santer?"

"Behind you, hunchback!"

Passepartout whirled about. A burly Indian strolled up over the summit holding a rifle on Brainerd and Passepartout. No stranger to disguise, Passepartout realized that the Indian was a white man with dyed skin and warpaint.

Santer smiled as he aimed his gun at Passepartout's stomach. "You should have taken my earlier offer Frenchman, now you will die slowly and painfully."

Brainerd moved in front of the rifle, forcing Santer to jerk his gun aside to miss him. As it was, the blast seared Brainerd's left shoulder.

Brushing past Brainerd, Passepartout attacked Santer with a kick to the midsection. But Santer was faster than he appeared, and he used the gun to block the kick. However, the kick knocked the rifle out of his hands. Passepartout advanced, bouncing on his toes and heels. Santer pulled a bowie knife out of a sheath on his back and kept the Frenchman at bay with a series of feints and lunges. He scored a slash against Passepartout's chest.

Johnny Brainerd tried to rescue Passepartout once again, thus proving the adage that often genius and common sense do not go hand in hand.

Santer grabbed Brainerd and placed the bowie knife against his cheek.

"I have to bring this *kruppel* to Herr Doktor Schultze alive, but not necessarily in one piece. He has to be able to talk and hear and see and think. Everything else is fair game, like his ears and cheeks. Tie yourself up and I'll not carve up the boy."

Brainerd slammed his head backwards and onto Santer's nose. The knife slashed Johnny's cheek as he jerked away from Santer. Passepartout leaped at Santer, knocking him to the ground. They wrestled for the knife. Santer's knee caught Passepartout in the groin and knocked the air out of his lungs. The villain's knife was inches away from the Frenchman's neck when it suddenly flew from Santer's nerveless fingers.

An arrow had transfixed Santer's shoulder, nailing him to the ground. Passepartout pushed away from the villain and rolled to his feet. The masked white man and his Indian companion had arrived. The Indian had nocked another arrow, aiming at Santer's chest.

The short, muscular white man put his hand in front of the bow, "No, Winnetou, do not kill a downed foe, it is not very Christian."

"Very well, Sharli, I will not kill him." The bow sang and an arrow transfixed the other shoulder, nailing that side of Santer into the frozen ground.

"Damn you, I have a bullet with your name on it!" Santer screamed writhing in agony. His eyes rolled back and he slumped insensible. The falling snow blanketed his still form.

Passepartout felt a flash of shame for enjoying the man's suffering, but only a flash. With a small smile, he turned to Jack Brainerd and said, "Who is that masked man and who is his friend?"

Brainerd laughed, "It's not who you might think. Actually, that's not a mask at all—it's my night-glasses. This here is Charlie, known as Old Shatterhand to the westerners and Indians. His friend is Winnetou of the Mescalero. I met them through Mr. Henry, a gunsmith and inventor in St. Louis who crafted some of my inventions. I designed a rifle that has twenty-five shots and Mr. Henry made it for Charlie. I also designed these spectacles that allow a person to see at night. How do they work, Charlie?"

"Fair, but not great, Jack." Charlie spoke and to Passepartout's shock, he also had a Germanic accent. "People and animals look like torches against a black night, but they hurt the eyes something fierce." Charlie removed the mask, which was actually a curved band of black glass with a nose bridge. "Henry sent for us when you were kidnapped and we have been trailing you for the last couple of days. We best get you back to St. Louis, and get this fella back to his train." Charlie pulled a half smoked cigar out of his cap and winked at Passepartout as he lit it. Talking around the cigar he said, "Winnetou's got a bet on your Mr. Fogg to win!"

Winnetou's hard black eyes bore directly into Passepartout's eyes. "Winnetou be very angry with palefaces if he loses bet. We go now."

Although the stone of Winnetou's face did not move, Passepartout saw a merry twinkle in Old Shatterhand's eyes. Winnetou might have been less than serious.

They left Santer still transfixed to the ground, deep splotches of red staining the snow covering his upper arms and chest.

Winnetou's and Old Shatterhand's lightning-fast horses caught up with two of the errant Indian horses. As Passepartout and Brainerd mounted, shouts and curses came from the top of the hill. Santer stood screaming invectives at them. Although arrows still transfixed his shoulders, he loudly vowed vengeance on Winnetou and his family.

Santer pulled the arrows from his shoulders. He stood, a lone figure in the white expanse, screaming in pain and rage. With a curse, he threw the bloody arrows in Winnetou's direction. Santer's display went unnoticed by Winnetou and Shatterhand for he was only a speck on the horizon by this time.

Shortly after leaving the hills, they encountered another band of Indians, some Arapaho. The Arapaho had three people with them whom Passepartout recognized as his fellow train passengers. The train passengers were bewildered, frightened, and confused about what had happened to them.

After a moment's conversation Shatterhand told Passepartout that the Arapaho had come across a small group of Cheyenne and Sioux, who were passing around bottles of firewater while taking turns cuffing and kicking some white men who were bound hand and foot. The drunken Indians also poked them with spears or threatened them with knives to great hilarity. When the Arapaho entered their camp, the renegades had either fled or attempted to fight.

After a short skirmish with the renegades, the Arapaho had picked up the nearly frozen palefaces with the intention of taking them to Fort Kearney. The Arapaho had been at peace with the Bluecoats and did not want war again. The Arapaho agreed to accompany Old Shatterhand, the enemy of their enemies, the Kiowa, to Fort Kearney.

Passepartout knew that Monsieur Fogg must have departed without him, and understood why. Fogg stood to lose everything if he lost the bet. Passepartout vowed to catch up if he could and double his effort to help Monsieur Fogg win the bet. For when Fogg won, Herr Doktor Schultze would lose a fortune. Passepartout hoped it would stop his mad plans to make Germany a world-conquering nation.

Winnetou broke Passepartout's reverie as he pointed to a cloud of white fog with a dark center rolling in from the east. "Cavalry comes."

"Well, this is where we part, Monsieur Passepartout. Them boys look like they are out for blood. The cavalry has a tendency to shoot first and sort things out later. I don't want to end up in a shooting match with some of my fellow Christians, so I will bid you adieu." Old Shatterhand bowed his head in Passepartout's direction and turned his horse towards the west.

Following Old Shatterhand, Johnny Brainerd waved goodbye to

the Frenchman who replied in kind. The band of Arapaho joined Old Shatterhand and Winnetou leaving Passepartout and the three other passengers behind.

Brainerd's departure brought a slight sting to Passepartout's eyes. He had grown to be very fond of the young man in the past few hours so renewed guilt flowed through him over what he had nearly done to keep him out of Doktor Schultze's hands. Passepartout was glad that they had safely escaped the clutches of Steel City. He hoped that Brainerd would be safe in Old Shatterhand's custody. He shuddered to think at what devastation Germany could cause if Prussian efficiency was married to such naïve genius.

The United States Cavalry soon surrounded Passepartout and the three other passengers. None other than Monsieur Fogg led the cavalry!

A mixture of elation and guilt ran through Passepartout when he learned that Fogg had paid the soldiers five thousand dollars to rescue him, and by personally undertaking the mission, had jeopardized his chances of winning the bet upon which his entire fortune had been staked.

The cavalry and Fogg were under the impression that the Indians had turned and run when they saw the soldiers, freeing their captives as they made haste to escape. Not wanting to depreciate his master's sacrifices, Passepartout omitted telling him that the rescue had not been necessary and that the Indians that had turned away from the cavalry had been friendly ones. He merely told Fogg that he had overpowered three of his captors; Monsieur Verne, elaborated, as he often did.

ABOUT THE AUTHORS

Jules Verne was born February 8, 1828, and was a French novelist, poet, and playwright. His collaboration with the publisher Pierre-Jules Hetzel led to the creation of the *Voyages extraordinaires*, a series of bestselling adventure novels including *Journey to the Center of the Earth* (1864), *Twenty Thousand Leagues under the Sea* (1870), and *Around the World in Eighty Days* (1872).

In addition to his novels, he wrote numerous plays, short stories, autobiographical accounts, poetry, songs, and scientific, artistic, and literary studies. His work has been adapted for film and television since the beginning of cinema, as well as for comic books, theater, opera, music, and video games.

Verne is a celebrated author in France and most of Europe, where he has had a wide influence on the literary avant-garde. His reputation was markedly different in the English-speaking world where he had often been labeled a writer of genre fiction or children's books, largely because of the highly abridged and altered translations in which his novels have often been printed. His literary reputation has improved since the 1980s.

For many years Jules Verne has been the second most-translated author in the world, ranking below Agatha Christie and above William Shakespeare. He has been called the "father of science fiction" and in 2005, on the centenary of his death, France declared that year "Jules Verne Year." Verne himself argued repeatedly in interviews that his novels were not meant to be read as scientific, saying "I have invented nothing." His own goal was rather to "depict the earth [and] at the same time to realize a very high ideal of beauty of style." Verne was made a knight of France's Legion of Honour on 9 April 1870, and subsequently promoted to officer rank on 19 July 1892.

One of Verne's most acclaimed works is *Around the World in Eighty Days*, an adventure novel first published in French in 1872. The story was published in installments with its ending timed to synchronize Fogg's December 21 deadline with the real world. As it was being published serially, some readers believed that the journey was actually taking place—bets were placed, and some railway companies and ship liner companies lobbied Verne to appear in the book.

Jules Verne died on March 24, 1905 but his incredible stories still live on!

Philip José Farmer was born on January 26, 1918 in North Terre Haute, Indiana. He grew up in Peoria, Illinois where he spent much of his childhood reading everything from the Bible and books on mythology to the classics by Baum, Carroll, Cervantes, Defoe, Dickens, Homer, London, Swift, and Twain to popular works by Burroughs, Doyle, Haggard, Verne, and Wells.

He sold his first story, a mainstream tale titled "O'Brien and Obrenov," to *Adventure* in 1946 before he decided to try his hand at science fiction. His next published story, "The Lovers," appeared in the August 1952 issue of *Startling Stories*, and is noted for breaking the taboo on sex in science fiction, as well as for earning Farmer a Hugo Award for "Most Promising New Talent."

Married and with two children, he soon quit his job to become a full-time writer, but after selling several more stories to the science fiction pulps, his career hit a stumbling block when he "won" the Shasta Prize Novel Contest. The grand prize was four thousand dollars (a lot of money in 1953), but he never received his winnings. Instead, the publisher asked Farmer for rewrites while the prize money was invested in another book, which bombed. By the time the truth came out, Farmer had lost his house and was forced to take up full time employment.

Farmer left Peoria with his family in 1956 and moved around the country working as a technical writer for the space-defense industry, eventually ending up in Beverly Hills, California in 1965. All the while he continued to write and sell science fiction short stories and novels, launching his popular World of Tiers series and even winning a second Hugo Award for the novella "Riders of the Purple Wage." Then, just before the moon landing in 1969, he was laid off from his technical writing job, so he decided to write fiction full time once again. This time it stuck.

In 1970, Farmer moved back to Peoria with his family and again his career began to take off, this time with a third Hugo Award win, for *To Your Scattered Bodies Go*, the opening novel in his bestselling Riverworld series. For the next few years Farmer sought inspiration from the popular literature he so loved, writing novels such as *The Mad Goblin* (a Doc Savage pastiche), *Lord of the Trees* and *Lord Tyger* (both Tarzan pastiches), *The Wind Whales of Ishmael* (a science fiction sequel to *Moby Dick*), *Venus on the Half-Shell* (written as if by Kilgore Trout, a character from the works of Kurt Vonnegut), and one of Farmer's greatest achievements, writing *The Other Log of Phileas Fogg* (the "true" story behind Jules Verne's *Around the World in Eighty Days*), the merged stories presented here for the first time. He also wrote two "biographies" during this period: *Tarzan Alive: A Definitive Biography of Lord Greystoke* and *Doc Savage: His Apocalyptic Life*.

The next two decades saw the publication of the Dayworld trilogy, as well as further installments in the Riverworld and World of Tiers series. Farmer also fulfilled his lifelong ambition to write an Oz novel, and authorized Doc Savage and Tarzan novels, with the publication of *A Barnstormer in Oz*, *Escape from Loki*, and *Tarzan and the Dark Heart of Time*. Late in his career, Farmer tried his hand at a different genre with *Nothing Burns in Hell*, a detective novel set in his hometown of Peoria.

After Farmer retired from writing in 1999, new collections such as *Pearls from Peoria* and *Venus on the Half-Shell and Others* continued to appear, as did new collaborative works such as *The Evil in Pemberley House* and *The Monster on Hold* (with Win Scott Eckert), *The Song of Kwasin* (with Christopher Paul Carey), and *The City Beyond Play* and *Dayworld: A Hole in Wednesday* (with Danny Adams).

Farmer passed on February 25, 2009, but his fan base is as ardent as ever, still gathering at annual FarmerCons.

M. S. Corley is a freelance illustrator and graphic designer specializing in book covers and character design. His interests include Jesus, folklore, weird fiction, video games, monsters, and the 19th Century. He's worked on everything from comic books to video game concept art, producing work for clients such as Simon & Schuster, Thomas & Mercer, Crossing, Skyscape, 47North, Valancourt Books, Henry Holt Macmillan, Dark Horse Comics, Houghton Mifflin Harcourt, Microsoft, Penguin Random House, and Meteor House (he designed the eye-catching cover and interior art for *Airship Hunters*, 2015).

Win Scott Eckert is a novelist, editor, essayist, and writer of short fiction. He is steeped in the works of famed science fiction writer Philip José Farmer, particularly Farmer's shared universe literary-crossover Wold Newton cycle and the Lord Grandrith/Doc Caliban series. He has a deep interest in studying fictional biographies, creating detailed chronologies of fictional characters and universes, and exploring the metafictional connections between seemingly unrelated works, which resulted in *Myths for the Modern Age: Philip José Farmer's Wold Newton Universe* (MonkeyBrain Books, 2005), a 2007 Locus Awards finalist, and the critically acclaimed, encyclopedic *Crossovers: A Secret Chronology of the World 1 & 2* (Black Coat Press, 2010).

Eckert has also chronicled the exploits of popular characters, including Zorro, Sexton Blake, the Phantom, Honey West, the Scarlet Pimpernel, the Domino Lady, and the Green Hornet, all of which can be found in the pages of anthologies from Moonstone Books, Meteor House (*The Worlds of Philip José Farmer*), Black Coat Press (*Tales of the Shadowmen*), and Titan Books (*Tales of the Wold Newton Universe*).

He contributed a new foreword to the 2006 edition of Farmer's well-known fictional biography, *Tarzan Alive: A Definitive Biography of Lord Greystoke* (University of Nebraska/Bison Books), as well as several forewords and afterwords to Titan Books' reissues of Farmer's novels. He played a key role in reissuing Meteor House's definitive editions of Farmer's fictional biography *Doc Savage: His Apocalyptic Life* (2013), and Farmer's authorized Burroughs novel, *Tarzan and the Dark Heart of Time* (2018).

Eckert is the authorized legacy author of Farmer's Patricia Wildman series (*The Evil in Pemberley House, The Scarlet Jaguar*). His latest releases are an authorized Avenger book from Moonstone,

Hunt the Avenger (2019); two authorized novels in the new Edgar Rice Burroughs Universe, *Tarzan: Battle for Pellucidar* (2020) and *Korak at the Earth's Core* (2024), and, as coauthor with Farmer, the fourth novel in Farmer's Secrets of the Nine series, *The Monster on Hold* (2021), furthering the titanic saga of Doc Caliban's battle against the dark manipulators who hold the secret to eternal life, the Nine.

Find him online at www.winscotteckert.com.

Henry G. Franke III is the editor of *The Burroughs Bulletin*, the publication of The Burroughs Bibliophiles, the nonprofit literary society dedicated to advancing the works and life of Edgar Rice Burroughs. The Bibliophiles has published *The Burroughs Bulletin* since 1947—the only fan organization and fanzine approved by Burroughs himself. Henry has been a past editor of the Edgar Rice Burroughs Amateur Press Association (ERBapa) and the North American Jules Verne Society (NAJVS). He was the contributing editor for, and author of the introductions to, IDW's four-volume archive set reprinting Russ Manning's Tarzan newspaper comic strips, as well as other comic strip archive editions published by IDW and Titan Books.

Dennis E. Power is a master at one of Philip José Farmer's favorite literary tricks: taking two or more apparently unconnected stories/novels/mythologies and finding a link between them. His real knack, however, is finding these connections between seemingly unrelated stories and novels by Farmer himself. Long active in Wold Newtonry, three of his articles appeared in *Myths for the Modern Age: Philip José Farmer's Wold Newton Universe* (MonkeyBrain, 2005), and eight of his articles appeared in *Farmerphile: The Magazine of Philip José Farmer*. Many of his essays can be found at www.pjfarmer.com/secret/content/secret-articles-alphabyauthorb.htm.

METEOR HOUSE TITLES

THE WORLDS OF PHILIP JOSÉ FARMER
Anthology Series edited by Michael Croteau
Volume 1: Protean Dimensions
Volume 2: Of Dust and Soul
Volume 3: Portraits of a Trickster
Volume 4: Voyages to Strange Days

Jesus on Mars by Philip José Farmer
The Stone God Awakens by Philip José Farmer
The Man Who Met Tarzan by Philip José Farmer
A Rough Knight for the Queen by Philip José Farmer
The Best of Farmerphile edited by Michael Croteau
The Philip José Farmer Centennial Collection edited by Michael Croteau
Greatheart Silver and Other Pulp Heroes by Philip José Farmer
Up from the Bottomless Pit by Philip José Farmer

SECRETS OF THE NINE SERIES
The Monster on Hold by Philip José Farmer & Win Scott Eckert
It's Always Darkest by Frank Schildiner

WOLD NEWTON SERIES
Doc Savage: His Apocalyptic Life by Philip José Farmer
Tarzan and the Dark Heart of Time by Philip José Farmer
Ironcastle by J.-H. Rosny & Philip José Farmer

THE KHOKARSA SERIES
Exiles of Kho by Christopher Paul Carey
Flight to Opar (Restored Edition) by Philip José Farmer
The Song of Kwasin by Philip José Farmer and Christopher Paul Carey
Hadon, King of Opar by Christopher Paul Carey
Blood of Ancient Opar by Christopher Paul Carey

THE PAT WILDMAN SERIES
The Evil in Pemberley House by Philip José Farmer and Win Scott Eckert
The Scarlet Jaguar by Win Scott Eckert

www.ingramcontent.com/pod-product-compliance
Lightning Source LLC
Chambersburg PA
CBHW020245030726
47499CB00001B/63